I0714090

ORPHAN FALLS

RUNNING WILD AND FREE

ORPHAN DREAMER SAGA
Episode Six
Volume One

A Novel

J. NELL BROWN

Orphan Falls: Running Wild and Free (A Novel)
Orphan Dreamer Saga: Episode Six; Novel Three; Volume 1

Copyright © 2023 by J. Nell Brown, LLC (Jeanelle Denise Brown)

All rights reserved. No part of this publication may be reproduced, distributed, or transmitted in any form or by any means, including photocopying, recording, or other electronic or mechanical methods, without the prior written permission of the publisher and author, except in the case of brief quotations embodied in critical reviews and certain other noncommercial uses permitted by copyright law. For permission requests, write to the author using the "Contact Us" page on www.JNellBrown.com.

Scripture taken from the Amplified Bible, Copyright © 2015 by The Lockman Foundation. Used by permission.

Scripture quotations are taken from the Holy Bible, New Living Translation, copyright ©1996, 2004, 2007, 2013, 2015 by Tyndale House Foundation. Used by permission of Tyndale House Publishers, Inc., Carol Stream, Illinois 60188. All rights reserved.

Scripture taken from the New King James Version®. Copyright © 1982 by Thomas Nelson. Used by permission. All rights reserved.

Scriptures taken from the Holy Bible, New International Version®, NIV®. Copyright © 1973, 1978, 1984, 2011 by Biblica, Inc. ™ Used by permission of Zondervan. All rights reserved worldwide. www.zondervan.com The "NIV" and "New International Version" are trademarks registered in the United States Patent and Trademark Office by Biblica, Inc. ™

Scripture taken from the Modern English Version. Copyright © 2014 by Military Bible Association. Used by permission. All rights reserved.

Scripture quotations marked MSG are taken from The Message, copyright © 1993, 2002, 2018 by Eugene H. Peterson. Used by permission of NavPress. All rights reserved. Represented by Tyndale House Publishers.

Bat Creek Stone: Thomas, 1890, Figure 7
This digital scan may be freely used with a link to this webpage.
https://www.asc.ohio-state.edu/mcculloch.2/arch/BatCrk/BatCreekFig7.jpg
Public Domain

The Beautiful and the Damned by F. Scott Fitzgerald
Copyright © 1922 Public domain

For ordering information, contact the publisher via the author's website, www.JNellBrown.com.
Printed in the United States of America.

First Edition: 2023

Cover by: www.whiterabbitgraphix.com and FrinaArt.com
Developmental Edit: Courtney Rae Andersson, Elevation Editorial
Line Edit: Sherry Clark
Judaic Consult: Ann Castro, AnnCastro Studio
Copyedit/Proofread: Judi Weiss
Typeset/Interior Layout: Lisa Gilliam

BOOKS BY
J. Nell Brown

NONFICTION

Shhh, My Father Is Speaking, and I Am Listening: A Bible Study on Hearing God's Voice

Blood Moon—God's Warning: Why Knowledge of Jewish Feasts Is Essential to Understand the Blood Moons of 2014 and 2015

America's April 2024 Solar Eclipse: What Does it Mean for America?

FICTION

Orphan Dreamer Saga

Novels

(A note on the reading order: please read even episodes in order)

Orphan Dreamer and the Glass Tattoo (Ep 2)

Orphan Tree and the Vanishing Skeleton Key (Ep 4)

Orphan Falls: Running Wild and Free (Ep 6—3 volumes)

Short Story and Novellas
(Read odd episodes in any order)

Orphan Dreamer and the Missing Arrowhead (Ep 1)

She Laughs Last (Ep 3)

A Generation of Lighted Evergreens (Ep 5)

House Guest (Ep 7)

Little Peach Lies (Ep 9)

COMING SOON

Orphan Star: The Mark

Orphan Seed: Desert Places

If Love's a Fish

Orphan's Horizon: The Lighthouse Leads

Orphan's End: The Beginning of Forever

How to Date a Demon During World War Two

Collector's First Edition Paperback

The Omega Journey: Blood Moons Whisper

Orphan Dreamer Standalone Thrillers and Mysteries

A Murder at the Harkness Table (Adelaide)

Coming Soon

The Storm

The Election

Pandemic

God Factor Saga (GFS) Trilogy

Frozen Prayers

Blood Moon Relics

Autumn Rains

The Rose of AD 30 (A GFS Compilation)

Dear Reader,

Welcome!

I hope you're excited to immerse yourself in the Orphan Dreamer's world—a story best read by adults and teens who have been exposed to mature situations and are trying to heal from the pain.

I wrote the Orphan Dreamer Saga as a sweeping transcontinental story heavily spiced with thrills, comedy, and a pinch of that horror-trope element called dread.

The saga reads as a contemporary epic that defies time, taking the reader from the predawn of humanity's beginnings to a future of what-ifs. It's a coming-of-age adventure on an epic scale featuring themes of friendship, inspiration, romance, and a fantastical twist.

Like the popular television show *This Is Us*, each episode of the Orphan Dreamer Saga follows three potential time periods of each character's story arc while solving a main plotline mystery. To keep track of time periods more easily, note the time and date stamps at the beginning of each chapter.

That's why I recommend reading any short story, novella, or novel in this saga when you're focused—distractions could cause confusion about the storyline. So consider turning off the television, brewing a cup of tea, playing a soft tune, curling up with *Orphan Falls*, and immersing yourself in the world of the Cavanaugh-Finns and the Darbyshires, and even the twisted tale of the Bushcrofts.

The saga should be read in order, starting with episode one, *Orphan Dreamer and the Missing Arrowhead*, a story that begins to answer these questions: What makes the main protagonist, Daniela Rose Cavanaugh, tick, and how does her mind work? Episode one reads as a nonlinear story that shows the experience of a schizophrenic—appearing as chaos and confusion to the outsider—yet it reveals how Yahweh sees the protagonist differently from how humans see her: as a child who hears His voice, unfiltered.

The Orphan Dreamer Saga is a work of fiction; however, a thread of truth weaves throughout the tapestry of words.

Orphan Falls focuses on the theme of truth versus deception. During one of my favorite movies, *A Few Good Men*, Jack Nicholson's character screams to his accuser—spit and all, "You can't handle the truth!"

Do we, as humans, prefer lies if that version of the story suits our agenda? Or maybe we prefer "facts"—a collection of manipulated semi-truths that validate our faulty beliefs—beliefs that benefit us even though they are rooted in a web of lies? In our modern world, we can consume a daily dose of our favorite brand of facts via social media or cable television, sometimes called "news."

But what if truth is the key that unlocks our mental chains, releasing us, and freeing our minds so we can soar to heights unexplored? Would we be brave enough to abandon our facts—our semi-truths—and our lies to embrace the truth?

Life has taught me that seemingly irrefutable facts will often contradict other ideas we also consider facts.

But truth never contradicts itself. Truth abolishes lies while illuminating our path as we walk in its light.

Truth is the Eternal Light.

An ancient Judean teacher named Paul—the bondservant and apostle of Jesus Christ, as he referred to himself—penned this warning over two thousand years ago as he wrote a letter to a group of truth-seekers known as the Followers of the Way: "They (people) perish because they refused to love the truth and so be saved. For this reason

God sends them a powerful delusion so that they will believe the lie" (II Thessalonians 2:11-12). What lie does this letter written to the Thessalonian Followers of the Way speak of? Well, if you'd like to find out, please add Paul's ancient letter written to the Followers of the Way living in Thessalonica to your reading list. The letter can be found in the New Testament portion of the Holy Bible, and the book is called First Thessalonians.

And this I know: truth—the Truth—will prevail no matter how ardently we embrace our half-truths, our facts, our lies.

Plain.

Definitely simple, as Daniela Rose likes to say. And so, we seek Truth as Truth seeks us—humble seekers.

All characters in the Orphan Dreamer Saga are fictional except God and Jesus, as well as the concepts of angels and demons. The proper Hebraic names of God and Jesus are used at times in this book: Yahweh (YHVH), Adonai (My Lord), Immanuel (God is with us), and Elohim (Supreme One) for God, and Yeshua for Jesus.

The Sons of Venus represent a conglomerate of religious, financial, and political secret societies and bear no resemblance to any one group.

When the last grain of sand slips through the narrowing of history's hourglass, Yahweh will stand triumphant in the spiritual battle depicted in this novel. He says, "For God so loved the world, that he gave his only begotten Son, that whosoever believeth in him should not perish, but have everlasting life" (John 3:16).

I am thankful for this truth. What would life be without God's love?

To me, nothing at all.

As an author, I believe God's love can be revealed even

in the pages of fiction, and thus, I believe storytelling is a gift, especially during the hard times such as pandemics and pestilence, wars, and rumors of wars.

So I gift you a piece of me—this story—as so many creatives have gifted me their stories when I needed a quiet way to touch God's heart, and as my own ancestors have gifted me with their rich histories.

It's true: I so enjoy sharing stories about my ancestors. Yep—I'm a human mutt, and I'm loving it!

When my character, Cillian Joseph Finn, reflects on his Daniela Rose, he is sharing part of my ancestral story:

> Her Cherokee forefathers walked the Trail of Tears. Her African ancestors crossed the Atlantic Ocean, packed end to end and side to side into a slaver's ship that, for some, would become a makeshift wooden tomb.
>
> Her Mongolian relations descended from Genghis Khan.
>
> Her English ancestors travelled on the Mayflower, escaping the yoke of the British Crown while seeking religious freedom in the New World. On July 4, 1776, they adopted the Declaration of Independence and cast their chains off forever, but then placed her African ancestors in shackles and ran her indigenous ancestors off their land.

If you'd like, check out your own DNA, and I hope you'll be pleasantly surprised and curious about your ancestral storyline.

Science has taught me that genetic variation is healthy for any species. Regardless of the ethnicity of our DNA, I believe we have been created in the image of God. We are all special—valuable, with a purpose, a destiny.

So, thank you also to my ancestors, and I hope to share a sliver of your stories—the good and the bad—in *Orphan Falls: Running Wild and Free*.

I hope you enjoy this piece of my soul and find truth amid the lies and peace amid the storms in the humble and honest words of the third full-length novel of my series, the Orphan Dreamer Saga, previously known as the God Factor Saga!

With gratitude to Immanuel for each day I've lived and that He's walked beside me,

J. Nell Brown

Characters and Pronunciations

Bushcroft: Bush-crawft
Cillian: Sih-lee-an
Daniela: Dan-yeh-la
Emmaline: Em-ma-line
Limy: Li-me
Jakob: Yah-kub
Legna: Lee-g-nah
Lucifer: Loo-suh-fer (Satan, Devil)
Nighean donn: Neein Down (Gaelic translation for Brown-
haired lass)
Yahweh Adonai: Yah-weh Ah-doh-nie (Lord God)
Yeshua: Ye-SHOO-ah (Jesus)
Yeshua HaMashiach: Yeh-SHOO-ah Ha-Mah-SHEE-akh
(Jesus the Messiah)

Definition of Proper Hebraic Names of God

Yahweh (YHVH)
Adonai (Master)
Immanuel (God with us)
Elohim (The Supreme One) for God
Yeshua (Jesus)

Spotify Playlist

https://open.spotify.com/playlist/
7F5OarSkGDfdfegTJAP7zM?si=a850bd0d18fe486a

Volume One

Time does not exist without Light, neither does darkness. Darkness is the absence of Light—a void of time and space. It remains powerless, succumbing to the presence of Light.

Who is the darkness and what is his name? His name is Lucifer, the falsely illuminated one.

More importantly, Who is this Light, what is His name? Given that our reality does not exist without time, and time does not exist without light—the Light of the World.

His name is the Timeless One. The Present. The Eternal One. Immanuel, God dwelling with us.

—J. Nell Brown

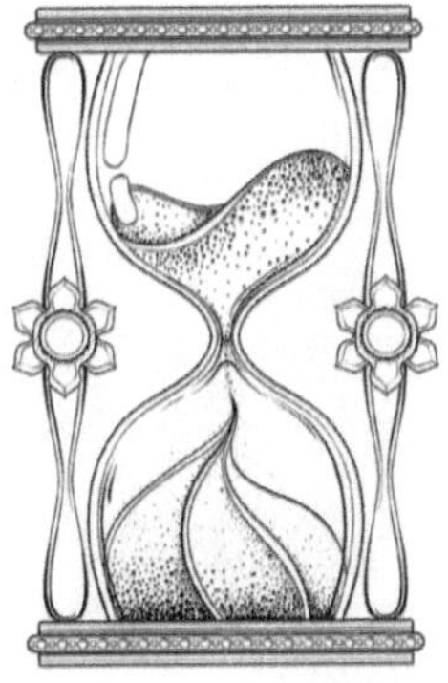

1—Orphan Dreamer

8:19 p.m., Thursday, April 1, 1993
Gainesville, Florida

THERE ARE GATORS IN THE Swamp—both humans and reptiles.

Tonight, above the Southern skyline splayed across Florida's swampy landscape, the sun is playing hooky, almost hiding beyond the western horizon of eleven-year-old Daniela's hometown of Gainesville, Florida—a place known for The Swamp, a football field, and its ivy league, college-town status.

Even in Gainesville—the home of the Florida Gators—it's a truth not widely accepted that living in a stone cottage near a Florida swamp means that a curious girl cursed with a set of spindly legs and inattention to her surroundings was nothin' but gator bait.

Ten feet behind eleven-year-old Daniela, a lily pad shifts.

A ripple forms just under the edge of a large, flat leaf,

then spreads across the surface of the murky pond. *Pay attention, Daniela Rose!*

But she is sleeping—plain ole' sleeping, no fancy Glass Tattoo in hand. It's true that cities, even countries, have been conquered while the city's soldiers slept.

And if Daniela is eaten alive by an oversize lizard hours before becoming the Orphan Dreamer and then securing the Glass Tattoo, what would become of the fate of the Eagle—the Biblical representation of America, Daniela's home away from home?

Ten feet.

Double the height of Earth's representation of the Eternal Light, the menorah. A relic lost to treasure hunters and thieves.

Ten feet. That is the totality of the space between a hungry gator and America's second chance: Earth's last Orphan Dreamer.

If Daniela survives this stealthy reptilian invasion, one day, she could attempt to solve the mystery of the origins of the Aniyvwiya—a segment of the real people, the first people. A mystery that must be solved before the sun descended for its final sunset on her homeland's second chance and the world's last chance before the Watchers return to Earth to take it back.

Beneath the illumination of the lost Jewish menorah, the Orphan Dreamer must discover the mechanism to neutralize her ancestors' curse triggered by their mistreatment of the Aniyvwiya.

Find the lost light.

Because tonight, America and Daniela Rose Cavanaugh both need another chance.

Because if America is destroyed, Daniela's mission of

saving the world from that dark force—the Watchers—would be next to impossible.

Find the Light—a bright and an eternal light—that would illuminate her path to God's powerful presence, the Ark of the Covenant, a place of miracles. The place of second chances. The place that leads to the place of redemption—Yeshua's cross—as her father, a chaplain, would tell his only child.

Beneath the moon's still glow, this eleven-year-old's only task tonight is to evade the devilish, leather-backed company lurking ten feet from her, rising on all fours on the bank of the pond in her parents' backyard.

Plain, but not so simple.

Wake up!

Pay attention, Daniela!

Fight!

But how does one fight a battle with Nomed, the most powerful of the Watchers?

The power of the Glass Tattoo seems cool unless you're the one charged to use it. Some dreams are sweet. Others not so much,

The arrival of the two total solar eclipses spread apart by seven years wouldn't wait for an eleven-year-old introvert to awaken and figure out how to fight.

Fight, Daniela Rose . . . even in your dreams, a quiet voice that sounds like her father's whispers into her soul. *Not by might nor by power, but by my Spirit, " says the Lord Almighty. For we wrestle not against flesh and blood, but against principalities, against powers, against the rulers of the darkness of this world, against spiritual wickedness in high places.*

Eight hundred years before the second total solar eclipse occurring on April 8, 2024.

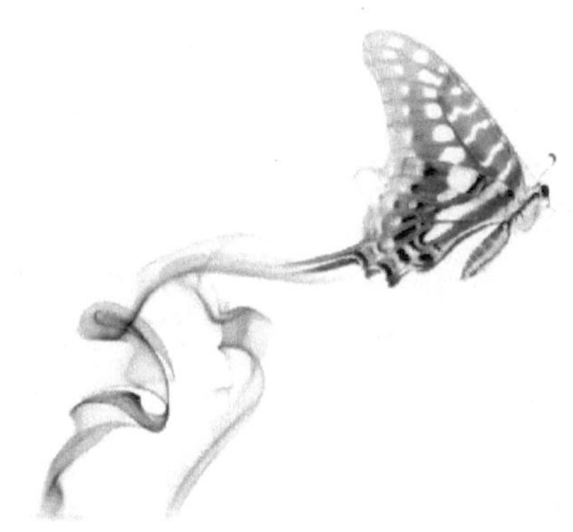

2—Fire, Hell's Candle

1256 A.D.
The Caspian Sea

THOU. SHALL. NOT. LIE.

It's true—a portion of the Orphan Dreamer's ancestors had mistreated the Aniyvwiya. *Mess with the Aniyvwiya, mess with God.* But who were the Aniyvwiya, and where had they originated before arriving in the Americas—North America, Central America, and South America?

No time to answer because tonight, even the moon was hiding from Genghis Khan's Mongolian army.

Before sunrise, four female spies lurked behind the seaside city's gates, waiting to open the spiked, metal, towering doors.

Then, one hundred cats, a thousand sparrows, and fifty horse-mounted mannequins would bring the wealthy city nestled by the sea to its hellish end.

But Genghis Khan's army wasn't waiting a field's length beyond the city's gates to merely conquer another village.

The warlord required a light. Because gold and bloodshed couldn't illuminate a tortuous path through the valley of death, only a light could. Though his main objective wasn't conquest, this night's battle was diabolical—Armageddon at the hands of Genghis Khan and his horde of ruthless soldiers, the devil incarnate with his demon throng.

The thud of horses' hooves would have been the first warning, if the citizens weren't still sleeping.

Beneath the cover of a moonless night, Genghis Khan pressed his torch into the chest of the first horse-mounted felt mannequin. Oil-soaked cloth drank in the fire, setting itself ablaze as the stallion beneath the flames whined and neighed, pulling at the leather reins.

Genghis Khan smirked as he remembered the little girl he'd run through with his blood-encrusted sword before stealing her horse, this horse. He inhaled deeply, sucking in the potpourri of war—human sweat, fear, savagery, and smoke.

Indeed, the Mongolian warlord was at home.

Behind the khan, his warriors brushed their torches across the chests of their own mannequins—five-feet-tall, two-feet-wide felt-covered bags of rice strapped to the backs of their enemies' horses, animals they'd stolen from the city they had conquered and burned to the ground seven days ago.

After the dummies were lit, each soldier slapped their horse on the hindquarters.

The stallions and mares charged toward the sleeping city as Genghis Khan's rear cavalry tied oil-soaked cotton balls to the tails of a hundred cats. With sticks of fire, they lit the cotton balls and then released the cats.

The felines scurried ahead, scampering across fields of tall, dead grass, eager to find relief from their hell. The cats wormed their way through the legs of charging horses, dodging the hooves of the angry beasts carrying their fiery payload.

Cats cried and screeched as the flames traveled up their tails and began to char their legs and haunches.

A lone archer shot a fire-tipped arrow across the horizon, the signal for the four female spies inside to open the gates. As the horses and cats approached, the city's gates opened. The spies had done their job well. Untouched by a man, even the khan. Loyal. Focused.

Everything was going according to his plan.

Chest puffed out with the hot air of dark satisfaction, Genghis Khan mounted his favorite steed, a smoke-colored stallion. As he stroked his long beard, his heartbeat slowed. He raised his torch and kicked the sides of his horse. The stallion leaped into action. The mounted soldiers galloped behind their leader.

Reaching the city gates, Genghis Khan paused, his breath coming easier as one cat brushed past a bale of hay . . . and then another . . . followed by another.

An orange cat whose haunches were now only seared fur and char hobbled into a wooden home near the gate. Genghis Khan sneered as the cat fought to climb into a bucket of water hanging by the home's door.

The pathetic animal climbed in, finding a moment's relief, but not before it had set the southern wall of the house on fire.

Won't be long, little one.

With his aching and arthritic knee, Genghis Khan nudged his horse to the right, allowing his generals to line up beside him.

At first, the blazes were small, popping up here and there. The flames soon spread from structure to structure, until an orange glow encased the city. And an unholy roar drowned out the screams of the damned.

A little boy tried to run past the khan and his generals. One of his trusted generals swung low with his sword, decapitating the boy with one strike. "It will be better for him this way," the general said as he watched the boy's body seize within the grip of a fleeting life.

"Showing mercy, Zev?" Genghis Khan rested his hand on his sword.

"I have a boy that age, my lord," his general replied.

Still, the warlord and his small army of specialty soldiers waited. Soon, the birds would fly.

Before the archers loaded their fiery arrows, they wrapped oil-drenched cotton balls around the neck of each sparrow in the flock, then ignited the cotton balls.

The birds screamed as they flapped their wings and flew toward the city. Some landed on wooden roofs and others on cloth tents. The town burned along with them.

Mothers ran out of their houses, clutching their wailing babies to their breasts. Husbands stumbled in the streets of the city illuminated by the hellish light. Still, Genghis Khan and his soldiers waited just inside the city's gates, slicing the heads off any pitiful souls desperate enough to escape.

Outside the city, archers launched volley after volley of fire-tipped arrows, penetrating deep into the city.

Men clutched their staves, swords, and spears, but, one by one fell to their deaths beneath the unrelenting barrage of arrows.

Felt mannequins, screeching cats, and squawking sparrows obliterated Genghis Khan's unsuspecting enemy that night. Hell and its devils had a way of creeping up on sleep-ing souls.

Still, Genghis Khan waited, his chin raised in a salute to himself and his battle genius. He and the specialty army beside him would need their strength for another task. No—the warlord had not come to the city by the sea to steal its treasure of silk, gold, and boats.

As he waited, the babies' wails quieted, replaced by the moans of fathers and mothers as they begged for a quick death to join those around them sinking into eternity's em-brace.

Genghis Khan signaled to his two most trusted gener-als with his thumb and forefinger. With the raise of their clenched right fists, his generals commanded the army to charge and finish what they had begun—death undignified.

But still, eight special warriors waited with Genghis Khan and his two generals.

As the fires finally dimmed, the khan signaled, and the eight soldiers and his two most trusted generals followed their leader on horseback into the smoldering city.

The rest of the army continued their murderous ram-page, assassinating all the city's occupants—men, women, and children—ending their misery, but not before indulging their carnal lusts.

Let them have their due. Their leader wouldn't stop them.

Genghis Khan pressed his knees into his horse's sides. The muscled beast jumped over a small ground fire before launching into a gallop. The khan pulled left on the reins, and the stallion careened around a burning carriage.

As minutes passed, they advanced unchallenged deep into the northern zone of the city. Genghis Khan and the ten men accompanying him entered a wide-mouthed cave, their torches lighting their path as the sound of crashing waves echoed inside the Caspian Sea cave and soothed the warlord's restless soul.

He rubbed his tongue across the top of his mouth, savoring the salty taste of humid air as he penetrated deeper into the earth. Water sloshed beneath his horse's feet, washing blood and dirt off the legs of his white stallion.

He patted the horse's mane. "Feels good?"

The horse tossed his head.

Deeper into the cave, man and beast waded through another pool that seemed to be lit from the rock bed at its base. "The light must be close," the khan assured Zev.

"Surely, the ancient man of the invisible God wouldn't have written lies," Zev replied.

They reached a high point and rose out of the water.

Water dripped from the cave's ceiling. Tapping the slicked stones beneath the horses' hooves brought an echoing rhythm—a song of peace irreconcilable with the fires raging just outside the cave.

Several minutes after exiting the clear pool, water no longer dripped from the ceiling. A holy hush consumed the confines of the cave.

Genghis Khan halted.

Ever loyal, his company continued to follow his lead.

Maybe this lingering, this sacred quietness, was a second chance from above, gifted to the leader's soul in this final moment of reflection. *Repent—turn around and go back. Then, seek redemption—a second chance.*

He clenched his jaw, having long forgotten about his fleeting and seared conscience. *No—never.*

In this moment, he did not need a conscience. A glint of

gold sparkling in the darkness beneath the intrusion of his torchlight had captured his attention.

Genghis Khan grinned, his eyelids pulling long and tight as a bowstring. Indeed, the man of God had told the truth. "Zev and Subedei . . ." He signaled with his hand again, and they came near. "Send the men forward to neutralize any snares. Should any member of the company fall prey to a trap, send his family a purse of gold."

"Yes, my lord." His two senior generals commanded the eight burly men to advance.

Only when the soldiers signaled with their torches that it was safe for the warlord and his generals to follow did Genghis Khan, Zev, and Subedei move forward.

The clomping of horses' hooves calmed the war leader. There in the distance, the glint of gold had grown into a five-foot-tall, solid-gold object.

"My lord, it's here." Zev's voice nearly vanished into a whisper. "You have found the Eternal Light—the lamp that will lead you on the treacherous journey when you close your eyes for the last time."

"The map was true. And until I die, with this light and my presence . . . we will conquer the world."

"May it light your path to an eternity of victories from one end of the Earth to the other." Zev sheathed his sword. "You will see all things and you will know all things. You will be a god among gods—all knowing, all powerful, your path in life and in death illuminated."

"Do you see what I see, Zev?" Genghis Khan inched forward.

"Yes—I do."

Another relic, large with hard edges, rested behind the Eternal Light in the recessed shadows of the cave. "It's the

Ark of the Covenant. It's here too." The warrior king moved quickly in the direction of the artifact.

"Wait, my lord!" Zev reached for his master's arm but stopped short, avoiding eye contact with the khan. "Legend tells us that the other relic possesses power—a power that can kill."

The khan stopped his pursuit. "A box that can kill. It doesn't need a snare."

"Secure the Light," Subedei commanded four of the men. The four soldiers, straining their muscles, lifted the ancient, five-foot-tall, solid gold lamp onto their shoulders. "Take it out of the cave."

Genghis Khan studied the light as it passed.

The ancient Judeans had called this Eternal Light, a light still shining dimly after all this time, the menorah. The khan smirked. It had all been worth it, snuggling night after night with his ugly wife, a descendant of the royal House of Li.

He had patiently listened to her bedtime stories, satisfied her passions, washed, and then studied what she'd talked about that night—the night the Jewish babe was born, and placed in a Bethlehem manager.

The House of Li's wise men had followed the North Star until they had found the child. His wife told him that the boy's mother had called her son Immanuel—God with us.

"God is dead," he whispers to the Earth. After the child became a man and was crucified on a Roman cross, his mother sent a flat, brown stone to one of the wise men who had visited her newborn son, naming it the Bat Creek Stone. The Bat Creek Stone would be the key ensuring a second chance for someone.

Supposedly, this Immanuel was the eternal Light of the World—a bright and blinding flame that could never be extinguished.

Flesh. Bone. Heart.

Was it true? Was the Jewish babe the Eternal Light promised by the ancient prophets?

According to the khan's wife, after Immanuel's arrival, the Judeans no longer needed a replica of the Light of the World—the menorah, the ancient golden light replica that was housed in Herod's Temple. The Messiah had come.

The original menorah was no longer in the Jewish temple. It had been hidden.

So, when the Romans took the curved-arm menorah during the Jerusalem siege and paraded it down Roman streets, they were parading nothing more than a fake. Genghis Khan had discovered that the original light had disappeared when the Babylonians conquered Judea.

"Carry it as I taught you." Zev commanded the last four men to secure the Ark of the Covenant. "Touch only the poles—or you will die and kill the rest of us." Each man gripped his pole and steered clear of brushing against the golden box. This was how the ancient Levitical priests had carried the Ark of the Covenant.

As the four soldiers waded into the first pool, the water lapped at their chests and washed over the boxy relic. The calmness of the water relented to the power of the artifact, and waves rushed over the men's shoulders. Beneath the surface, the water glowed a deep blue-white, and the soldiers' bodies violently shook.

One man clamped down on his lower lip. Blood oozed. Another grimaced. The third groaned, and the fourth remained stoic even as blood drained from his left ear.

"Keep going," Zev commanded as he, the khan, and the second general waited for the stirring waters to calm. "The ancient power is still present in the Ark of the Covenant, my lord."

"I can see that." Genghis Khan scowled.

He had conquered the world and had no need for another God to rule his kingdom, nor had he a need for the Jewish Messiah.

His wife's bedtime stories, the Copper Scroll, and Ezekiel's blueprint had led him to King Solomon's treasure—the Judean's solid gold and seven-armed, straight-branched menorah and the elusive Ark of the Covenant—Earth's power center of Yahweh's presence. "When I die, Zev and Subedei, bury me with the Light so that my path will be illuminated in the afterlife."

"And what of the Ark of the Covenant?" Subedei mounted his horse.

"Take it away from me—even now."

"Where to, my lord?"

"You will take it here." Genghis Khan slapped a scroll into Zev's hand. "I'll not have that thing killing my people as it did the Philistines. I don't need the presence of the Judean God hovering over me, judging me. Punishing me. Send the four men carrying the Ark to this place this night."

"It's a long trip of sea and land."

"Do it."

"Yes, my lord." Subedei bowed his head. "And the treasure of the Copper Scroll? Shall we use it to finance our battles that we must continue to fight even after your death?"

"Keep some of the treasure but bury most of it with me, in case I have to appease the Judean's God in the afterlife." Genghis Khan chortled. "I did steal His things."

"Yes, you did, my lord." Zev softly laughed as well.

★ ★ ★

MESS WITH ANIYVWIYA, TRIGGER THE curse. Colonizers of South and Central America had done just that. But so had Genghis Khan on the night he attacked the sleeping city by the Caspian Sea, then stole their sacred treasures. Shortly after this conquest, the Bubonic Plague killed him.

And the Spanish colonizers . . . well . . . look at South and Central America, even Texas and how the Comanche warriors drove back the Southwest Spanish colonizers.

Be not deceived, God is not mocked. Whatever a man sows that shall he also reap.

But what about America—Daniela's homeland?

Beneath the oak tree by the pond, Daniela awoke as the gator approached, hissing and spitting death.

3—Orphan Dreamer

7:46 p.m., Thursday, April 1, 1993
Gainesville, Florida

DANIELA. ROSE. CAVANAUGH. THAT'S MY name. And I'm eleven years old.

Claire's been bustin' my chops all day at school, so I escape my bedroom, go outside, and drink gallons of fresh air to calm down. Who cares if it's dusk. I'll only be out a little while because I don't like nightfall.

But after I escape into my parents' backyard—my sanctuary, a church house where most of the saints are moss-laden oaks, crickets, and butterflies—I soon fall asleep beneath my favorite oak tree.

When I wake up, my mouth is a tacky mess of bad breath, dehydrated spit, and sand. I rub sleep from my eyes and blink.

The stars are out tonight. Big and bright. But images

of burning cats, birds, and horses linger in my memory, a horror movie forever seared into the sulci of my eleven-year-old brain.

Sulci are the grooves on my brain's surface nestled between the gyri. They increase the surface area of my brain. I learned this from Encyclopedia Britannica.

Sometimes I think I have too much surface area.

For starters, my dream about an ancient prince and his arrowhead hadn't been this frightful. When I think about the cats, the birds, and the horses, tears slither down my cheeks without my permission.

Trails and tears . . .

Some of my ancestors had experienced tears because of the long and arduous trails. With trembling hands, I gather my things—a quiver that holds one blunt-tipped arrow, my bow, and my tattered journal.

I glance around, taking in my surroundings. Ever since I can remember, I have despised loneliness. But I never asked for this kind of company.

Not then.

Not now.

Not ever.

Red-eyed, cold-blooded, armored with leathery scales, something devilish from the pits of a dragon's fiery underworld moves through the dark water . . . then out of the water, toward me!

It is true.

I have begged God for a kindred spirit just like the fiercely independent orphan girl Anne Shirley, who met and then fell into platonic love with Diana Barry—a beautiful crow-head girl who lived in Avonlea, the magical lands of *Anne of Green Gables*.

I am not anything to look at, but I am a crow-head. God

drenched my curly locks with the same black ink that soaks a crow's wings, and for that bit of goodwill, I am grateful.

The gator rises on his legs and runs away.

But something tells me that I'm running out of time to find my friend and gift her my homemade friendship bracelet—a chevron pattern of emerald hues woven next to black, then plum and lavender, and finally yellow, before starting over at emerald again.

Because one night, they will take me to save you. My rafiki—*friend*, a.k.a. my dad—told my mom that last night.

Who knows if I'll be sleeping or awake when they come, but here's to hoping that tonight is not that night. According to Dad, after I am taken, strangers will call me the Orphan Dreamer.

I shiver as I sweep the butterscotch glow of my flashlight back and forth, searching through the cattails by the pond in the middle of my backyard where I ate lunch earlier today. *Did I lose the ancient arrowhead here?*

How am I going to find a black arrow in the dirt . . . at night?

I squint and keep searching.

Honestly, I don't clearly remember ever possessing—much less losing—an ancient relic gifted to me by a prince. I admit it all sounds a bit like a fairytale. Some days, I'm a bit confused about what happened . . . what's real and what's not. My teacher says I have a big imagination.

My math teacher accused me of lying.

No, ma'am. I. Do. Not. Lie.

Trust me! Something deep inside—my knowing—is telling me that a prince gave me a priceless artifact last night after I'd slipped into a vivid dream. Again, I have been a bit confused lately. It's the new medicine.

I think.

It's true. I'm not exactly the kind of girl a prince would even notice, unless he was the prince of nerds and the awkward. Suddenly, death warmed over stinks up the sticky air that clings to my skin. Cattails rustle, whispering a warning.

But I haven't found the lost relic yet. And I have to, to prove to Mother that I'm not imagining things again. The arrowhead is proof that Jeanette Cavanagh's only child isn't crazy.

I glance over my left shoulder. Grody. To. The. Max. The company I never wanted . . . it's back!

Heart pounding, I clutch the handle of my quiver. *Only one arrow left.* It's not ancient. Not special. Not gifted to me by a prince. And it's as blunt and dull as Harry's IQ. But this arrow might save my life.

Beneath the yellow sweep of my flashlight, the cold-blooded reptilian belly crawler cursed with a mouthful of jagged, foul-smelling chompers charges out of the pond toward me. I would've been safer in Evergreen Cemetery, lost among moss-laden oak trees, headstones, tombs, and dead people.

Storm!

I bolt across the red, wooden bridge that splits the four acres behind our stone cottage in half. Fire shoots up the back of my legs and settles into my calf muscles and thighs. Just two more acres to go. *You can do it, Danny!*

I must.

Zigzagging, I slosh through a low-lying area of our backyard. Cold mud slings around my ankles, attempting to suck me into the quagmire. I keep pushing forward, focusing on my goal—home, safety.

At least for now.

An amber glow flickers behind the windows of our stone cottage. Mom's probably still up reading. No arrow though. So much for being able to prove I'm not a lunatic.

I grit my teeth and propel myself through the ankle-deep sludge. *Should I scream for help? Never. Wimps lose their marbles, then whine about it.* The beast slaps its tail as it snakes its way through the mud, letting me know it's still on my trail.

One more acre to go.

Zigzag!

My lungs scream.

I'm tired. So, time for Plan B. I launch my body, reach up, grab an arm of a moss-draped oak, then scamper up the stairs of the treehouse anchored in the one-hundred-year-old giant's crooked branches. *Snap!* I glance over my shoulder. The gator has slapped its jaws shut, wishing he could gnaw on my right leg for dinner. I'm not a chicken, gatorman.

A timid smile wishes me blessings and good fortune. "Th-th-thanks, Grandpa." Grandpa Cavanaugh died a few years ago, but his legacy—a Swiss Family Robinson fortress—remains.

It was a birthday gift to me before he took his last journey to a faraway place, across the River Jordan. Grandma Gertrude always says, "It's a place where more angels live in the neighborhood than people. It's fancy, too. Streets made of clear gold. Mansions only. No cottages in that neighborhood. And the gators are herbivores."

It wouldn't be a bad place to move to, especially if the neighbors are nice, unlike Claire Underwood and her brat cousin, Harry. *What do angels look like?* I try to let my breath catch up with my legs. Gasping for air, I sure could use an angel about now, and definitely another arrow.

At the base of the tree, the gator waits for me. Hissing. Snarling. Letting me know my end has arrived. But if that's true, what about Mother and Father? And what about all that Orphan Dreamer stuff I overheard my parents talking about last night?

I need to survive.

For their sakes. Not mine.

I check my pulse. Not dead yet. Mission accomplished.

For a few minutes, I rest while hoping and praying the reptile will grow bored of teasing me, the awkward kid with big hair and a gap-toothed smile. My school bullies usually do. But past sundown, the gator must not have anything better to do than add me to his dinner menu. It keeps its beady, red eyes trained on me.

Make a plan. First, gather the facts. Fact one: according to the science special my teacher showed in class, gators move slower on land than in water. So stay out of the pond! Fact two: the vulnerable parts of an alligator are its eyes and its palatal valve.

"Sour milk and mushrooms!" I whisper because the palatal valve is located at the very back of a gator's throat. The only way I can punch through the palatal valve is if the gator opens its mouth and I stick my arm inside.

Note to self: don't let this situation get to the hand-in-mouth stage. It's what we call a major fail. Yep, I've seen CPR performed during my two hours of weekly allowance of television watching, but I'm pretty sure that's different than hand-in-mouth gator resuscitation.

And don't get caught in a death roll either. That's an epic fail!

My pounding heart knocks up against my rib cage, sounding just like our rickety screen door on a stormy day.

"Here goes nothing." I reach into my quiver, retrieve my last arrow—tipped with a blunt wooden arrowhead—then load the practically useless projectile into my bow. *Do I try*

*to kill the gator? Especially after the butterfly? That would be a
double murder in one day.*

Has my life already deteriorated into this—the life of
an assassin? It sounds exhilarating and powerful—killing
things—but murder is never really the act of bravery. I grip
the rise of my bow, pull the string back, and fire.

Bullseye!

The arrow thumps the gator in the left eye. It rears back
its ugly head, bellows, then charges past the oak tree.

With the beast out of sight, I scamper down the treehouse stairs and keep running until I climb onto our back
porch, open the screen door, and dive onto the dining room
floor. The rickety door cannot close fast enough, shielding
my trembling, mud-caked body.

What a fine kettle of a mess I've found myself in, looking in the near dark for an ancient arrowhead that I don't
remember having or losing and then getting chased by a
gator—as though the reptile was telling me, "Girl, get your
behind home. Your momma's waiting for you."

Maybe the inquisitor is right—I'm not all there.

I'm lying to myself . . . not really living in reality. I shrug
as I stand up. Maybe I don't want to be there anyway.

But since the obsidian arrowhead supposedly belonged
to a prince, my finding it could gain me entry into Claire
Anne Underwood's Untouchables.

It's almost nine o'clock, and it's past my bedtime because
it's a school night. I take off my muddy tennis shoes and hide
them by the back door of the dining room before I sneak
through the kitchen and living room. Still feeling breathless,
I arrive at my bedroom and slip on my pajamas.

A bath will have to wait.

My parents cannot know what I was up to.

I wasn't supposed to be eavesdropping last night, either.

It's true: I'm a swamp girl. I live on the fringes of a swamp. A place where water moccasins, rattlers, and gators hide between cattails.

But technically, I live three miles from The Swamp. A field where the Gators—the orange-and-blue variety—dress out in their University of Florida football jerseys before running into The Swamp to fight Georgia's Bulldogs, Florida State University's Seminoles, or Alabama's Crimson Tide.

We Gators are used to sitting at the top of the food chain, just like our namesake, the alligator—an apex predator, according to my science teacher—so our football team and other athletic teams at Florida's oldest university try their best to keep our town riding on top of the coveted tidal wave of the Southeastern Conference.

Or so my rafiki says.

He loves sports. I'm only a lukewarm fan; it's something for a girl to do with her dad on a Saturday afternoon.

When I grow up, I am going to attend college at the University of Florida, where I'll study something scientific like physics, biology, nutrition, chemistry, or mathematics.

Then I'll get into the College of Medicine.

That's my ten-year plan—to become a medical doctor and take care of sick children. That is, if I survive 7112 S.E. 221st Avenue—my parents' loving but dangerous lair, a house of secrets. Secrets that, according to them, matter for everyone's survival.

Of course, I can't sleep. I'm bugg'n out.

Not because of the swamp, snakes, bugs, or gators. I'm used to those creatures. Have arrows, will travel. But I'm not even a teenager, and my Cinderella daydreams have already vanished—only to be resurrected as mutated Frankenstein nightmares.

According to my parents' conversation last night, my

destiny has been decided. Plain and simple. The blueprint of my future doesn't even include the one thing I have begged for—one single, solitary friendship bracelet.

I am not picky.

The girl who gifts me my very first friendship bracelet doesn't even have to be Claire, the most popular girl in my middle-school class. I know I'm not good enough to join the Untouchables; but as I said, that ancient arrowhead could give me a fighting chance.

But do I really want to join the Untouchables? All I ever wanted was my very own *Anne of Green Gables* best friend—a kindred spirit, someone who likes me just as I am. I'm pretty sure the Untouchables don't have a "come as you are" policy.

Tonight, my dream of finding my kindred spirit must be a universe away, rocketed into outer space faster than I depleted my bank of clever 1980s slang words. Words I learned by listening to Claire.

Blonde.

Tall.

Skinny. But a lightweight in the brain department. Chad Prevington doesn't seem to care if Claire isn't smart though. He thinks she's cool, pretty, and fun. Maybe boys don't like smart girls.

Mom and Dad call me precocious, even genius.

I think that's my main problem. Who wants to talk to a precocious genius? It sounds worse than a period—and not the punctuation type either. Haven't had one yet, but I know about them. Claire's had one.

Doesn't matter.

I'm only eleven, and I'm not allowed to look at boys or even acknowledge their existence—except for Ethan's. I press my shoulders into my mattress and jut my chin into the air. But getting to know Ethan was an exception. He's wheelchair-bound, so my rafiki felt sorry for him.

I especially cannot talk to boys who look like Chad—rich, pale, and blessed with a Hollywood smile.

So my rafiki says.

I don't know all the reasons why.

I sigh.

I wouldn't know what to do on a date anyway, but all my fourteen-year-old classmates have gone on at least one. Even coke-bottle-glasses Sherry Sanders. That makes me a total dud—a rocket with no fuel to launch.

But could I try to be more like Claire?

No. It'd be too hard; she's fourteen, perky, and cool. It's easier to act like myself. Satisfied, I tuck the thought behind a gap-toothed smile. I've got bigger problems.

One day, someone graveyard scary will take me.

When?

How?

Why will they take me?

I don't have a clue.

Or at least, I don't know the real reason—the unfiltered, unparented, PG-13 *Raiders of the Lost Ark* version.

Last night, while I eavesdropped on my rafiki talking to my mom, I overheard something about me becoming the next Indiana Jones. That must have been a joke. I'm so not brave. Definitely not swashbuckling-Harrison-Ford brave.

I'm just a girl. Small. Awkward. Brown. Mom and Dad had whispered something about an ancient puzzle and finding a mysterious key to unlock it. I am good at solving riddles and finding lost things. Ask my mom. When she loses her keys in the morning, I'm her go-to kid. Actually, I'm the only kid in the Cavanaugh house. My shoulders slump.

The mysterious key supposedly will allow me to conquer an invisible planet called Wormwood. Yeah right!

I understand.

Really, I do.

Every parent wants their kid to grow up and become a hero. The Andersons brag about their son to my parents all the time. Bobby's doing this. Bobby's doing that. My mom and dad say nothing. But I don't fight, much less conquer planets named after invertebrate animals invading a piece of wood.

Who names a planet Wormwood?

Creepy.

Pluto may be small and losing its planet status, but the name at least sounds planetary.

Last night, after the conversation died down, when my parents had cuddled together on the living room couch, sipping lemonade and whispering into the night, I stood hidden in the hallway. Dad had whispered to Mom, "Chi-Xi-Stigma."

What the heck?

Then, he talked about taking me on an archeology dig to look for the lost Ark. At best, dirt and I maintain a love-hate relationship. I can be a tomboy, but only when I need to be.

For instance, when running from alligators.

But my parents lost me when they were talking about my traveling to exotic worlds of the past and future. Don't know how I'm going to travel to other worlds, much less afford anything exotic. Dad earns $17,000 a year. I saw his tax return.

Mom studied at Spelman College to become a teacher but chose to stay home with me until I grew up. My allowance consists of five dollars a week. We're poor, but I'm okay with that because we won't always be poor.

Promise.

My rafiki said something about math problems, too. At least I rock at math. But he also mentioned a pandemic. The thought of diseases makes me nervous and itchy all over. My parents call my dislike of viruses, parasites, and bacteria OCD.

OCD. Obsessive compulsive disorder—or any other acronym that forms a speed bump in my path to becoming a medical doctor—prepare to be flattened.

Then there was the vilest part: the part about the orphan.

Orphan and Dreamers.

It's an odd combination.

4—Orphan Dreamer

9:01 p.m., Thursday, April 1, 1993
Gainesville, Florida

OKAY. MAYBE I AM A bit sheltered, even naïve.

Can I share a secret?

I have never met or even seen an orphan, at least not while awake. The idea of meeting someone who was given away—a kid who doesn't belong to anyone—scares me to the bone.

Because if someone doesn't belong, they have nothing to lose.

Right?

It's the law of nature . . . I think. Maybe I'm also a bit jaded.

Mom explained that jaded means overly negative; the word *jaded* reminds me of turquoise-tinted diamonds, so I use the word at every opportunity. My dad swears that the men in prison commit crimes because they have nothing to lose. No love. No family. No hopes or dreams. Just … plain nothing.

I toss and turn, hoping for sleep, but it evades me.

If I meet an orphan, will that orphan infect me with their I-don't-want-you-anymore disease? Will I become an orphan if I befriend one? Could an orphan's misfortune rub off on me, making my parents die or choose to give me away to the universe or to a stranger?

Anne Shirley was an orphan, too, so no matter what swashbuckling adventure my parents predict for me, one day I will find my very own *Anne of Green Gables* kindred spirit. Red hair, freckles and all.

Plain.

So definitely simple.

I like orphans like Anne.

I try to swallow, but my mouth turns cotton dry. Clutching Grandma's quilt, I bolt up in bed. They call him—the eyeless boy who has been turning my dreams into nightmares for the last six months—the Orphan.

Not an orphan, but *the* Orphan.

As if he is the only one. Sort of like the University of Florida Gators are called The Gators, not *a gator*.

During their not-so-secret conversation, Mom and Dad called me the Orphan Dreamer. My slight frame quivers more violently than the 1960s Valdivia earthquake I learned about in Ms. Bender's science class.

I chew the inside of my lip while I think about the Nazca Plate gyrating and grooving across the South American Plate to the tune of 9.6 on the moment magnitude scale, a.k.a. the new Richter scale for humongous quakes.

Tectonic plates dancing in the middle of the ocean . . . ? Scary lousy idea, by the way! That's how tsunamis start, and once they start: Oh. My. Goodness. They cause a mess.

Well, the Nazca Plate went and danced atop the rocky floor of the submarine Peru–Chile Trench in the eastern Pacific Ocean that reaches a maximum depth of 26,460 feet below sea level.

A place of dark, cold, and suffocating death.

What do you think happened?

I crash onto my fluffy sheets and dig my toes into the mattress, trying to anchor myself, but I keep shaking. I pull my grandma's patchwork quilt over my chilled, sweat-drenched body.

Someone opens my bedroom door.

My heart skips a beat. If it's Mom, should I lie and tell her I found the obsidian arrowhead—my ticket to non-crazy? I squeeze my eyes shut and practice my lie. *I found it, but I want to wash it before showing it to you.*

Should I tell her about my other dream? The burning cats and birds?

No—I'll be committed forever.

Then I'll never become the Orphan Dreamer, and if becoming this person will lead me to my kindred spirit, I can be the Orphan Dreamer, or at least I'll try. Hopefully, I can figure out why I'm having dreams about burning animals and Mongolian warlords.

I slip my sheet down and peek over the line of cotton. My rafiki enters my bedroom, holding a jar. Shriveled-up yellow wings cling to the bottom of the glass tomb.

Corn shuck and hay! Forget the arrowhead. Dad found it—the other thing.

Warmth fills the back of my nose, then slips down my throat. The hot liquid tastes like nails. "I-I-I didn't mean to kill it, Rafiki. Honest, I didn't!" I sniffle hard and then swallow a slimy mixture of blood and mucus. Gross.

"I believe you, darling."

He believes me—always does. I take a deep breath.

"Always tell the truth even if you're scared."

"Yes, sir. But I didn't mean to hurt it."

My rafiki gives me his handkerchief, then chuckles. "You're a gentle soul. A bit absentminded at times, but you couldn't swat a bumblebee even if it stung you. But why did you do it, Danny-girl?" He sits on the chair beside my bed.

"I had to help . . . I just had to, Daddy." My voice falls to a whisper. "Sunflower-yellow wings. Miniature black eyes. Dainty feet. She is . . . I mean was . . . so b-b-beautiful." My face flushes. I hate stuttering. So unladylike. Claire would never stutter.

"God rest its little soul."

I sniffle again. "It's not fair. Buried alive. Suffocating. Being forced to begin as a slimy green worm and then hide its ugliness inside a dark, cramped cocoon. The apricot sulphur didn't deserve to struggle anymore. Being buried alive part is enough misfortune for such an exquisite creature." I dab my nose with his handkerchief.

"But by helping the insect, you crippled it."

"I know that now, and I'm sorry. Devastated, actually. Promise I am. Cross my heart, hope to die."

"I hope you live!" My big, brown eyes find his—kind, understanding, fatherly. "Our lives depend upon your staying alive, Danny Rose."

"Really, Dad."

"I'm telling the truth."

"It's not right to make up such stories. I'm not special."

"You are special, and I'd never lie to you." Daddy smiles wide. "And this is the truth: beauty and life without strength—without suffering—can be a crippling, or even fatal, flaw. Ask Claire. She should know."

Instinct tells me to laugh at my dad's joke but looking

at the dead insect stifles my humor. "I'm not beautiful. If that's what you're saying." I divert my gaze from my dad's kind eyes.

"But you are, and the struggle, baby girl, strengthens the part of the insect that allows it to fly." My dad's voice cracks. "Robbed of its strong wings, it died. Remember this lesson, Danny Rose."

"I will—promise, pinky swear."

My dad links his chunky fifth finger with mine, crushing my pinky like an anaconda suffocates its prey. He smiles at me, and initially, warmth consumes my shivering frame, but I know the truth: I killed that apricot sulphur—innocent, beautiful, and packed full of sunflower-yellow hope. Cold dread consumes my mind.

Even my rafiki agrees with the verdict: I am a murderer. My heart plummets, sinking 30,000 feet into the dark-blue depths of the Peru–Chile Trench.

A bone-crushing depth.

Flat-as-a-pancake squished.

Dad's right.

I should feel sadness, because a kid who kills helpless things by crippling their wings no longer deserves empathy.

Guilt and darkness fill me. I face my newest reality. I am no longer Daddy's little innocent girl—I am an impatient murderess, a convict just like the men locked behind bars at Florida State Prison, where my dad serves as assistant chaplain. But unlike the inmates, I don't have an excuse. I belong to loving parents, Austin and Jeanette Cavanaugh.

The apricot sulphur was my first victim.

"Dear God," I whisper beneath my breath. ". . . Let it be my last! I don't want to become a serial killer. It's true: I deserve a death sentence, but maybe I can make up for my fatal mistake?" I stop praying and look at Daddy again. "Rafiki, how much time do we have left?"

"Lord willing and the creek don't rise, enough time for you to change our fate. If you choose to accept your destiny, that is."

"Maybe I will," I whisper.

"Look out, Harrison Ford, a new Indiana Jones is in town!" Dad laughs.

"Not funny, Dad . . . Fate," I whisper, then sigh. "Definitely not my long-lost kindred spirit, is it?"

"Don't be ugly, Danny Rose."

But I am ugly. My face. My skin. My attitude. My future. Horned-lizard ugly. Beyond my window, two hundred billion stars form a posse and chase away the final bits of sun's warmth and light. Matching the turmoil churning inside my mind, darkness the color of black ink seeps across the once happy pale-blue sky.

Do the stars even like me?

But as always, as it sets, the sun whispers over its shoulder, "Goodnight, Danny Rose," swipes a kiss with painted lips of golden lavender across Earth's horizon, then skitters down the back side of the western sky—out of sight and out of mind, leaving only the darkness for those eager to get on with their diabolical plans.

It's my least favorite time of day.

Nightfall.

"Don't let them take me, Daddy. Not yet. Please." My lower lip trembles. "Make them wait at least until after my birthday party. Even if all my classmates refuse to come, let me stay normal until then."

"Why?" He sits beside me on the bed.

"Because maybe I'll open a big box"—I stretch my arms

wide—"that's been tied shut with red ribbon and royal-blue wrapping paper." I wipe a big, fat tear from my right cheek and grin, my chin quivering. "And maybe . . ." I whisper, "I'll finally find my very own Anne Shirley—a girl with matchstick-red hair who chooses to be my friend in spite of my nosebleeds, big hair, and brown skin. Okay, Rafiki?"

Dad says nothing for a long while. "It's not my choice, Danny-girl." Dad sniffles and rubs my arm with his calloused thumb. "Never has been." He folds the handkerchief soaked with my blood, hiding the evidence of my nosebleed. For the third time today, my face flushes volcanic hot.

He kisses my forehead, then turns off my lamp. "Sleep well, darling." The nightlight clicks on. "After you become a big girl, you'll be asked to decipher when, who, what, where, how, and why."

"Then I'll stay small—invisible."

"Not possible." He tucks me beneath my grandmother's quilt. "You're our Orphan Dreamer. So dream, my darling one. Spread your wings. Fly. And if the good Lord has a kindred spirit tucked away for you, she will be the lucky one." He winks.

"What about me meeting a nice boy and kissing him—on the cheek," I immediately compromise, "before I have to decipher ancient codes and be brave? Maybe I can be brave and go on a date."

"Absolutely not, Daniela Rose!" A scowl shadows his darkened features. "Your mother and I will pray for rapture before you ever reach puberty. That's what we'll do!"

"But who will decipher the riddles and save the world, Daddy?"

"Let someone else do it." He stands as he clenches and then unclenches his fists.

"Okay." Daddy's afraid of something bigger than the

dark. No longer daddy's little girl, I am left alone in the dark as he shuts the door behind him. I'm a butterfly, and I have to open my wings all by myself. And this brave butterfly likes to dream happy dreams. "So darkness, go away—no more orphan. No more scary faces."

I click on my flashlight and study my rafiki's newest word search puzzle, which he made especially for me.

The title reads *Your mission, should you accept it: solve the riddle.* Find the words that will remind you of your destiny: WHEN, WHO, WHY, HOW, WHAT, WHERE.

```
S V W O S Y Y
R E H O B H A
L W E N H W M
O O R B W G I
F N E H B V D
R G E P B H I
Q N T A H W L
```

I solve the puzzle in ten seconds flat! *Easy-peasy.*

"Daniela."

I jump. "Mom. I-I-I didn't hear you enter."

"It's okay. I was looking for you earlier. Where were you?"

"Outside."

"Did you find the arrowhead?"

I gulp hard. Here goes nothing. Best get up, dressed, and ready to be sent to the kids' mental ward ASAP. I blow a long breath from my mouth. "No, ma'am."

"It's okay, Daniela. You'll find it in time, and when you do, write about it, okay?" Mother reveals what she is hiding behind her back. I thought it was a straitjacket—but instead, she gifts me the most beautiful pink, leatherbound journal.

"Wow!" I launch from my bed, spilling waterfalls of cotton at my bare feet.

"Happy early birthday, my cinnamon-spiced bumblebee. You're almost a teenager, and you've always been our dreamer, and one day you won't just dream . . . you'll go places. Far. Far. Away. And when you go and then come back, write the details of the journey in your journal. You may need the information in the future."

"Yes, ma'am." There she is, so beautiful as she sits on the edge of my bed dressed in her pink silk pajamas. "I love you, Mom. One day, I'm going to look just like you."

"No. You'll look like yourself. Beautiful as a sunrise." Mother smiles then leans down and kisses me before she reaches for a small, leather-bound book next to the base of my table lamp.

She thumbs through the thin pages and then reads, "'Then the Lord answered me and said: Write the vision And make it plain on tablets, That he may run who reads it.'" She flips to the back of the book. "'In the last days, God says, I will pour out my Spirit on all people. Your sons and daughters will prophesy, your young men will see visions, your old men will dream dreams.'"

"So my dreams and visions are normal—even Biblical?"

"For God's girl . . . very much so."

"I'm not mental, then?"

"You're not a schizophrenic. Just because you hear His voice and see His plans before the rest of us experience them doesn't make you crazy. It makes us deaf and blind."

With her words, a weight the size of a boulder floats off my chest. She—my beautiful and kind mother—believes in me. I sigh, my lungs filling easily with air. "Thanks for believing me, Mom."

"Always and forever. Close your eyes, darling. It's time to go to sleep." Mom turns off the light and slips my bedspread up to my chin.

Mother and my rafiki want me to dream, too. "Maybe I'll write my own movie script."

"Why?"

"Fantastical books and movies are super popular. *Star Wars, The Lord of the Rings* and even *Jurassic Park.*" I tick off my top three.

"Makes sense that stories featuring exceptional and vivid worlds where justice is just, and honesty is honest, a place where love resonates in its purest tone—*agape* love, a selfless kind of love—are the most popular."

"Okay. If I don't go to medical school, I'll become a movie person."

"So then, sleep, and as we both remain enamored by the fantastical, we will remain grounded, searching for a place of truth illuminated by an Eternal Light."

I smile on the inside. I'm not crazy. I know about the Eternal Light—the Jewish menorah. "Mommy, the Eternal Light is a thing, right?"

"No—it's a person, and that light is Yeshua."

Maybe I am crazy. "Could it be a thing, too?"

Mother furrows her brow. "What do you mean?"

"I think I saw something in my dreams . . . a big, gold light with straight arms. Fire burned on the tip of each arm."

"That's the description of the original menorah—though most people describe the original menorah to look like the artifact chiseled into the Arch of Titus . . . Any more details, darling?"

"Not much," I say as her inquisitive bright brown eyes search mine. I look away. She can't know about the burning animals. She'll think I'm a sicko and commit me for sure. "Mommy, where is this home—a place of peace, love, and truth? Where is heaven—exactly? Do you have the address?"

"You'll go once it's your turn, okay? The Light will take you there. But not tonight."

"Okay. I can be patient. I'll wait my turn."

"I know you can. You're a good girl." Mother closes my bedroom door with a soft thud.

"Yahweh . . ." My voice is nothing but a breath—a last exhale drawn from my inner strength. "Shine a light and take me to this safe place, a world better than my happiest and most fantastical dreams—past Claire's lies. . . take me to the stars beyond, Papa."

A voice whispers into my soul, "My Word is a lamp unto your feet, and a light unto your path . . . so go, then."

Bravely, I climb out of my bed, grab my flashlight, and sneak out of the house to our backyard. I return to the pond, the shadow of death now dispelled with the illumination from my light.

I might as well be wading into the raging waves of the Jordan River as I eagerly seek to find the Truth in the midst of the darkest sea of lies.

No more lies.

I will face and then embrace the truth. Mom says, "Truth will lead us to freedom, and freedom leads us safely home."

An hour later, with the obsidian arrowhead secured in my right hand, I fall asleep and dream without shame and fear. I don't go anywhere like Mommy promised I would go one day. I wake up and write the details of my visions and dreams inside my new journal. Because one day, strangers will call me the Orphan Dreamer.

Daniela Rose Cavanaugh. Orphan Dreamer. And one day, a doctor.

What's in a name?

My purpose.

My contribution to the world—my legacy. The name given to my darling daughter, Adelaide Rose Cavanaugh-Finn.

If I call my daughter's name, Cavanaugh comes first, before Finn.

If her father calls her name, Finn comes first . . . at least in my dreams.

Twenty-three years later . . . Eight years before the second total solar eclipse, occurring on April 8, 2024.

5—Orphan Dreamer

06:20 a.m., Sunday, September 11, 2016
Florida

IF THE UNITED STATES OF America succumbs to the curse of the Bat Creek Stone because Daniela Rose Cavanaugh—Earth's last Orphan Dreamer—never learns how to swim or finds someone who can, well, some will think it's a cryin' shame.

But others will be pleased, positively thrilled.

China.

Russia.

Iran.

Governmental vultures awaiting the eagle's demise.

How could Daniela—who as a non-swimmer at the tender age of twelve was pushed by her middle school nemesis over the edge of Newnan Lake dock—a rickety, wooden thing suspended over murky, black, gator-infested waters—be expected to dive beneath an Indian burial mound and journey through an underwater cave to satisfy the curse of the Bat Creek Stone?

Daniela thinks of the hissing laughs, puffs of oxygen delivered through the diver's regulator during her intro to diving class.

A major fail!

She thinks of the regulator as nothing more than a poisonous serpent's jeering wheeze, *You're dead, Danny Rose, buried alive in a soup of stagnant water and decaying plants and animals!*

This expedition—navigating the nooks and crannies of an ancient, underground, mysterious room nestled beneath the lakes and foothills of Tennessee's Great Smokey Mountains—is a journey where her lifeline is a set of dueling oxygen tanks delivering miserly gifts of oxygen.

This girl, whom the world had tormented, is not expected to think with a clarity that directs her to find the destination on the map tucked inside her leather journal.

Daniela Rose has satisfied one quest. She is a medical doctor—an anesthesiologist—not a contortionist or magician. She rolls her eyes. Raising the dead is so much easier than swimming in tight spaces.

She'd done it before.

Why expect this thirty-five-year-old, single woman to face her fears only to save a gaggle of strangers?

That's only if she succeeds at her next quest of searching, then finding, and opening the entrance of a submerged Indian burial mound where she must race against a clock, triggered by a booby trap.

Before the clock runs out, she must solve an ancient puzzle that would satisfy the demands of the Bat Creek Stone curse and secure America's second—no, her final chance . . . the world's final chance.

This stuff is Indiana Jones's job! She sighs deeply.

The overnight call is almost complete. She rubs her shoulders as she exits the operating room for what she hopes will be the final time for the last twenty-four-hour shift.

Physicians' twenty-four-hour calls are inhumane . . . bright light; the lack of sleep, food, and water; and constant stimuli sounded like something out of a POW camp. And yet the medical system expects the most educated and dedicated portion of Earth's population to possess supernatural powers and not require sleep, food, or water.

Which is worse? Overnight call or wading through spider web–coated caves? Both could be on the résumés of Doogie Houser and Harrison Ford. A faint smile creases Daniela's lips.

Forty. She's five years shy of the significant birthday—a birthday she never believed that she would reach. *Rapture before puberty*, that was her parents' wish.

And then there was the constant sadness—depression as the psychiatrists had called it.

Forty. She glances at her watch.

Almost there.

Only forty minutes before her twenty-four-hour call shift as an anesthesiologist ends. She grins, pushing shallow dimples into her fatigued facial muscles. The lack of sleep has riddled her body with prickly numbness. Daniela stumbles through the corridors of the dimly lit operating room, the idea of the impending cave dive releasing waves of shivers and rivulets of perspiration down her five-foot-six, Pilates-toned body.

She slides the back of her hand across her forehead.

Did she have a fever? No—please, no! She can't be getting sick—not now. He's coming this morning . . . and this is her second chance.

Death-warmed-over was never a good look on her.

Forty . . . almost forty years old . . . forty minutes. It's true: forty minutes can span an eternity for the in-house trauma anesthesiologist covering a Level I trauma hospital.

Gunshot wounds.

Car accidents.

Stab wounds.

Yep—the evidence that the world's gone plum crazy.

Daniela walks with purpose—sure footing, a steady pace—until she reaches her call room, a place to be herself and not the heroine so many expect her to be. She's been trained to handle the anesthetic concerns of life and death but learning how to swim is a summit she just cannot reach.

Then find someone who can, a voice resonates deep inside her soul. Someone—a kindred spirit—but when did she have time to find her someone, a quiet man? A man who cares.

Find someone who can, Rosebud, the wolf within repeats. It's her knowing—God's voice, whispering into her spirit because she's one of God's girls. A sheepish smile replaces her sullen expression, and she whispers into the nothingness, "Okay."

She punches in the code, then stumbles into her call room for the first time during her grueling shift, praying that she can sleep for thirty minutes before he—that possible someone—arrives at the hospital's front entrance to pick her up and keep her safe from the coming storm.

She climbs beneath thin, starched white sheets.

Still single, unwillingly so . . . she thinks. Too busy. And too timid. Unwilling to grab the bull by the horns, as they say, when it comes to falling in love. She inhales and releases a sigh. Daniela closes her eyes, shutting her window to the present—and embraces her dreams, her reality, singleness without a family, a spigot without running water. *Grabbing a bull by the horns . . . what a silly idea!*

The dingy white walls of the small, square room close in around her, images of being buried alive invade her imagination, feeling all too real.

Then, the events of her trauma call play out like a horror movie inside her mind: gunshot wound to the face. A stab wound to the neck. Semitruck versus a motorcycle, and the passengers mangled. *Breathe, Daniela. Just breathe. It's not your fault. The world is a messy place with messy people, and you cannot save them all . . . even if you wanted to.*

She slows her breath. Inhale—*2, 3, 4, 5.* And out through her nose—*2, 3, 4, 5.*

The edge of a lifelong dream—motherhood, a loving marriage—blurs the edges of her reality.

This dream—a nightmare, a vacancy—haunts even the quietest moments.

An analog clock resting on the small, beat-up table next to her bed ticks down to 07:00—the hour of her release from trauma call, but there is another clock ticking down, and at the end of that clock, the world will end.

"Don't let it be my fault, Yahweh."

I need a swimmer, Rosebud, so be brave. Swim, darling girl.

She says nothing to the wolf within for a full three minutes. "Fine." Her focus would need to shift to marriage, and maybe even motherhood.

What would it feel like to give birth to a little baby girl and then get to teach, celebrate, and love her to pieces . . . and what about a son? She would teach, celebrate, and love him, too, raising him to adore his God, his mom, and his country—America, her home.

"Trauma alert. Trauma alert," the hospital operator announces over the intercom in a frazzled staccato pace. Lying on her belly, Daniela's heart sinks to the front of her chest. *Not another gunshot or stabbing victim—please, no.*

All knives and guns should be banned . . . no—she has a better idea. Cut off everyone's hands. Then, the brutes would succumb to headbutting, and she'd be taking care of patients all night, providing anesthesia as the head butters underwent surgery to evacuate brain hematomas. A sardonic chuckle tells her that she is losing touch with her practice of medicine.

A lack of empathy is a hallmark sign of a burned-out physician.

Make it go away.

She waits . . . a minute passes. "Level I trauma has arrived in the ER," the operator shifts her message and makes a call to action. *It's not going anywhere.* She grinds her teeth. So much for rest. She rolls out of bed. It squeaks beneath the shifting of her thinning frame.

She slips on her face mask and eye-protective glasses—no telling what bodily fluids will be flying around the trauma bay of the emergency room—then shuffles one foot in front of the other out of her call room.

Daniela joins her on-call nurse in the hallways. "Good morning, again, Janice."

"We have to stop meeting this way, Doctor Cavanaugh."

"You don't say. Breakfast at IHOP after work?"

"Yep—the OR techs and I figure we'll hit it up one more time before Hurricane Josephine arrives."

"Good deal. That place is a mainstay to the beachside, and it may not be there after that Cat 4 hits," Daniela delivers the glum news.

"I know, Doc. The trailer may get washed up this time."

"If it does, you can use my spare bedroom. A promise is a promise."

"Thanks, Doc."

"You're welcome. I'm sorry nature seems so out of control these days."

"It's not your fault, Doc."

"Sometimes I feel as though it is." Daniela fingers the Glass Tattoo at the base of her neck. She and Janice pick up their pace, walking briskly down the harshly lit halls toward the emergency room.

She inhales sharply, and lint escapes her mask, making her sneeze. The barely filtered antiseptic scents that seep through are both familiar and sterile. Daniela punches the silver-metal plate on the wall by the double doors, and two steel doors open outward. She and her nurse exit in the back hall of the operating theater. They turn the corner, exit another badge-secured door, and Janice presses the elevator button. "What're you thinking about, Janice? You look deep in thought."

"Surviving this call, then eating pancakes and sausage, and drinking orange juice."

"We'll survive the call, Janice—though, we may just be the worse for wear."

"What about you, Doctor Cavanaugh? What are you going to do?"

"Take a shower, then sleep." Daniela leaves off the part about meeting Cillian at the entrance of the hospital, then letting him take her home—her talents belong to the health-care community. Her private life, well, it's private.

Plain.

Definitely simple.

Ten seconds later, the elevator arrives at the lower level of the hospital. *It's go-time.* "Let's see what's cooking." Daniela transforms from the shy introvert into the professional who knows what her abilities are and what they can do . . . save a life.

The elevator doors open, and she bolts out of the steel box, rounds the corner, swipes her badge, and runs into the ER. Janice is right beside her. She dashes into the first trauma bay on her left, her breath controlled as though she sprints every day.

In the first trauma bay, she sees a teenage boy. In the next, another. Two boys, abdomens ripped open, spilling blood like they're the sole donators to the fountain of youth. "Goodness gracious alive," she mutters. Their blood soaks through the white sheets beneath their bodies.

What if they were her sons? She tries to swallow, but the maternal thought has sucked all the spit right out of her mouth.

"Gunshot wounds." The trauma surgeon glances up at Daniela.

"You don't say . . ." She purposely adds a dash of sarcasm to stifle the other emotion—grief.

The trauma surgeon knows this, of course she does. "You okay, Doctor Cavanaugh?"

Daniela nods. "What can I do to help you?"

"Intubate this one and then prep the operating room." The trauma surgeon points to the young male in the other trauma bay. "He's done, but we'll try to save his brother."

Brothers. Daniela blinks back a stray and inconvenient tear, then smoothly intubates the first boy. Janice makes a call, notifying the trauma operating room team of the plan.

Daniela and Janice assist in the resuscitation of the young male as the trauma surgeon places a femoral central line to measure the blood pressure and then another to give blood rapidly.

After starting an intravenous line on the patient's left arm, Daniela pulls her scrub jacket tight, hiding her flat stomach—proof, nothing in the motherhood category has ever occurred beneath this belly button.

Motherhood.

A blessing to some. A curse to others.

A curse . . . it was fifteen years ago—the morning radical Islamic terrorists attacked America, and the same day Daniela met Genghis Khan, the infamous Mongolian warlord. She lay on her backside, vulnerable in front of her accuser and judge—a handsome medical school coed. His name was Morgan. She had collapsed inside the University of Florida's formaldehyde-drenched, basement-level cadaver lab.

After meeting Genghis Khan, one thing was clear: the ancient light mattered to her success in saving the world. When the second of two total solar eclipses, both crisscrossing North America's sky, penned the letter *X*, the final countdown will be complete—the end of America's second chance.

Her final chance.

Find someone who can swim.

It's the only way to save America, and eventually the world.

She studies the boy's face. It's true: humans don't seem to want to be saved. Maybe this was the someone who would swim the last lap of the race? But he's dying now. No—this young man is someone's son, left to his own devices, and the streets had raised him. Maybe his parents were to blame, maybe not. But they hadn't helped this young man succeed, and neither had society.

When would Daniela have time to find this messiah swimmer, unafraid of the water?

Daniela works—works, and then works a bit more. But what has she accomplished . . . really?

It's true. Daniela did something counterproductive for an introvert and a woman who longed—no, still longs to become a devoted wife and an even more a devoted mother. She should have refused the promotion.

Plain.

Definitely simple.

But she didn't. The hospital needed a doctor—a leader. And Daniela was just that. After securing the new 14-guage peripheral IV, Daniela moves closer to the head of the bed. Her heart pounds. Is this trauma exercise all for nothing?

Please, God, make it not so.

Standing above him, Daniela shifts her gaze to the boy's eyes.

The young man's bloodshot, vacant glare looks past her. His expression is one of terror. His pupils are no longer re-sponding to light—black pupils fixed and dilated, filling his brown irises, the tell-tale sign of brain death. Just because a patient has a heartbeat doesn't mean they are alive.

Heartbeats could tell lies, too. "He's brain dead, Doctor Conner," Daniela says in a deadpan voice to the trauma surgeon. Yes—their work had been for naught.

"I know, but he's young . . . has a pulse. We must give him a chance."

"A chance at what? He's brain dead."

"Daniela . . . Dr. Cavanaugh." The trauma surgeon pauses for effect. "What if this patient were your son?"

A clump of emotion forms in the back of Daniela's throat as she reflects upon the question. What if this brain-dead patient were her son . . . or her daughter?

No—this could never be her son or her daughter.

She wouldn't allow it.

Motherhood takes time, and if one day she should be

fortunate enough to become a mother, her career would take a backseat to motherhood.

Plain.

So very simple. The choice is hers, and she slides it from the shelf of possibilities and places it in her heart.

"I'll go and prep the operating room . . . see you there, Ruth." Daniela and her nurse return to the operating room. They prepare the surgical and anesthesia equipment and medications for the patient, this brain-dead boy. As they quietly work, Daniela pens a letter to her daughter—the little girl she still holds in her heart, inside her dreams.

Adelaide, my darling daughter,

It's time to be quiet . . . to reflect. Never be afraid to dream, even if the dream is dark and you're afraid to close your eyes again. Life is a vapor blown away by the winds of time. When my time ends, I'll say goodbye, and then I'll fly away, my most darling daughter. But I'll see you again, in another time, and in another place. Address unknown. But the Light knows how to find His home beyond the stars. Please do not perform heroic but futile medical interventions on my corpse.

No matter how afraid you are, swim to the destination. This is our second chance, America's second and last chance . . . Earth's last chance. Be brave and be kind.

Daniela Rose Cavanaugh—The Orphan Dreamer
Your Mummy

6—Orphan Dreamer

06:32 a.m., Sunday, September 11, 2016
Florida

"DOCTOR CAVANAUGH, IS THE OR ready?" The trauma surgeon bursts into the operating theater with the patient on the gurney, snapping Daniela out of her internal conversation.

"We're ready." She slips her cell phone from her scrub jacket pocket and dials her on-call CRNA. "Hey, Natalie. GSW in OR seven. Intubated. Lined up. Blood transfusing via the Belmont. See you soon."

"Coming, Doc," Natalie says.

The last twenty minutes of her call shift, someone would be murdered.

Four minutes shy of 06:40 a.m.

7—Orphan Dreamer

06:36 a.m., Sunday, September 11, 2016
Florida

FOUR MINUTES UNTIL 06:40 A.M. If Daniela had known the tragedy about to unfold before she transfused another unit of blood to her brain-dead patient, she would have saved the donor blood for another victim.

After Natalie arrives, Daniela and the certified registered nurse anesthetist transfuse three more units of blood and start medications designed to raise the patient's blood pressure.

The patient's vitals stabilize, but his pupils still tell the world, "I am dead."

"Let's give two units of fresh frozen plasma," Daniela tells Natalie.

"Will do," the CRNA reaches for the cooler holding blood products. Suddenly, a loud bang ricochets, sending echoes through the sterile air of the operating room. Daniela pivots on her left foot, her gaze focusing on the door behind and to the left of her position. "Sounded like a gunshot."

Shaken, her team continues its resuscitation attempt on the teenager. She glances back at her patient, noting the teardrops tattooed at the angle of his right eye. She hadn't noticed those before.

They represent how many people the gang member has murdered. Where was his mother . . . where was his father? She clenches her hands as blood pounds into her neck arteries.

Pow. Pow. Pow.

"Call security, Janice! Someone is coming to finish the job." Daniela barricades the door with her anesthesia cart, trapping them inside, determined that the medical team will not lose their lives.

Daniela controls her breath to keep from hyperventilating. Breath in—*2, 3, 4, 5.* And out again—*2, 3, 4, 5.*

"I'm going to pack the belly so we can get out of here." The trauma surgeon packs the belly with surgical sponges. Daniela decides that now is not the time to question the surgeon's odd choice of packing material. The nurse scoots the heavy cart away from the external operating room door, opens the large steel door, and peeks down the long hallway.

"Active shooter." Janice slams the door shut again. Panting, she repeats, "Active shooter approaching our OR."

"Opening the door wasn't in the plan of defense, Janice," Daniela snaps as she draws up a mixture of succinylcholine—a powerful paralytic. "Now, the shooter knows where we are." She mixes it with two milligrams of Remifentanil, an opioid that will stop a human from breathing.

Her CRNA and the rest of the team continue to care

for the patient as Daniela positions herself near the door to protect the team.

Thud! Before Janice can reposition the cart, the door hits the nurse in the face, and she falls backward. A large man, face littered with teardrops, charges into the room and aims his gun at the surgeon.

Daniela ducks.

"Let him die." The gangster turns his gun on the nurse.

"Mister, he's already dead—eyes as fixed as the stock market." Daniela clutches the loaded syringe with a trembling hand, tucking it slightly behind her right thigh.

"If he's dead, why are you working on him? Using up taxpayer money."

"I doubt you're a taxpayer." Janice's careless comment is all it takes to raise the ire of a madman. The gunman pulls the trigger and shoots her in the head. Daniela grips her syringe tightly; a deep breath fuels her muscles. She flinches with each shot as the gunman unloads his gun into the patient's chest. The beeping of the heartrate monitor slows, fading into monotone.

What is a life but a vapor?

The gangster reaches for a reload. *Big mistake!* Daniela lunges and stabs the gangster in the right shoulder before unloading her anesthetic concoction. Within seconds, the combination renders the man helpless. Twitching beneath the spell of the depolarizing paralytic, he falls to the ground near Janice.

"Good job, Daniela." The trauma surgeon un-scrubs, then checks to see if Janice has a pulse. "Nothing."

Quickly, Daniela intubates the gunman and gives him several breaths through an Ambu bag. Belatedly and breathlessly, hospital security arrives. *Just in time*, she thinks. "When the drugs reverse in ten minutes, he'll be crazier than a lunatic, so keep him secured." Daniela assists the security team in lifting the gangster onto the gurney, where his wrists and ankles are handcuffed to the metal railings. "All she wanted was to eat a stack of pancakes with a side of sausage and to drink a cup of OJ after work."

"Don't even know why we save people like this." The security office's face flushes with an eggplant hue, a mix of hypoxia and rage.

"It's not fair," Daniela admits.

The gunman's limp arm falls over the edge of the gurney. Before she places it back onto the stretcher, Daniela notes another marking—a brand . . . like Cillian's.

The room spins. She belly-breathes, fighting the urge to pass out. It's a barcode, like Cillian's!

A waterfall of empathy washes over her as she retrieves a warm blanket and places it over the gunman.

"Dear God," she whispers. "What's his story?"

8—Orphan Dreamer

07:27 a.m., Sunday, September 11, 2016
Florida

THE DRIVER OF THE IDLING SUV—a charcoal-gray Land Rover with tinted windows—is waiting in the hospital parking lot. She dials his number and lets the phone ring. "I'm almost there."

She's late.

As usual, Cillian is on time.

She smiles, wanting to release a girlish grin and giggle. But vulnerability isn't her biggest talent. Dressed in green hospital scrubs, Daniela stumbles from the bowels of the inner-city hospital.

The rain pummels the sidewalk just beyond the hospital entrance's overpass, washing grime into the foul-smelling sewer. Eager to wash away the horrors of the night, she runs into the thick of the rain. The torrent splashes her pants, soaking her feet and legs. Fat, wet drops pimple her skin.

She focuses on the raindrops sliding down her scalp beneath her curly hair, the clothes clinging to her skin, the pavement slicked with oil and rain and denying her clog-shod feet a firm grip—anything to distract her from the fear and anger. Janice shouldn't have died this morning.

The Land Rover rolls toward her, just beyond the overhang.

There had been another gunman . . . years ago. During that ordeal, as Daniela was recovering in the ICU, Valerie—her ICU nurse—instructed her then to find someone who could swim.

That someone exits the SUV and saunters toward her—broad shoulders, dressed in an army-green button-up shirt and black Bermuda shorts.

He stops in front of her. The taut muscles beneath his clothes twitching with anticipation . . . anticipation of her, or she hopes.

Thick, black hair.

Freckled, pale skin.

A megawatt smile that could illuminate hell and outer space at the same time. Maldives, almost unnaturally bioluminescent blue eyes. She has long believed him to be something otherworldly. He's too perfect. Maybe an angel . . . Like Legna?

"Daniela, how are ye, lass?" His voice is but a whisper—so quiet and Irish with a hint of a Scottish burr, a soft blowing in her direction, a gentle breeze carrying all sorts of possibilities from his homeland of the ancient Gaelic lands. "Why did ye not call me again then wait for me inside? Ye'll catch yer death in this rain."

"Then, we'll die together." She tries to be funny, but he furrows his brow. Then asks again, "Are ye all right, lass?"

She says nothing for a full minute. He waits, not pushing,

just present. Supporting. "Ah, lass." He sees straight through her fatalist attitude. "Are ye sad, then, Daniela?"

She nods, trying not to cry. "I am. I'm so very sad . . . and unhappy, Cil."

"Ah, lass, yer as kind as ye are brave." He swaggers toward her, closing the distance before he takes her into an embrace, holding her, shielding her from the rain, an umbrella of muscle, grit, and determination.

She quietly waits for him to finish his thought, and even though he is naturally a quiet man, he finally responds, "But I'm afraid yer kindness may verra well be yer curse, Rosebud."

Daniela pushes away from his embrace, then sweeps a clump of rain-soaked stray curls from her tired eyes. "Really?"

"It's the job, Daniela—the daily crucifying of who you really are . . . a quiet woman. A woman of substance who has forced herself into a position where it's all noise—clanking pots and pans. This new job takes all yer time. Each wakin' hour, yer toiling for strangers. Takin' care of patients is one thing, Daniela. But takin' care of a gang of ungrateful employees is another. Yer an introvert. A person who relishes quiet and peace."

"But so are you," she protests, feeling so inadequate in front of him. He has amassed a fortune. A Bernard Arnault–sized fortune while owning and managing thousands of employees. She blinks back tears, but even among the raindrops, he notices.

"Ah, lass." He flashes his flawless smile—shy, pink lips evenly pulled back over bright white teeth. "Yer goin' to hate me for sayin' this. But yer tender—a woman meant to be adored by her man and her children, not worked to the bone by strangers."

She doesn't protest. He is right. Women-lib. Strong Black woman. All those false labels about her were nothing more than spikes nailing her coffin shut. "I don't know what to do, Cil. I don't want to fail."

"You must make a choice. Decide." He pauses. "But before you do, I'll be givin' ye a bit of advice if ye'll be takin' it and placin' it in yer heart."

"Okay. I'll try."

"Be verra careful that ye dinna spend all yer talent, time, and kindness on behalf of strangers who willna be holdin' yer hand when yer takin' yer last breath."

"Oh, Cil." More tears fall. She prays rain will wash them away, too, hiding her vulnerabilities, her failures—time wasted. Seven weeks prior to this moment, she did something so very foolish. She accepted a leadership position. What is an introvert doing talking to people, much less leading them? "I was asked, Cil."

"Of course, you were, lass. Yer a woman of many talents. But ye'll remember that I asked, too, Rosebud . . . and ye said no."

Be brave, Danny Rose. Don't blubber. She repeats the internal mantra over and over, but she fails to enact it. Proof trickles down her cheeks, barely masked beneath the raindrops splattering her face—a mask of fake bravery, the Orphan Dreamer's more commonly told lie.

"I shouldna ha' said that." He cups her face between his warm, strong hands.

Tears fall untamed onto his fingers. "The truth, you mean? You should always tell me the truth, even when it hurts. You're not judging me. You're protecting me."

"That's true. Yer safe wi' me, and ye needn't be strong when yer wi' me." He pulls her into his chest, then says,

"Cry for a while, lass. It's good for yer soul especially in the rain."

She did.

She knows she is safe when Cillian is near, but his powerful presence—his form, his character, his impossibly beautiful face—makes her feel overwhelmed, like she wants to pull away.

No—Cillian isn't judging her. She's judging herself. And the verdict in the court of Daniela Rose versus Daniela Rose is always guilty.

Cillian judging her? Never.

Protecting her? Yes.

Comforting her? That too.

Giving her joy? Always.

But the idea of loving him and being vulnerable . . . yielding her innocence to him—the idea terrifies her. What would that feel like . . . naked with nothing to hide behind? Allowing him to penetrate her defenses in places she'd allowed no man.

She would rather take swimming lessons in Boiling Lake and receive third-degree burns over her entire body than be vulnerable to Cillian in that way. Daniela had endured the burn ICU once in her lifetime—she knew what to do with physical pain and scars.

Cillian lets her cry until they are both soaked to the bone. Then, he sweeps clumps of hair from her eyes, wrings the water from her water-logged curls, then places them into a bun at the base of her neck. "I like to see yer eyes . . . beautiful and brown, *mo nighean donn*." With his kindness, he draws her out of her dark cocoon of introversion.

She lets herself fall into this moment. Her gaze makes its way upward from his muscular abdomen to his chest.

She finds his face—scars of the childhood pain still etched into the depths of his ocean-blue eyes. She allows him to see her tear-lined face as their gazes lock.

Two days ago, she had gazed into these same eyes and lied to herself. Lying to him and God, she had betrayed their future together, and her happiness. Too busy with a career she was beginning to loathe, she hid from his love, afraid of what it would do to her, so she declined Cillian's hand in marriage.

Cillian Joseph Finn.

Somewhere in a list of synonyms inside an archaic book of definitions, his name, essence, and legacy would be found next to these five words: Kind. Brave. Reliable. Trustworthy. Honorable.

In a rendering of his likeness, the artist would paint a ravishingly handsome, Einstein-intelligent, and Bernard Arnault–wealthy figure. Even though Cillian is quiet, he can also be funny with the people he trusts.

Trust, something that flourishes in the absence of lies. He's a dream, Daniela's dream. *What have I done? Why?*

She knows why.

Daniela Rose, Earth's last Orphan Dreamer, is afraid to allow herself to be happy. Denial. Sacrifice. Mental anguish. Loss. These words feel familiar.

Rapture before puberty, her parents prayed every night when she was a little girl, but now she has eclipsed puberty. It is as though she was designed to be alone. But Cillian, unlike Morgan, would have been patient—in every way.

Yep, Daniela Rose.

You're a certified idiot.

A wave of nausea rises from her gut with a tsunami of negative thoughts that shake the foundation of her psyche—a mind that is, at times, disorganized and depressed.

The pediatrician had diagnosed her with childhood-onset depressive schizophrenia.

But her mother and father had fought the diagnosis.

A headache pounds in her temples. She deserves the pain, the throbbing.

She had caused Cillian pain.

As though the sky is equally as tired, the rain stops falling, but the sea's winds increase in strength.

A gust blows humid breath in Daniela's direction. She tumbles backward, almost falling.

No—it isn't hurricane-force winds trying to knock her down. *I asked, too, Rosebud . . . and ye said no.* It is the truth of his words sinking in, fracturing her emotional dam—her hiding place for too long.

But his words had found her soul, too.

Simple, yet exacting and precise—a force more powerful than the winds of the approaching hurricane.

But even while telling her the truth, Cillian makes her feel safe, holding up a mirror while turning down the lights.

He catches her as he always has, with a gentle but firm grip. "Breathe, Daniela. Just breathe. There'll be another time when I'm brave enough to ask ye again."

"Please be brave, Cil."

His hand presses into the small of her back, nudging her toward him, a place of safety and acceptance—a fortress of unconditional love, a love that almost killed him. He guides her toward the SUV. "Ye need to dry off."

"I need to do a lot of things, Cil." Daniela takes heavy, labored steps to the passenger door, knowing she has been a fool and a liar.

She has deceived herself.

Facts: Daniela Rose Cavanaugh is not that important in the task of healing this broken world.

It's true. Yahweh chose her to be Earth's last Orphan Dreamer—the one chosen to wield the power of the Glass Tattoo.

But Daniela could have chosen Cillian, too. She could have chosen happiness instead of a life of only service to strangers.

It's not a sin to be loved well.

Jesus loves well, and He is blameless. In the darkness, Daniela keeps her gaze on the freshly washed asphalt, avoiding Cillian's penetrating gaze—an ocean of pale blue light, illuminating her path. But maybe he's not even looking at her any longer? Maybe he's seeing another woman.

The world hasn't always been kind to him.

He has a past, as most people do.

Even in the night, his eyes sparkle with an otherworldly light, a fire fueled with kindness and gentleness so rare in a man, or in any human for that matter. They are illuminated sapphires—brilliant even in the absence of light and despite the horrors they have witnessed.

Daniela says nothing because her heart is broken, unable to pump blood into Broca's area—the part of her brain responsible for speech.

"I've not been kind, forcing ye to stand in the rain." He opens the passenger door. "And yer drenched."

"So are you." She pauses before getting in. "Besides, you've never forced me to do anything—sometimes I wish you had."

He crinkles his brow. "No—I would never do that, Rose-bud."

"Take me home, Cil."

"If ye'd like me to." A fine tremor ripples through his jawline and settles into his voice. Cillian releases her bun then squeezes the water out of her rain-soaked locks. He shakes his hands, then scoops her hair back up into a bun before ushering her into the passenger seat of his Land Rover.

Spook—his Belgian Malinois—nuzzles Daniela's wet face as she climbs in. "You're a good boy." She yields her face and neck to his wet nose.

Cillian closes her door, walks around the truck, and climbs in. He reaches behind the driver's seat and retrieves a hand towel. "Dry off. Ye'll be wantin' a proper, hot shower if the power is still on."

"You could do with one, too." She winks.

"Do I smell, lass?"

"No—but your complexion is a pale-blue, and I doubt that's healthy." Daniela gingerly smiles. "I'll run a hot bath for you. I know you prefer baths."

"That's true." He winks at his lass, and she reaches for his hand and finds it. He drives out of the parking lot, navigating large rain puddles.

"Thank you, Cil."

"Yer welcome, lass." She towel-dries his head and back before drying herself. Daniela turns her attention to Spook and gives him a scratch behind the ears. Cillian's quiet presence cocoons her in a sacred silence.

Fifteen minutes later, he parks inside her seaside condo's underground garage, and they ride the elevator up to her penthouse floor. She unlocks the door, and they enter the empty house with Spook in tow.

Faith—her Maltese—is gone. Cillian and Spook don't immediately leave; they never leave before she tells them she's okay.

Spook follows Daniela to the kitchen, and she gives him a treat—a roll of turkey meat. If the power is going off, the fresh meat will spoil anyway. But the threat of a power outage hadn't made her such a softie in this moment. She regularly slips the dog bits of fresh meat.

Daniela fetches Cillian her biggest and fluffiest towel before running him a hot, Epsom salt bath. She emerges from the master bathroom a few minutes later. "Your bath is ready." She will take a shower in the spare bedroom.

Thirty minutes later, Daniela towels off and finds Spook waiting for her at her bathroom door. "Where's your daddy?" She dresses in a flannel nightgown. "Cil, are you done?"

"It smells of lavender and peaches, lass." He strolls into her bedroom from the master bathroom. His black hair slicked back.

Dearest God! She wants to gasp but doesn't. *Why did You have to go and create something like that?*

But everything beneath her skin is reacting—boiling, tingling. Fine hairs stand at attention down her slender, scarred forearms. A pleasurable sensation settles deep inside her pelvis, and her skin flushes as her heart thrums. "Lavender and peaches . . . that's me." She blushes and looks away. Can he tell she wants him?

"Makes me want to eat dessert." He smiles, knowing exactly what he is doing.

"It's hot in here." She skedaddles, heading toward the thermostat.

"Cooling it down, Daniela . . . willna make a bit of difference." He grabs her from behind.

"It may help." She looks up. His neck and face are flushed. "Wh-wh-what did you have in mind—for dessert?"

"Peach pie, Rosebud." Mischief twinkles beneath his gaze.

"Umm," she stutters. "I don't have any peach pie, and Publix is closed."

"Then I'll wait for another day." He pulls back the sheets, and she quickly jumps into bed then yanks the covers up to her chin, burying her damp body beneath a thin layer of cotton.

"Okay—then."

He simply surrenders to her wishes. He's a patient man. She's not patient. She's afraid. There's a difference. "Get some sleep, lass. Spook and I will pick ye up before daybreak tomorrow morning."

"Okay."

"Pack what ye want, and I'll come back before the hurricane arrives."

"Promise?" She grips her cotton sheets as though she might float away if she were to let go.

"I do. Ye'll stay wi' Spook and me in the mountains where ye'll be safe."

"Thank you," Daniela simply says as Cillian tucks her covers around her. While he plunges her sheet and bedspread under her body, she sees his lips move without uttering a sound. "Are you praying for me, Cil?"

He blushes. "Guess I am." Cillian Joseph Finn—the Orphan—is praying for her, the Orphan Dreamer.

"Ironic but comforting." For years, she had prayed for him.

"I pray for you—for us, every night, lass." He leans over and pecks her on the forehead.

"What about?"

"Things." He doesn't elaborate, then changes the subject. "Dinna worry yerself. If ye decide to step down from job or even if ye decide to keep it, I'll take care of you . . . and provide for you."

"You'd do that for me?" She wrinkles her forehead.

"Yes—I would." He pauses while tracing the outline of

her lips with the back of his forefinger. "When yer takin' yer last breath, Rosebud, I'll be there to hold yer hand . . . if ye'll let me."

"I'd like that." Though the fear is suffocating, Daniela refuses to break the trance of their gaze. "Cil, what about pacifying the curse—swimming, then finding the underground cave—what about that?"

"Ye dinna ha' to be the Orphan Dreamer to everyone. Least of all me." He releases a reluctant smile held captive by his sadness at her refusal of his hand in marriage. She unburies her left hand from beneath her sheet and rests it on his leg. He places his hand over hers. "Am I not the orphan boy ye were dreamin' of, lass? The one ye were prayin' for?"

"I think you are."

"And now you've met me. Touched me."

"I have." She squeezes his hand and pinches his arm, still refusing to believe he is real and not a figment of her imagination.

Cillian laughs. "Ye still think I'm a ghost—a wraith?"

"That's what Paul calls you sometimes." She shrugs and tucks her lower lip between her teeth.

"Well, lass, he's my wee brother, so he calls me many things."

"You're so perfect—can you really be real, Cillian?"

"Aye then, I'm real all right, lass."

"I'm not calling you a liar. It's just that I don't trust myself. My pediatrician diagnosed me with delusional thoughts as a kid and even said I'm a schizophrenic."

"What does God call you, Rosebud?"

"His child, one who hears His voice unfiltered."

"Believe Him. He's the one who created you, and just because yer dreams are more vivid than others doesna mean yer a split personality." He gestures at the reality of her home—the bed, the television, the small desk that was her mother's and now anchors the corner of the room. "If this is the only kind of reality, reality is boring. But ye should know this, lass: ye dinna ha' to dream of me anymore. I'm wi' ye now. And that pinch . . . it hurt me, *mo chridhe.*"

"I'm sorry."

"Don't be . . . I long for yer touch, Rosebud, even if it hurts." He pauses, swallowing his injured pride and his unfilled needs and emotions. "I'm here. I'm real. Dinna deny yerself a happier reality just because yer afraid—okay? I know how to hold a lantern still."

"Find someone who can swim," she whispers, then closes her eyes. "You can swim like a dolphin. I've seen you."

"I can, *mo chridhe,*" he replies in a tone with a rugged edge of desire. "And so can other parts of me waiting inside my body." He chuckles, then rests his left hand on her abdomen and gently presses down. "We can swim together. I'll teach you."

Swimming together . . . that's what it would take to become a mother. She glances at her clock, and Cillian lowers her black-out shutters.

At 9:40 a.m., Cillian walks out of the Orphan Dreamer's home.

The lie she's telling herself about what is most important in her life—the strangers, the patients, and the staff in a hospital—is nothing more than a moth-eaten, small-pox-laden security blanket.

Please get rid of it, the wolf within warns. *Blankets made of lies will kill you.*

The warning is there, but so is the fear of the unfamiliar. Daniela is used to strangers rejecting her, but what if Cillian rejects her just after his seed takes a swim, leaving her alone to be a single mother?

Catch the butterflies, Danny Rose. Stop the self-sabotage!

The self-sacrifice and self-sabotaging martyr's complex . . . they both started on July 8, 1993, the night of Daniela's twelfth birthday. The night of her poorly attended birthday party, when her classmates had rejected her, Yahweh chose her.

He chose this unlikely child to become the next Indiana Jones. That night, Daniela Rose Cavanaugh became Earth's last Orphan Dreamer.

But heroines, heroes, and even villains need a kindred spirit—someone who loves them as they are.

Someone they can trust.

Someone who can withstand the pressure of the flame and not run away.

It is up to the heroine to learn to trust her God-gifted kindred spirit, allowing him to swim the last leg of a race and cross the finish line.

Teamwork. Trust.

Friendship. Romance. Marriage.

Even Abraham, the Judean patriarch who entered the blood pact called the mystery of the Bat Creek Stone, trusted Eliezer to find a wife for Isaac—Abraham's promised son.

As Daniela falls asleep, her scattered thoughts shift between vivid scenes of lies and truth.

Lies, nothing more than a hammer in the hand of the Father of Lies, killing dreams for an eternity.

Truth, it is everything—the Liberator Who came to Earth to set hearts and dreams free, butterflies released for eternity from their dark cocoons.

Daniela knows about butterflies. Because when she time travels as the Orphan Dreamer through Ellesmere, sometimes she assumes the form of an apricot sulphur butterfly—her favorite butterfly.

The Father of Lies sees a butterfly as what it used to be: a dirt-eating worm that has just emerged with fragile wings from a dark place. But The Liberator sees cocoons and butterflies for what they will become.

Cocoons—a second chance, a final chance.

Beginnings. Endings. How would Daniela have lived her beginning if she had known her end?

Earth's last Orphan Dreamer would have fought for a second chance—the bravery to trust Cillian Joseph Finn to swim the last leg of the race.

After she solved the mystery of the Bat Creek Stone curse, he would appease the demand of the curse and save America, and ultimately the world.

Teamwork.

Marriage.

It would be a cryin' shame for the world to end because Daniela never learned how to swim or found someone who could. Almost lost to sleep, she rests her hand on her abdomen, imagining Cillian's essence exploring . . . then, the fruit of his exploration swimming deep inside her, finding its other half, then making Adelaide Rose. Their daughter. Their child. Their legacy.

Daniela would like that.

She runs her tongue along the rim of her lips. She is ready to face her fears and become a wife and a mother.

Three years later . . . Five years before the second total solar eclipse occurring on April 8, 2024.

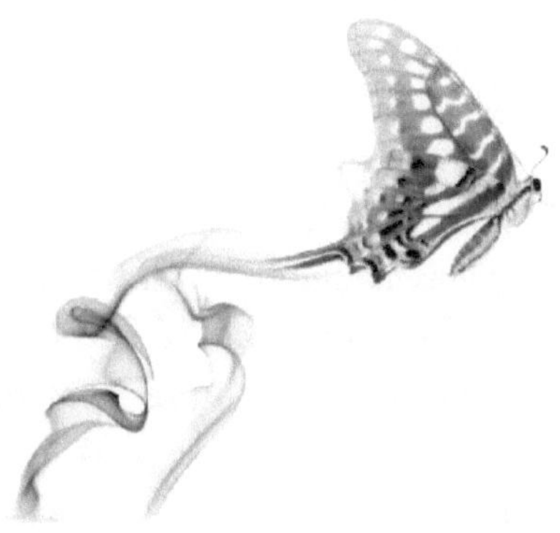

9——The Bat Creek Stone

4:00 a.m., Monday, July 8, 2019
Amalfi Coast, Italy

BLACK WATERS MUSCLE AGAINST THE powdery-white beaches of the Amalfi Coast—the place where thousands of years ago, under the eyes of God, the Tyrrhenian Sea and the Gulf of Salerno wedded during a beachside ceremony then went on honeymoon and became one flesh of pale blue waters, Southern Italy's Mediterranean Sea.

At dawn—when the light bleeds into the darkness, abolishing it from the devil's playground—the grieving parents will begin their arduous task.

Even after the sun rises, the prince of darkness will still be horsing around, watching as two devastated parents, Earth's last Orphan Dreamer and her billionaire husband, take Kian out to sea for the last time.

Captain Rolly makes good use of his time. He plants

the last of the nuclear tracking device onto the hull of the luxury sailing yacht—a sleek, midnight blue crown of the sea. Claire Amilee's submarine will be looking for Mister Finn's yacht.

Cillian and Daniela shouldn't have messed with us, the captain thinks as he chews on the end of a Gurkha Black Dragon, a Christmas gift from the Chairman of the Sons of Venus—a secret society of secret societies.

Beneath him, the depths of the water roar—bass booming, rattling the subwoofers of the sea.

The waves calm Captain Rolly as he works the ropes, freeing the luxury sailing yacht from the moors before the stars take their leave. And the day awakens.

As the captain checks his maritime maps, he notes the weather: mild, calm seas. *Perfect for a funeral.* He grins.

Here, the ridges of Italy's Lattari Mountains coalesce to form the rocky backbone of the Sorrentine peninsula of the Amalfi Coast. A summer breeze lifts then soars, swooping down from the emerald-breasted Lattari Mountains, no different than a bald eagle taking flight.

The eagle's going to fall out of the sky soon. The chairman of the Sons of Venus believes it to be so, and Captain Rolly cannot tell if Asher Bushcroft is happy about the eagles' fate or devastated about his prediction.

With the yacht's ropes secured to the deck, the captain pulls anchor then maneuvers the Finn-Cavanaugh's brand-new yacht, *The Rose of the Ocean,* out of the harbor while the parents still sleep.

"Captain Rolly, do they know yet?" a nosy deckhand blessed with mousy hair, plump hips, and a pair of equally jelly underarm batwings drills the vessel's captain. His eye twitches, an outward representation of his inner annoyance.

The captain wants—no needs, to focus on the process of navigating the yacht past the rocky coastline.

"No, Inspector Holmes—they don't," he snaps, his tone laced with the sharp edges of sarcasm. He clears his throat before sucking another drag from his cigar. "Cillian and Daniela are still sleeping."

"Good on them," she says as she clumps her thinning hair into a ponytail that looks more like a half-plucked cattail.

He smirks, amused at his own foul sense of humor. "The package . . . do you have it, Sherlock?" The captain blows a nose full of smoke, not bothering to direct it away from his subordinate.

Without answering, she jogs across the deck, down a set of stairs descending into the ship's bowels.

Those knees are shot, he thinks and chuckles. But he isn't anything to look at either. Splotches of red and rough patches mar his skin. Bad dentition from years of smoking. And a set of small, poorly set eyes. All add up to plain ugly.

She returns and offers the captain a manilla folder. Captain Rolly snatches it from her hands, rips open the folder, and flips through the photographs. "You sure this photograph is of the authentic Bat Creek Stone?"

"I am."

"And the marking on the back . . . it's a map?"

"It's there, Cap. Hidden except for those who know how to bring it to life."

"I can see that," he snarls. "You sure it's accurate and will take us where we need to go?"

"My brother says it is."

"How is the rabbi—the former rabbi, now a secular man . . . a professor." Captain Rolly hocks a wad of spit and swallows.

"Fine. He got a promotion. He's director of Israeli antiquities." She puffs out her chest.

"Those triple-D trash bags could use a plastic surgeon's knife, and until then, those bags could use a set of power poles to prop them up. Don't you think?"

With an agility that defies her body habitus, she pivots, reaches down and then around, slapping him diagonally across his pocked face before resting her hands on those massive hips. They wobble beneath the sudden movement of her hands. "That's not what you said last night, Cap."

"Wow!" He shakes his head—exaggerating the action as though he's a cartoon character that's just received a roundhouse slap. "Like it—like all of it, Big Momma. Bring that to the birth next time."

"Call. Me. That. Again." She narrows her eyes and shoots lasers through his chest.

"Oh—so you also like to lie to yourself, too." He shrugs. "So be it. Then, we must get to the relic before the Orphan Dreamer does."

"You're wrong—we are going to make sure she and the professor get to the relic first. They already found it once."

"Well, help them find it again, so she can teach us how to use it."

"You are a conniving little feller," she says.

"I'll take that as a compliment."

"Captain, do you think she's dreaming right now?"

"Of course, she is! She's the Orphan Dreamer, dim wit." The captain hocks and snorts down another mouth full of tobacco-laden mucus before swallowing and then releasing a litany of coughs.

"You really should stop smoking, Cap." She wags her head.

"Why? The world's ending in a little over five years."

"America's not the world, Cap."

"She is to me." He grunts, then barks a command to his subordinate. "Go swab the decks and stop eating so much cake and ice cream. The boat's going to sink. Then, go to the comm room and activate the cameras and tracking devices. Those nukes need to be able to find their way when Claire Amilee gives us the command."

"Aye, aye, sir." She fakes a salute and abandons the captain who is steering the yacht from inside the cockpit. *Too eager to please.* He despises that kind of woman. But that backhanded slap . . . that was his kind of woman.

The deck hand pops her head back into the cockpit. "Claire Amilee." She says the name with an ample amount of disgust. "Be careful you don't end up as one of her targets."

"She doesn't hold a candle to me in the intellect department." He punches in a set of new coordinates, and the sails adjust.

"Cap, you think the Orphan Dreamer will find a way to give America a second chance?"

"I hope so." The captain takes the yacht out to sea, knowing that in five years, the second total solar eclipse will occur. And on this day, the moon will wedge its girth between the sun and the earth.

According to the Orphan Dreamer, after the second total solar eclipse crosses over North America, the end of the eagle's dominance of the sky will arrive unless the curse of the Bat Creek Stone has been pacified.

'Bout time. Captain Rolly grins, revealing a set of stained and broken teeth. *Yeah—I know. Thought I was a patriot. I am—just of a different country. We were here before you were. And we're going to take our home back. That's all.*

Monday, April 8, 2024.

A Monday is as good a day as any for the world to end. No underpaid worker needs to return to their chosen, lifelong corporate plantation; no student needs to endure another lecture in school about . . . pick an annoying topic.

"Of course, she's dreaming." He grips the yacht's helm. "That's what the Orphan Dreamer does—time travels while she sleeps. No wonder she looks dead-possum-tired."

But when she returns, tired or not, she is ready for a fight. Captain Rolly tightens his grip around the helm until the blood drains from his pale fingers.

Is he ready for the fight?

10—Orphan Dreamer

4:12 a.m., Monday, July 8, 2019
Amalfi Coast, Italy

INSIDE THE AFT MASTER STATEROOM of *The Rose of the Ocean*, the Orphan Dreamer has been travelling even though she appears to have been sleeping.

The yacht rolls, tethered to the off-beat rhythm of the sea, waking Daniela to a view of limoncello-colored lights twinkling against the backdrop of a predawn morning.

"Four hundred," Daniela mumbles as she rouses, rolling away from her husband who's still sleeping.

Still half-asleep, she halts her log roll just before she falls off the edge of their king-size, pillowtop bed.

Daniela squints, the morning fogginess from a disturbed night's sleep cloaking her brain. She moans, loathing the next action on her to-do list: climbing out from her cocoon of dreams and bed covers to face the reality of her present—a reality without Kian.

"Four hundred," she mutters again. "Forty multiplied by ten," she mumbles as though she's speaking with someone while still emerging from Ellesmere, a place far away.

And no differently than a bird migrating south, she is coming home from a faraway land with a vital clue clutched inside her beak. On the fourth day of creation, Yahweh created the sun, the moon, and the stars—the timepieces of the world.

The number forty, a multiple of four, in the Hebrew Scriptures and the New Testament signifies the end of a time of testing.

For four hundred years, the Israelites were slaves in Egypt.

Moses was an exiled prince of the house of Pharoah and lived in the Sinai Desert for forty years before returning to Egypt.

After God spoke to Moses through a burning bush, God raised the former prince up to lead the enslaved Hebrews out of Egypt. After the Hebrews were freed, complaining was their constant practice, so God allowed them to wander the desert for forty years before they were allowed to enter the Promised Land.

Jesus was tested in the wilderness for forty days and forty nights.

Four.

Forty.

Four hundred.

Four and multiples of four are important numbers.

They pertain to the timing of the end of the old world and the beginning of a new world. The end of one superpower and the beginning of another superpower. Daniela reaches out and removes the Skeleton Key from the bedside table next to her side of the bed. Its head is made of pure gold, its chest and arms of silver, its belly and thighs of bronze, its legs of iron, and its feet of part iron, part baked clay. Each metal represents a historical superpower.

Ten toes made of clay and iron, representing the last of the human kingdoms.

Most Americans believe America began in 1776 during the year the Declaration of Independence was signed while rejecting the 1619 Project—launched in August 2019 to commemorate the 400th anniversary of the arrival of the first enslaved Africans in the British colony of Virginia.

America's Declaration of Independence was penned in 1776. The Revolutionary War ended in 1783. But when this project that acknowledges European colonization began in 1607 and ended en masse in 1783, the true age of America will be revealed—over four hundred years old.

Four

Forty.

Four hundred.

The end of something.

It's also true: four hundred years ago, in North America, the Aniyvwiya were displaced, triggering the Bat Creek Stone Curse.

What's next for America? Prosperity or the apocalypse or Armageddon?

What's next for the world? Peace or the Tribulation or a nuclear holocaust?

The pain of the impending loss of her home rips through Daniela's soul, and she trembles, her sweat-misted frame rippling beneath her cotton nightgown. The shredded remnants of a tangle of cobwebs still ensnare her brain.

Danger. Wake up!

Her heavy eyelids snap open.

If the apocalypse is on the way, what's the plan? She rolls

over and faces her husband, thinking to wake him and talk. No—let him sleep; it's the antidote for unrelenting mental anguish. They can brainstorm later after they honor Kian.

What's the plan . . . wanna rush back home to pack a go-bag?

It's tempting.

Maybe even rational. But the action will be futile.

No forest or jungle is thickened enough by canopies of trees to hide a human from the sun when it catches an attitude and starts flicking off solar flares—like a smoker tossing lit cigarette butts into a patch of dry grass.

When the sun hurls a solar flare toward Earth at more than two million miles per hour, the sheer electromagnetic power will disturb Earth's ionosphere, disrupting radio communications, interfering with internet connections and the power grid while heating Earth's outer atmosphere and causing it to expand.

The Carrington Event released approximately ten megatons of exploding TNT. Compare the Carrington Event solar flare to the Tsar Bomba, the most potent thermonuclear weapon ever detonated, and the explosion power is about five billionths of the power of the Carrington Event.

It's true that Earth's magnetic field protects the planet's population from death by solar flares.

But what happens if its magnetic field is destroyed?

Daniela is a scientist, and she knows the answer. That's why she asks: why pack a go-bag? It's useless. No one can survive the power of a rogue solar flare.

But she'll tell her secret: There is a way for a person to escape a solar thermonuclear apocalypse.

And the Orphan Dreamer knows the path to safety.

It's true: She's an introvert and prefers peace and solitude over chaos and company.

But she's not a narcissist. She'll share her exit strategy—It's simple: *Beam me up, Scotty.* Just have to know Scotty personally.

Daniela does.

His name is Immanuel, God with us. Jesus. Massaging her throbbing temples, Daniela does the inevitable—she rolls out of bed and faces her reality—a life without her son, Kian.

She gingerly sits on the edge of the bed, careful not to wake Cillian, who is barely coping. If Cillian survives the emotional battle of their loss, he will possess one more option of escape than his wife.

Claire Amilee, Daniela's childhood and adult nemesis, has offered Cillian a place in *The Hive.* But he would have to go without his family. *The Hive.* Haven't heard of the place?

Of course not. Didn't cut the muster.

Few have been invited—only five million persons out of Earth's population of over seven billion.

Unless a person has been genetically blessed to be beautiful—but not too pretty as to intimidate Claire Amilee—they would have less than a one-percent chance of being granted an interview, much less a pod where they could wait out the nuclear blasts and Earth's pause.

Yes—a handful of invitees are hopelessly unattractive, but they're Oppenheimer-level geniuses or titans of industry, possessing a bank account to prove it. A space home located far from the sun's wrath costs a lot of money to build.

Otherwise, if a person cursed to face the sun's rage isn't like Cillian, there. Is. No. Room. In the inn.

Cillian ticks off all the boxes.

It's okay.

Daniela wiggles her toes and then stands. There's another inn, which sits at the end of the cul-de-sac of time and space nestled between streets of gold. Want the map—Daniela's exit strategy?

Here you go.

John 3:16. For God so loved the world, that he gave His only son. Immanuel. God dwelling with us.

11—Orphan Dreamer

4:34 a.m., Monday, July 8, 2019
Amalfi Coast, Italy

FOR OVER A YEAR, SHE'S been dreading this day.

He's not here—not anymore. She blinks back her tears. *Don't look,* she thinks, but her doe-brown eyes track beyond the foot of their bed to the dresser. The small wooden box is still there, resting quietly where his father placed it last night, atop a mid-modern design of teak wood and bronze pull knobs.

Yes, she's the Orphan Dreamer, but Daniela has failed to dream her nightmare away—the presence of that wooden box.

She melts into a puddle of quiet sobs. *Don't wake Cillian!*

The devastated mother requires an immediate distraction to keep her grief from escalating. She strolls to the rear side of the stateroom, looking past a wall of windows while focusing on the ancient Romans' architectural work.

Both she and Cillian adore exploring abandoned castles.

Back at shore and beyond the stateroom's wide and equally long windows, the Amalfi Coast is dotted with the architectural work of the ancient Italians. In times of old, they must have tucked amber torchlights onto the underbellies of the village's stone bridges.

But why? What had they hoped to illuminate? Secrets, or the path for weary travelers who could stumble on their way home.

Light.

Illumination.

The amber light spills upward, casting an ancient glow across the network of arched bridges that underpin the seaside village. The pathways run beneath jagged spikes of dark-green mountains that look down like sentinels watching over the people and the happenings of the village.

It was here, a summer ago, Cillian introduced his wife, Daniela, to the delicate nature of fine Italian food. Ripe tomatoes. Plump green olives. Pungent garlic basking in a drizzling of olive oil. And the freshly baked bread. *Ah—the bread.* Daniela rests her hand on her abdomen.

It's okay. A few extra pounds at her age are a sign of health, right? She glances back over her shoulder, noting the wooden box. The room seems to close in on her.

Gasping, she opens the sliding glass door then inhales deeply.

The sea's breath rushes in, mixing with her own. It's wet, doused with predawn humidity, and laden with scents of life: wild-caught fish, baking bread, and garlic wafting from the kitchens dotting the coastline.

A scent that would usually make her mouth water now makes her nauseated.

She gags.

Daniela wipes her face with the shirtsleeve of her pajamas. She gags again then retrieves an Italian soda from the stateroom's wet bar. She sips the carbonated blood tangerine liquid until her stomach calms.

Beyond their stateroom, rows of white villas topped with Sedona red tiled roofs are anchored to mountain ledges that lean back from the meandering coastline of the Tyrrhenian Sea and the Gulf of Salerno.

After the sun rises, it will bleach the black nighttime waters into a shade of marine-blue. The same color as Cillian's eyes.

Still, the sun sleeps, not ready to bleach or destroy anything, yet. Two total solar eclipses. The last occurring on April 8, 2024, a date that seems a long time away.

Even the seagulls are not fishing at this hour.

Daniela adjusts her nightgown, evening out the cotton material clumped around her slumped shoulders. She closes the sliding glass door, a mechanical motion, then abandons the view. Still unwilling to awaken Cillian only to watch him grieve, she tiptoes toward the master bathroom of *The Rose of the Ocean*.

Life is a series of possible realities, and only God knows the path that should—and will—be taken.

Theologians call this attribute of the Almighty omniscience or foreknowledge.

Daniela's story isn't one of theology.

But even the founders of America's most esteemed academic institutions respected the omnipotent and omniscient Creator as they explored Earth and its world of questions—science, mathematics, and philosophy in concert with the spiritual, not in antagonism with the Creator and His creation.

To be one with theology and science is natural, a comprehensive study of the whys of the world.

Yale—was it not founded by conservative Connecticut Congregationalists? Princeton—was it not founded by pro-awakening New Jersey Presbyterians?

Brown—was it not founded by devout Rhode Island Baptists? Dartmouth—was it not founded by mission-minded New Hampshire evangelicals? And even Harvard—was it not established by Puritans?

These academic visionaries possessed intellectual minds well-seasoned with humility. They understood that there must be Someone who knows all the answers in a world so full of questions.

Find this Someone. Find the truth. How else could the principles of geometry, calculus, algebra, physics, chemistry, and biology come together and form the universe with all its complexities?

To reject truth is to embrace the lie.

Daniela undresses, preparing to freshen up. Grief weighs down her already-sloped shoulders as she steps into the warm streams of the shower. Her heartsong—Cillian—continues to sleep beneath the spell of Ambien mixed with a father's grief.

If life is a baseball pitcher, it's only been throwing curve balls to the Finn-Cavanaugh family. But this isn't a game.

Daniela sighs deeply, resigning herself to the depression stage of grieving. She and her depression have met before. They've gone shopping together. Starved themselves together. And even pointed a gun to their heads.

Emmaline's gun hadn't been loaded, though.

A second chance. It's a God thing.

12—Orphan Dreamer

6:03 a.m., Monday, July 8, 2019
Amalfi Coast, Italy

CILLIAN IS AWAKE—FRESHLY SHOWERED, BLACK hair slicked back, barefoot and dressed in lightweight gray cargo shorts and a crisp white golf shirt that clings to his thick, cut biceps and triceps.

Daniela reaches for his hand and holds on as though her very breath depends on it. She's dressed in leather sandals and a simple white tunic—Christmas gifts from Kian.

The couple emerges from the master bedroom. They walk in solemn unity up the parlor's steps and stroll across the yacht's teak-wood deck.

Captain Rolly is drinking coffee, standing on the boat's portside near the bow. Daniela notices the sun peeping up just beyond the coastline's horizon as they walk toward him. Kian is still sleeping, though. He won't ever wake to see the sun rise again.

The captain pops a toothy grin onto his face, rests his mug on a table, then approaches the headsail, mainsail, and jib. Cillian loves watching the sails open, and Captain Rolly knows this. The captain releases the three sails, exposing their apple-red hue, with the push of a button.

Each sail gulps the wind, then bows backward like a ballerina performing a backbend on the world's stage. The bowed sails push the yacht further away from the coastline. "His ashes should not be disturbed, Mister Finn."

"Agreed."

"Breakfast?" The captain gestures to the alfresco dining area that sits aft on the yacht, covered by five red canvas sails.

"Later, Rolly—after the deed is done and my boy is at rest." Cillian releases his wife's hand. He clings with both hands to his son's remains sealed inside a small wooden box made of Kauri wood. The same wood as Daniela's future casket. Life could be cruel, but death was much crueler.

"Yes, sir." The captain chews on an unlit cigar.

"Yer not smokin' on my deck, Rolly."

"No, sir." The captain dips his head, showing respect as his boss nears.

Daniela's right hand trembles as it clutches two boxes of Kleenex to her chest. With her free hand, she fidgets, twisting the time-and space-defying Glass Tattoo that rests at the nape of her slender neck.

The snowflake diamond sparkles against the cinnamon-brown hue of her skin—a delicate and delightful gift from her myriad of ancestors, a birthday gift she'd not always appreciated or adored as she grew up in a community where others loathed her skin-deep blessing.

Yes—her skin had been an inconvenience in certain spaces. But not in this one—out at sea, walking beside this man, the kindred spirit who had accepted and loved her just as God had created her to be. To be loved—and being loved well is not a sin.

Now, she embraces the story of her skin, the journeys of her ancestors who lived before. Skylark. Blossom. Grandma Gertrude. Jeanette Cavanaugh. Austin Cavanaugh.

Cillian's shoulder brushes his wife's.

Throbs of electricity pulse throughout her being, leaving her in a confusing state of grief and desire. *Let the desire last. Remove the grief, Yahweh,* she silently prays, then inches closer to Cillian, wanting—no needing—to touch him even if for the briefest moments.

Their footsteps are heavy and strained as the parents continue their journey toward the tip of the bow that juts out over the ocean.

The captain follows.

The sea air clings to Daniela's damp skin like her grandma's blanket, but its touch is impersonal, not comforting like her grandmother's. She takes a deep breath. Lavender-scented shower gel still radiates from her skin.

The scent calms her. She's determined to finish what seems like a death march. Finally, she reaches out and grips the brass railing.

It's cold, unaccepting.

She closes her eyes, no different than the truth of the matter.

It's over. He's not coming back.

Blinking back tears, she forces her mind to imagine Kian is still here and this reality is a lie.

Her boy following close behind, giggling and teasing his older sister, Adelaide Rose. Children—her children—at play in a safe place with their parents. The happy memory rips through her soul as the heavy air rattles the powerful headsail. The yacht launches forward, shifting her balance.

She stumbles. Cillian reaches for her just in time before she falls. "Thanks, Cil."

"Yer welcome."

Daniela rubs her arms, realizing that even the invisible jet streams seem to be pushing against her family and their future. She leans into the wind—air thickened to the consistency of fresh honey. And as Daniela leans in, she pushes back the darkness with flickers of a light burning from within.

Honey.

Kian's favorite.

The corners of her lips upturn into a faint smile as she recalls Kian's love of her Saturday homemade biscuits, whipped Irish butter, and fresh honey—harvested from the family's beehives.

Instinctively, Daniela parts her lips, hoping to taste the sweet nectar. But the sea's breath forces its way into her mouth and rests upon her tongue, tasting of brine. She snaps her mouth shut, wipes her lips as she opens her eyes, and faces what needs to be done.

The morning air thickens until the sky cries and forms a mist. Her unrelenting grief spills onto her psyche, and like rain made of bleach, would be expected to erase the colors of the flowers, leaves, and ocean. The brightness of Kian's memory begins to fade into the background.

Her smile disappears.

She pleads with God, *please, don't let me forget his beautiful face.* At that moment, Daniela ends the bargaining phase of her grief.

Grinding her teeth, she asks the question: another family member lost—no, taken . . . and for what? To secure a stranger's second chance against the Nephilim and the Watchers? What she wouldn't give to have Kian back in exchange for 10,000 strangers falling at the Watcher's hands.

"My cinnamon-spiced bumble bee, it was never going to be a fair fight." The warning from Daniela's late mother, Jeanette Cavanaugh, had proven true more times than Daniela cares to count, but she is sickened by casualties of the fight—her family, her son.

Catch the butterflies.

Distraction—please. Her disorganized mind attempts to cope with the emotional battering ram of a mother's loss.

Numbers. Math.

Anything.

It's true. Daniela possesses a love affair with numbers, even gematria—the substitution of numbers for letters of the Hebrew alphabet intrigues her to bridge science, mathematics, and faith.

Facts versus Truth.

Sometimes their realities align, and at other times, diverge.

The fact and the truth: at times, life disappoints. But life remains as a series of possibilities and even second chances.

God did not send His Son into the world to condemn the world, but to save the world. Fact—nope, it's truth.

Fact.

Daniela is a crack shot archer, usually hitting the bullseye every time she nocks, aims, then releases an arrow from the taut string of her Fred Bear Grizzly Recurve Bow—a gift from Cillian that features a riser made of walnut, white oak, and maple harvested from the hardwoods nestled around the Cavanaugh-Finn Blue Ridge Mountain chalet.

Daniela watches Cillian's Adam's apple rise and fall, so lazy and so anemic in action. She barely breathes as Cillian turns to look down at his wife.

His usual bright, aquatic-blue gaze is dull, a lifeless and vacant stare. Does God truly love like a waterfall—cascading down so wild and so free upon the broken hearts and minds of His kids?

Does He see his son Cillian? Does He feel His child's suffering?

Daniela loosens the belt of mental discipline that she secures around her mind and emotions. She recalls a few of the memories so carefully buried in the attic of her mind—slivers of his pain, a constant companion haunting Cillian's life since he was a babe.

Cillian was a product of rape. Fatherless. A child rejected and abused by his mother and her litany of men . . . and then the brothel.

A quake forms in Daniela's muscles, making her shudder.

Cillian reaches for her again, and she thinks to whisper a prayer to drive the demons away. But her prayers don't seem to hit the broadside of a barn—not even heaven's sky-wide barn anymore.

The evidence?

Kian, her only son, is dead, years before he was allowed to walk through the hallways of his sister's boarding school—Phillips Exeter Academy, one of America's most prestigious boarding schools.

Could there be a future for Daniela without Kian? Despite her gut-wrenching question, the Creator is here. Before dawn breaks, His eye is on the sparrows—two sparrows with broken wings embodied in the form of two devastated parents.

And as the sun rises, He brushes long and purposeful strokes of light across the deep berry-blue morning of the horizon, painting a watercolor that erases the darkness.

The sky is so blue that Daniela could drown in it. Within

the early morning light, tendrils of fog release their grasp, and the horizon clears.

Kian is home . . . forever.

Earth's last Orphan Dreamer wipes away a coating of stubborn tears from her long, brown lashes. She blinks and then glances up into Cillian's eyes. He looks away.

It's true.

Kian would never again ask Daniela to cook from-scratch oatmeal—apple-cinnamon spiced. Nor would he beg her to let him take a sip of her cucumber-apple-protein shake before spitting the gritty beverage into the sink.

He wouldn't sneak a taste of his father's hot Irish tea and scan his father's newspaper's cover story while waiting for Cillian to arrive at the breakfast table.

Cillian's body trembles beneath an invisible curtain of cascading emotions.

Daniela rests her hand on the small of his back.

A stiff ocean breeze cuts over the Tyrrhenian Sea and charges into the side of the yacht, spinning it aft.

Daniela fights to stand beside her man.

Cillian turns into the wind and clenches his jaw, his rugged and masculine grit steeling him against the headwinds tumbling down from the peaks of the mountains that tower behind the shoreline.

The Finn-Cavanaugh family will survive this. Cillian holds a small Bible in his left hand, then flips to a passage of Scripture, his Scottish-Irish accent underpinning all the inflections just right, "'I heard a loud shout from the throne, saying, Look, God's home is now among his people! He will live with them, and they will be his people. God himself will be with them. He will wipe every tear from their eyes, and there will be no more death or sorrow or crying or pain. All these things are gone forever'."

No more pain.

Faith—the substance of things hoped for, the evidence of things not seen.

Truth—God's promises.

Religion—human promises about God.

Fiction—the figments of our imagination.

In this moment, the prosperity gospel preachers, those who promised a false religion, a life where the faithful parishioners who gave a bit more money would experience a life where only blessings were added and multiplied …

Well, they are proved to be liars.

Because of late, Daniela's life resembles a subtraction table, taking away more than it has given.

And while the Orphan Dreamer slept and dreamed, defying time for the benefit of strangers, Nomed kidnapped her son.

I shouldn't have fallen asleep that night.

But it's also true that Kian's eternal Father never fell asleep—ever. And so He rescued the frail boy's spirit and soul, protecting them from Nomed's punishment of death.

Yahweh will stay with Kian until his mother and father arrive.

Daniela Rose takes her final and silent step, standing beside her husband.

Cillian stabilizes the small box in both hands.

She leans down and kisses the top. Cillian does the same, and in what seems to be slow motion, Cillian rotates the wooden box upside down and drops it into the sea, off the bow side of *The Rose of the Ocean.*

Death.

Life. Eternal life. How does one obtain eternal life?

The way … the Truth. Truth—a concept so rare these days—but so vital. Wading into the shark-infested waters of a sea of Cancel Culture, somebody as brave as God has to tell the truth.

But fighting for strangers . . . after this? Daniela thinks she will be sick. She gags, swallows, then gags again.

Cillian pulls her close. "It's okay, lass."

"But it's not okay, Cil."

"It will be."

Daniela isn't always brave, but she is a fighter. She has people to fight for—Cillian and their daughter, Adelaide Rose, her treasure, just like Daniela Rose was her late mother's treasure.

Now, she's a devoted mother.

Loyal wife.

Dedicated physician—an anesthesiologist, one of the medical doctors who would, in a year sacrifice their safety to save lives as COVID rampaged through communities, inflaming then plasticizing lungs and rendering them useless.

As she watches the small box float out to sea, she thinks to jump in and grab Kian into her arms—or what remains of him.

But she's a pathetic swimmer; she can't even tread water. And God knows that anytime Daniela steps foot near anything but a kiddie pool, she's begging to drown. Too bad this mission's success requires a strong swimmer's services.

I've sacrificed enough, Yahweh. Facing the water isn't a sacrifice I'm willing to make. I'm sorry.

She prays, completely unaware that the choice may not be hers.

It is a truth not known and thus not acknowledged by Daniela Rose—the gamma rays that she has been exposed to when travelling through Ellesmere via the Glass Tattoo, have chopped up a critical portion of the DNA inside her ovaries and uterus. The same reproductive organs that have refused to listen to her pleas to God and allow her to bear children have betrayed their owner, becoming treacherous monsters with a name: ovarian cancer with metastasis.

Ignorance is bliss, until it's not.

Daniela Rose Cavanaugh-Finn's body is harboring its own ticking time bomb even as America and the world are relying on her to pause the countdown to the end of humanity. Which countdown would approach *00:00* first?

If Nomed has his way, this will be Earth's reality.

He's gotten his way before, or so it seems.

13—Orphan Dreamer

7:06 a.m., Monday, July 8, 2019
Amalfi Coast, Italy

THE SUN CONTINUES ITS ASCENT, and Cillian watches Kian float away until his only son disappears beneath the undulating surface.

Unceremoniously, sunlight sparkles and dances on a dance floor of deep blue waves.

Daniela balls her left hand into a fist. Agatha Christie once said, "Evil is not superhuman. It's something less than human."

No—evil is human, a human.

And Asher Valerian Bushcroft is his name. A media mogul billionaire who presides as chairman over the elusive Sons of Venus. He was Kian's exact bone marrow match, but the handsome, tinsel-haired titan of industry had refused to donate his life-saving bone marrow to her dying child.

The refusal wasn't the issue—his bone marrow belongs to him.

It was the way he'd refused, the way he'd written back to Daniela. Without Cillian's knowledge of their communications, Bushcroft had informed the desperate mother in a penmanship featuring fine calligraphy that he would need to preserve his good-stock blood for his only remaining family—a long-lost sister, Natalia.

Ballerina. Violinist. Asher's one-time best friend. According to Bushcroft, Natalia had been taken by Nomed when she was a teenager, and the Bushcroft family lived in the Hamptons.

"Sometimes the weak need to be euthanized," he'd written to Daniela, and then continued to inform Daniela through his letter that he could not sleep at night if he wasted his bone marrow on someone who was not bone of his bone or flesh of his flesh.

She tightens the strip of muscle anchored to her jaw. "Payback isn't a female dog," she whispers to Asher. "She is a mother—me." Daniela unclenches her left hand and finds the Glass Tattoo dangling from a dainty platinum chain hanging from her slender neck with her left hand. "This is how I fight my battles," she whispers, but the wind immediately consumes her veiled threat.

That night—the night Kian died and before they'd gone to bed—Cillian had been furious when he found the correspondence between Daniela and Bushcroft, his former enslaver.

She had hidden the letter where she hid everything— beneath her delicates. Her husband had found the stack of letters when he put away the folded laundry.

Daniela should have hired a maid when Cillian suggested it.

"Bushcroft blood will never course through the veins of my son . . . not ever!" The volume of his voice had saturated the room, decibels pushing against the walls as though they might break through. But when he'd said *never*, the Earth shook loose from its iron-fortified foundation, and Daniela was sure the whole planet would lose its gravitational pull and be flung into space. "Never, Daniela. D'ye understand me, lass?" She was sure he'd put her over his knee and mete onto her backside some form of punishment.

But he didn't that night . . . and never had.

The same man who had raged that night is broken now.

His hands shake as he watches the box take on enough water to sink beneath the waves, and his grip on the misted handrails slips. He wipes his hands on his shirt then rips his golf shirt in half as though he's Samson getting ready to fell the temple.

Without warning, Cillian swings one leg up and prepares to jump into the ocean from the fifty-foot-high bow.

"Stop, Cil!" Her voice is hoarse, raked raw by pain. *Dearest God, no. I can't swim*, Daniela prays as Cillian arches his back and screams her name as though he's exorcising his demons. "Daniela!"

She grabs his leg and plants her feet into the wood. Fine splinters catch the bottoms of her flip-flops as she holds onto her raging bull. "Stop! Stop!" she screams, but he's still in momentum, and her bare legs slam into the boat's edge.

Micro-sized splinters dig into her bare flesh. "You're hurting me, Cil. Stop—please. I can't swim," she says with more of a gasp than a voice.

The special ops warrior freezes as he finally sees his wife amid his animalistic rage. He tilts his head back and releases a wail so raw, so vulnerable that it guts the ocean from the inside out.

A school of dolphins propels their lithe bodies out of the sea. Brightly colored fish rise to the surface and seem to linger there. A gray cloud shifts over the corn-blue sky as a cold wind whistles, snaking a path between the yacht's sails.

Cillian sways with the wind like a boat unmoored.

Nausea washes over Daniela. Do. Not. Gag!

She grips the railing with her left hand, rests her right hand on her abdomen, then draws in several long, Pilates-trained breaths.

Her muscles release, and her vagus nerve stops firing. She moves behind her husband, planning to catch him if he collapses beneath the rhythmic waves of visceral pain pulsating through his soul.

But how would she catch a six-foot-four, hundred-and-ninety-pound man with ropes of muscle covered in a fine layer of taut and freckled pale flesh?

Plan B. Coach him back to a place of self-control. "Breathe, Cil . . . please, just breathe. I can't lose you, too."

He obeys his wife, his wails disintegrating into a muffled cry.

Gingerly, she wraps her arms around his waist.

During a storm, a ship needs an anchor. Daniela presses her cheek into his back, careful not to overstimulate the jagged, crisscrossed scars. No plastic surgeon could erase his past as a trafficked child.

Asher Bushcroft hadn't missed one square inch of Cillian's pale flesh with his braided whip.

Daniela's heart thumps against her chest. The volcanic heat of rage builds and flushes her face.

That man has inflicted enough pain on my family. Time to pay. But how?

Without an immediate answer, she closes her eyes and begs God, "When I open my eyes, give me back my son . . . please."

One. Two. Three.

She opens her eyes.

Nothing has changed except the direction of the wind.

Summer winds whip her brunette locks into a frenzy.

Then the rain begins to fall.

Today is still Daniela's and Cillian's thirty-eighth birthday, and what a birthday gift! Time to accept what she could not change. Yeshua's promised peace in the middle of the storm. "Cil, I'm afraid we will have to move on . . ." Her voice falters. "I'll need to survive this, and you must do your best to survive this."

"Why, lass . . . why survive?"

"Adelaide," she says, then watches a lone tear slip down her husband's right cheek. "Our daughter needs us, Cil . . . and so does everyone on Earth."

Cillian opens his mouth, gasping for air while trying to voice his heart, but his heart has been torn to shreds, and no words will come until . . . "I canna say that I give a damn about everyone who lives on Earth."

"Cil!" She playfully slaps his arm, but she feels the same.

"I dinna say that I'd not do my best." He pauses. "For you. For Adelaide *mo chridhe*." He clenches his fists to his chest, fighting to catch his breath. The will to live, much less be of use to a world without his son living in it, is proving too much for him.

Time to be honest with the man she sleeps beside every night. "The feeling is mutual . . . so then, Cil, we will complete this mission for Yahweh and out of love for our daughter and each other."

"Aye, then." He winks at his lass—*me*. And Daniela grins as a blush creeps into her quivering cheeks.

14—Orphan Dreamer

Two Months Later . . .
5:03 p.m., Sunday, September 08, 2019
New Zealand

THE HIGHEST WIND SPEED EVER recorded on Earth was 253 miles per hour. It occurred during a tropical cyclone crossing Barrow Island. The cyclone scraped all vertical objects off the face of the remote island.

Death by fire or by water . . . which was worse?

Standing at her farmhouse-style kitchen sink nested beneath a large west window, Daniela sighs while washing the dishes inside the white-cabinet kitchen of the Cavanaugh family's seaside New Zealand home.

Thirty minutes ago, she cleared the dinner table after cooking dinner for three—her husband, her daughter, and herself.

Homemade hamburgers—her specialty, made with

grass-fed ground beef, onions, mushrooms, green peppers, and salt-and-pepper seasoning bound together with one egg and accompanied with Daniela's thin-cut, oven-baked sweet potato chips.

She pours the last few ounces of her homemade lemonade into a glass and drinks it—sweet and sour, just like her life. The Orphan Dreamer slips her hands back into the dishwater. It sloshes as she scrubs the last dinner plate and her glass.

Beyond her kitchen sink, beyond the rocky plateau where her home sits above the ocean, lays an endless horizon of aquamarine water.

Water.

Its surface.

Its depths. This she knows: perception rarely equals the truth—just too many missing parts.

A story usually begins as it was meant to end.

Except for this story.

No, in this story, the roles about beginnings and endings, those will reverse. The people who cried in the beginning will laugh in the end. The ones who laughed in the beginning, they will weep in the end. In the beginning, the Aniyvwiya—Daniela's people—wept.

And because they cried, one day, after two total solar eclipses crisscross North America's sky, the eagle would cry as it falls from the heavens.

In the Holy book, the eagle represents The United States of America.

The countdown has been activated.

Daniela's homeland is set to nosedive into a sea of forgetfulness, pulled down from soaring above Earth as the chief bird of the planet's blue-jay skies. Stifling a guttural cry, she grips the sink until her brown skin deepens to a hypoxic purplish-dusky shade. The first total solar eclipse has already travelled across North America's sky on Monday, August 21, 2017. And the second . . . it would complete the second arm of an X-pattern on another Monday—April 8, 2024.

And today is September 8, 2019.

Five years. That's it . . . to appease the Bat Creek Stone curse.

Some days, months, or even years soon after the last total solar eclipse, Earth's molten iron core will slow and eventually lose its magnetism.

After this, Earth's polarity will flip, and some of Daniela's kinspeople—those who laughed at the beginning of this story—will weep bitterly. Because while Earth is in the process of flipping its polarity, the planet will stop spinning at its usual 1,500 miles-per-hour for a brief, but unknown period.

And if Earth's electromagnetic shield weakens during this reversal, the planet will become vulnerable to solar flares. A flare could warp Earth's magnetosphere, wreaking chaos on the power grid.

During this polarity reversal, it is uncertain what will happen to a technologically dependent civilization.

During the last moments of the flip, as the planet slows, objects in motion—such as water—will keep moving at their previous speeds of close to 1,500 miles-per-hour.

Daniela's mouth dries, a dryness that all the water in the ocean could not quench. She towel-dries her hands, then reaches for her real estate agent's business card. This place is surrounded by the powerful Pacific Ocean. Is it time to place the New Zealand house on the market? She shakes her head. Moving further inland would hardly make a difference.

Just a longer wait until the inevitable arrives . . . the apocalypse in the form of oceans and lakes charging across the planet's water-soaked face at 1,500 miles-per-hour, scraping and scouring every bit of life from Earth's face.

In effect, the sea would sanitize the Earth, extinguishing humans—forever.

But what about the rainbow—Yahweh's promise to Noah that a flood would never cover the entire face of the earth at the same moment?

It's true that the Orphan Dreamer isn't a meteorologist or a weather magician like Yeshua, Jesus, when He spoke to the stormy winds and white-capped waves while His disciples were sailing with Him on the Sea of Galilee.

He said, "peace be still," and then the winds and the waves obeyed the voice of the Creator and fell silent.

She towel-dries the last dish.

Secure a second chance for America—her home. But that isn't her only mission. Secure a last chance for planet Earth. She takes in a deep breath then blows it out with the force of a gale.

She gazes beyond the window, up at the sky. Heaven seems so far away. Distance. Prayers for wisdom, a strategy. How much time remains to solve the mystery of the Bat Creek Stone? Is there a grace period if she misses the deadline of April 8, 2024? And if this grace period exists, can she secure victory in the invisible war between humans, Nephilim, and their powerful fathers—the Watchers?

Darkness. Light.

Light defeats the darkness. And her weapon is light, but where would she find a physical light so powerful to prevent the Nephilim and the Watchers from taking Earth from all of her people, humans.

All she needs is illumination.

The Eternal Light. A lamp unto her feet and a Light to

guide her path. She picks up a silver-framed photograph of her late son. Kian. Such a beautiful boy. Gone too soon. Asher refused to give her son a bone marrow transplant. They were a perfect match. But why? Her son was perfect. Innocent. A gift to humanity.

"Asher Bushcroft has to be a Nephilim." She speaks to an empty room as a scowl etches its way across her face.

Finding the light would be her payback to the darkness of Bushcroft's soul. And after she lit the long-lost light, she would place the light on the hilltop, exposing Bushcroft's and the Son of Venus's plans for humanity to the world.

Discovering an ancient light and placing it on a hilltop will be her vengeance for her son. One day, the Light will banish the darkness. Forever.

"Hi, Cil." Daniela glances over her shoulder as her husband swaggers into the kitchen, comes up behind his wife, and kisses her neck.

"Come to bed."

"Only if you promise to sort out the details of the mission."

"Not fair." He pecks his wife on the cheek. "But fine. What did Professor Jakob tell you?"

"Eclipses are heavenly signs." Her mentor, Talmudic Professor Jakob Cohen, taught her according to the Talmud.

"Aye, then, lass. Yahweh is a genius—a master mathematician. If the sun is 400 times larger than the moon, how could the moon block out the light of the sun during a solar eclipse?"

"The sun must be 400 times further from Earth than the moon." She gazes up into his mysterious deep-blue eyes. Cillian grins, flashing those pearlies and melting every bit of resistance pent up in Daniela's small frame. Breathless, she responds. "It's a relationship of distance exactly parallel to that of size."

"Aye, then, yer a genius, too. You once told me that the Jewish rabbis taught your professor that an eclipse of the moon was a bad omen for the Jewish people."

"Yes—and an eclipse of the sun was a bad sign for the non-Jewish world," she finishes the parallel.

"What about the number 400, lass? What of that?"

"According to Professor Jakob, in the mystic tradition of Kabbalah" —a teaching Daniela hasn't explored or embraced— "the number 400 is meant to alert the Jewish community to a special meaning, usually the end of a time of testing . . . Moses spent forty days on Mount Sinai. Noah's flood lasted forty days. For forty years, the Israelites wandered in the wilderness before Joshua led them into the promised land."

"And what about the number four, Rosebud . . . what important event happed on the fourth day of Creation?" His eyes twinkle with genius-level sexiness.

"God created the sun, the moon, and the stars on the fourth day of creation." She gasps and covers her mouth with her hand.

"I dinna believe this is all a coincidence . . . d'ye?"

"No." She fist pumps the air.

"Aye, then, lass. The relationship between the sun and the moon predicted 400 years that the ancient Jewish people would be enslaved by the Egyptians and taken away from their land in Israel."

"Cil!" Daniela screams his name then runs to her laptop.

"I was hoping . . ." He stops in midsentence as she focuses on her mission.

"Egypt," she whispers as she types a hundred words a

minute, and he walks up behind her, attempting to pull his wife into his body. "It's important, Cil." She points at her laptop's screen. "You see."

He gives up and sits on the edge of the chair with her then reads the text out loud. "Carbondale, Illinois is referred to as 'Little Egypt', and it is here that the crux of the total solar eclipses occurring seven years apart will form."

Daniela types in—*Why was Carbondale nicknamed Little Egypt.*

Cillian reads the results of her search, "Its river system mimics the Nile Valley. Partly because slavery was practiced even though it was illegal in Illinois. And because the area has a number of cities named for ancient Egyptian places such as Karnak, Cairo, and Thebes."

"It's true then! The fate of the Jewish person and the Gentile person has been written in mysteries of the con-stellations—the sun, moon, and stars—since time began, for all the world to see."

"Good job, lass." He kisses her, his soft lips lingering.

She presses in, and then he says, "You must decode these ancient messages before a catastrophic event heralded by these celestial warnings of the seven-year total solar eclipse strikes America and annihilates the rest of our family—our legacy, and every other human who lives on Earth."

"That's a mouthful." She brushes her lips against his. "I know, Cillian." The Orphan Dreamer closes her eyes and fully kisses her husband—their passion dulling the constant ache of their parental grief. A parent never stops missing their child.

Plain.

Definitely simple.

But they can celebrate.

15—Adelaide: #TheEyeofTime

The Present, the End . . .
8:21 p.m., Tuesday, December 31, 2019
Charlotte, North Carolina

A JUNIOR AT PHILLIPS EXETER Academy, I am nursing my broken heart, so I decide to play hooky—escaping the New Year's Eve party of my on-again-off-again boyfriend, Gabe, and finding a place of peace.

And anyway, he's hitting on another girl, again.

Maybe none of this stuff really matters in the end.

Because on the afternoon of April 8, 2024, according to Mummy, the celestial clock ends its seven-year countdown as a seventy-mile swath of darkness will make its way from Oregon to South Carolina.

My brother is dead . . . didn't live until Christmas. Mummy, Da, and I celebrated a quiet Christmas this year. Kian was the jokester—the life of Cavanaugh-Finn holidays.

My heart aching, I climb into the backseat of my midnight-blue Range Rover.

Dressed in a Balmain black leather jacket, dark pencil jeans, and black leather flats, I—Adelaide Rose Cavanaugh-Finn—scoot beneath the blanket left in the backseat. I pull my curly, red hair out of my face and back into a ponytail.

Biting into my lower lip, I refuse to cry as long as Theo, my driver, is studying my every movement in the rearview mirror, watching but never brave enough to say anything.

Tonight, the world feels like it's already falling apart, way before 2024.

Maybe 2020 will be a better year. A year of health and prosperity. I slip my freckled fingers into a pouch attached to the back of the front seat, remove a tissue, and dab my eyes.

"Would you like to visit my church, Miss. Adelaide?"

Here we go, but what do I have to lose? "I guess."

"Okay." He says nothing more. Two hours later, my driver stops in front of a beautiful building. *Guess it's a church; doesn't look like one though.* Elevation Church. Okay. The place could be featured in a modern architecture magazine.

I exit the car. I tilt my chin up a little higher to not betray the anxious feeling I stuffed into a corner somewhere inside.

"I'll park, then wait in the foyer," Theo says.

"Okay. But you don't have to. It's your church."

"I can listen on my phone. Enjoy."

I approach the entrance alone, feeling awkward while walking behind the couple in front of me. I find one of the last seats in the back of the building. Where will Theo sit in the foyer?

I keep quiet and take it all in, listening, searching for something or someone bigger than myself, an anchor to weather this storm and then the next, and the next, until infinity.

Around me, church goers clap and sing during the New Year's Praise Party 2019. "God, say something. The silence is killing me. Speak to me like I'm Mummy . . . and like I'm listening—finally."

Silence.

God isn't a puppet. He doesn't speak on demand.

At the midpoint of a rousing rendition of a song named "Surrounded," Pastor Steven Furtick walks onto the stage and begins to pray. "You are our only hope." He pauses, taking in one deep breath and then another.

Pastors and prophets experience pain, too, speaking truth when others want to keep embracing their lies. It's not a calling for wimps.

Bigot. Radical. He's so close minded.

She's so judgmental.

Crucify her! The newest method of crucifixion is cancel culture. I see what my mother deals with as she walks the Orphan Dreamer's journey.

"You are the source of our strength," the pastor continues his prayer. "You are the strength of our hope."

His voice drops, then picks back up as his tone changes—determined, purposeful, as though he's preparing to declare war. The drummer pounds out a rhythm that could chase the devil and his demons from Earth and back into the bowels of hell.

"We came here tonight not for a performance or an event, but to encounter the One who has been carrying us all this way. If it had not been for You on our side" —the pastor's voice rises— "we surely would not be standing.

"And, God, we thank you not for only what You have

done for us but for who You have been for us. You've been really good to us. You drew close to us. At times when we needed comfort, you were there to dry our tears. At times when we needed counsel, you were there to give us wisdom. In moments when we needed a big brother, you threw a right hook and knocked the devil back twenty feet. We thank you for it. And tonight, we realize that the weapons of our warfare are not carnal but are mighty through God for the pulling down of strongholds.

"So we bless your name, your great name, Jesus. Your name is above every feeling! Your name is above every disorder! Your name is above all division! Your name is above all evil! Your name is above injustice! Your name is above anxiety! And we bless your name because this is how I fight my battles: in the name of Jesus . . . will ya'll help me fight? If you've got a battle, fight it like this." The music swells as Elevation Worship team sings the melody of "Surrounded". "This is how I fight my battles . . ."

Pastor Steve Furtick continues to inspire the church crowd with his words as the musicians play and the singers sing. He shouts, "This is how I fight my battles . . . with my hands up . . . We end this decade with the blood of Jesus and the testimony of the saints. Come on, give him a shout of praise like you've got the victory."

Without fully understanding why, I weep. And with my elbows pinned to my waistline, I raise both hands in surrender.

But it doesn't feel like I'm losing a battle. It feels as though I'm winning. As though I'm accepting the victory of a battle already won on my behalf.

Salvation.

A knowing takes seed, telling me something terrible

stalks the horizon of my future, *but I will never leave you, nor forsake you.* A shadow temporarily dims my view. It's the shadow of the monster waiting in my future and holding a sledgehammer in its left hand and a sickle in its right.

What's the meaning of this vision?

Next year will bring the beginning of intense sorrows—pelvic-ripping labor pains that occur just before the birth of something ominous and sinister.

The devil even comes to church.

But now, I have an anchor.

Upon exiting the church, a shroud of inexplainable peace overwhelms me as I stroll to the parking lot where my driver is waiting. He opens the back door, and I slide in. "Thank you, Theo."

"You're welcome." In silence, my chauffeur drives his charge home.

I am at peace, even though so many questions tug at the corners of my mind. *No need to call Gabe.* He couldn't tell me if he'd eaten his dinner yet, much less answer any of my moral or theological questions.

But my mother—well, that's a different story. Daniela Rose is a walking encyclopedia, thesaurus, and Biblical commentary all in one. I ring my mother, and after a few minutes of small talk, I share my evening's divine experience, then I ask questions:

Did Jesus really die for my wrongdoings?

Does God really love me?

Would He really fight my battles?

In my mother's calm voice, she replies, "It's a date, darling."

"I'm asking serious theology questions, and you're talking about a date?"

"Your father's gone to South Africa on business, so it's a date—girls' night, and we're going to watch three movies—okay?"

"Why?"

"To answer your questions."

"How?"

"Three questions. Three movies. The first one we'll watch is *The Passion*. And after watching that soul-wrenching movie, you'll hardly ask yourself ever again: 'Does Yeshua love me?'"

"Okay."

"Then, we'll watch *The Shack*. You'll see that God loves Mack so much and is willing to shift into the person Mack needs to see in order for the grieving father to heal. 'God is spirit . . . I will become a Father to the fatherless and a Mother to the motherless. . .' You'll see for yourself that Yahweh loves you."

"The third movie?"

"Ah—then, after you're convinced of the Holy Trinity's love for you, we'll watch *War Room*, then you'll learn how to fight your battles."

"Thanks, Mummy," I say then think, *there's hope*. "Mummy, don't forget the popcorn."

"You'll need more tissues than exploded kernels of corn," she says, and I can imagine the twinkle in her eyes as she winks at me. "See you soon, darling."

"I love you, Mummy."

"I can't believe you're mine, darling."

"I'm glad I'm yours . . . and Father's."

The present time . . . Twenty-six years before the second total solar eclipse occurring on April 8, 2024.

16—Orphan Dreamer

9:00 a.m., Tuesday, July 8, 1998
Palatka, Florida

THE GIRLS EXITED EMMALINE'S JEEP and approached the country church, strolling past a group of parishioners dressed in all black. "Where's the President's security detail?" Daniela asked her best friend, Emmaline.

"Don't know." Emmaline completed a 180-degree turn, taking the details of the parking lot into her analytical mind. "I still don't believe the President is coming."

"Claire's father was a senator."

"*Was*, the qualifying word."

White paint littered the grass around the steepled building like flakes of dandruff, and Daniela wanted to scratch her scalp to shreds. *Don't mess up your curls.* Her mom had applied a curling iron to her wayward locks.

After they entered the church, Earth's last Orphan Dreamer, dressed in all black, sat next to Emmaline Georgiana Winterlyn Darbyshire—her kindred spirit, a girl steeped in a hot brew of mixed Scottish and English royalty.

Mary, the Queen of Scots, capstoned Emmaline's ancestry, making her technically a member of the English royal family. And possessing an excessive number of last names seemed to be a thing for the house of Windsor royals, as well as nerves that were more like ropes of steel—no tungsten, the strongest metal in the world. "Are you nervous, Dannygirl?" Emmaline casually asked Daniela.

"Of course, I am. Claire Amilee Underwood is the purveyor of all things I-hate-Daniela-Rose-Cavanaugh," Daniela whispered to her best friend. "Yet here we are, attending her mother's funeral."

"Thoughts?"

"Life's strange."

"And most days, strange is normal." Emmaline winked then leaned in, pressing into Daniela's shoulder, her warm yet bright green eyes shining past a galaxy of stars and planets, bringing a celestial light back with them. "Besides, some will never like you because of you."

"Why? I'm wonderful." *Definitely joking.*

"The God in you rouses their restless demons."

"Rousing demons . . . ?" Daniela winked to hide a quivering right eyelid, all nerves and adrenaline. "An eerie visualization at a Podunk country funeral." Daniela squeezed her best friend's hand, waiting for the church organ to inflate its rubberized lungs before transforming air into a sound so hauntingly magical.

"And so not your problem."

"How's that?"

"Dealing with demons, that's a job for priests and pastors. They signed up for it." As plain as plain, non-vanilla yogurt, Danny-girl."

"Thanks for grounding me . . . again."

"Anything for you."

"But I am the Orphan Dreamer . . . sort of complicates things."

"I know." Emmaline flashed her bright smile as the organ filled its pipes and then sang a morbid solo.

"'Toccata and Fugue in D minor,'" Daniela whispered.

"Breathtaking. Beautiful."

"Agreed." Daniela slipped her hand around Emmaline's then whispered into Emmaline's right ear, "Who plays a tune in D minor at a funeral while it's raining, on a pipe organ of all instruments?"

"I guess they didn't check the weather report before making the song selection." Emmaline bit her lip, until a pop of laughter earned her a stern look from the woman sitting in front of them.

"Funerals are scary and spooky all on their own, no need to add the minor keys. That's all." Daniela squeezed then released a handful of cloth—her father's handkerchief.

"You'll survive, but I may not survive that stare down coming from church lady. I didn't mean to laugh," Emmaline whispered.

"I'll fight for you."

"I think I can survive until you beat up church lady."

"Surviving's one thing, living's another." Daniela forced herself to exhale.

"You've got to win the battle in your mind first."

True.

Black humor . . . let's go. Daniela's post-funeral shopping list: Buy a gothic castle. Install a pipe organ. Paint Daniela's brown face with Queen Elizabeth I white lead paint. Dress in a vampire's black cape lined with red satin.

Classic attire.

Finally, wait for a stormy night, invite Emmaline to the haunted house, and play "Toccata and Fugue in D Minor" on a pipe organ as thunder claps and lightning flashes. Daniela raised her hand to her mouth, stifling another giggle. Didn't want church lady to have to stare them down again. Her head would explode.

"What're you up to?" Emmaline elbowed her friend, bringing Daniela back to reality as the choir sang "Amazing Grace."

A tune so much less spine-chilling . . . but so out of tune that Daniela cringed. How does a choir mess up "Amazing Grace"? A simple three-quarter time signature, fifty-three beats a minute. "Nothing," she whispered, her voice rising a few octaves on her own minor chord scale.

"You're lying. I can hear it, and I can see it in your eyes."

"I'm sorry, Limes." Her mouth dried, and her gut churned. Never tell a lie! "I won't lie to you again—promise."

"Forgiven." Emmaline's eyes twinkled as she leaned into Daniela. "Even?"

"If you want." Daniela Rose's mental antics had worked. For an onlooker, the proof could be seen as her shoulders relaxed. The funeral dragged on, but by finding the black humor in the situation, Daniela broke her rising tsunami of morbid fears into miniature and manageable rippling waves, creating a mental situation that resembled a well-tamed lake instead of a seiche.

Her mind no longer brimming with fear, she focused on the monotony. Another off-key solo followed by a long-winded sermon, then a contrived eulogy. She rubbed her eyes.

Wake up! Stay alert! Someone seemed to whisper to the Orphan Dreamer.

Claire Amilee Underwood's mother had been murdered—her warm blood spilled all over the front steps of the Underwood's antebellum Florida mansion, across the park from Daniela's family's cottage.

The killer was still at large, lurking in the shadows of Florida's swamps like a cottonmouth ready to strike. Daniela glanced at Claire and the emotion rimming Claire's lower eyelashes.

Even though Claire had incessantly tormented Daniela during grade school, Daniela believed that no one should be forced to watch the horror of their mother being stabbed and then strangled to death.

Daniela's skin chilled to a deathly cold, her goosebumps vanishing as a scruffy man dressed in a black coat, a baseball cap, and dungarees plopped down on the other end of their pew near a duct-taped stained-glass window.

Who is he?

A gust of body odor snaked down the pew and slammed into her. She gasped for air as evil spilled from his pale eyes. Grinning, he leaned down and reached for the floorboard.

Daniela froze. *Where's security?* Claire's father was a powerful senator, and the president of the United States would be attending the graveside service later—at least according to Claire.

Claire . . . that girl could lie like a dead possum.

Keep hope alive, Daniela. The President's entourage was most likely scouring the grounds, looking for troublemakers. She wanted to scream: *Potential troublemaker in here!*

The man picked up a hymn book, opened it, snapped to attention, then focused on the eulogy. *See, there.* She'd been wrong to judge. *Catch the butterflies, Danny Rose. Calm down.*

Daniela released her breath, then greedily took another and then another until her heart rate slowed.

An hour later, the funeral service mercifully ended.

"Shall we walk to the graveside and lay our dear sister to rest?" the pastor asked, and the choir answered by singing "Nearer My God to Thee."

"I guess that means yes," Daniela whispered and smiled.

"About time we did something." Emmaline leaned closer to Daniela. "How near exactly are we to God?" She raised her brows and moved her eyes in the direction of the stench, indicating the man it belonged to, before focusing her gaze back on the pastor.

The scraggly man bent over again, reached for the floor, and lifted the red carpet. Glaring at the Orphan Dreamer, he removed a long, black object from a hidden compartment.

"Gun." Barely audible, Daniela's voice sank between waves of fear that seemed to paralyze her, making her doubt herself. Was she dreaming? After blinking twice, she reached for the snowflake diamond beneath the neckline of her funeral getup.

The Glass Tattoo was still there.

Nope, not dreaming!

The man aimed the gun at the back of a young girl sitting in the pew in front of him. With blonde hair and a round face, she resembled a younger version of Claire Amilee. He glared at Daniela, lips barely moving as he growled, "You shouldn't have come."

How does he know me? Her stomach lurched with nausea.

Then, with a mouthful of tartar-stained teeth, he shouted, "You people wanna see my young'uns and wife so bad?" The churchgoers turned toward the voice. "Join 'em both in hell!"

Time froze.

Scraggly Beard grabbed the helpless girl's ponytail and yanked her up over the bench onto his lap. She wailed, and gasps echoed throughout the church.

"Put her down!" the minister said.

The monster jumped to his feet and backed up against the wall. "Consider me doin' the world a favor by cleanin' up God's house. Ain't no need for a bunch of Jesus freaks runnin' around this town, muckin' up the politics. We've got to drain the swamp! And I'm about to do just that, getting rid of the holy rollers."

Was that Claire's father? His dialect had been one of a refined Southern gentleman, but now he sounded like . . . a drunk hillbilly.

Claire Amilee pivoted on her pew and screamed. "Daddy, let Polly go!"

"Stop!" The minister pounded the podium, then charged the assassin. "In the name of Jesus, I say—"

With the pull of a trigger, the scraggly man dispatched the pastor into the open and accepting arms of Yeshua. Bullets pummeled the baptistery. Water sloshed down the pulpit.

Claire Amilee and her boyfriend took refuge on the floor.

Daniela's mouth felt parched as she said a prayer, "Dear God, be with us, Immanuel."

Parishioners scattered, but few who moved escaped. Daniela stayed still, melded to her pew. Blood splattered the walls, and stained-glass windows shattered. Mute but no longer paralyzed, Daniela yanked Emmaline beneath their pew.

They crawled under church benches toward the door. Bullets splintered wood in their wake.

Then came silence . . . until there wasn't. "Daddy, you're hurting me," the little girl whined. "I'll be good, promise."

"Shut up. Yo mamma wudn't nuthin' and your brat sister ain't nuthin' but a hussy, but Claire had a sweet little mouth."

On her hands and knees, Daniela gasped, then froze. Images of the sad boy—her oily boy—trapped inside the hell of her nightly dreams flashed through her mind. He had been abused physically, mentally, and even sexually.

Shamed. Abandoned. Forgotten. The Orphan Dreamer's hands curled into fists. "Limy, wait . . ."

"What now?" Emmaline paused her crawl toward the vestibule to glance back at her friend.

"How does Claire's dad know how her mouth tastes?"

"You're a smart girl, Danny. Add it up!"

"I've done the math." Bile shot into Daniela's throat as reality hit her square in the stomach. Claire's father had raped his own daughter!

Narcissists, sociopaths, and psychopaths—bullies roaming Earth, and they all seemed to be nothing more than Nephilim, half-breed demon-humans.

"Come on, Danny-girl. Now's not the time to pontificate." Emmaline continued crawling beneath the pews.

Daniela followed, then suddenly reached forward and grabbed her friend's foot, stopping her escape. "We have to help."

"Jiminy Cricket! Come on! The President's security team won't waste time killing anyone who appears to be a threat. We have to get out of here before they come in."

"Is the President really here? I doubt it."

"No time for fact-checking Claire's messed-up reality. Come—now!"

"I don't think anyone else is coming . . . and we're here, so we have to help."

"We will. It's called helping ourselves to safety."

Inside the quiet church, flesh slapped flesh. Daniela stood

as Claire Amilee bolted to the back of the church, tripping and falling, all tangled up with her beau while abandoning her sister.

"Well, we don't have to worry about saving Claire and her man." Daniela sneered at her childhood bully.

"No—Daddy!" Polly screeched. "Please . . . I'm begging you, don't do that to me again." The little girl's cries ripped the momentum out of Daniela's escape. "I'll be a good girl. I promise, Daddy."

"Is he doing what I think he's doing?" Daniela's face flushed hot with untamed rage.

"He's raping her, Danny-girl. Right inside God's house." Emmaline's voice faltered.

"I hate him, Limy." Daniela's voice broke in two. "I wanna kill him."

"The devil's crashed into heaven on Earth, and he's not leaving until he destroys everything and everyone." A tear slithered down Emmaline's right cheek. "And he won't think twice about killing us too . . . and maybe he'll even want to have a bit of fun before doing so. We have to storm, Danny-girl!"

"No!"

"Remember . . ." Emmaline paused, hesitating. "You're a virgin, and he's probably a Nephilim, according to you. Goodness knows how big . . ."

"Don't." Daniela's world spun, and she briefly closed her eyes. "Don't do that. Using words to make me afraid."

"We have to go. Do you smell that—did he bring a bottle of hell's perfume with him?"

Daniela sniffed. "Gasoline. Fire." She peeked above the last pew. The front pews were burning, shredded with bullets. Her blood ran cold. *Be fearless.* Standing, she glared Death in the face.

"Are you crazy?" Emmaline tugged at her friend's leg. "Get down."

"Run, Limy. I've got to help this little girl."

"No—I won't leave you!"

"Then go to the vestibule, get the gun I know you have in your purse, and help me!"

"Well, then, Annie's got her gun." Emmaline turned, preparing to run out of the church, but stopped. "But Annie doesn't have her best friend . . . you."

"Go. I'm ready to die, but you aren't." Emmaline had never donned the life raft, Yeshua. Emmaline left her friend behind to do what she did best: be a gun slinger.

Would this be the last time they saw each other? A lump expanded inside Daniela's throat as she ducked beneath the pew. She inched toward Claire's dad, her sights trained on his bowed and hairy legs.

Gross!

Daniela got her own gun. "'For the weapons of our warfare are not carnal, but mighty through God for the pulling down of strong holds'. Second Corinthians, chapter ten, verse four." Mentally empowered by God's promises, the Orphan Dreamer stopped and peeked above a pew located two rows from his.

Belt unbuckled, the man had hoisted the whimpering girl under one arm and was sprinkling gasoline on the altar with the other.

Bare buttocks clapping in the wind, he knelt in front of the communion table and retrieved a clump of dynamite that had been taped under the wood table. *So irreverent!* "Coming back to worship, Daniela?" Claire's father mocked, not even looking over his shoulder. He was a devil, and devils could sense the presence of God or one of His children.

For some odd reason, Daniela just wanted to laugh.

When her nerves were frayed, she always did, but instead, she gave her first order. "Let. Her. Go."

"Make me, nigger girl." He paused the abuse of his daughter, making way for his tired and worn-out racial insult to sink into Daniela's psyche. He waited and waited some more, smirking.

Finally, he broke his death stare and doused the altar with gasoline. Somehow, when a man who raped his own daughter in God's house and then set fire to his wife's casket calls you the N-word, it's a rock-solid compliment.

Plain.

Definitely simple.

"Mister Underwood, you call me a derogatory term, yet you're the one with your pants unzipped, hanging your things in God's house after raping your daughter. That makes you some kind of crazy stupid, sir," Daniela mocked.

"Some say it's best to die while laughing. So keep on laughing, little girl, because you're next. I'm gonna teach you a big lesson." The human demon struck a match, lit the stick of dynamite, and dropped it next to the pool of gasoline.

Fire exploded in the fuel, then climbed up the wick. The intruder retreated from the fire, his backside toward Daniela.

She took cover from the fetid stink of pimpled butt-flesh as well as the impending explosion, but something inside her refused to allow her to leave Claire's baby sister behind.

She deserved a chance at life—a second chance. She was the angel balancing out the evil residing inside Claire.

The young girl screamed, startling Daniela. "King of the fight," Daniela said, drawing in breath and fingering the Glass Tattoo that hung from her neck, "be with me, Immanuel. Empower me to defeat this beast!"

She marched down what was left of the center aisle.

The altar exploded, and the foundation of the clapboard church rumbled, sending shards of stained glass in all directions while propelling the Orphan Dreamer up and through the air like a hand grenade before slamming her into a pile of rubble.

After a dazed moment, Daniela stumbled to her feet, ash raining down on her face while a hellish heat cooked her exposed arms.

The demon-possessed man dropped his youngest daughter, charged across the decimated house of God, grabbed Daniela's wrist, and flipped her onto her back. "You asked for it." He straddled her, preparing to strip Daniela of her feminine dignity and innocence.

"Run!" Daniela arched her back and screamed at the little girl.

But covered in ash, the girl just sat on the floor, confused and shocked while calling for her sister. "Claire! Claire! Claire!"

Claire never came back.

The devil incarnate encircled Daniela's neck with his hands. His breath, drenched in wine and cigars, landed hard and heavy in Daniela's face. She tried to yank herself from his grip as he fumbled at her clothes. He spat as he spoke, "You could've just given me the Bat Creek Stone."

"The what?" She'd never heard of the thing.

"Don't act innocent. You're the negro girl Father told me to find." He encircled her neck with his grimy, sweat-slicked hands then squeezed.

Help, Daniela silently prayed.

Outside, lightning flashed. Thunder clapped. The heavens rumbled, and a wall of rotating black sky screeched then careened toward the chapel.

A firecracker exploded by Daniela's ear, pinning her to the floor.

The force lifted the monster into a crouched but standing position. He stumbled about, blood spilling from his right ear. Two bloody holes pierced through his right shoulder.

"Legna?" Daniela whispered as she looked over her shoulder at the vestibule.

At the entrance of the sanctuary, Emmaline stood, legs spread and firing off rounds as though she were Doc Holiday defending turf at the OK Corral. Smoke twisted upward from the tip of her Glock.

Annie got her gun! "Thank God," Daniela whispered.

An eerie quiet permeated the space, and the abused little girl dressed in a thin, white dress ran from the bowels of hell into Daniela's embrace.

"Polly, right? That's your name." Daniela asked as she quickly surveyed the child's body for injuries.

"Yes."

"Polly, you're okay, but go with my friend, Emmaline." She gestured toward the door, and Emmaline lowered her weapon.

"But I want to stay with you. I'm scared."

"I am too—but I need you to trust me and go with my friend."

"Okay, if you say so."

"I do." Daniela crawled with the little girl protected beneath her body.

Sirens wailed outside, and voices echoed within the chaotic noise.

"Danny Rose, watch out!" Emmaline raised her gun.

Behind Polly and Daniela, the devil cloaked in sagging and jaundiced flesh sprayed bullets into the church fire, murdering his own demons before turning the gun toward his daughter's angel, Daniela.

Emmaline braced her stance, aimed the gun, and *click*. She looked at the gun, confused. The posh gun slinger had run out of bullets!

Daniela released Polly's hand. "Limy, take Polly—now!" The Orphan Dreamer's thoughts raced faster than the little girl's legs. *What now?*

As Polly ran to Emmaline, Daniela yanked the Glass Tattoo from around her neck. Would activating the time-travel device cycle her into a dreamlike state, leaving her vulnerable to Claire's daddy's evil intentions?

Or would the snowflake diamond open the portal in a different way this time, granting her the power to save, like Harriet Tubman and her narcolepsy episodes?

Time to find out what the activated Glass Tattoo would do to her mortal body in a desperate situation.

Daniela palmed the powerful diamond. It sank into her flesh, darkening into its usual midnight blue snowflake tattoo. Besides a warm feeling, something electric and pulsating filled her body.

Her muscles hardened into steel cables. Bones solidified to iron. Her legs felt like they could carry her body faster than a gazelle.

Now, unto Him who is able to do exceedingly and abundantly above all that we ask or think . . . She stood razor-blade straight and stared evil in the face. "It's my party now," she said in a calm voice, then ran straight toward the assailant.

She jumped and in midair, dove into a somersault. Flipping her body upright and in a strong midair stance—right leg straight, left leg tucked, and both arms straight—she threw a punch toward the base of his neck and a simultaneous kick that cracked bone. He screeched in pain. The devil's neck twisted ninety degrees.

His head hung at an angle incompatible with life. Defying death, he reached inside his jacket and removed a brassy, round object—a grenade.

All is lost. Storm!

She turned to retreat.

Whoomph!

Something invisible slammed the pervert so hard into the church's concrete foundation that his body splintered the floor ten feet in each direction.

Daniela imagined an NBA All-Star slam-dunking him into the subbasement. Then that same something—or someone—grabbed Daniela from behind, expelling her from the church at the speed of a launching missile.

Legna's words flooded her memory: *You may not see me, but I'm here—fighting, protecting. All you need to do is call for me.*

The glass front doors of the church were closed. She was heading toward them at rocket speed. She squeezed her eyes shut and tensed her muscles.

In the last second, the door must have opened, because she was suddenly standing outside, drenched by torrential rain, but glass free. Daniela stood alone gasping for breath, fire and smoke burning her throat and eyes as spectators gawked at her.

The familiar warmth that had accompanied the angel's presence ebbed. The rain began to cleanse her skin, washing away the ash.

Camera flashes blinded Daniela as her body screamed with pain. Microphones held by eager reporters pummeled her face. She stumbled back, then raised her arms as police officers rushed to her side.

No good deed goes unpunished.

Did they suspect her of attempted murder of the President of the United States of America? "I-I-I didn't do it."

"You're a hero." A burly officer flashed a handsome smile. "You saved that little girl—she's my niece. Thank you."

"You're welcome . . . but where's the President?"

"Washington D.C. I guess." He shrugged.

Just then, an Asian woman, her face mangled and bloodied by shrapnel, brushed against the Orphan Dreamer. "Daniela. Don't trust anyone."

"Yes, ma'am?" How did the stranger know her name?

The woman fell into Daniela's arms. "Take this."

Daniela crinkled her brow. The stranger's fingers slipped something into her pocket and slid it down her thigh. "Don't lose it. It's a replica of Skylark's keystone—the second authentication device. But you'll need the original."

"What—what are you talking about?"

"You need to find the original!"

"Why?"

"Or America, and then the world, will be destroyed."

Daniela gulped down her fears. "But how do I find the original?"

"Aren't you the Orphan Dreamer?"

"Yes, ma'am. I am."

"Then dream and time travel through Ellesmere to your exotic worlds of the past and the future, and when you find Skylark's keystone, bring it back with you, place it in an underwater lock inside a cave after the moon hides the sun . . . or you'll be too late—understand?"

"I do, but I can't swim—much less in a cave!"

"Then, find someone who can swim, Daniela." The woman coughed hard, almost coughing up her alveoli. "I'm almost dead, so listen. Skylark's keystone will guide you to the light." She gasped between each word. "The keystone, in the presence of the light, the Bat Creek Stone, and the Skeleton Key, will guide you to Yahweh's presence, where you'll find the power to defeat your enemies—Nomed, the Watchers, the Nephilim, and the Father of Lies. This, Daniela, is the only place where the world's second chance can be found. Hebrews, chapter twelve, verse one and two. Read it, then follow the instructions."

"Yes, ma'am," Daniela said. "But—"

The woman fell limp, slipping into the arms of eternity.

Boom!

A blast catapulted Daniela, the dead woman, and several reporters across the lawn, tossing them into a heap of debris. Daniela's head ached as air buzzed, then a black curtain slid down, 360-degrees around the stage of Daniela's final act, obliterating her world and her future.

The Orphan Dreamer was dead.

Game over!

But how?

And what about second chances—Yeshua's specialty demonstrated when he raised a four-day-old corpse from the grave?

Dead man. Dead man. Dead man. He had brought Lazarus back to life. And this dead man—Jesus, Yeshua—died on a Roman cross, went to Hades, then conquered the grave, bringing back the keys of hell and the grave with him.

It. Is. Finished.

Truth. Life. And it's true that Lazarus was a friend of Yeshua's. But Daniela was a friend of God, too. So would Yeshua gift the Orphan Dreamer a second chance as well?

Her father had thought of his daughter as a snowflake—unique, beautiful, but temporarily chilled and aloof because of her introvert personality.

According to her father, the day his only child was born,

one snowflake fell from heaven—Daniela Rose—to extinguish hell's fire. But could a melted snowflake become a snowflake again?

Daniela's heartbeat slowed until even a hibernating bear's heartbeat would've been faster at eight beats a minute. Her parents' only child, Emmaline's kindred spirit, Ethan's Rosebud, and oily boy's Orphan Dreamer closed her eyes, then sank beneath the surface of a bottomless, cold, black river—the Jordan River . . . but she possessed an invisible life raft, Yeshua's sacrifice.

Oh death, where is your sting? Oh grave, where is your victory? The sting of death is sin. The strength of sin is the law—a set of rules that requires humans to be perfect. But thanks be to God, Who has given us the victory through our Lord Jesus Christ.

God's girls don't fight for victory; they fight their battles from a place of victory. Just then, a voice captivated her waning consciousness. "Dinna be afraid," a Scottish baritone voice said. This was not the voice of Legna. Whose voice was it?

"It's almost nightfall," the mysterious voice continued, "and the river's a wee bit deep, but across the River Jordan, weel be findin' a waterfall, fallin' wild and so free. Ye'll see it soon, and she'll be our reward—together forever, *mo chridhe.*"

Mo chridhe, she somehow knew, translated to *my heart.* Her ability to translate a language she'd never heard was because of the wolf within, as a Cherokee tribal leader had called her ability to clearly hear God's unfiltered voice.

Her mother called this ability, as well as the ability to decipher and understand ancient and modern languages she'd never learned, the filling of the Holy Spirit and the gift of tongues.

But . . . who did this new voice belong to? Did the voice

belong to her oily boy—the tormented boy who'd transformed her dreams into nightmares for the last five years?

Sucked deeper by a strong current into the Jordan River, Daniela was gulping down mouthfuls of water, unable to tread her liquid grave any longer. "I can't swim," she tried to reply, but the water choked her words into her throat.

Find someone who can swim . . . The dying woman's voice rose from the depths of Daniela's fading memories. "Help me," Daniela seemed to scream.

"Take my hand, Rosebud," said the baritone voice that had been touched with an accent from a region where people spoke with a cream-with-very-little-coffee accent. "I'll not be lettin' ye drown, then."

"But in my dreams, you always look so weak—" She fought her rescuer.

"Looks can be deceivin', lass. I'm a strong swimmer, and in time, ye'll see I'm strong, not scraggly, and definitely not weak."

"It's definitely you then, oily boy?"

"Aye, it's me. And I'm here wi' ye, now."

"I'm supposed to be scared . . . of you. You could be the antichrist!"

"I dinnae ken who that is."

"Six. Six. Six. The antichrist—you know, the son of perdition! The megalomaniac who ends the world as we know it!"

"Whoever he is, he seems to be havin' one too many names." Her oily boy laughed as he lifted his *chridhe* from the rippling waves. She laughed, too. "I'm not plannin' to end anything, so dinna be afraid of me—not ever."

"I'll try . . . but then, you'll have to prove yourself to me."

"How, then?"

"If you're not the guy with one-too-many-names, help

me stop the antichrist from killing everyone with his mass pandemic."

"Dinna worry, lass." He pulled her into a strong and safe embrace, then began to tow her to shore.

Daniela relaxed in his arms. Her toes brushed the sandy bottom of the massive river. Fighting to stand, she instead faceplanted into the cold, shallow water.

He lifted her up.

"You can swim . . . but can you be trusted? That's the question." She cinched her arms around her shivering body.

"Aye, lass, I can be trusted. I'll be the ruthless one, pushing back the darkness so ye can be kind. Earth will be balanced once more because of yer compassion, Daniela Rose, *a rún mo chroí*—the secret of my heart." She once again understood the translation. "Trust me, *mo nighean donn*."

With the power of the Glass Tattoo and her gift of tongues, Daniela translated the Scottish Gaelic again—*mo nighean donn*—to English: *My brown-haired lass.*

His brown-haired lass.

That was who she was to the orphan boy trapped inside her head. He'd even called her Rosebud—Ethan's nickname for her. Maybe he could be trusted. And boy, could he swim! She grinned wide.

Her oily boy.

What's in a name? Everything. A lifetime. Character. Reputation. The truth. A name was a legacy—an explanation of the past, a place in the world of the present, and a promise for the future.

"You ready to swim with me, lass?"

"I am." Submerged beneath water, Daniela grinned from ear to ear, then pursed her lips and blew the air from her lungs. Trusting. Hoping. Dreaming.

It was then that she fully exercised her faith, remembered that she had donned a life raft at the age of four. The water rippling under her body parted no differently than Moses's Red Sea, accepting her into its liquid and patient embrace. "Yahweh, may oily boy take me to stars this time—do You trust him to keep me safe?"

"I do, and like a father surrenders his daughter to her groom, I give you to him."

She swam through the Jordan River beside her oily boy, the Glass Tattoo taking them to a faraway place.

Then, something unexpected happened. The orphaned boy swam ahead, and she found that she had been returned to shore, watching him from a distance. "Bye—stay safe. I'll see you again . . . I hope." She allowed herself to dream that one day—not today, but after her burns healed then scarred over—oily boy would come for her.

He would one day become her heartsong, the man for whom all love songs had been penned, at least in her dreams.

A dream.

Sometimes that was all a girl could expect or want. She wrapped her arms around her chest, choosing to keep oily boy close to her heart as though he were real.

Pray for your kindred spirit, Daniela Rose, her dad had said.

Yes, she would pray for him—if she was given a second chance to live. On her knees and with an open heart, she returned to her Father's side. "Take me to the stars, Yahweh."

Then, she sank into Ellesmere, the place of dreams, a place accessed by only God's girl—Daniela Rose—the place where the Orphan Dreamer, via the Glass Tattoo, experienced Yahweh's supernatural presence. It was a place like the Holy of Holies, hidden deep inside Moses's tabernacle and King Solomon's temple, the place where the Ark of the Covenant was kept.

God's presence—it was truly another time and place.

Daniela and everyone she cared about must get to that place, the place where God's presence was unfiltered—heaven.

Daniela opened her eyes and having eyes to see, she saw; having ears to hear, she heard God's voice—the voice of a doting and loving father—unfiltered . . . uncut. "Find the light, Rosebud. Earth's representation of My perfect light—a light that was present before I created the sun, the moon, and the stars . . . it's My son, Yeshua. The Light of the World."

"Why, Yahweh? Why do I need to find an Earthly representation of Yeshua, when I've already found the Person the replica represents, Your son, Yeshua?"

"Because the light illuminates the path to my presence on Earth, the place where the Ark of the Covenant rests, the Ark must be found for one last temple to be erected in the Holy Land—the place where Yeshua came to meet man. Some are afraid of a light so pure, so bright—My son. They're so used to the darkness—its coldness, hopelessness, death and its grave, but this is their second chance, a miracle. Again, find Earth's original representation of my Son, the Light of the World, and it will lead you to the Ark of the Covenant—a place where truth wins and a place where miracles and second chances can be found."

"What is it—Earth's representation of your Son?"

"It's an artifact. It's made of pure gold, and its seven solid-gold arms have six tributary arms branching off from the main stem at straight lines. The center stem is the center of the world, My Son—the Word made into flesh, Yeshua."

"The menorah—the original Jewish seven-branched menorah featured in the desert Tabernacle of the Jewish people when Moses was still alive," Daniela whispered, understanding. "It's five feet tall and solid gold."

"Yes, my darling daughter. And it represents the Tree of Life—a tree whose fruit was not desired by Adam and Eve."

"They chose to eat of the Tree of Knowledge of Good and Evil."

"Yes, Daniela. And look at the world now."

"Adam and Eve were kicked out of the Garden of Eden, where the Tree of Life remained. Why?"

"I couldn't allow the mother and father of humanity to remain in that state after they ate of the Tree of the Knowledge of Good and Evil—falsely illuminated by the deceiver, Satan, yet living eternally. My angels on My command banished Adam and Eve from the Garden of Eden, and because they embraced knowledge instead of truth, my relationship with humans was fractured." The sound of rushing waters filled the vastness of outer space.

But there were no oceans in outer space . . . *is God crying . . . over rebellious humans?*

Daniela did what her mother did when her father became emotional: she distracted him with a question, saving him from embarrassment. "What path would the ancient light illuminate?"

"My Word—Yeshua—is a lamp to your feet and a light to your path. The Light will lead you to the truth about the Aniyvwiya. The Light leads to a path of repentance. Repentance gifts a second chance and protection from the Evil One. Repent and be saved, for the Kingdom of God is at hand. Tell your neighbors—everyone, both friends and enemies—what you discover. Lead them to repentance and back to My presence," Yahweh whispered into her spirit. "Keep the eagle flying high."

"America?"

"Yes—your home, Daniela."

"And if I fail, America and the rest of the world are destroyed?" Daniela asked urgently. A long pause was her answer, until finally the voice spoke.

"Yes."

Her speech pattern changed—rapid, like the rat-tat-tat of a Gatling gun. "The representation of your presence on Earth was the Ark of the Covenant—right?"

"Correct."

"Finding the ancient relics would be a miracle indeed and would get the attention of God's people—the Jewish people as well as the Gentiles. So I need to find both—right?"

"Yes. The Menorah is the representation of Yeshua, while the Ark is a representation of Me. I want humanity to know all of me—the trinity, three parts, one God."

"I understand. Everyone wants to be known." She thought for a while. *Even me.* "Yahweh, who were the Ani-yvwiya?"

"You'll figure it out, Daniela. I cannot give you all the answers. Live. Dream—bend time and travel. Remember that I will never leave you or forsake you. I will be here, holding your hand when you take your last breath—the moment before you come to live with me for an eternity, Rosebud."

Daniela opened her mouth to speak, but Yahweh spoke again, and what imbecilic girl interrupted God? "Seven is the number that represents perfection—completion. Six, a number just shy of seven, represents imperfection. It's man's number." He paused.

"Six-six-six . . . the unholy trinity." Daniela's voice lowered. *But who is six-six-six? Ask. Go for it!*

Saving the world is more important than cheating . . . right?

"Adonai Yahweh," she timidly asked, "who is six-six-six?"

"I'll give you a clue. Remember that my son told His

twelve apostles that the identity of six-six-six would be revealed after the One who restrains is taken away."

"I remember."

"I—we—Yeshua, My Spirit and Me, the Holy Trinity, we never lie . . . we can't, so I cannot tell you who six-six-six is."

"That's not fair. I'm doing so much leg work to solve all of these mysteries."

"If the One who restrains, the Holy Spirit, is gone, you won't be here then."

"The first pandemic—the escape hatch."

"Exactly, and know this, darling girl: the One who restrains is the Holy Spirit. The Ruach, the feminine voice of the Holy Trinity—like you, She speaks comfort, but Her voice is so powerful that She can separate the Red Sea, shut a lion's mouth, and speak wisdom to My church. And the gates of hell will not prevail against Her.

"So worry less about the identity of six-six-six and focus on preparing your friends and even your enemies to not be deceived by the lies of the unholy trinity. Some will be left behind and not raptured, but that's their choice. I give out second chances, but I don't force myself onto humans." Daniela nodded.

"Catch the butterflies," her Father whispered, no differently than her earthly father would have said.

"Yes, sir." She blushed as she refocused her wandering thoughts. "Abba Father, if six-six-six will not be revealed on Earth until after the Holy Spirit is taken away . . ." Daniela paused, looking up into the void of space, expecting to see her Father riding on a gush of winds. But who could see the face of God and live?

"Once again, you'll be gone by then—raptured, taken to safety." The stars gyrated with the waves of Yahweh's mirth. "Legna, finish up, then come and take Rosebud back to the lands of her ancestors—my people, the seed of Abraham, Isaac, and Jacob."

"I'm part Judean?"

"You're a lot of things, Daniela Rose Cavanaugh, so is everyone else. That's why racism puzzles the dickens out of me."

"Me too." When the voice stopped speaking, she could feel a vacuum where it once had been.

Legna's got tour duty today. Suspended in a place of timelessness, the Orphan Dreamer giggled, excited to see the archangel once again.

It had been too long.

As the powerful angel approached, the stars played the lead into Brandon Lake's "Graves," the tenor crooning the intro.

The otherworldly African—Legna, a.k.a., Raphael, the number one archangel in the universe, the lethal warrior, seemed … distracted.

She could see him in the distance.

Dark head draped in a hoodie. Head low.

Lightning flashed behind a bank of clouds, illuminating his silhouette—legs apart, hands buried inside his pockets—inside a haze of fog.

Her heartbeat raced. She waited, but he didn't move.

Legna never abandoned his charges. He stood firm, as though something was beneath his feet. How could she have known that Legna was a bit busy, protecting her future heartsong?

Makes sense. Legna's master possessed all authority, effectively placing all demonic principalities beneath His feet.

And until Legna arrived at Daniela's side, she danced in space—alone—to the tunes of KB, Lecrae, and Kingdom Muzic. Her forehead glistened, dotted with sweat.

Music—the rhythm and mathematics of her soul. The numbers never lied, but humans could manipulate them.

Lies. They were human things.

Find someone who doesn't lie. "Yahweh," she prayed while dancing, "protect my oily boy. Make him a man who tells the truth."

Second chances. A God thing.

Instead of Legna, someone else came. *Oh. My. Goodness!* Dread ambushed the Orphan Dreamer. It was Nomed and his plans . . .

No one cares how much you know until they
know how much you care.

—President Theodore Roosevelt

Twenty-four hours after the second total solar eclipse, occurring on April 8, 2024.

17—Nomed—the Human's End

A Cosmic Revolution
Immortals—Time Without End

IT SUCKS TO BE CROSSED out, but that's why the letter *X* was designed.

Twenty-four hours ago, the moon stuck its butt in the way of the sun's light, blocking sunlight from reaching Earth and forming a total solar eclipse that wrote the last arm of an *X* across North America's sky on April 8, 2024.

Nope. I'm not a meteorologist.

The name's Nomed.

What's up?

Who am I? What's in a name . . . my name? Well, my name tells people everything they need to know about me. But only if they are paying attention—close f-f-four-letter-word attention. Let me spell my name out, N-o-m-e-d.

Pay attention.

Focus on the letters . . . there are only five of them.

Oh—so you figured it out. Good.

Still want to hear what I have to say? A clever and ambitious person would listen, no matter who I am.

Asher Valerian Bushcroft listened and look at him now. Powerful billionaire media man and the chairman of the Sons of Venus.

Skull and Bones, the Bilderberg Group, the Bohemian Club, The Club of Rome, and all of those other exclusive societies for people whose mothers didn't hug them enough, and so in adulthood they still need to belong . . . to feel special. These secret societies pale in power and scope to the history and the all-encompassing power of the SOV—as Asher refers to the Sons of Venus.

The SOV got their power from the Watchers—my kinsfolk—and our descendants, the Nephilim.

Scared?

Should be. I . . . we—my people—lived on Earth before the humans arrived. I—Nomed—lead the charge of Watchers and Nephilim, flying above *The Rose of the Ocean* as it sinks to the bottom of the Indian Ocean.

What a beauty . . . *The Rose of the Ocean.* But not more beautiful than her passengers, Adelaide and Cordelia. The first is the daughter of the elusive Cillian Joseph Finn.

She needed to die.

Why are they on the boat . . . and where are they going?

So many questions about a sinking luxury yacht owned by a billionaire assassin—in both the economic and physical sense. I shake my head. *Where?* For the most part, I have always loathed the *where.*

Where have I been?

Where have I lived?

Where am I from?

Where am I going if I fail in this final moment and on this last mission against the humans?

Sometimes God likes to give the humans a do-over . . . on His account.

But not today!

Sink the boat, sink the girl—drown her and her option to act upon her Elohim-gifted second chance—America's last chance, entrusted, rather foolishly, to the girl by her mother, the Orphan Dreamer.

If you want it done right, do it yourself, mothers!

I take in ten small breaths, then blow them out together, so I can start thinking clearly again.

Finish the mission. This. Is *where* I am!

The mission is a man. Break him. Tear him up. Cillian was born then became an orphan, but now, he's an Orphan—made one by a man more devilish than me, Asher Valerian Bushcroft.

Nomed—that's my name. Who am I?

A thief and a liar?

I shrug. Maybe.

Telling no lies. I steal things—second chances—but that's because I never got one.

Remember my name, Nomed. The oldest five-letter word in the dictionary of horrors! The day I was born, the infamous horror character, Count Dracula, didn't even exist in the mind of Ireland-born author, Stoker.

Ireland. Yes. That's right. Cillian Finn was born on the Emerald Isles. He was conceived in Ireland, too.

Asher Bushcroft—he knows Ireland well, too. I can't help but smile because I was there that day with Asher, ever present as his HouseGuest.

But a good HouseGuest keeps the secrets of their host,

so whatever happened on Ireland's Rathlin Island, well . . . it stays on Rathlin Island.

The mast of *The Rose of the Ocean* disappears beneath still waters.

Ahhhh. They're gone.

At least I think they're gone . . . I hope they're gone. Adelaide and Cordelia are two of the five occupants plummeting into bone crushing ocean depths—trapped inside Cillian's glossy, midnight-blue sailing yacht.

Good riddance! Cillian adored that girl, his Adelaide . . . his daughter, his Rose. Time to party.

Cracking.

Whizzing.

Buzzing.

I dance to the beat of heaven's drums, corrupting its rhythm with my own. Rivers of undulating green-blue lights—the aurora borealis—snake around my twisted form as the stars expand and contract.

We, the Watchers, are many—plasma-hot shapeshifters slithering through the night, fighting to reclaim the space as our own, but the vast and starlit sky is Legna's domain . . . for now.

Legna—the brightest star among the stars of heaven. I'm so jelly.

It's true. The stars are sleeping angels, resting until Elohim awakens them and declares war on me and my kind.

Go ahead.

Make war, and we will fight.

We are not cowards.

And once my warriors and I ambush then conquer Legna and Elohim's other sleeping stars, forcing them into a supernova, we will easily pierce the Kármán line, unharmed and dressed in our new accursed bodies. Bodies that look like yours, but better. Hollywood beautiful.

Humans—nothing but dead men walking . . . so *haute couture.* Ugh.

The zombie apocalypse has already arrived. But my people aren't zombies.

I leave Earth, travel past the Kármán line, and return home—my temporary home until all the humans are gone.

War. Pestilence. Natural disasters. Whatever works.

I shrug.

Where? Where are the humans going after my kinsfolk take Earth back?

Good question. But the answer ain't so good.

18—Nomed—the Human's End

A Cosmic Revolution
Immortals—Time without End

"THE HUMANS EVAPORATED FIRST, MY lord," Nomed—the chief Watcher—gloats as he watches the retreat of his undulating dragon-red snakes.

"Did you collect any humans from the shipwreck to torment down here?" The falsely illuminated one—the deceiver—smirks.

"No, my lord."

"Why not?"

"Their spirits were alive and thus claimed by another."

Nomed's master scowls. "And the half-breeds? Were they punished for their betrayal?"

"The Nephilim vanished second, my lord." Nomed tucks

his chin to his chest, then lowers to one bloodied knee. "As you know, they're harder to kill." A tear slips from Nomed's right eye. His only offspring had been a Nephilim—a half-human, half-fallen angel, yet still his son. His only son. Sacrificed.

But his barren wife, Aglaope—a Greek siren—had never known of that child.

Humans. Aliens.

Nephilim. Extraterrestrials.

Angels. Demons.

What's in a name?

Stupid humans invent labels for things they can never understand. Besides, Nomed truly cares nothing about the nicknames assigned to the players in this game of life and death.

Win!

This is his only goal.

But win what?

Power? The humans are gone—vanished, evaporated. And without slaves, an overseer's power is powerless.

"You're weeping!" Loathing and malice weigh equally on the falsely illuminated one's deep, bass voice. "Are you sad about their demise?"

"I rejoice in their demise. But some of the humans were raptured and others evaporated after a series of nuclear blasts."

"And your unwavering allegiance, is it mine?"

"Yes, my lord." Nomed slams his right arm across his broad chest. The tellurium armor wrapped around his forearm clanks as it strikes his chest plate. Fluorescent, green-black blood oozes from a gash that zigzags across his right shoulder, sizzling as it splashes onto jagged, lava-hot rocks.

"And Legna?"

"Legna and his hordes were formidable foes. But success is ours." Nomed grips his blood-slicked sword in his left hand while clenching his right hand into a punishing fist.

"Excellent! They deserved their end. Their final chapter . . . our beginning."

"But Earth . . . she's gone." Nomed's shoulders slump.

"An unintended victim, if one ever existed." Nomed's master stands over his charge, offering no assistance to dress his seeping wounds. "But now all is quiet on this summer's night."

"A silent, unholy night." Nomed echoes his boss's sentiment.

Nomed's master shakes his head. "They never deserved that planet. Lush fields. The deepest oceans. The prettiest flowers, and the sunsets—oh, the sunsets. Masterpieces of art day after day, but how many ungrateful humans stopped and smelled the roses . . . or gave credit to the master artist?"

"Few, my lord. The Orphan Dreamer and her family are one of those annoying few. Their incessant worship of Elohim." He scrapes his bleached-white tongue with his jagged nails. Green oozes.

"Focus," the boss barks.

"Yes, my lord." Nomed dares to lock his eyes with the condescending gaze of his master. "And us? Where do we go, my lord? Where do we go if we desire to escape hell and its icy cold fire?"

"We stay here, and we wait."

"For?" Nomed raises his right brow.

"Elohim."

"Why?" Nomed holds his breath.

"He may become creative again, speaking another water and oxygen-drenched planet into existence." Physically beautiful yet morally ugly and deceptive, Satan paces the halls of their prison, the underworld.

"Then, what, my lord."

"We'll be ready—ready to invade, deceive, and occupy once again."

"What if we're not invited next time?"

"How else will He test their love for Him?"

"I forgot! He doesn't want robots. He wants family—relationships." Nomed's emphasis on *family* drips with disdain.

"A million angels fall . . . their faces to the floor singing, 'holy, holy, holy,' and yet He wants a family." Satan shakes his head. "A husband. A wife. And little whelps. Disgusting."

"You're pleased with me, then?" The soldier waits for his master's verbal acknowledgment.

Every fool does.

Needing an immediate pat on the back, the warrior mentally ticks off his accomplishments during the awkward silence. A week ago, he dove headfirst into the fiery belly of an underwater volcano to retrieve the artifact—the one lost in the wreckage of *The Rose of the Ocean*. The seed.

The volcano's magma had inflicted his worst wounds—until this morning, when he'd stood at ground zero, and his human minion, Claire Amilee Underwood Covington, detonated the first nuclear bomb from her submarine.

An underwater fish fry spiced with radiation. Nomed chuckles on the inside.

Then all hell broke loose. China and Russia believed the wife of the president of the United States of America had initiated a nuclear attack.

Asher Bushcroft had trained Claire Amilee well as his top Sparrow. But Cillian Finn had been Asher's top Raven. Sexpionage. It had been the human's idea—not Nomed's, just evidence that humans can be evil all on their own. Nomed shifts his weight, wincing as black char flakes off his muscular right thigh.

The intense heat and the scalding glacial cold of his forever home had never scorched him like this. Earth's fury had scarred him for an eternity, scalding his once beautiful Earth form with her fiery rage as she crumbled back into the abyss of darkness—a world that had originated from a dark, formless void, now cursed with inattention and the lack of a kind voice to speak into it, "Let there be Light . . ."

Light—a second chance ringing throughout the annals of human time—chronos, chronological time.

No sun.

No moon.

No stars.

No light.

No food. No humans.

Humans were fools, denying Elohim, the Creator, his due credit. He's the only reason why they exist and haven't annihilated each other. Nomed thinks to spit, wishing one of the groveling humans had been lying at his feet, begging for mercy as he showered them with his acidic, fire-laden disdain. Then, he'd take his fill torturing the human, getting drunk on their screams for mercy.

No. More. Second. Chances.

Redemption gone. It is finished! Nomed's upper lip curls into a sneer and settles into a twisted smile.

Afterward, Nomed would smother his own burns with a healing salve. But not in front of his master.

Aglaope would tend to his injuries and comfort him in the way only a wife could. Or at least, she'd try. In the past, he had tended to her wounds—the ones he'd inflicted during their last act of passion thousands of years ago, after the

Tower of Babel had been erected and Elohim had confused the languages of the humans, then scattered the nations.

Distraught and full of rebellion, Nomed had abandoned his wife, returned to Earth, and seduced a human woman. She had conceived, bearing him a son nine months later.

Altair was a beautiful and intelligent child.

Human scientists would later call Altair a Neanderthal, a creature responsible for human's intellectual leap.

But Altair's human DNA weakened him.

Located inside the Hive, the descendant of their coupling is now attached to life support—like a human with a breathing tube in an ICU—immersed in a liquid medium that feeds his dying cells.

Created in the likeness of the International Space Station but much larger, the Hive is a self-sustaining man-made planet floating in space, safe from Earth's destruction inflicted by the humans and their nuclear bombs. Claire Amilee runs the place.

Aglaope would be pleased with his success while influencing Claire's actions and the subsequent annihilation of the humans. In her naïveté, she'd cry about Earth's demise. She'd been fond of the place.

Then, he would console her, telling her that the universe would now be safe enough to raise their offspring—if Aglaope could ever conceive.

Despite his wife's barrenness, Nomed had been one of the few lucky ones. He had experienced the reckless and unrestrained love of Aglaope before their fall—in the beginning, before Elohim spun the Earth into His starstruck universe then created and deposited humans on the luscious planet.

Nomed had experienced Elohim's love for the angels

before Nomed and his rebellious hoard fell then became Watchers and before Elohim created His pet humans.

Patience, Nomed. Is patience not a virtue for the wise? But when had Nomed or his kind been wise? Wisdom requires humility, not pride.

Pride always preceded a fall—the big fall, the day when one-third of the angels rebelled against Elohim, seeking to become gods themselves. Demons didn't possess the capacity to demonstrate humility.

The humans followed suit, with puffed out chests, they rebelled against their Creator, building the Tower of Babel to reach God, then again as they built their Fourth Reich, duplicating the Tower of Babel in the design of the Strasbourg Parliament building. Human stupidity on repeat.

Claire Amilee's first bomb had hit that building as the nuclear warhead rose like Leviathan from the deepest and blackest ocean. Nomed smiles on the inside. He is no different in his most passionate state. Rising. Exploding. Just before he spills his seed.

"I am pleased." The awkward silence finally ends when, after several moments, Nomed's leader levels his verdict and snatches his subordinate out of his self-congratulatory state.

So dramatic! Nomed catches himself before rolling his eyes. He dares to glance up again at the face of the falsely illuminated one. A tremble more subtle than an earthquake passes through Nomed's taut, muscular body. "You promised—"

The Bearer of False Light snatches a bloodred stone from a glassy black pouch that hangs from a metal belt slung across his shoulder, then tosses the stone in Nomed's direction. "You found it in the depths of that volcano, so it's yours—for now."

The warrior catches the relic in his right hand. A grin spreads across his face as he massages the edges of the Philosopher's Stone—the desiccated and last remaining fruit of the Tree of Knowledge of Good and Evil, the nidus of the human's fall. The seed of deception . . . of a lie. Satan had eaten from the tree the same day Eve ate, and after the fruit's seed passed through his body, the bloodred stone came into being.

"The humans are gone . . . what will you do with it now?"

"I'll wait," Nomed says flatly.

"For?"

"The passing of a thousand years if I must."

"And?"

"If Elohim should decide to create another Garden of Eden, I'll be ready for the arrival of a second Eve."

"Why?"

"The seed inside the Philosopher's Stone will sprout and grow another tree." Nomed grins—as hopeful as every devilish being should be as they embrace their false reality. Lies. Deception. Treachery. A sordid second chance. He pauses, then says, "She'll become hungry, too."

"Then you'll feed her?" Nomed's master strokes his chin.

"I'll feed her until she and her offspring grow fat with knowledge—knowledge that outpaces their morality."

"Good, Nomed. Don't they all lust for a taste of the Philosopher's Stone and its promise of power?"

"Yes, and like us, they never yearn for the illumination of the Light because their actions are continuously evil. Instead, they flounder, unable to stomach the consequences of their ill-conceived motives—wars, rumors of wars, famine, discord, hatred. Then they blame Elohim for their wrongs. The joke's on Him, their inventor. The Creator."

"Ironic and humorous. A masterful plan." The falsely illuminated one nods approvingly. "Why would you do this . . . for me?"

For him? Goodness, no! To himself, Nomed speaks his most fluent language, a lie. "They insulted us, nicknaming our kind extraterrestrials." Nomed's emphasis falls on *extra*. "As though we're the supporting actors in their play." His heart pounds, beating out the drumbeat's rhythm of a death march. A heart? If that's what the thing beating inside his chest could be called. "Aglaope was insulted. Devastated. Moved out of the way for the likes of them."

"You must defend her honor?"

"Yes, my lord."

"And you?"

"I was amused at the humans' foolish theories. They think their science rivals absolute truth, but it doesn't," Nomed explains. "How could science be absolute or something to boast about when the p-value—a five percent chance that the hypothesis is wrong—stands as an obstacle to certainty? And in their dim vision, they raise their social lies even higher than their science."

"Knowledge does not always lead to wisdom." Satan consoles his underling. "Many are informed. Few are wise like the Dreamer's parents. And the humans who believe they are the wisest are the proudest and usually the most deceived."

"Deceived humans never know they are deceived." Nomed smiles. "Humility is the lamp that lights the path to truth and the mirror of self-reflection."

"And Elohim's word," Satan tacks on his observation, "but the humans didn't want wisdom."

"Neither did we." Nomed glances over at the reading

room, where seances took place. He remembered what happened inside the room across the expansive cavern before he found his host.

That night, he and Satan had consulted dark magic to secure a human agent who would mark the Orphan Dreamer and the boy she would dream of for assassination. So Nomed became the HouseGuest of Asher Valerian Bushcroft. And over the years, they'd both become comfortable with the arrangement.

The Orphan Dreamer is a liar, too. No different from Nomed and his master. But unlike them, the Orphan Dreamer had been redeemed—forgiven and given a second chance.

"The reverence of Elohim is the first step to gaining wisdom." Nomed thinks to weep but refuses to release another tear. The one he'd shed already was too much. Watchers weren't supposed to cry. "Like us, humans embrace their arrogance and call it strength. But perception rarely equals a concept as lofty as truth."

"But unlike us, their arrogance renders them weaker." Satan boasts.

"Their pride blinded them, then they embraced your lies—the darkness—and called it light." Nomed kisses the stone and licks his lips. *Power. It tastes like nothing else.*

"Humans adore playing the opposite game, twisting the truth to suit their feelings and vain imaginations." The illuminated one's mouth contorts into a hideous show of mirth. "Choosing to believe a lie, they even denied our existence until we abandoned Wormwood and invaded Earth."

"They were overwhelmed. Confused. You would've thought an alien invasion would've united them." Nomed strokes the Philosopher's Stone.

"It's not a pet." A sneer passes over Satan's face.

"No. It is not, my lord." Nomed drops the stone into his leather satchel.

"Their love of hatred proved to be our Trojan horse." Nomed's master starts pacing, his webbed feet leaving imprints in the boiling hot lava.

"True. And our success in winning this war was mostly dependent upon the humans denying the existence of their only Friend in this invisible fight, their unseen Ally, YHVH—Elohim."

"In the end, without His army's assistance, they could never have defeated us, Nomed. They asked the Orphan Dreamer to call on Legna and his battalions too late in the war."

Nomed shivers at the mention of the powerful warrior's name. "True, my lord." *Where is Legna?* It's true that Legna and his hordes were formidable foes, but it is not true that success had been Nomed's.

Lies. Lies. And more lies.

"As I said, they deserved their fate. Tell me, Nomed, did you witness the Orphan Dreamer's demise? How did she die? And what about her child—the girl cursed with a cap of hair as fiery red as the flames of hell? Did you pulverize the Bat Creek Stone, the Skeleton Key, and Skylark's keystone, making sure they could never be used again as the world's last chance?"

"Yes. The girl drowned. I saw the ship go down. And the Dreamer . . . trust me, my lord, she's dead."

"What?" Satan's lips pull back into a feral snarl. "Me . . . trust you—a demon?" He guffaws, then focuses his deadly glare in the direction of his powerful warrior. "Answer my question, Nomed." He raises his chin. "Did. You. See. Her. Die. With. Your. Beady. Little. Pale. Blue. Eyes?"

"No, my lord," Nomed whispers. "I think . . . she was snatched away—raptured."

"Then, you have failed." His voice is quiet, a whisper of death. "You're worthless." Satan spits fire from his jagged maw. Nomed ducks as his master screams, "Give me back the Philosopher's Stone! Give it back! Give it back! Give it back!" His command echoes throughout the cavernous space, bouncing off jagged cliffs of granite.

Hand trembling, Nomed returns the crimson stone.

In a flash, his master finishes his transformation from his Earth-bound body—a body designed to disarm, seduce, and deceive—into his truest form. Black-green scales flicker over his neon-green eyes. His razor-toothed maw widens.

The humans would have been terrified of Nomed and his kind if they had presented themselves in their true forms.

Instead, wanting to be powerful and beautiful, humans embrace demons because of their false beauty and telling of honeyed lies.

Nomed follows his master's lead. Transforming into his snakelike form, he rises like a king cobra. The transformation eases the throb of pain pulsating beneath his burns. This body was made for hell.

His master's iridescent form slithers at lightning speed through the underworld, vibrating the thick, stagnant air.

Nomed runs behind him on webbed feet overlaid with fingerlike claws. *He better not harm Aglaope.* As they travel deeper into the bowels of what will likely become their forever home, black smoke belches from a cauldron of burning sulfur while screams of lost souls reverberate from its depths.

For what shall it profit a man, if he shall gain the whole world, and lose his own soul? Tsk. Tsk. "This," Nomed whispers between jagged breaths, answering the centuries-old question of Yeshua's apostle, Mark.

Eerie, dissonant tones erupt from a contraption that resembles a splintered pipe organ. Deep inside a vein filled with glacial ice, on a path leading to the heart of the abyss, the falsely illuminated one sheds his iridescent scales. They clatter to the floor, the sound of hail pummeling glass. Bloodred claws erupt from his tail as legs protrude from his slithering form.

He's ugly, fetid, and foul. But who is Nomed to judge?

Rust-brown hair sprouts through Satan's scarred flesh until a lion's mane borders his crimson eyes, set in a gargoyle-like face.

The lion's mane! Satan is transforming into war mode, a roaring lion seeking whom he may devour—he behaves as a cannibal, preying on his own.

Find Aglaope at once! Nomed slinks back.

But where would he and Aglaope escape to?

Earth's been decimated. *Are there any planets remaining in the universe that are as breathtaking as Earth?*

No. Elohim gave the humans His best. Still, they'd been ungrateful and entitled.

Besides, what alien kingdom would open their borders to Nomed's dark presence as the humans had?

What about Asher? Where is he?

Ahh . . . that's right—the Hive.

Asher Valerian Bushcroft had proven himself a true friend. Keeping his word, he had housed and protected Nomed, providing the fallen warrior a home when he needed to work among the humans.

And since Asher had survived the nuclear blasts before Earth stopped spinning and solar flares after Earth stopped spinning, would the leader of the Sons of Venus allow Nomed to be a HouseGuest again—at least until Nomed could find another host, a new home?

Probably not, so Nomed charges through the under-world, dodging in and out of all his and Aglaope's hiding places.

His heart races. Where is she?

Asher didn't know it yet, but Natalia was gone—forever. Always had been. The hope of her survival is yet another lie. And what would Asher do to Nomed when he realized the truth about his dead sister?

Have him exorcised? The demon required a Plan B—a second chance . . . and someone else owed Nomed a favor. "Claire Amilee Underwood," he says beneath his breath. "She'll serve as my second host."

The First Lady of the United States of America, Claire had betrayed friend and foe, frying up Earth the same way she cooked her morning eggs—scrambled, burnt to a crisp.

A snake bites.

A liar lies.

A murderer murders.

Claire had been all three. Completely reliable to the under-world's master planners.

As for learning how to effectively kill humans, Beelze-bub—Lucifer's warlord charged with training an army of Watchers sequestered on Wormwood—had scheduled a trial run of a viral pandemic during the Gregorian calendar year of 2020.

It had worked.

Mayhem. Selfishness. Everyone had an opinion.

Then, basking in the promise of unlimited power, Claire had agreed to be the human agent Nomed's soldiers worked through.

Meanwhile, Asher's multimedia corporation had turned the nations against themselves by wielding the power of divisive words. *Divided, then we conquered.*

The humans didn't see the Watchers coming.

The whole world had been focused on a Chinese president with a King Herod complex and a Russian leader with a bad temper. Lies spoken and then embraced by the masses had injured the powerful wings of the eagle nation charged by God to protect the unwanted humans. Nomed whispered the aging poem to himself . . .

The New Colossus
Emma Lazarus

Not like the brazen giant of Greek fame,
With conquering limbs astride from land to land;
Here at our sea-washed, sunset gates shall stand
A mighty woman with a torch, whose flame
Is the imprisoned lightning, and her name
Mother of Exiles.
From her beacon-hand Glows world-wide welcome.

her mild eyes command
The air-bridged harbor that twin cities frame.
"Keep, ancient lands, your storied pomp!" cries she with
silent lips.
give me your tired, your poor,
Your huddled masses yearning to be free,
The wretched refuse of your teeming shore.
Send these, the homeless, tempest-tost to me,
I lift my lamp beside the golden door!

The eagle people had forgotten their purpose in the world, their vision, and without a vision the people perished. Infected with a special kind of selfishness, the citizens of the eagle nation laid down their torch, refusing to illuminate the world any longer.

But Nomed had made one fatal mistake: he had trusted the Father of Lies.

And now Venus, a dim planet cursed with the intense heat of volcanic activity trapped beneath an impenetrable and toxic atmosphere would be Aglaope's and Nomed's forever home because Earth was destroyed.

Aglaope didn't deserve this!

It's Satan's fault. That con. Nothing but a liar! Hell, such a wretched place to live . . . to exist . . . to survive. It was a place void of love. Dark. No light—only raging heat.

No Son. No Light of the World.

Aglaope and Nomed had lived on Earth before the humans arrived, when the planet was still without form. And yes, Aglaope loved him very much. They even saw love up close. Real love. Not the Hollywood lust.

The kind of love that compelled a heavenly King to journey to Earth and become a servant. Agape love. Then, He spread His arms wide as sweat-drenched Roman soldiers nailed him to a splintered cross—the place where he paid for human's failures . . . but not Nomed's.

Nomed turns a corner and gasps when he finally sees his quarry. "Stop it!"

What the heck is that fool doing!

He charges Satan. The lion has grown teeth, and he is gnawing on Aglaope's deformed arm.

The Word—God in the spoken form—had always been Legna's most formidable weapon when fighting Nomed and his horde of demons, so Nomed stated the truth, "Satan, you've been defeated. Jesus—He paid for it all!"

The lion whips his bloodied face around, then levels a hellish stare in Nomed's direction.

Bravery oozes from Nomed's voice, "Jesus has won. On Golgotha's Hill, He crushed your head. So. Get. The.

Hell. Off. My. Wife." Nomed fights his master with the only thing that could defeat the powerful ruler of the dark underworld—the Light, Truth. The Word of God is sharper than a two-edged sword.

He continues quoting Elohim's words, "O Death, where is your sting? O Hades, where is your victory? The sting of death is sin, and the strength of sin is the law. But thanks be to God, who gives us the victory through our Lord Jesus Christ." Nomed's voice trickles to the breath of a last and dying whisper.

The powerful words—the Word of the Creator—are meant to shine an effervescent light, defeat evil and create good . . . but these words affect Nomed, too.

As he fights for his wife's second chance, he stumbles backward and then collapses to the ground beside his love— his wife, the woman he couldn't stay faithful to.

Both demon and master devil have lost their power. Satan is gasping for air. Puffs of smoke exhaled with each breath.

Their evil is overcome by the truth interwoven in the rays of the Light of the World.

Light—the Sun . . . the Son—makes all things live again.

A second chance. *Oh, grave, where is your victory . . .?*

The heartbroken demon nudges the side of his mauled wife. She will die if her arm, which is festering with hell's worms, isn't removed now. Nomed leaves Satan behind and takes Aglaope to a sparsely occupied space in hell where he conjures up the last tendrils of his strength and reverts to his more palatable Earth form.

"Nomed," he hears his wife's plaintive whisper. "Don't leave me, not while I'm dying."

"I'll never leave you again."

"Again . . .?" The fading light behind her eyes begging him to tell her the truth, but the truth would kill her.

He takes his sword—the same sword that had slaughtered so many humans—and dunks it into a cauldron of fire, holding it fast until the dried human blood evaporates and the silver loses its shine, dimming to a pale white.

He severs the lower part of Aglaope's arm in one quick motion, leaving a stump below her elbow.

She shrieks with pain. He fights to transform back into his underworld form, so he is protected from the heat of hell's fire—a fire that in his hellish form, feels like a bath of glacial ice. Nomed gazes at his wife.

Limp and drenched with pain, she moans.

"It's okay, Agla." Possessed by anger more intense than the fire suffocating the cave ignites inside Nomed. Irrational, feeling powerless, and full of hatred, he declares his threat to the remaining humans hiding within the Hive. "You all must die. Cowards, unbelievers, corrupt, murderers, the immoral, those who practice witchcraft, idol worshippers, and all liars—this is your fate, the fiery lake of burning sulfur. You refused your second chance—the first pandemic, the escape hatch, the rapture—Yeshua's sacrifice. Claire and Asher, I'm coming for you too. Asher Bushcroft a friend?" He huffs. "I have no friends, especially human friends."

Aglaope moans in agreement with her husband.

"For you, darling," he promises. "Yes. They tried to escape from the second death—the pandemic the Orphan Dreamer had tried to keep at bay—but all the Hive members deserved to succumb to the deadly disease. The citizens of the Hive refused her overtures of love." He weeps. "It's only fair that they get hell instead of Earth. We didn't get a second chance."

"Don't cry, Nomed. Not here . . . please. I need your strength, not pity and sadness." Aglaope stirs, her head lolling, refusing to follow her twisted body. "Hold my hand. Please."

He obeys. "I despise all humans."

"No. You're jealous of them. There's a difference."

"It is true. I'm jealous of their second chance."

"We are a jealous bunch." Aglaope chuckles weakly. "The second death, living in hell . . . it sucks really bad." A rawness that often accompanied death rakes the back of her throat, rendering the tone of her voice into a sound that mimicked claws scratching along sandpaper.

"As it should." Thoughts taunted him. *Could the humans have tricked him? Could his reality be the false one? Had he and his people actually won the war—Armageddon? Or had the Watchers only won a battle within the warfare?* He massages his temples, kneading the ache out of an alternative possibility: had he lied to himself?

Had the humans—Claire and Asher—tricked him, a prince of telling lies? "No. Humans are not that clever," he speaks his dreaded thought.

"Don't get trapped inside the web of pride," his wife urges.

"But it is in the embrace of pride where I do my best work, Agla." A sneer mixed with disdain spreads like curdled milk across the fallen angel's face. "No, Agla." He pauses. "This isn't going to be how Nomed's story ends. After all, I was the one who masterminded the plan to manipulate the humans into bombing one another to smithereens."

Most of you deserved it.

Probably all of you.

Nomed squeezes Aglaope's hand. He would wait for her to heal. That's what the Light did, even in the presence of pure dark evil—it healed. It resurrected. It redeemed. It restored.

Love—agape love defined within three simple words uttered by a crucified King: "It. Is. Finished."

It is finished!

The supernatural healing needed time to manifest from kairos time—God's infinite time into present time. The Word still speaks the truth—forever and ever and ever, Amen.

And as for Satan, Nomed and his Watchers . . ., yes, they had deceived the humans about the Light's motives before, telling lies about Yeshua and assigning false labels. Religion had been one of the main methods.

If given the chance, Satan and his Watchers will deceive again.

It's their nature. It's in the nature of their offspring, the Nephilim's, nature, as well. How could one find a Nephilim? When he speaks, he tells lies.

> For such men are counterfeit apostles, deceitful
> workers, masquerading as apostles of Christ.
> And no wonder, since Satan himself masquer-
> ades as an angel of light. So it is no great surprise
> if his servants also masquerade as servants of
> righteousness, but their end will correspond
> with their deeds.
>
> —I Corinthians 11:13-15

Two hundred days after the second total solar eclipse occurring on April 8, 2024.

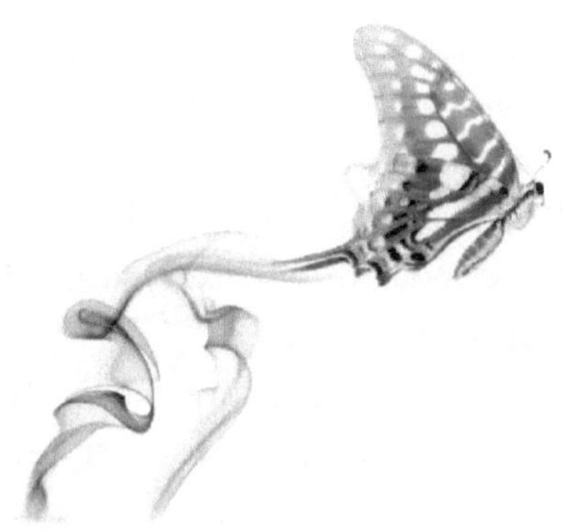

19—Cordelia Gray

8:56 a.m., Wednesday, October 30, 2024
Dunedin, New Zealand

TWO HUNDRED DAYS HAVE PASSED since the Great American Solar Eclipse blotted out the sun's face, preventing it from shining above America. Seventy days after the eclipse, something evil—a presence and then a person—overran America.

But four hundred days had been the grace period before the final showdown.

Cordelia finishes drinking her daily ration of coffee as she ponders her best friend's mother's saying, that every tyrant believes himself to be utterly reasonable if he is getting his way.

And he will make peace with Israel for three and a half years . . .

Peace before tyranny.

In the one-hundred and thirty days he'd ruled, six-six-six, the antichrist, had made Stalin seem like an amateur in the theatre of tyranny.

Sheldon Covington's predecessor had reclaimed the presidency, then pardoned himself, executing a checkmate in the game of political legal chess.

The United States Constitution didn't prohibit a felon from running or winning the presidency. And the US Constitution granted a president the right to pardon any person who had committed a federal crime—but not a state crime.

After Covington's predecessor won the US presidency, the Second Civil War ensued. Another repercussion of Adelaide's failure to reverse the curse of the Bat Creek Stone.

United we stand.

Divided we fall.

Some said that hell has no fury like that of a scorned woman.

They were wrong; they must have suffered from a bad case of hippocampal failure and forgot about all the wars started by those possessed by the Y-chromosome. Testosterone could render brain cells deaf to rational thought. Payback was rarely a woman or the derogatory term for one.

It was a man—usually was.

Hitler.

Genghis Khan.

Mao Zedong

Many of Rome's Caesars.

Some of America's presidents.

Six. Six. Six.

Few survived on Earth in the days following the spring of the second total solar eclipse. And those who did survive wished they hadn't, envious of those who'd been taken, protected by the first pandemic.

Nuclear winters rained snow and ice onto every continent in the Northern Hemisphere. Antarctica's ice caps were melting faster than ice cream in mid-summer.

Seventy-one days after the eclipse, Cordelia set sail across stormy seas to arrive in New Zealand, Adelaide's family's most private and coveted estate of the nine they owned.

Her heart aches for Adelaide more than her sprained back as she climbs off the kitchen bar stool, crosses the living room, and enters her bedroom. In the attached bathroom, aqua-glass tiles glint in the rays of the morning sun. Passing by clear glass windows, she steps with bruised bare feet into the shower of the Cavanaugh-Finn's empty seaside cottage.

The Cavanaugh-Finns are gone. Vanished. Poof, like a vapor. "Come back!" Cordelia cries as clean, hot water needles her scarred flesh, cleansing her skin while her tears attempt to cleanse her soul.

She begs to forget her best friend, but the harder she tries not to remember, the more vivid the memories of Adelaide become. So, she compromises and mentally sorts through her notes that she wrote down last night when she couldn't sleep—again.

The notes would serve as breadcrumbs necessary to guide the plot of her epic story. A remembrance. A memory. A legacy.

She sighs, long, deep, inhaling then exhaling one tragic breath after another.

After her shower, she would write the next scene in her novel—a timeless story of hope, love, and the promise of second chances. This story is her catharsis. She's named it the Orphan Dreamer Saga. It would be a story about her best friend, her best friend's mother—the Orphan Dreamer—and the orphan she had dreamed of, Cillian Finn.

This family was—no, is—her muse.

* * *

The Present, the End . . .
6:23 a.m., Monday, June 19, 2023
Blue Ridge Mountains, NC

SOME CITIZENS WERE FREE ON July 4, 1776, and others tasted freedom on June 19, 1865—Juneteenth, when Texas enslaved people got wind of the news of liberty from Union soldiers.

Nah. Texas plantation owners weren't going to tell the truth. Who would toil in the fields under a Texas sun if they did?

That was then, and this is now. All remaining Americans were going to—or had—lost their freedom, paying for the sins of their ancestors.

It's the last day, the day before forever.

Daniela Rose slides her damp fingers across the face of the smaller stone—Skylark's stone—then rests America's lifeline inside her daughter's trembling hand.

She closes her daughter's pale fingers over the cold rock. "It's our second chance, Adelaide. But it's America's, and the world's, last chance. Do you understand me?"

"No—I don't. A rock! I mean . . . how in God's green Earth does a rock save us all? It's as silly as 'one ring will rule them all'." Tears slip down Adelaide's face.

"It's not just any rock."

"Mummy, please." Adelaide reaches for her mother and then falls to her knees. "Please, not me. I'm not that brave or clever."

"But you are, and you can swim." Daniela gestures toward the swimming medals hanging on Adelaide's bedroom wall. Then kneels before her daughter. "Let me tell you a story about justice. For thousands of years, the Aniyvwiya—*the real people*—lived in Loudon, Tennessee . . . until they were taken." She traces the edge of the keystone lying inside Adelaide's open left hand.

"Who took them?" Adelaide studies Skylark's stone.

"The kidnappers—invaders. They penned lies about the Aniyvwiya on their talking leaves, lies used to assuage the guilt of the kidnappers for their atrocities against these people. These talking leaves whispered a dark tale, a diabolical plan—the premeditated murder and the near-extinction of the Aniyvwiya."

"That's evil." Adelaide looks away from the relic and finds the eyes of her mother.

"Worse than evil, Adelaide." Daniela traces the edge of Adelaide's jawline. "You see, there was a major problem with the invaders' plan."

"Only one?" Adelaide says, and her mother smiles.

"You're right, but I only have enough time and enough breath to tell you about one."

"Then tell me everything." Adelaide tugs on her mother's sleeve, pulling her to her feet and leading her to the couch. "Because I want to hear your voice . . . for an eternity."

Daniela smiles and sits beside her daughter. "One spring day that was almost lost in the heat of a Mesopotamian desert, the One Who had spoken into a black and formless void—the predawn of Earth's ordered universe—causing light to come from nothing, made a promise that would reverberate throughout the annals of time."

"What was this promise?"

"Yahweh said to Abram, 'Abram, take your family and leave the safety and wealth of this land. I am taking you to a new land, the Promised Land.' Abram replied, 'My lord, we are small in number and vulnerable to our enemies.' 'Go, Abram,' God said, 'and I will bless those who bless you, and I will curse those who curse you. And your name will now be Abraham—the Father of Many Nations—and all the earth will be blessed through your seed.' Abraham obeyed, got up, packed, and left the familiarity of his small but prosperous kingdom. Then, he set off on an unfamiliar journey to an unfamiliar place. That day, a powerful blood pact was sealed."

"What does Abraham have to do with the Bat Creek Stone or this total eclipse you keep telling Father and me about?"

"The Bat Creek Stone curse is triggered by the conditions of the blood pact made between Yahweh and Abraham in 2068 BC—four thousand ago."

"But that's four thousand years ago. What does that have to do with us, now?"

"The kidnappers executed their diabolical plan—the premeditated murder and extinction of the Aniyvwiya. The Aniyvwiya were Abraham's descendants. This mass genocide of God's people triggered the divine curse, and a countdown was set—the end of the countdown will be signaled by two total solar eclipses. And the last solar eclipse will occur on April 8, 2024. Less than a year from now."

"What happens when the clock stops at zero?" Adelaide scoots to the edge of the couch and turns to face her mother.

"The end of a beloved empire—our homeland, America, gone. And soon after this refuge of freedom is gone, the end of the whole world."

"That sucks." Adelaide pauses. Daniela stays silent, allowing the information to sink in. "A promise is a promise and meant to be kept—right, Mummy?"

"Yes, darling." Daniela nods. "Especially a vow made by God." She pauses. "Unlike humans, God cannot lie."

"And you don't want America to be destroyed? Even

though it hasn't always treated people who look like you kindly?"

"No, I don't want America to be destroyed. It's my home, too."

"There's still the rest of the world, Mummy. With Dad's billions, we could live somewhere else . . . like New Zealand."

"That's true, but America holds a special beacon of light for the world to see, and even though it's shining rather dimly at the moment, this light still holds possibilities, giving hope to so many who are hopeless."

"Our leaders as of late have been pot-stirrers, basic duds, and dark lampshades, so no one can see our light, Mummy. They just see our butts." Adelaide's smile dims.

"You're right. But our leaders have simply reflected the values of America's citizens, Adelaide. Never forget this. Be someone different from the masses. Tell the truth. Be reliable. The fate of America depends upon it."

"Must be nice, though." Adelaide smiles.

"What?"

"God and his inability to lie. He would never have been grounded in my parents' house, or worse." Adelaide chuckles. "If I can survive telling a lie in the Finn-Cavanaugh household, America can survive this total solar eclipse countdown and whatever follows." Adelaide chuckles again. "Trust me."

"Trust?" She pauses. "It's not that simple. You see, America must not only survive, but she must also thrive, remaining strong in a world that values freedom. As so, we Americans must right the wrongs of our past. Humble ourselves. Because redemption—a second chance—only comes after repentance, admitting our wrongdoings."

"You mean pray . . . ?"

"Yes, pray," Adelaide's mother confirms. "Is that so bad?"

"No."

"What is prayer to you, Adelaide?"

"A protest," Adelaide responds. "It's ironic that those who say they are Christians so abhor protesting for freedoms here on Earth, yet they ask for everyone to pray for them when they need God's help." Adelaide smirks.

"Pay no mind to them." Daniela stands and tugs Adelaide's arm, signaling her to follow. They move into the master bedroom. "Fortunately, the Martin Luther King, Jrs; the Rosa Parks; and the Harriet Beecher Stowes of the world didn't listen to those telling them to shut up. And so, Adelaide, we must not listen to the Father of Lies who tells us not to protest—to pray. We must repent for our sins against Abraham's people—the Aniyvwiya. Only then may we be a radiant beacon of light in the world. Humility, not pride, is the fuel to our lamp of light."

"Mom, you should've become America's PR manager instead of the Orphan Dreamer." Adelaide burst into laughter.

"It's nothing to take lightly, Adelaide."

"I know, Mom, but your neck vein is getting ready to explode. Count my humor as a pressure valve."

"As the Orphan Dreamer, I am humanity's PR person." Daniela gazes into the distance as she walks past the master bedroom suite's floor-to-ceiling windows, then circles around to the king-size bed, running her fingers down the thick, fluffy, white comforter. *He was here.*

"A martyr's complex isn't healthy, Mummy," Adelaide teases.

"Be serious, Addy Rose!" Daniela huffs. "Look around you! Take notice! Not everyone lives in a 20,000-square-foot luxury mountain chalet. Ukraine's President Volodymyr

Zelenskyy did not go to France, England, Australia, China, India, Africa, Central America, South America, or Japan. No—he came to America to request an alliance in his fight against tyranny." After she finished speaking, both hands were balled into fists.

Adelaide whispers, "Lucky us." She rolls her eyes. "That support could cost America everything. It could incite another World War that would force young American men and women to abandon their colleges, their farms, their jobs, their hopes, and their dreams and instead spill their blood so the people of Ukraine can be free and shake off the chains of Russian tyranny."

"You're right."

"Let. Them. Fight. Their own war, Mummy."

"Battered and scarred by a whip studded with barbs of lies, stoked divisions, and hatred—it's true that America's heart is bleeding."

"Do we even have a heart?"

"Of course we do." Daniela leaves her daughter at the foot of her bed and removes something from the bedroom safe tucked in a false wall behind the fireplace. "Yet with her bleeding heart still beating inside her chest, she clutches a torch of light and freedom, raising it skyward within the grasp of the Statue of Liberty. Without America's light of freedom, what would the world look like?" Daniela shudders at the thought of that pervading darkness, then reaches for her daughter's hand.

"Mom, are you okay?"

"Adelaide, promise me this: before you set sail with Cordelia, return the Bat Creek Stone to its proper place—Mound Three, Chief Know Nothing's burial site in Loudon, Tennessee. Place it under his skeletal head, and after you do this, use this smaller stone as a key . . ." Daniela squeezes Adelaide's right hand containing the smaller stone. "It's called Skylark's keystone, and it is named after a very brave girl."

"What exactly will it do, Mummy?"

"Skylark's keystone and the Bat Creek Stone will work together, behaving like a two-factor authentication code used to log in to important online accounts. Used together, they will abort the impending disaster coming to America."

"Mummy, I'm scared."

"I know you are, and so were your father and I."

"Are you scared now?"

"A little. I'm scared for you. But now the Light, the original menorah, is in its proper place. Your father and I made sure of it. The keystone, in the presence of the light, the Bat Creek Stone, and the Skeleton Key, will guide us to Yahweh's presence—the place where the power lies to defeat our enemies. This is the only place where our beloved country's second chance can be found. The time is now, darling. And you're the one I choose to complete this task. You're a great swimmer. Our family's final task, our family legacy, is to ensure America's second chance, and the world's last chance."

"A light in the darkness."

"Yes."

"Where is this mysterious light?"

"Somewhere safe. And as the light shines, we must make sure Yahweh's presence is seen and then felt in all the Earth."

"But the light . . . where did you find it?"

"Your father and I relit the eternal light inside a tomb, and this special fire burns to this day, illuminating an underground maze connecting America to Mongolia."

"A fire lit inside a mountain?" Adelaide furrows her brow.

"It is no ordinary fire—it's a powerful fire that can siphon the water of all the oceans of Earth to keep them from rising above land." Daniela holds a velvet-covered object in her hand.

"This fire is trapped somewhere safe?"

"A sacred place. When you place the two keys in their rightful locations, this act of unification will demonstrate to Yahweh that the new owner of the keys—you—have made America's wrongs right with the Aniyvwiya."

"Okay, Mom." Adelaide studies her mother's pain-etched face, then brushes stray curls away from her mother's big, brown eyes. "Why do you care so much?"

"I'm the Orphan Dreamer. It's my duty to care."

"No, Mom. This is different."

"Some of my ancestors were the villains . . . and others were the victims."

"Super complicated."

"Making things right usually is, Adelaide. And when you're successful, you'll know it. This sacred fire opens the underground spillways, siphoning the radioactive floodwaters away from North American lands. Then, the Eternal Light will cleanse the poisoned waters, cool them, and return the water to its proper place—the ocean."

"Radioactive? Is someone going to set off a nuclear bomb underwater?"

"Yes—Claire Amilee will. Her act will trigger massive earthquakes—one close to Tennessee where the Bat Creek Stone needs to be replaced, so promise me that you'll do as I ask, before she sets off her bomb."

"I promise, Mummy."

★ ★ ★

IT'S TRUE.

Adelaide could make a promise then not keep it—no, she's not God, just the daughter of a dreamer and an orphan and Cordelia's best friend. Cordelia scrubs her scalp, working up a lather, the hot water forming a foggy film on the glass doors.

How does one escape the long arm of the Creator? The young author's heart races as she towel-dries her damp skin. She dons a thick cotton robe before sitting at her favorite desk, the pink one that faces the sea.

This morning—finally—she is emotionally ready to remember her best friend, her Addy Rose. Her high school roommate at Phillips Exeter. Her shipmate. Her kindred spirit.

So, she sits at her typewriter, prepared to remember. She writes another draft of her novel—*Orphan Falls*, the third novel in the Orphan Dreamer Saga, a tome telling the story of the Orphan Dreamer, Daniela Rose Cavanaugh.

And Daniela's heartsong—Cillian Joseph Finn, the orphan she'd dreamed of.

And the hottest man to ever tread across Earth's face. No way that man was human. Cordelia smiles. He had to be extraterrestrial, something angelic and magical.

Addy Rose would kill me. A lump grows in Cordelia's throat as she wishes her best friend back to her side. Instead, she sits alone as her left forefinger strikes the first letter of the next scene—a Mother's letter . . .

The Eyes of Time

Adelaide Rose possesses old green eyes—eyes that have seen too much and could tell a story if one has the time to listen.

Do you?

What if your life depends upon listening to her story and hearing the truth?

But the truth is, time is gone.

Beginnings are gone. Middles have ceased. And the end has come.

It's true. Adelaide's patinated copper eyes had once shown as bright a green as the lush fields draping the Emerald Isles of her father's ancestral lands of Ireland and Scotland.

Now, at the end, her once bright eyes have dimmed into the shade of the paltry vomit-green of a pitted olive streaked with flecks of copper. Their superficial beauty may have dimmed, but they still tell a rich and beautiful story—a story about second chances. Her story. They also speak a truth that even daughters born as beautiful as Adelaide would one day die.

Plain and simple.

Time. Beginning . . . and the end.

A life spent well equals a legacy. Time poorly spent equals infamy and regret.

Sinners in the hands of an angry God.

Sinners in the hand of a merciful God.

Rewind . . .? Is it true: is Someone gifting second chances?

Yes. It is. But only this once—and only in this way. Why this limited path? Redemption requires a sacrifice, and one cold dark day, Yeshua whispered to His father, *Father forgive them, for they do not know what they are doing,* and these heartrending words ensured us a second chance.

No sane person wants to relive their difficult past. Even if reliving that dark and confusing past guarantees another person a future. Yet the Orphan Dreamer's story will reset, defying time, so that Earth's humans can experience a second—and last—chance.

Second chances. Use them wisely. "For what is our life but a vapor that appears for a little time, and then vanishes away?"

Poof. Time vanishing into the fog of eternity, a place on the other side of Ellesmere, where the Orphan Dreamer hunts for clues to solve ancient puzzles that will save her friends and her enemies from a diabolical force—Earth's previous occupants.

Second chances . . . this is Adelaide Rose Cavanaugh-Finn's story, her mother' story, her father's story.

And your story . . . if you'd like a second chance.

If you had known your ending, how would you have lived your beginning?

Writing to remember,

Cordelia Gray Anderson

Author of the Cavanaugh-Finn story and Adelaide Rose Cavanaugh-Finn's best friend

20—Orphan Dreamer

2:23 p.m., Wednesday, July 9, 1998
Gainesville, Florida

NOMED'S REALITY WILL BECOME EARTH'S reality if Daniela doesn't succeed in her mission to pacify the Bat Creek Stone curse and find the long-lost ancient light, the menorah. Outside Daniela's hospital room, lavender was blooming, and birds were chirping, reminding those who were listening that the world was still very much alive.

"Mom! Dad!" Sweat clung to Daniela's skin until rivers of perspiration ran down her back and chest.

"It's okay."

"Mom! Dad!" she screamed over and over.

"Daniela, wake up. You're having a nightmare. It's okay. Wake up."

"She's in trouble! Mom, help me—Adelaide's heart is broken!" Daniela tossed and turned. Suddenly, a bolt of pain dug into her left hip. "Ouch!" She threw off her covers and started hollering. "There's a scorpion in my bed. There's a scorpion in my bed, and it bit me!"

"Sorry," someone said.

"For what?" Daniela's eyes roved wildly, unable to focus.

Finally, she blinked away the rivers of emotion that had been blurring the edges of a face—brown, a wide-bridge nose, full lips, and a tidy afro hairstyle capped with a starched white cap and matching uniform.

"I'm sorry for pinching you."

"Where am I? Who are you?"

"You're in the hospital, and it's Nurse Valerie—your favorite."

Daniela inhaled deeply. Antiseptic mixed with the sweet stink of healing burned flesh assaulted her nose, triggering a bout of dry heaves. "Where am I? I'm afraid."

"You've been dreaming." Nurse Valerie steadied a puke basin beneath her patient's mouth. "That's all. You're still in the burn unit. Remember? The church fire. You were burned." Nurse Valerie sat beside her patient on a plastic hospital chair and rested her hand on Daniela's. "You're okay. I promise."

"No—it's not okay."

"But it is. You're healing."

"I don't care about me. It's my daughter, Adelaide Rose . . . she's sad—some mean boy broke her heart, drowning her in pain. Such a horrific situation . . . at seventeen, and I wasn't there to punch that boy in the face."

"Breathe, Daniela . . . just breathe." Valerie stroked deep brown curls away from Daniela's moistened brow. "If she was just drowning in romantic pain, it's better than drowning in the middle of the ocean."

"That's mean, Nurse Valerie!"

"But true. You've been sleeping, maybe even dreaming. You're awake now. Safe. Inside your hospital room."

"I-I-I'm not a liar."

"I didn't say you were."

Daniela reached up and grabbed the starched lapels of Valerie's white shirt. "I know what happened, and I wouldn't lie to you, Ms. Valerie, promise!"

"No one is accusing you of lying. Your daughter may exist in the future, Daniela, but she's only hurting inside your nightmare."

"I'm not crazy either."

"How did she look?"

"That's the oddity of it; I don't know how she looked, except that she had red hair and freckles. I think she was beautiful."

"Every mother thinks that about their child."

"I know she was there. And, Ms. Valerie, I'm not cross with her for going to that New Year's Eve party . . . she left, went to church, and began to search for God. I just want her to be okay. And then there was Legna. I remember how he looks."

"And?" Valerie's voice upticks.

"He's so dreamy, Nurse Valerie."

"I bet he is." Valerie tilted her chin, giving Daniela a look that was expectant—concerned, confused. But there was something else—a knowing.

"I'm not crazy—right?" Sleep's cobwebs began to release Daniela's brain from her nightmare. "I promise, and I don't care what Claire's said about me. I'm not stupid, either."

"I don't think you're crazy or stupid." Daniela's nurse gently dabbed Daniela's brow with a cool washcloth, sopping up the fear along with the sweat. "Besides, you're only seventeen. How could you have a daughter of seventeen?" Valerie chuckled. "Much less be married."

"Where am I?"

"You're in the hospital—the burn unit. You saved a little girl's life. Remember? At the church. At the funeral of the disgraced senator's wife. Reporters are still outside. The President was there."

"Where is Emmaline?" Daniela bolted up in bed, gasping for air. "Where is Polly, Claire's sister!"

"Okay. They are both safe."

"I'm glad." Daniela began to cry. "Please, Nurse Valerie. Help me sort through all of this. I feel so crazy . . . even though I know that I'm not."

"We'll be rational together, special girl. Remember last night when you were so worried about the scars? Saying that you were ugly and no boy would date you in medical school because of the scars?" Valarie touched Daniela's forearm bandages. "I asked you if you've ever had a boyfriend, and you told me that you hadn't even kissed a boy—right?"

"That's right." Daniela blushed. "The nosebleeds would make things a bit awkward. And my parents, well . . ."

"You don't have to explain. My parents were strict, too— as parents should be. But how could you have given birth to a baby girl who is now your seventeen-year-old daughter when you're only a teenager? Let's do the math together. You said you love math."

"I'd be zero years old."

"That's right, and you're starting the early medical school entrance program soon, so you know that isn't possible." Nurse Valerie winked.

"I do." She sighed. "But the dreams were so real." Daniela wiped away her emotions, still moving between the reality of now and the reality of her dreamworld—the world accessed by the Glass Tattoo. "Will the two ever coincide?"

"Do you want them to?"

"Yes." Daniela's voice could barely be heard above the hum of machines in the burn ICU. "I'd like to be a mom." Daniela smiled. "Maybe fall in love with a boy and marry him."

"Give it time."

"And if I cannot save my Adelaide Rose in the end, what's the point of fighting, or living in the present?"

"Don't talk like that. You're accomplishing your dreams. You are more than someone's wife, or mom. You're attending medical school at the University of Florida in the fall, and you're going to become a physician." Nurse Valerie's tone changed to pride in Daniela and their shared struggle as women—brown women. "You make us all so very proud."

"Thank you." Daniela's clumsy grip slipped as she fingered the bandages wrapped securely around both forearms. "Ouch." Beneath the gauze, tendrils of pain stung like jellyfish tentacles. "Did you place the gauze to hide the burns?"

"To protect—there's a difference. I've been meaning to ask . . ." Nurse Valerie pointed at Daniela's right palm. "What's that?"

The Glass Tattoo had spilled dark blue ink into the center of her palm, leaving behind a beautiful midnight-blue snowflake tattoo. Daniela giggled nervously. "Mother hates tattoos. But it's something odd and powerful enough to defy time."

"Naughty Daniela Rose Cavanaugh." Nurse Valerie chuckled. "I didn't know you had it in you."

"I guess I'm a naughty girl."

"G-rated of course."

Daniela's lips peeled back into a Cheshire Cat grin as

she curled the fingers of her right hand over the snowflake staining her right palm.

Then, she opened her fist. The tattoo faded, and the snowflake diamond ejected from her skin, flushing the details of the nightmares from her mind.

"What in the world?" Nurse Valerie stumbled backward, knocking over Daniela's tray table before surrendering to the plastic recliner.

Daniela laughed as the water jug clanked and bounced across the floor, spilling water as it went. "Nurse Valerie, are you okay?"

"I'm okay." She waved her hands, minimizing Daniela's concerns and faking her adult bravery. "I hate seeing anything coming out of the skin: pus, sebaceous cysts, scabies, you name it."

"Are you sure?

"Stay in bed. You're a hero—my hero. And one day you'll be Adelaide's mother, so I can't have you slipping on this water and breaking your neck." Nurse Valerie sopped up the mess with a towel, threw it in the laundry bin, then sat in the chair next to Daniela's hospital bed.

"Did it hurt when that glass crawled out of your skin?"

"No. Don't worry."

"Does the mission ever hurt?"

"Sometimes I hurt if my oily boy gets hurt . . . flogged, slapped, punched and even . . ." Her voice trailed off into oblivion. Maybe she wasn't a virgin any longer? "I guess it's normal."

"Hardly, child." Nurse Valerie's forehead creased as she secured a glass syringe from the metal tray resting on the bedstand. "You're an empath, feeling other people's pain as though it's your own. You're gonna have to learn how to protect your heart. Or it'll kill you one day, Daniela."

"I don't want that—please, Ms. Valerie. I don't want to be forced into another nightmare. Please. I won't talk about Adelaide anymore . . . or even my oily boy." A single tear escaped Daniela's right eye. "Please." Her final plea puffed from between her dusty-rose lips.

The nightmare of Daniela's teenage daughter drowning in the pain of rejection brought back a tidal wave of pain— one that had begun in Daniela's childhood, at school and in church, at the hands of Claire Amilee and her cousin, Harry.

Rejection.

Polly. Polly's dead mother.

Even people inside Daniela's dreamworld had experienced rejection.

Legna. The Aniyvwiya. Who were the Aniyvwiya? And the Bat Creek Stone curse Legna had referred to . . . was it connected somehow to the Aniyvwiya?

How did these mysteries fit together as puzzle pieces of her Orphan Dreamer destiny? She'd seen what would become of Earth if Nomed had his way.

Total destruction.

Professor Jakob could help her solve the Bat Creek Stone curse mystery, and maybe even the mystery surrounding the Aniyvwiya. He was the Director of Israeli Antiquities and happened to be her archeology professor and mentor from college.

She must contact him—and soon. If America was somehow in trouble because of an ancient curse, she must protect it.

"Yahweh," she whispered, "help me find the light that will illuminate my path to your Earthly presence—a place of power and clarity."

"I knew you would come around."

"Around to what?"

"Your prayer. It's simple but pure and beautiful. You're brave, Daniela," Nurse Valerie said.

"No. I'm not that brave."

"Well, then like it or not, the Orphan Dreamer must learn to brave her nightmares, slipping between three realities in order to find her next clue." She smiled wide, and Daniela saw how beautiful the dark-skinned woman really was. Nurse Valerie winked at her patient. "Seems like a perfect job for a childhood-onset schizophrenic by the way—because others can't see Him or hear Him, they think you're crazy. You're not."

"Thank you, Nurse Valerie. I don't want to be crazy. Honest I don't." Daniela's mind wandered—again. "The Eternal Light," she whispered.

"What did you say, Daniela Rose?"

"The point of my dreams—my next mission."

"Which is?"

"Find Earth's original representation of the Eternal Light, and it will lead me to God's presence on Earth."

"Which is?" Nurse Valerie repeated.

"To find the Ark of the Covenant—God's ancient Earthly presence, something the Judeans will relate to." Daniela looked up at her caretaker. "Any ideas of where to start?"

"Well, if a person wants to find something in the darkness, they need a light. But if it's dark, how do you find the light? And I imagine if you're looking for a special light in an especially dark darkness, you'd need a whole lot of faith to step into the darkness and find the light."

"Catch the butterflies, Nurse Valerie." Daniela crinkled her nose as her nurse burst out laughing. "You're talking in circles."

She kept laughing, holding her side now. "I sound like a politician, don't I?"

"I guess." Daniela shrugged. "Don't really know any up close and personal."

"Claire's father."

"Oh—that's right."

"Light represents knowledge and wisdom to me, so ask someone wiser than you what to do—and maybe, just maybe, the Light will find you . . . like on the mountain."

"Wiser . . ." Daniela tapped her chin. "Like Mom or Dad, or Professor Jakob?"

"I like your parents, but who's this Professor Jakob?"

"He was my archeology professor at the University of Florida. He taught a class in Judean antiquities—he's Jewish and my late friend Ethan's uncle." Daniela bolted up and slid to the edge of the bed, adrenaline and excitement propelling her forward, ready to make her one phone call from inside her prison of the burn ICU. "I'm starting medical school soon, and he took a promotion and lives in Israel now." Her voice rose an octave. "I hope the hospital allows for long distance calls. It's so time for another archeology dig!" She lowered her voice and her head. "After I heal."

"Sounds riveting!" Nurse Valerie clapped her hands, then stood up. "But this isn't the local jail, so no, you don't get one phone call. You need to heal first before crawling into some dusty hole in the earth. You'll get infected then die of sepsis."

"But, Nurse Valerie . . ."

"No, ma'am."

"Can I call my dad, then?"

"Later. I want you to sleep. Besides, your parents were here earlier, and you sounded like a mad hatter." She pressed on Daniela's forehead, pushing her onto her pillow. Then she pulled up Daniela's sheets and bedspread. "I have to attend to my other patients—nope, they're not my favorite. But while I'm doing my job, you my dear, have some travelling to do."

"But I don't feel rested after my travels."

Nurse Valerie removed her hands from her hips and pointed at the snowflake diamond resting in Daniela's right palm. "You may not be healthy enough to go to Israel, but you can time travel through Ellesmere."

"How do you know about Ellesmere?" Daniela's mouth dried stickier than years-old glue.

"You don't think Yahweh would give you any old nurse— do you?"

Honey and cream with salt poured in! No. He would not. She just wanted to daydream, to control her thoughts instead of risking experiencing a nightmare while traveling through Ellesmere. But she would do the right thing. The hard thing. She would time travel again.

She'd have to sort out the details after travelling to God only knows where. Daniela had already obtained other ancient relics during her time travels: an ancient Judean prince's arrowhead, the Glass Tattoo, and the Skeleton Key.

Why not add Earth's representation of the Eternal Light to her collection . . . or even the Ark of the Covenant? But none of those objects would fit into her dresser drawer beneath her panties.

She blushed.

"I just want to make a quick phone call first. May I use the phone?"

"No—you need to rest. You're not calling anyone." Nurse Valerie removed a syringe from her pocket and reached for her IV.

"I don't want the drugs." Daniela clamped her bandaged hand over her IV stopcock. "Please, Nurse Valerie. I won't cause any more trouble. Don't give them to me."

"Sleep is the key to healing both the mind and the body. This medication will ensure deep sleep and sweet dreams." Nurse Valerie unloaded the contents of the syringe into Daniela's intravenous tubing. "Besides, in the morning, a famous reporter is coming to interview you. I don't want you looking tired and crazy, so sleep, child, then find someone beyond Ellesmere—a partner, a kindred spirit powerful enough to help you swim." Valerie winked.

"Wait!" Daniela held up her hand, but it was too late. "I have Emmaline."

"No—go find your orphan."

Daniela fought the embrace of the drug. "The best-selling book of all time begins, 'In the beginning, God created the heavens and the earth,' and it ends with a promise . . . ?"

" 'Surely, I am coming quickly. Amen.' " Nurse Valerie completed the passage, proving to Daniela that she was her ally.

The mission of her collective dreams had become clear: Find Earth's representation of the Eternal Light and figure out who the Aniyvwiya were. Then, figure out this Bat Creek Stone curse thingy. Maybe all this was related . . . but then maybe not?

Few thoughts in a schizophrenic's world are orderly or even related. So why start now? But how would she find her way to a light without the illumination of a light? Her world began to slip away . . .

"I'll be close by until your parents return in the morning. I can't have anyone or anything hurting my Daniela."

Hurt me? "Who . . ." The medication locked onto Daniela's brain cells, effectively handcuffing her body and her brain to the hospital bed. She whispered in slow motion, "Who would want to hurt me?"

"The investigators never found the body of the disgraced

senator, but don't you worry, ain't no backwater politician messin' with my hero."

Daniela's world dimmed.

She gripped the Glass Tattoo as though it were a security blanket, and she was still a little girl afraid of the dark. While she navigated the tangles of her vivid dreamworld, she longed for a protector—Legna.

But she found someone else.

A ghost.

21—Orphan Dreamer

A Cosmic Revolution
10:30 a.m., Tuesday, July 8, 1998
Lake Khukh via Ellesmere

BEFORE I LEFT FOR THE funeral in Palatka, Florida, it was my seventeenth birthday. Seventeen, an age of discovery, a part of growing up when life can be confusing all on its own without the inconvenience of time travel.

Now, the last bursts of a balmy sunset toast my cheeks a deep plum as I soar, cruising higher than the eagles above a series of mountains and lakes that shimmer in the sunlight. I inhale crisp, clean cold air as clouds fly past my face and my thoughts clear. My knowing—my wolf within—tells me that here, in Khukh Nuur, in 1189, Temujin received the title Chinggis Khaan, Genghis Khan.

A name. A destiny. A legacy.

A name changes from Abram to Abraham. From

Temujin to Genghis Khan. From Daniela Rose to the Orphan Dreamer . . . a name possesses destinies.

I glide toward the highest peak of the Khar Zurkhen Mountains located north of Lake Khukh, which I also know is called the Blue Lake of Black Heart, where the Black Heart is the highest peak of the mountain located north of the lake. The ridgeline of the Khar Zurkhen Mountains towers over 5,000 feet above sea level.

I land on the ridgeline and look down.

My feet are wrapped in Mongol gutals designed with upturned toes, so I do no harm to nature. I stand at the precipice of a deep gorge carved between the mountain slopes of Mount Kharzurkh, a part of the Khar Zurkhen Mountains.

Could such a dark and cold place lead me to Genghis Khan's tomb and the ancient light, the menorah?

And would this menorah truly light my path to solving the Bat Creek Stone curse?

A sliver of light penetrates up through the lake's still waters, reaching beyond the dark embrace of the gorge. Something is hidden beneath, and the wolf within howls, screaming a warning.

Winds whistle through the gorge.

Up from a distant forest, leaves are rustling and waving to the One who created them as they gather invisible currents of algid air that push them up the sides of the mountain.

Chilled to the bone and still dressed in my funeral outfit—with the addition of the gutals—I crouch low, determined not to let the wind blow me down the slope of the mountain. There is no one else to keep me from stumbling, from falling.

Or is there? Suddenly, the wind stills.

And it's pure serenity.

So, in the quiet stillness, I wish upon a star, "Let me never leave this place. I don't want to go back to where I must endure the pain of healing my burned body."

A voice resonates within. "There are fires everywhere, Rosebud. Even here."

On cue, a fiery volcanic pain sweeps a flame up and down my arms and my left flank. I squeeze my eyes shut and breathe deeply. *Distraction—you need a distraction.* So I allow my ever-present curiosity to make me ask, "Yahweh, where am I, and why am I here?"

A gust carries my question away but brings back silence.

Will I believe in the silence, too?

Snow begins to fall and coats my poorly clothed body with an arctic balm. The gentle touch of the Master's hand. A relief. It soothes the searing ache bubbling beneath my brown skin's epidermal and dermal layers while hammering a chill deep into my bones.

I inhale, and the air, frigid and tinged with scents of evergreens, quenches the fiery tangle of nerves smoldering beneath my breasts. This isn't Ellesmere . . . at least I don't think it is. Because if this is Ellesmere, where is the giant spider the size of a bear?

My body tenses.

No.

This can't be Ellesmere.

There's no dread wrapping its tentacles all around my bravery, constricting and twisting until I beg to leave.

No smell of death that lingers as I defy time, cutting through the expanse of history, the present and the future. The stench of decay and death . . . Ellesmere has always reeked of the potpourri of hell.

I glance at my palm. The stain of a midnight blue

snowflake is still etched into my flesh, confirming that the Glass Tattoo has been activated.

I'm so confused.

"Yahweh, why am I here—wherever here is?"

"Go out and stand on the mountain in the presence of the Lord, for I am about to pass by." The voice carried on the wind is so quiet, so serene, I almost miss it.

Seconds later, on the other side of the gorge, a great and powerful wind tears through the mountains, rending the earth, shattering boulders, and splintering giant trees. "God . . . are you there?"

Silence.

No—he's not in the raging winds.

The winds gusts, again blowing strands of my usually curly, but now bone-straight and coal-black hair across my eyes, hash-tagging my world into bite-size pieces. "Please, just speak with me. Don't kill me. I didn't do anything wrong . . ." I beg.

An insulted silence answers my false accusation. I'm the one who wanted to stay here.

His mercy—kindness shown toward me when He could punish.

His grace—the unmerited gift of the divine favor.

Mercifully, the winds calm, settling into a spring breeze filled with the chirping of birds and the batting of butterfly wings.

I gather my wayward strands into a ponytail, then walk down the descending spine of the mountaintop along a narrow path as I search for the Serene One. The Prince of Peace. The Light of the World.

A crow caws in the distance, warning me.

The ground shakes beneath my feet.

I stumble, kicking loose rock down the side of the mountain as I fight for balance. I engage my Pilates core and right myself.

Across the gorge, a bear roars, standing on its hind legs as it taunts me from across the ravine.

I pray, "Please don't let that bear jump over the chasm and attack me!"

Just then, the gorge narrows. The bear charges, galloping at full speed. It launches into the air, crossing the chasm, its lips pulled back, revealing yellowed and broken incisors.

I smell death.

The earth trembles again. I drop to all fours, preparing for impact. The bear leaps. The ground rises toward me. I curl into a ball and peek from under my right arm.

Behind the bear, a shadow moves.

The calm azure lake bundles up into a heap, forming a tsunami wave, and pushes a wall of water over the ledge and the bear along with it.

A beautiful waterfall, running so wild and so free, remains.

A waterfall. It has protected me from death. The sound drowns out my fearful thoughts as the water crashes to the bottom and hits the rocky surface beneath. "Thank you." I stand up once again, smiling as an apricot sulphur butterfly rises out of the mist formed by the waterfall dashing against the rock beneath.

With wings fortified with steel, it navigates the fine mist, flitting from one green leaf to another as it climbs up from the chasm. I stretch out my arm and open my hand, inviting the weary traveler to land inside my palm. To rest. It lands, and its miniature feet tickle my palm as it dances on the snowflake tattoo.

The butterfly speaks, a feeling rather than a voice, "When

you dream to solve the next mystery, you will feel as though you are me. You will experience life as I do. But do not let the weight of life crush your fragile wings—your dreams."

"Okay." I grin as I take the time to adore the butterfly's delicate buttercup-yellow wings. Feeling stronger and more hopeful, I tuck my other thumb beneath the leather strap of my archer's quiver.

I didn't have the bow and arrow at the funeral, but something tells me that I'm stronger now—a warrior—so my weapon has come to me.

The butterfly leaves my palm and lands on my shoulder.

Rubbing the old scar across my side, I promise myself that the fanged spider will not surprise me this time with its venomous bite, eager to sink its poison deep beneath my skin. Besides, Mom and Dad—maybe even the world—are counting on my success.

I still cannot fathom that I'm important to the whole world, but Legna insists it is so. At least, I cannot fail my parents.

They have never failed me.

The ground shudders, and rocks topple over the side, disappearing into the blackness of the gorge and diving into the deep blue lake. I widen my stance for balance and stay standing this time.

The earth quivers and quakes, again and again, but Yahweh is not in the quake.

Still, I hug the scant tree line. Becoming foolish and bold with the adrenaline of a silly form of bravery, I run as the mountain ridge narrows and rocks fall into the gorge below. My gaze darts left and right, looking for wild animals hidden in the trees' winter-stripped limbs—wild animals that may kill me and prevent me from accomplishing my mission as the Orphan Dreamer.

It's a day of contradictions. Snow falling while steam rises from the cavernous gorge, dilating my pores. Sweat dripping onto my collar. Within the belly of the gorge, the foreboding sound of an angry sea booms.

I pause, then look over the edge, through a cloud of mist.

Water churns at the bottom, and the frothy white caps tell me the lake is angry.

I hate water, unless I am drinking it.

Is the alpine lake's water temperature scalding or arctic cold? Nothing is making sense. How could an alpine lake be hot?

Duh. Basic science. It's hot if a volcano is located beneath. I tiptoe around a fallen log, but not carefully enough, and my foot catches on a wayward branch and I lose my balance, barely managing to right myself before slipping to my parboiled death.

Breath hitches inside my lungs, and my heart goes limp, hanging like a condemned criminal inside my chest.

Focus.

Be methodical.

You're a wannabe scientist. When a scientist examines a new slide through a microscope, they zoom out first before zooming in. First, I zoom out, seeing the evergreens rising into pointed steeples against a slate-gray sky. Then I see the sliver of light tucked away and out of sight down the ridge, hidden behind ash and pines.

Standing on the ridge exposes me to the night, so I hike deeper into the forest—down the slope of the mountain, eager to find the Light and hide from the night.

As night falls, stars waltz across their dark stage.

The light in the distance burns brighter; it calls me to it. Motivated by fear, I kneel and whisper into the forgotten forest, "Speak with me, Yahweh. Don't leave me alone. I'm afraid of the dark."

"Go out and stand on the mountain in the presence of the LORD, for I am about to pass by," the same voice says again.

"God . . . is that you? I'm going toward the light—I'm coming to You." But the voice stays quiet.

As I move, a fog deepens its grip on my path. I near the source of illumination, so my path should be clearer . . . right? But above me, the trees wave goodbye and foliage blurs into fuzzy lines of green.

The ground trembles, then marches.

The drumming bass lick of nature collapses all around me. Trees jump out of the ground, their roots exposed, before crashing to their deaths, falling and splintering in front of and behind me.

I run.

Red and ochre-yellow leaves on their way to dying bounce beneath my feet, dancing and drumming out a death march across the forest floor as the ground shifts. *It's an earthquake!*

Angry to be woken from its slumber, the earth opens, showing its fiery core—a volcanic chasm, rotating around a solid core of *NiFe*, a.k.a., nickel and iron. The outer liquid layer—the place where the circulating conducting liquid generates Earth's geodynamics—the force responsible for the planet's magnetic field.

Truly, Earth has a heart of iron. Has to! She's constantly putting up with feckless humans. But wisely, she shields her heart with layers of rock and metal, pressure, heat, and radioactivity. No human will ever reach her heart.

Only God . . . in time. When she stops spinning, dancing

on the dance floor of space among the stars created by her Creator.

Earth's molten chasm at the bottom of the gorge reaches for me. It's my punishment for leaving the ridge and hiding from God.

Swells of ink loom in the chasm's abyss, backlit by magma. I slip, falling toward Earth's fiery belly . . . is this hell?

But I am a child of God. Why am I going there? I claw at anything, everything, and then nothing. Dead leaves shift over wet soil, mocking my frantic attempts to find purchase and climb back up.

Pain shoots through my fingernails and lingers in my hands. Blood seeps from my burn wounds and scratches.

Until now, my vision of heaven resembled the Swiss Alps—thick woods, snowcapped mountains, and a light, hopefully a lamp, hidden inside a cabin or a shack on the lake where I could meet Jesus.

But my vision of bliss has quickly deteriorated into a living nightmare. I arc my right leg back at the hip joint, then slam my toe forward. Finally finding a foothold in the vertical ground in front of me, I stop my descent.

But the temperature continues to fall, and frost nips at my ears. A cold hell? The fiery visuals are incongruent with the temperature. What have I gotten myself into by leaving the ridge?

I dig my fingers into soil. Gaining traction, I climb like a tarantula rising from the dead. Now, I'm the spider! One inch, and then another. Muck coats my face, and I spit out mouthfuls of dirt and petrified leaves.

"You're not in the wind! You're not in the quaking of the earth!" The wind pushes my voice back into my throat. "Then where are you, Yahweh?"

All remains quiet. I break the silence with my crying prayers. "Listen to me . . . please! Where do you hide when a human disobeys and goes their own way?"

With each ragged breath, cold stabs my nostrils. But my hands are busy grasping hungrily at the earth, so I cannot clamp my nose shut to prevent the blood pouring from each nostril.

I roll my eyes, then keep pinching soil between my tired fingers and hands as I pull myself upward. Icicles latched around leaves and rocks start crackling and popping as though they have a bad case of arthritis, like Dad's knees.

Finally, I rise over the ledge as ice suffocates the forest. I yank the sleeves of a hospital gown up my arms—where are my funeral digs—jump to my arms and knees, then crawl like a begging dog.

Behind me, tree branches snap. The crackles grow angry, then begin to roar. Smoke fills my lungs and burns my eyes. I turn. A fire devouring everything in its wake is barreling toward me. What?

Now there is fire and ice? Ice strangulates the forest. Fire consumes it. Seriously, can You give me a break, God!

Make something here real . . . and then I realize what I'm asking. I'm asking God to make my facts—my construct of reality, a lie—into the truth. Lying. Well, that's something He could never do.

God cannot lie.

Plain.

And simple.

So, I do what Adam and Eve did . . . I run . . . totally stupid to run on this narrow ledge in the dark, but fear shrouds any sensible thinking. So I storm, bolting toward the unknown. I charge along the edge of a cliff, risking a look behind me as ice yields to the fire.

Exhaustion wrings sweat from my pores. My legs cramp from dehydration, but I push through the pain.

"Are you in the fire, then?" My voice softens from a warrior's demand to a little girl's plea.

"No, Daniela." The voice escapes my consciousness and speaks into my ears. It's the voice of a patient but divine and all-powerful Father.

Then, the voice of a mother . . . my mother, I think, and it floods me with hope, *A strong wind tore the mountains and broke in pieces the rocks before Yahweh; but Yahweh was not in the wind. After the wind, there was an earthquake; but Yahweh was not in the earthquake.*

Fathers and Mothers—the divine ones and the undivine. They are our teachers. The fire closes in around me, toasting spruce and pines to ash. "I'm going to be roasted alive."

I'm only dreaming.

It'll be okay, Daniela Rose.

But the dried blood on my palms and the ache inside my hands tell me that while I am dreaming, my dreams are real and that, actually, it won't be okay. If I survive, I'll have more scars and bruises than those I incurred in the church fire.

And if I die in this mysterious place that looks and feels like Mongolia, then fail to return to Earth's realm and my present-day reality, Earth is toast, too. My only purpose for defying time is to search for clues, the keys to solving ancient puzzles that will prevent a dark force from annihilating Earth. That was my life's mission, my destiny, and, if I survive the process, my legacy.

I am Daniela.

I am the Orphan Dreamer. Sorry. I didn't choose me, either.

"But I did," a voice pushes through the whisper of wind.

I know that voice. "But I can't swim. You know that." I huff and keep running.

"Yes—with My strength, you can. Stop running. Stop disobeying me. A divergence from My perfect path leads to death."

"How did I disobey you?" *Did I have a choice to be blown up at a church funeral?*

"You focused on what you thought I was or would be—the dim light burning in the distance."

"If that's not you, then who is it?"

"A false light—a false illumination—the moon, but not the Sun."

"Huh?"

"It's a copy of the true light meant to deceive the disobedient. Remember. I told you to stand on the mountain."

"True." My voice is almost inaudible.

"I would have brought the Light to you—found you, protected you, rescued you—given you a second chance no differently than when I came to Earth as Immanuel that silent night. So don't run like Jonah did . . . and yes, Rosebud, you can swim." A breeze nudges me, pushing me over the edge. "It's behind a waterfall, Rosebud."

"No fairrrrrrrr!" My voice echoes off the walls of the gorge as I plummet. "Are you trying to kill me just because I didn't want to walk the ridge?" I clench my fist, my jaw, and every orifice on my body.

"I came to give you life, not death." The voice is speaking Truth. *"O Death, where is your sting? O Hades, where is your victory?" The sting of death is sin, and the strength of sin is the law. But thanks be to God, who gives us the victory through our Lord Jesus Christ.*

The Scriptures are the Word. And the Word was manifest

in Jesus Christ—God in the Flesh. The Word of God and Jesus—Yeshua—are the same.

I'm still falling.

Speak the Word . . . and Speak Jesus. If I'd paid more attention to my Sunday School teacher instead of Claire's sarcastic remarks, I would have remembered these Biblical proverbs. A spark licks my left forearm, then my calf.

My skin bubbles with fresh heat. As I fall, a wall of fire waits less than a football field before me. *Please don't do this to me!*

Where's Legna?

But I pass through the fire unscathed. As though Someone was waiting for me in the fire, waiting to protect me.

I roll onto my back, looking up and away from the rush of water.

My prayers echo off the mountain's stony guts as I fall. Am I right back where I started? Running usually does that, boomerangs a person right back to the beginning. Frigid air cools my skin.

I imagine hitting a shallow pool of water at the bottom of the gorge and think of a beached whale with a broken neck trying to swim—that'll be me, if I survive the fall.

Mother's Biblical words flood my mind, reminding me of how to access a second chance—*If my people, which are called by my name, shall humble themselves, and pray, and seek my face, and turn from their wicked ways; then will I hear from heaven, and will forgive their sin, and will heal their land.*

"Immanuel," I whisper. "Are you there? I'm sorry for not listening to you and going my way—a wide path leading to destruction."

Silence answers my supplication.

"I will stand on the mountain and wait for you now." Peace calms me even though I'm falling to my end. "You say I should call to You, and you will answer me, and show me great and mighty things, which I do not know . . . so I'm calling on you, Immanuel—God with us."

"Ready for Plan A?" a masculine voice says with the sound of a freight train crashing through the distance. Boom!

"Anything—even a Plan B!"

"Not necessary," the masculine voice says, the sound of the freight train still chasing it. *Boom!* The deepest bass on one of the baddest Christian raps, "Addicted to Jesus," rattles the cavernous walls of the gorge.

I move to the beat.

Yep—I'm dancing amid my storm.

Bright white flashes against the dark mountainsides, disappearing within the shadows that loom beneath me. My heart wedges inside my throat. I close my eyes, stiffening my body for impact. I am no Olympic diver, not even an average swimmer.

Still, the portal permanently resides in deep waters.

A wall slams into my body; it's the waterfall, sucking me toward my watery tomb.

A moment passes, and a vice locks around my waist, stopping me from falling further. I fight for breath. The hand yanks me to the surface, and I resurrect to new life.

I've been baptized.

The hold softens.

My lungs expand. My mind clears. I realize the snow-white down feathers cradling me within this embrace belong to the one and only Legna.

Suddenly, I'm grinning while floating above a volcanic ocean. Bright orange lava spews upward from the torrid bath.

His being sucks up the magna; then he log-rolls like an F-18 fighter evading the guns of a pursuing jet. "Miss me?"

That voice! Smooth, baritone, and bass in all the right places, with no hint of ear-grating, nasally vibrato.

"Yes. I have." I investigate the face belonging to the voice, and Legna's coal-black eyes lighten to an iridescent violet. I want to kiss him. "It's really you. Where were you?!"

"Helping someone reach a lighthouse."

"Why didn't you come and help me sooner?"

"Wasn't my time, Rosebud." His eyes twinkle with an irresistible sensuality . . . and he's not even trying.

"Who were you helping out?"

"Someone who will matter to you one day . . ."

"Don't leave me in suspense."

"Then fly with me." *Gladly!* He pulls me close, and we pull Gs, climbing up the chasm's walls in less than ten seconds before leveling out.

He's basically a bad-a. Dot. Dot. Mmhmm. And he knows it with that cocky smile. My head's spinning from his threat to gravity. At the top of the chasm, water swells as though the force of his presence is yanking the lake up with him. The bass drops, and the subwoofers of heaven sing their African-inspired praises.

The lakes form a waterfall that defies gravity. A cool mist clings to my skin, then water consumes my lower body.

"Where did all this water come from, Legna?" I hold onto him for dear life.

"Human geologists call it a seiche, or a lake tsunami." He grins, tucking his lower lip between teeth that dazzle with a white I've never seen before. *This dude's doing this on purpose. Oh storm—he can read my mind.* But he says nothing, too busy enjoying the moment, I guess.

"A tsunami on a lake?" I ask, playing along.

"An earthquake shakes loose rocks, trees. . . well, basically, the side of a mountain, dropping tons and tons of dirt and rock into a deep lake. The rock and soil displace the water, creating a seiche, or a lake tsunami. You want another factoid?" he says as he flies.

"Sure, why not?" Anything to prolong his embrace.

"This is why the seas are rising. Your scientists call it climate change and blame the rising seas on the use of fossil fuel. Wrong answer!" He winks at me. "It's a seiche due to gravity and Satan's bad sense of humor."

"But you must admit the seas are warming and expanding, Legna."

"I never said there wasn't global warming." He winks at me as I look past him at nature's backdrop.

On the other side of the now-placid lake, snowcapped mountains tower ever so innocently around the crystal blue water. Awe becomes my blood, faith my oxygen. "It's beautiful. The million-dollar question: Where are we?"

"You were right before. You are on Earth above Mongolia. But you were wrong, too, because you're close to heaven."

"Am I dying?"

"Aren't you all?"

"I guess so." I shrug and then rest my head on his shoulder. His muscles quiver beneath my intimate touch.

"Shh," Legna says. "Elohim's speaking. Listen."

A still, small voice whispers, "Rosebud, I love you." Yahweh's breath dances across my neck. It is a sweet aroma, the fragrance that brings life. "You are mine, and I am yours. Rest now as Legna takes you to the waterfall. Try not to fall. There you will find the light . . . a gift to the Aniyvwiya that represented my coming presence in the world. The light will illuminate the path back to me—my presence, represented on Earth by the Ark of the Covenant."

"One of the most searched-after lost relics! Legna will take me to see it?"

"No, Rosebud—not Legna, but Legna's mortal competition, the orphan, your oily boy who will one day become your heartsong. He'll help you if you don't fall for a dud in medical school. My advice. Wait for oily boy. Don't settle for the substitute."

"Okay. I'll try." I blush while passing a glance up at Legna's face. It registers intense sadness. The look rips my heart out by the root—my aorta flailing in the air. "I will." I choke on my words.

"It's okay," Legna mouths.

"I'm sorry."

"Nothing to apologize for . . . except, if you would've listened to Elohim's instructions and stood on the mountain and waited for Him, I wouldn't have needed to come rescue you, only to hear about my mortal competition from the mouth of God. Think about the consequences next time you make a choice . . . okay? Listen, then obey."

"I'm sorry." My weak apology does nothing to rid my face of my tears. "I'm so sorry, Legna, but I-I-I will listen and then obey next time. Promise."

Legna grins, and all of heaven lights up.

I close my eyes, filtering out some of the light while embracing him, selfishly taking a share of his joy for myself. Joy lightens my burden.

"He's always been in the still, small voice, not the earthquake, hurricane, or fire. Remember this when life's earthquakes rumple your spirit and your courage." Legna flaps his wings, gaining altitude and catapulting us over another ridge of sharp black edges. He's taking me on a tour of the mountain range, and the view is magnificent. "Have faith in God—even when you cannot see Him. Okay?"

"Okay." I rest until my mind kicks into high gear with a

barrage of questions. "If not carbon emissions, what instigates natural disasters?" I ask.

"People inspired by the chaos starter. They make stupid choices—usually motivated by greed and narcissism."

"By the chaos starter, you mean Satan?"

"Yep . . . I want to introduce you to someone."

"Satan?" I dig my fingers deep into Legna's sides. "I'm not ready for that introduction."

"Why would I ever do such a thing? Give me some credit, Rosebud." He shakes his head.

"I'm sorry. What's his name?"

"Her name is Rebekah."

"I don't want to date a girl."

"I wouldn't ask you to, nor would my master."

"And I'm too exhausted to find another clue," I admit.

"Relax. This journey is for you, to give you hope. You'll need it."

"Sounds ominous, like a roller coaster. And I hate them. It's the sudden drops for no reason except to inflict a spinal cord injury maybe." We both chuckle at my pathetic joke.

"A good roller coaster ride starts slow, and this dream will ease you into the roller coaster ride called romance."

"I'm going to fall in love one day? Yahweh's going to let me meet oily boy?"

"Adonai wants you to experience romantic love, but meeting your oily boy as you call him depends upon you. You'll meet him if he doesn't die before you get to him."

"Pray for him." My voice upticks half an octave as though I'm asking him a question.

"Yep. Your dad said it all those years ago, and Rebekah will show you how to spot a real man—one that will respect you, cherish you, and protect you."

"Okay, Legna."

"Rosebud, don't waste your time chasing vermin. You don't have to chase down a good man. He finds you."

"He finds me," I repeat.

"Remember this as you meet coeds in medical school. Nor do you have to scour the Earth looking for your oily boy; he will find you or send someone to find you through his prayers."

"Thank you, Legna. I understand."

"But first, he must meet God and get to know Him enough to ask for your heart. That's your job: to introduce him to the only pathway to Elohim. The menorah represents the light but isn't the light. It's simply a tangible platform to reach those who shy away from the actual Light—Yeshua. Representation. Mercy. Yahweh said He would be a father to the fatherless and a mother to the motherless. Good parents do what is necessary to protect their children."

"Got it. Legna, do you know where my oily boy is?"

"Of course, I do."

"Can you tell me?"

"No—you just obey Elohim, and that obedience will keep you on the narrow path where you will find your oily boy in God's appointed time."

"You absolutely know for sure that God wants me to fall madly in love?"

"I don't know about the madly part." Legna tosses his head back and laughs. "Yes—he does want you to fall madly in love. Don't you know Elohim is love, and love is Elohim?"

"Sometimes I forget."

"I'm going to send you on a little trip through Ellesmere so you can learn about the how-tos of romance."

"But I'm so tired. I couldn't bear to go on a walk, much less another adventure."

"Even as your favorite butterfly—an apricot sulphur?"

"I'll have wings? And I can fly on my own . . . ?" Excitement increases the pitch in my voice.

"Yep, and then you'll see that Elohim cares about more than just sending you on missions to solve puzzles to save the world. You're the apple of his eye, Rosebud." Legna dips low and exits the bank of thick clouds, exposing us to the oranges and pinks of dawn.

"Perspective," Legna says as the lush forest floor bleaches into the khaki sand of a desert horizon. Beige specks become camels.

"Where are we?"

"The Desert of Haran, 1673 BC—when Immanuel came to Earth and asked a righteous man named Abram who lived in the east to leave his home and travel to a new homeland, Judea. Then, Adonai renamed the man Abraham—a name that means—"

"The Father of Many Nations," I finish.

"You were paying attention in Sunday school class." Legna drops me, but something odd happens.

I don't fall. Instead, I become lighter than a feather. "I did pay attention."

"Then another piece of trivia, butterfly—are you ready?"

"Go for it." I fly away from the gorge, and this time, he follows me.

"According to legend, who said this to his faithful followers before he died: 'I have conquered for you a large empire. But my life was too short to take the whole world. That I leave to you.'"

"Genghis Khan."

"Okay, genius girl . . . so you wanna meet him again?" Legna teases.

"For real?"

Legna shrugs, jerking his wings upward as he rolls into a spin, taking on an altitude my butterfly wings cannot reach, but his voice echoes back to me. "Why not?"

"He burns animals to fight his wars, Legna . . . I think I'll pass."

"It takes angels to fight demons, Rosebud. You'll meet him all right . . ."

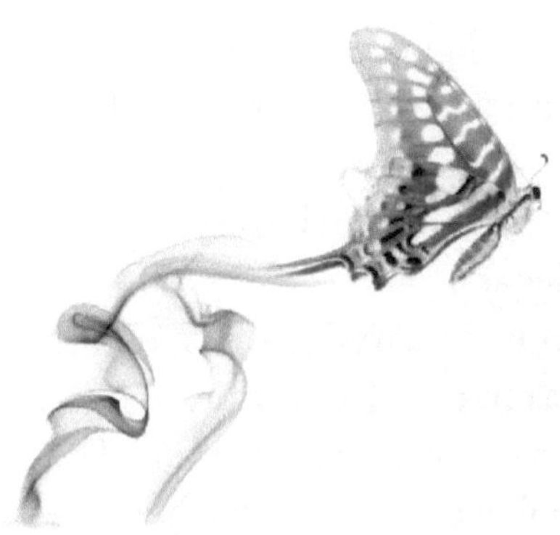

22—Abraham: The Blood Pact

1673 B.C.
The Desert of Haran

THE DESERT SUN BEAT AGAINST the wrinkled leather of the old man's face. Mesopotamia's hot desert sand shifted beneath the toes of Abraham's sandaled feet as he walked beside his trusted advisor. Abraham lived in the unforgiving Mesopotamian lands. He was a wealthy man and beloved of God; not that poor men were not loved of God, too—men like Eliezer, Abraham's manservant.

Many years ago, Abraham freed an orphaned boy from an Egyptian slave caravan. The orphaned boy grew up into a man, and Abraham trusted Eliezer more than any other person in the world, including his wife. Eliezer would secure Abraham's legacy.

Above, the sun was beginning its monotonous task of rising from the east and setting in the west. Pink flaming arrows of rogue light shot across the golden horizon, seeming to promise a hopeful heart that first-time love was on the horizon.

That hopeful heart belonged to Abraham's son, Isaac. Abraham's legacy.

Abraham had shared his instructions with Eliezer of where he was to travel and what characteristics to look for in the handmaidens of his kinsmen. The sun began to illuminate the village below. Rows upon rows of sand dunes encircled Abraham's village—a desert village made up of one hundred beige tents.

From the heavens, the tents must have appeared as copper waves riding a bleached-white sandy surf. And all around the two men, a gentle wind blew, stirring up the fragrances of the desert—earth-spiced scents, floral hints of sparse flowers, and the musk wafting from the stable of camels, goats, sheep, and stallions.

A scorpion scuttled beneath a tent's edge, pursued by a slithering snake getting on with the grisly business of surviving in the desert. A hawk soared overhead, cawing, mocking those not blessed with wings, altitude, or cooler air streams.

You will be the father of many nations, Yahweh Adonai had promised Abraham before he and his aged wife, Sarah, had conceived Isaac.

Many years after the promise, Isaac was born.

Isaac had then grown into a man. At the age of forty, there were no prospects of a wife within his father's luxurious sprawling tent village. No wife. No children. No legacy. Abraham's lineage and name would abort.

Find Isaac a bride.

This was Abraham's mission, which had now become Eliezer's mission. "Eliezer, look first for a wife within the house of my distant relatives who live in Nahor."

"Yes, my lord."

"And no matter how beautiful she is, you shall not force her to come back with you and marry my son." Abraham stopped, turned, and faced Eliezer. He leaned heavily on his staff, his tinsel-tinged beard draping well past his thinning waist. "The future wife of my son must not be forced; she must come willingly."

"I will execute your wishes."

"Promise me . . . on your life. I will not have my son married to a woman who dreads his touch and presence." Abraham glared into his manservant's eyes; he was entrusting the care of his son's heart into the capable hands of the overseer of his estate, but his worry remained.

"My blood shall shed if I break my vow to you. I would not . . ." Eliezer bowed his head, averting his eyes, ". . . ever force a young maiden to please my whims or the whims of another man—not even Isaac's."

"You are a good man."

In the distance, a tall man with olive skin and a handsome, chiseled jawline peeked beyond the flap of his mother's tent. It was Isaac. Savory scents of fire-grilled leeks, olives soaked in dry wine, and freshly baked bread wafted from the open tent.

Abraham's mouth watered. Eliezer swallowed, then straightened, flexing his back muscles as his face became rigidly solemn. Now was not the time to indulge the belly. Then, he removed his right shoe and gave the sandal to his master, sealing the terms of the vow.

Truth was, Eliezer was still a slave, and Abraham was still a master. He owned Eliezer's person and his wishes, no matter how much he trusted Eliezer.

"Hashram, pack wine, bread, oil, and leeks for Eliezer."

Another slave scurried into the cooking tent.

"Come, then." Abraham strode beside his manservant beyond the tents and into the desert place next to the stables where a caravan of camels and well-groomed servants waited for Eliezer to begin their journey. "Gold, silver, and a rare ruby . . . gifts for the bride-to-be's family." Abraham rested a small leather purse inside Eliezer's scarred, calloused hands.

"I will gift them to the handmaiden—if she is worthy." Eliezer stood beside his master. Several moments of silence passed.

"Don't bring her back to Isaac if she is not worthy."

"I will do as you say." Eliezer glanced up and into the far-off gaze of his master. "The promise, my lord. Tell me about the promise again," Eliezer asked as he hid the leather purse inside a saddle bag resting against the flank of his camel.

"The vow is this—made by Adonai to me when He commanded me to leave my previous home. 'I will bless those who bless you, and I will curse those who curse you.'"

"The fiercest kind of protection, my lord."

"It is." Abraham rested his hand on his manservant's boxy shoulders. "Adonai will extend to you this protection as you serve in this mission—you are protected."

Hashram returned with a package of warm food. Abraham gifted the box to Eliezer. "Eat it when you long for home."

"Home is far away."

"Ah. You're right."

"But thank you for the sustenance and the protection, my lord."

"We thank Adonai for the protection and the food." Abraham smiled.

"Always."

"Before you go, Eliezer. You must understand this contract between Adonai—the Creator—and me does not open a path of oppression for us."

"Yes, my lord."

"So we will not force the handmaiden or any others to do our bidding. Nor will we deceive. Trick or manipulate. We will not be known on the earth as the ones who deal treacherously." Abraham stroked Eliezer's camel's flank. "Surefooted. Faithful."

"I understand, my lord."

"Adonai, help us if we ever become the oppressors. Because we have no privilege to abuse the pact."

"Yes, my lord." Eliezer walked around his camel for a final survey. "Does this blessing and this cursing gifted from Adonai to you also apply to and provide protection to your maidservant's illegitimate child—Ishmael, your seed but not the one Adonai promised?"

Adonai had promised to give Abraham and Sarah a son, but they'd had to wait many years for Sarah to conceive. During this period of waiting, the couple grew impatient. So, Abraham had laid with Sarah's handmaiden, Hagar. Hagar conceived and bore Abraham a son, whom he named Ishmael.

In His kairos—God-appointed—time, Adonai fulfilled His promise. Sarah and Abraham, in their old age, conceived their son, Isaac.

Hagar and Sarah fought, and one day, Sarah banished Hagar and her son Ishmael to the lifeless desert.

Hagar cried out to Adonai, having nothing to feed her hungry son.

But even amid painful consequences brought on by human disobedience, Adonai promised the desperate and homeless mother, Hagar, that even though Ishmael was not Abraham's promised son, Adonai would make Ishmael and his descendants powerful and wealthy.

And He had—he made them very wealthy, gifting them a buried treasure. Oil. God cannot lie.

"Adonai promised me that the descendants of Ishmael would be wild men, but that they would be wealthy."

"Wild and rich . . . not the best combination."

"It's my fault. I disobeyed Adonai, and my actions created a forever war between brothers—my sons, Isaac and Ishmael. I made a wrong decision, and now we must all pay the consequences."

"A harsh sentence for us all, indeed."

"I should have waited . . . but Sarah asked me to go into Hagar, thinking she would take the child and raise him as her own. What man would say 'no' to this request?"

"I've seen Hagar . . . few men, my lord." Eliezer chuckled.

Abraham shook his head and released a deep sigh. "Adonai promised me a son through whom all the world would be blessed, but I failed Him—I failed future generations when I acted on my own will. As for Adonai giving Ishmael the same protection of cursing those who curse me, and blessing those who bless me . . ." Abraham thought for a long time. Then, a solitary tear slipped down his weathered cheeks. "I don't believe so, even though I want to believe it, but I will leave the details to Adonai."

"I should go . . . Isaac's bride is waiting to be found and continue your lineage."

"You speak in faith, Eliezer."

"It's hard to become a father of many nations if your seed dies with Isaac."

"This is true." Abraham raised his veined hands and rested them on the side of Eliezer's head. "'The Lord bless you and keep you, Eliezer. The Lord make His face shine upon you and be gracious to you. The Lord lift up His countenance upon you and give you peace.'"

Abraham's countenance fell, acknowledging that this was a spiritual blessing for masters and their children, not servants.

Eliezer bowed his head, a tear slipping from his right eye. "Thank you, my lord." Eliezer knew the blessing well.

"And may Adonai's angels run before you, protecting, guiding, and illuminating your path with Adonai's eternal but invisible flame. Then, one day, this Light whose origin is without beginning and end—the Light of the World that preceded Adonai's Earthly lights of the sun, the moon, and the stars—will come down to Earth and dwell with us."

"Immanuel?" Eliezer understood the Torah seemed to promise an eternal light to illuminate Earth, pushing away the darkness and showing the path to an eternity without evil's darkness.

"Yes, Eliezer. His name shall be called Immanuel—the Light of the World. He will be our eternal priest, in the Hebrew tradition, our Melchizedek."

Eliezer's eyes glistened. He opened his mouth to speak, only to choke on the swell of emotion. He composed himself. "My lord, I hope to be alive when Immanuel comes to Earth."

"Now, go! Be vigilant. Watch for cowards, zealots, and a lion that roars, looking for whom he may devour while they traverse the desert." Abraham then handed his manservant a small scroll stamped with the wealthy man's seal. "Open it."

Eliezer obeyed, stunned at its simple message. "My freedom, my lord?"

"*My friend* will do." Abraham patted his friend on the back. "You, too, must be free, Eliezer, just as the girl must be free. Free to love. And as Hagar is now free. And just as I am free because I am Adonai's friend. You are my friend, too." Abraham bent to his knees to worship, his bones creaking as he did so. "Pray with me."

Eliezer knelt beside Abraham—for the first time as a friend, not an enslaved person.

After a moment of silence, a familiar language between friends, the men parted ways. The freed man climbed onto his camel, then nudged his beast to stand. "Through your seed—through Isaac's and his future wife's seed, then and only then will all the nations of the world be blessed . . . my friend."

"My friend," Abraham echoed, and then the 140-year-old man wept as he watched Eliezer begin his months-long journey, a path that promised love and a future for his son.

The caravan, loaded with gifts for a princess, followed Abraham's friend into the horizon, toward Mesopotamia and the city of Nahor. There he hoped to find that good thing—a wife for Isaac, the promised son of Abraham and Sarah in the lineage of King David, whose seed would birth another king one silent night.

But what would happen when both Isaac and Ishmael married, their wives bore children, and their descendants multiplied until nations were formed?

A story usually begins as it was meant to end.

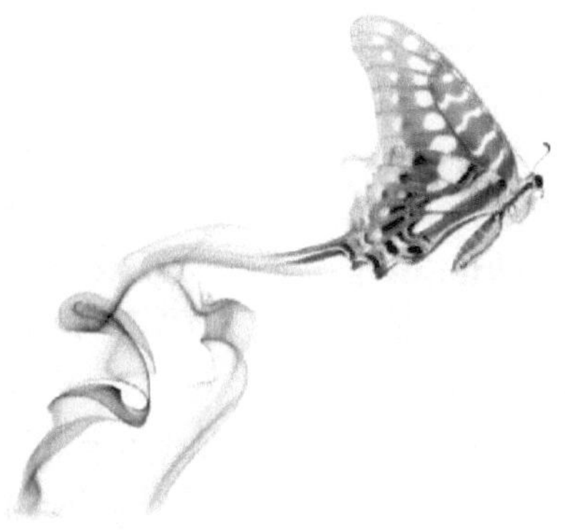

23—Abraham: The Blood Pact

1673 B.C.
The Desert of Haran

WEEKS HAD PASSED SINCE ELIEZER departed Abraham's camp. He clutched the thick gold coin purse hidden beneath his tunic as he remounted his camel.

Trapped in the throes of a midday desert sandstorm, Eliezer wrapped a cloth around his leathery face. He secured two goat's skins around his slight shoulders—one still full of wine and the other half-filled with goat's milk. Eliezer nudged his camel, and the beast lurched upward. Swaying left and right, the camel finally stood on his padded feet before plodding through the thinning veil of hot sand.

As they traveled, Eliezer's anticipation rose.

The manservant entered the bustling city of Nahor several days later, tired and caked with days-old dust.

After sending the other members of his caravan into the

village to buy food, he rested with the camels just beyond the stone gates.

Next would come the day-long task of watering the camels from the well. He bowed and prayed a simple prayer, "Adonai, show kindness to my friend's son, Isaac. Whoever offers to water my camels and offers me a drink, let her be Isaac's future wife."

While the sun still stood at the top of a cloudless blue sky, a young girl strolled toward the well. She was beautiful.

Eliezer puffed out his chest and watched her every move. But she filled her pots and left. Another lady, and then another, arrived, filling their pots and then leaving.

Should he modify his prayer? He remembered the consequences of Abraham's and Sarah's impatience. Eliezer shivered beneath the baking sun. No—patience. Stand on the mountain and *wait* for the Lord to pass by.

Mountains, a place of waiting.

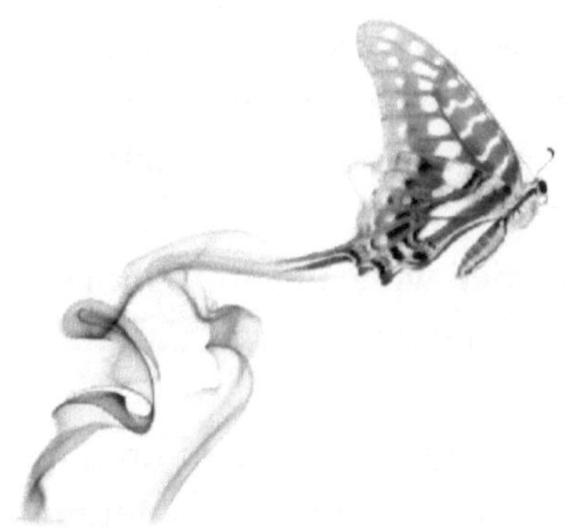

24—Abraham: The Blood Pact

1673 B.C.
The Desert of Haran

THE GLINT OF HONEY HIDDEN within the strands of her thick, henna-brown curls caught his attention first . . . and then her easy smile, the sway of her wide hips, the grace beneath each step, and finally the ripple of muscle beneath tanned skin as she lowered her pot deep into the well. Excitement coursed through Eliezer. He jumped up, intending to ask the young girl to allow him to borrow her pot to water his camels.

Patience.

He shook his head, sat down, and rested again, but he refused to take his gaze off the natural beauty.

She balanced the pot on the top of her head, then walked toward Eliezer and his camels. Her big curls brushed her narrow waistline and the tops of her generous hips. Her olive skin glowed beneath the noon sun. She glanced at him, then fixed her gaze on the task of emptying her water into the trough in front of his camels. "They look thirsty," she simply said.

Eliezer nodded while inwardly smiling.

Quickly and quietly, she poured a jug of water into the camels' trough.

As the camels greedily lapped up the refreshing water, she returned to the edge of the watering hole. She dipped her jug into the well's mouth and drew it back up, her thin arms showing their strength. Water sloshed over the edge of the clear pool. This jar, followed by many more, went into the camel's trough. The beasts snorted as they guzzled the cold water.

After she finished watering the camels, she glanced at Eliezer.

He looked down and away, guilt riddling his weary bones. "Are you thirsty, my lord?"

He was, but he should get his own water. But the quest—find the girl who would water his camels *and* offer him water. "I am." Eliezer's hand trembled as he held out his cup made from clay—a gift from Sarah. He must swallow his masculine pride and allow her to give him a drink, too.

This was his fleece—a test that a man asks God to take to verify something to be true. Was this girl the right partner for Isaac?

The young girl filled his cup, which he cradled as he gulped down the water, never taking his gaze from the beautiful and selfless girl.

Yes—she's the one!

But now he must convince her family. The brown-haired beauty didn't stop until her task was finished and the camels had finished drinking a second time.

Her face glistened with perspiration—beads of sweat dotted her forehead. And that blush never abandoned her rosy cheeks. Eliezer approached the girl and quietly opened his satchel as the other girls watched. He retrieved two gold bracelets from the pouch. "Please, may I?"

"You may."

Gently, he reached for her hands and cradled them inside his larger, calloused hands.

Lavender-blue petals of fresh bruises were blooming inside her palms. Watering his camels had not been easy, but the task of becoming the mother of Isaac's blessed seed was not easy.

Adonai had prepared her. Because Isaac required a wife—one of noble character, who feared and trusted Adonai, and invited confidence. Eliezer peeled back her fingers and slipped one gold bracelet on the right and the second on the left of her delicate wrists. "What's your name?"

"Rebekah."

"To tie, or to bind. That's the meaning of your name. And your family—who are they?"

"Of the family of Bethuel."

He smiled. *Yes, Nahor's kinsfolk.* "I'm Eliezer, the servant—I mean, the friend of Abraham." He bowed.

"A friend of Abraham's is a friend of my family."

"Is there room in your house for me and my men?"

"Yes, my lord. We have extra provisions and room in our house." *Perfection. A girl who knew the details of her father's house—smart, beautiful, and wise, the ultimate answer to his heartfelt prayers.* Eliezer prostrated himself.

"My lord." Rebekah gasped and backed away.

"This position is not for you, even though you are a gem to be found among lesser gems," he said, confusion spreading across her lovely Mediterranean features.

"Explain, my lord."

"I bow before Adonai because he has answered my prayer."

"If I am the answer to prayer, let me give thanks with you." Rebekah bowed next to him as the other village girls and women watched.

"Blessed be Adonai, who has shown mercy to Abraham and me."

After his offering of thanksgiving, the manservant arose, then followed the damsel to her home, a village of bright tents and flat khaki buildings. Eliezer and Rebekah approached a large white tent on the outskirts of the northern part of the village. Date palms pregnant with fruit swayed in a stagnant breeze.

"Laban," Rebekah called out. "We have a visitor, brother." A wiry man ran out from the middle tent with his stave drawn. "Who comes with you, my sister?"

"It's okay, Laban." She shifted her gaze to their guest. "He loves to fight." She flashed a bright smile. "This is Eliezer, Laban. The friend of Abraham. He's family."

"Abraham—the wealthiest landowner in Mesopotamia?"

"Yes, brother."

"Adonai has blessed my friend because Abraham is a righteous man. He possesses lands, flocks, herds, silver, gold, and many servants." Eliezer bowed his head.

"Welcome." Laban lowered the stave, then beckoned the guest into his tent. After they entered, Laban clapped his hands twice. Servants flocked inside, tending to Rebekah's guests by washing their feet and offering drinks as the weary travelers reclined atop pillow-topped beds.

They feasted, sopping bread with oil and olives. "You've travelled far?" Laban probed.

"We have."

"Why?" Laban asked.

"Abraham has sent me to seek a wife for young Isaac, and Adonai's angel led me to this house."

"And?" Laban stopped chewing, his gaze solidifying into a glare.

Eliezer swallowed. "Your sister . . . she's a maiden?"

"She is." Laban gestured wild and big. "You've eaten, but you've taken no wine to drink. And my sister . . . she's young."

"I will drink only when I know my journey is a success."

"I love my sister, Rebekah. I will not just give her to any man."

"Isaac is the promised one—the man whose seed Adonai will raise up and protect. Seed that will one day bless the whole world. Immanuel will come through Isaac's seed."

"God with us?"

"Yes. Adonai is our midst."

"Eliezer, let her stay with me a few more days. Then, if she chooses, she will depart to your master's home to meet Isaac, but if she despises him, you will return her at once."

"I promise to return her if she does not desire Isaac, but I beg of you, do not keep me from fulfilling my mission. Tell her your wishes."

"Her ears aren't filled with beeswax. She hears from Adonai better than most men . . . so shall we not inquire of her?" Laban stood, then called his sister. Waiting, he rocked back on his heels. "I'm already missing her."

Eliezer nodded but stayed silent, allowing Adonai to do the persuading. Rebekah rounded the corner, balancing a platter of leeks, figs, and flat bread on her right open palm. A yellow butterfly sat on her right shoulder.

"Ah—here she comes." Laban tugged his sister's waist-length braid once she neared him, and she giggled. "Still have that stinking butterfly glued to your shoulder." He clapped his hands, acting as though he would crush the insect.

"Stop, brother." She pulled back. "Besides, I'm not a little girl anymore. I can choose my own destiny as well as protect this beautiful creature, so if you hurt this butterfly, you're dead."

"I believe it." He winked at his sister. "Okay, protector of the butterflies. Are you old enough to travel with this man to a faraway land, marry his master, and bear his children?"

She gulped hard. "That's plainly spoken, brother."

"That's what I thought." Laban studied Eliezer. "She's not ready."

"No—Laban." Rebekah glanced at her shoulder. She lifted her hand, and the butterfly flapped its wings and rested on her finger. "Maybe traveling with this man is my destiny."

"Did the butterfly tell you that?"

"No . . . but I don't feel so alone after it arrived yesterday morning. And traveling to a faraway place with a friend at my side isn't as scary."

"Then, take it with you, and may you become the mother of thousands of millions . . . children, not butterflies." He chuckled, and his sister blushed.

"I wouldn't survive that ordeal, either, brother," Rebekah joked, and Laban laughed again before kissing his sister on the cheeks.

Guilt crept into Eliezer's soul. How could he separate this loving brother and sister pair?

After their feast, Laban stood then helped his sister stand. Her head reached her brother's shoulder, so he cupped her face between his calloused palms and said, "Rebekah." Tears invaded the corners of his eyes. "Let your seed prosper before those who despise you." He kissed his little sister on one cheek, then the other.

Late into the night, the trio broke bread and drank water treated with wine.

After the celebration, Rebekah retreated to her tent. She pulled the cloth tent doors shut and lit a candle to drive out the darkness. After glancing around, she opened a trunk and removed a flat black stone. She heated the stone, pressed the face into a square of leather, then traced the details of the inscription etched into the face of the leather with her fingers.

The yellow butterfly left her shoulder and walked across the face of the map before taking flight and circling just above the map. "You're studying the inscription, too . . ." Rebekah smiled. "What does it mean, little friend? You don't seem like an ordinary butterfly. Your eyes are keen, and you arrived just in time . . . don't you agree?"

"Who are you talking to?" a strange man said, pushing his way uninvited through the tent flaps and unsheathing a knife. A scar ran diagonally from his right brow to his left chin.

"Who are you? Get out!"

"Make me." He licked his fat lips.

Rebekah dashed to the other side of her bed. *Where's my knife?*

The intruder dove for the table. His massive left hand opened, ready to crush the butterfly and steal the flat stone with the inscription.

"Run, my friend!" Rebekah screamed.

But the butterfly didn't fly away. It launched itself onto a charcoal powdery substance that Rebekah had been preparing for her arrow tips. Tilting right and left, it dipped its wings into the poison, took flight, and doused the man's eyes with its payload.

He screamed, stumbled backward, dropped the stone, and jabbed his fingers into his eyes in a vain attempt at relief, driving the poison deeper. He would be blind by morning.

Rebekah finally retrieved her knife as her brother and Eliezer ran into her tent. Laban easily pinned the intruder, still attacking his own eyes, on the floor.

"What is your business here?" Laban demanded of the man, then punched him in the gut. The thud of flesh meeting flesh vibrated throughout Rebekah's tent. Laban punched the man again.

The man gasped, "She's not leaving this village with that stone."

"What stone?" Eliezer inquired while shielding Rebekah. Laban tied the intruder's arms and legs. In the morning, he would flog the man to extract more information.

Rebekah would be glad to be gone from this place with her butterfly and her stone. She despised the sound of leather cutting human flesh. She stayed silent, dodged past Eliezer, and rushed to the well to fill a basin with water.

The butterfly would die if she didn't clean its wings.

★ ★ ★

IN THE MORNING, ELIEZER WAITED by his camel.

Clothed in a lilac silk tunic, Rebekah mounted her waxen-colored beast, her hands trembling as she slipped a palm-sized river-smooth black stone into a leather satchel mounted on the camel's side. In the distance, her brother tied the blind intruder to a post. *To be whipped while blind.* She shivered.

Eliezer noticed the pouch. "What is it?"

"Adonai has given me other missions besides bearing

children, Eliezer, but the details are private, my lord. So, forgive me."

"You need not ask for my forgiveness if your actions are Adonai's will."

She slipped a bright white veil across her eyes and followed Eliezer into the horizon, cringing at the sound of the lash fading behind her.

Several months later, Rebekah and Eliezer approached a grouping of tents. A man exited the largest tent and ran toward the caravan. Desert currents travelled through his long, brown hair. Eliezer turned toward the young bride. "That is Isaac, my friend's son."

"He's handsome."

"Indeed."

An old man stood framed in the door of the tent. "And that's Abraham, his father . . . and my friend."

"You have your secrets, too?"

"You never asked."

"Is he a righteous man—Abraham?"

"Adonai seems to think so. After He chose him to be the father of many nations, Adonai promised Abraham, 'I will bless those who bless you, And I will curse him who curse you; and in you, all the families of the Earth shall be blessed'."

"We are protected," Rebekah said, removing the leather satchel that held a small tomb—a wooden box where a dead yellow-winged butterfly lay.

"We are."

"Then ask Abraham to pray for this butterfly who saved my life. Ask for my friend to be set free, too."

"You ask him. You're his daughter, now. You don't need a human priest. Look at the smile on Abraham's face. He will surely grant you any request."

"Then I will."

"And the stone?" Eliezer gestured at her saddle.

"It's my mission to protect and preserve it." She dismounted her camel and followed Isaac back to the largest tent.

Isaac welcomed her into his tent, where her first request was to have a private audience with Abraham. Rebekah's friend—the butterfly—must be set free before Rebekah basked in the sweetness of a new love.

For it was no ordinary butterfly. And this unique butterfly took a trip back to the future . . . the world of the ghost, Wraith.

One year before the second total solar eclipse
occurring on April 8, 2024.

25—The Orphan

THREE MEN. TWO CHANCES. ONE truth. Wraith—the pale ghost—known as Cillian Joseph Finn to his wife Daniela, tightened his jaw. He knew what was coming next, just after the sun rose.

Sunrise—the desert morning's fire-drenched lips kissing the cold, black, starless night sky that hung low above Afghanistan's mountains until a pale-blue sky interrupts their affair.

The sun could be a persistent lover. Or at least, Wraith's Daniela Rose would have described the desert sunrise in such a manner as it climbed onto the camel's hump of the Afghanistan mountain peak.

In and out. He focused on the simplicity of his oxygen intake, then exhaled his body's waste of carbon dioxide.

Nothing else to do but wait on his mountaintop.

"Cillian, it's a simple plan." The President of the United States of America had arrived and was pacing the well-packed track of dirt next to the Humvee.

No one would find Cillian's body but his dog, Spook, if the desert didn't kill the animal first.

"I need you to take this one on the chin—tell your dog-gone voice of a conscience to shut the heck up and stick with the plan—our plan, America's plan. I need you to do this for me—for us. The Hive is the only hope people like you and me got!"

To lie or to tell the truth.

The horizon stretched into an eternity behind the president of the greatest country that had ever existed, to Cillian's mind anyway.

It was an endless horizon and a vast desert that was as unwelcoming as President Sheldon's wife's bed when it came to her husband, but not to Cillian. "I canna do what yer askin' of me, Mister President." A tear welled up in the warrior's right eye. Would he ever see Daniela Rose again?

"Why do you have to be so stubborn? So honest?" It was an odd problem when the President of the United States possessed an allergic reaction to telling the truth.

Wraith's wife had called this deadly reaction anaphylaxis. And his physician wife carried an EpiPen that she used to treat her allergic reaction to latex gloves. He'd learned about that the hard way after using a latex condom on their wedding night.

"Yer askin' me to take a trip down a slippery slope, an incline that's too steep for me to be climbin' back up."

"It takes bravery to tell the truth, Cil—nothing but the truth, so help you God."

"I know, Mister President."

"Call me Sheldon. We're friends."

Cillian didn't respond. If they were friends, what had the world come to?

"You're a brave man, Cillian. Ain't no argument there."

Cillian simply nodded.

"But you're too stubborn." Sheldon stopped his pacing. "Last chance . . . think about Daniela—your wife and that beautiful daughter of yours . . . fatherless, an orphan like you."

"I ha' been thinkin' about both of my girls since the day I first saw their faces, Sheldon. And I'm thinkin' about both of them now."

"I need you to forget about pacifying that Bat Creek Stone curse—okay?"

"No, I canna do it, sir."

"Is this your final answer?"

"It is, Mister President." Cillian swallowed, but his tongue stuck to the top of his mouth. This was it.

The president slipped on his sunglasses, and the Delta Force soldier standing behind Cillian cocked his gun. *Guess that was the cue—sunglasses going on.* The president looked past Cillian and tapped the rim of his Ray Bans.

Wraith—the pale ghost—sucked in his last drag of hot, desert air, then exhaled the pain of this betrayal, coming to terms with his fate.

"I've heard heaven's a nice place." The president backed away.

"So have I, and the Good Book also promises that the truth will set a man free. I was a slave once, as a wee lad. But standin' here now, I believe the Good Book is telling me the Truth."

"This day, you shall be free—forever, and the truth will be your liberator." Sheldon Covington reached up and rested his trembling hand on the shoulders of the six-foot-four special-ops soldier. Ten seconds later, he stepped back. "What a shame. What a loss."

The soldier standing behind Wraith raised his Sig Sauer, aimed, and pulled the trigger. Stagnant air shifted behind Cillian's right ear—like a puff of air from the nostrils of his loyal Belgian Malinois named Spook.

Something growled.

And then a giant of a man . . . a hero . . . a husband . . . a friend . . . a brother . . . a soldier . . . a father . . . a true American patriot . . . and one of Earth's great citizens fell, crashing into the desert floor.

Was it a chest wound, his blood spilling out of its flesh-and-bone cage? His essence soaking through dry-caked sand, weaving deeper until the fragments of his soul had found the eternal place—the place he hadn't deserved but had gotten anyway. Grace—God's unmerited favor. Grace, nothing but a second chance.

His breath slowed as though his lungs were travelling through a bathtub filled with warm honey. Wraith visualized his wife's face first, then his daughter's, and lastly his late son's beautiful, boyish, innocent face. "Daniela. Adelaide. Kian," he whispered as his lungs collapsed, breath expelling.

The utterance of their names thrust him into a memory, a visualization gifted only to a soul that had been set free, unshackled by the keys of Truth and launched from Earth's surly bonds as it reached out to touch the face of God.

Cillian smiled.

* * *

"BUT, MOM!" ADELAIDE STOMPED INTO the kitchen until she stood a foot away from her mother, her hands resting on her narrow hips, her face flushed with jolts of anger, and her voice raised to an octave even Steinway piano soprano keys dared not tread.

Cillian shifted his weight, threw his kitchen towel over his right shoulder, then abandoned the sink.

He moved closer, three feet behind his daughter, ready to intercede and defend the mama bear of the Finn-Cavanaugh clan—his clan.

"Babe, that's not a good idea." Daniela stopped mixing the carrot cake batter, her tone still calm and metered as she gazed at her only daughter.

Adelaide took a deep breath and paused, most likely feeling her father's towering presence behind her. "Okay—so maybe it wasn't a good idea back in the olden days, but people lie all the time nowadays." She shrugged.

"By olden days, you mean the era when dinosaurs roamed the Earth?" Daniela flashed that flawless, coy smile. Cillian pinned his lower lip between his teeth, stifling what was surely to have become a hearty laugh—a sound his family would miss after today.

"I guess." Adelaide huffed.

"Adelaide, in case you haven't noticed, the dinosaurs are dead now—right?" Daniela started mixing her cake again. "Maybe things would've turned out differently if they would've listened to their mothers." Daniela winked.

"Really, Mom?"

"Of course."

Silence filled space and time, until Adelaide broke into laughter. Cillian leaned in and embraced his daughter. "Yer mother's right, Addy Rose. Ye should never lie—even if telling the truth makes you look bad. Even if ye'll suffer for tellin' the truth."

"Why do my parents have to be girl and boy scouts?" Adelaide scooped up a finger of cake batter and licked it.

"Adelaide!"

"Sorry, Mom." She pecked her mother on the cheek. "I need to find a way to make an A."

"Aye, then, Addy Rose. Do the work. Ye didna even start the assignment, much less complete it, and then lost it."

"Your father's right, Adelaide. You can recover from the temporary state of looking bad. But you only get one chance to tell the truth . . . the first time. So don't throw that opportunity away."

"So much for second chances," Adelaide said under her breath. "Fine. You win, Mom. All your infinite, motherly, and annoying wisdom. It's checkmate."

"Didn't know we were playing chess, but I love you, darling girl." Daniela kissed her daughter on both cheeks. "Get me a pan. I'm ready to pour the cake." Cillian pulled his daughter into his chest, leaned over her shoulder, and kissed his wife's face, a ravishing beauty that not even sadness could mar. A cherry pink flushed her cheeks.

Indeed, she was an easy woman to love.

"Exciting . . ." Adelaide ducked out of her parents' embrace. "Mom?"

"Yes, darling?" Daniela pushed back into her husband's chest as she poured the cake into the Bundt pan. He rested his cheek against her head.

"What is the Bat Creek Stone?"

"What? You're kidding me. You haven't even completed the research portion for your archeology research paper for school?" Shock registered across Daniela's face.

"No, ma'am . . . but at least I told you the truth." Adelaide winked at her mother.

* * *

WRAITH'S BREATH CAME FASTER . . .

And the first thing he smelled was . . . dog breath. *Spook?* The first sound he heard was the voice of President Sheldon Covington. "Welcome back, Cillian. You passed the test."

Wraith opened his sand-dusted eyes. The sun's light was bright and penetrating.

"It was a dart of Remifentanil, a potent opioid. Chad—" President Sheldon motioned to the Delta Force soldier "—is also an anesthesiologist, so he intubated you until you were ready to breathe again."

"Why?"

"I needed to know I could trust you. Claire Amilee—my wife," Sheldon's voice faltered. "She's plotting against me . . . and America. I need you to handle her for me—okay?"

"Okay." Wraith took Chad's hand, and Spook nudged his master's leg, telling his friend, *I love you. I trust you.*

Cillian noted the bandage on the dog's back leg.

"That dog always finds you." The president tapped the edge of his Ray Bans again. Just a nervous tic. Cillian laughed.

Perception was oftentimes the culprit of lies.

A lie can travel halfway around the world while
the truth is putting on its shoes.

—Mark Twain

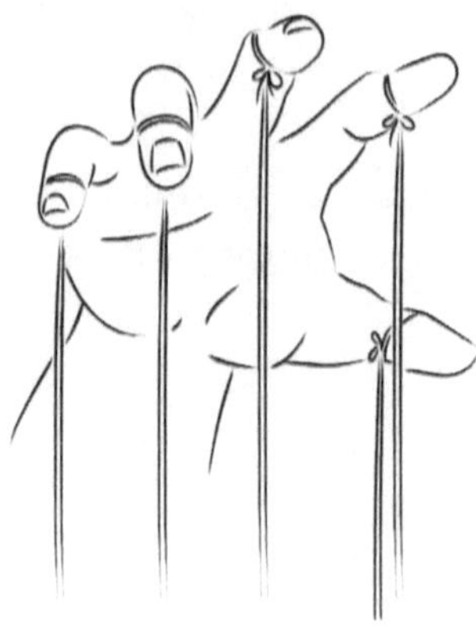

26—Asher

The Present, The End . . .
10:31 a.m., Tuesday, May 9, 2023
Hallstatt, Austria

BEYOND THE WINDOWS OF A quaint Bavarian café, the sun was taking its place as the rightful tenant of the morning sky. If the First Lady of the United States of America, Claire Amilee, had her way, ninety-nine percent of Americans would vanish next year.

And if Asher Bushcroft got his way, this bright morning would be no ordinary day. He slid a sheet of scented linen paper toward Claire as they waited for their breakfast. "Tell me what you see."

"A map of North America." She shrugged then sipped her hot tea.

"And what else?" He rearranged his silverware, putting his fork to left of the spoon—a nervous habit.

Claire scrunched her manicured bleached-blonde eyebrows. "Two dark lines."

"Correct. It is a map of North America—but it's no ordinary map." With his equally manicured forefinger, he traced the curve of the first arm that seemed to have been dragged across the continent, leaving a trail of smut as it crossed from northwest to southeast. Lastly, he traced the second curved arm that had travelled from southwest to northeast, leaving its own trail of darkness.

"Where did this drawing come from?"

"My artist created this rendering from an ancient drawing found on a scroll penned by a Hebrew prophet. The two dark lines are curved arms formed by the trajectory of two solar eclipses."

"Okay—so what? Who cares?"

"I do."

"Why—because you found something ancient, another artifact?" She rolled her eyes. "Something else to spend your billions on?"

"That, and I believe the sun is speaking to us."

"You've finally lost your marbles, Asher." She stirred a cube of sugar into her tea.

"I never liked marbles, so I never played with them. Listen to me, Claire. I think this celestial phenomenon is a final warning. I think it's a countdown clock placed in the sky so everybody can see it, especially after the invention of social media."

"If this is a warning or a countdown, what are we counting down to?

"America's end," he stated matter-of-factly.

"That's interesting." Claire's words took on a bland tone, her attention captured more by the melting cube of sugar in her tea than the conversation. "But how would you know?"

Asher removed his smartphone from his inside jacket pocket, tapped on the screen, then began to read an ancient passage, "'The earth quakes as they advance, and the heavens tremble. The sun and moon grow dark, and the stars no longer shine. The Lord is at the head of the column. He leads them with a shout. This is his mighty army, and they follow his orders. The day of the Lord is an awesome, terrible thing. Who can possibly survive?'" Asher paused and sucked in a long breath, giving Claire time to butt in.

"Sounds ominous. But when did you start reading the Bible?"

"You mean the Hebrew Scriptures. My father taught me to read Hebrew . . . in Germany. No, I'm not religious. But I am a scholar and a gentleman."

"You must be playing the opposite game," Claire muttered, then spoke in her normal voice. "I went to Sunday School, you know. Hebrew Scriptures. Bible. Same difference. " She spoke in an irreverent tone. "Besides, the Bible is a Jewish book written by Jewish people. Never could figure out why Jewish people got so worked up about the writing of Jesus and Paul—both men were Jewish."

"You? Sunday School? I never could've guessed." A smirk peeled back his lips, a small piece of insanity escaping his natural, timeless appeal.

"You're not one to judge . . . what about all of those orphans?"

"I know, darling girl."

"Just making sure you do."

"Yes, the passage is ominous until . . . 'That is why the Lord says, Turn to me now, while there is time. Give me your hearts. Come with fasting, weeping, and mourning. Don't tear your clothing in your grief but tear your hearts instead. Return to the Lord your God, for he is merciful and compassionate, slow to get angry and filled with unfailing love. He is eager to relent and not punish. Who knows? Perhaps he will give you a reprieve, sending you a blessing instead of this curse.'"

"If you believe the Bible, that passage sounds a bit more hopeful."

"In this case, I can't take the chance by not believing. A second chance is just what the Orphan Dreamer wants for America . . . for all citizens of the world."

"Why do you care what she wants? You were supposed to assassinate her, and you failed."

"I changed the mission. That's not a failure. And I care about making what she doesn't want a reality, so I need you to assure me that the first passage—the part about the painful portion of this promise, retribution for all past ills—will last as long as possible."

"Why?"

"The bad guys don't deserve to quickly escape their due—their misery. You Christians call this time the Tribulation Period, and if it's real, I want it to last much longer than seven years. Extend the pain."

"You do enjoy watching people writhe in pain." Claire sipped her tea.

"And you don't?" he said. She didn't deny his accusation, so he continued. "That's what I thought. But I also enjoy beauty, so I consider myself to be a well-balanced human. Are you?"

She ignored his statement. "Tell me. When do these solar eclipses occur?" She cocked her head, her interest piqued. "When does the countdown begin?"

Asher tapped the face of his phone, then turned the device so Claire could look at an image. "See the dates?"

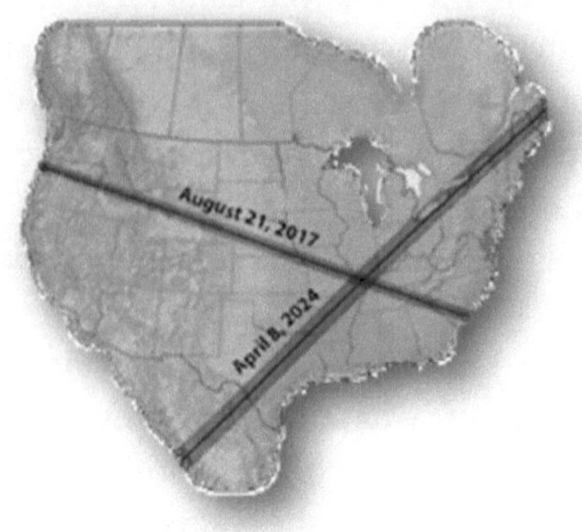

"I do." She nodded. "August 21, 2017, and April 8, 2024."

"The sun and its light can be beautiful but get too close and it will kill."

"April 8, 2024, is less than a year away from today." A grin eviler than the devil's scowl twisted Claire's skin-deep beauty.

"I know."

Claire burst out laughing. "And to think I was going to have to do this all by myself—scrub Earth clean of all of the baggage and unnecessaries."

"You see? The Sons of Venus are your allies. And I—as the SOV's chairman—want to be given the opportunity to watch and enjoy the process, after what they did to my people."

"I won't need your Sons of Venus. I've got my own plans."

"Oh, but you do need me."

"We'll see about that. We go to the Hive in two months because this thing is about to blow." She shifted in her chair, and the legs scraped across the black-and-white-checkered tile floor, grating on Asher's nerves and snatching him back to his last day of school in World War Two Germany. His teacher had scratched her nails down the backside of a chalkboard to get the class's attention.

"No—wrong. You work for me." Asher leaned forward and leveled his pale gray-blue gaze at her.

"We work together."

"Keep telling yourself that, Claire. But know this: we—you and I—are not going to allow the Orphan Dreamer to lead the people to repent of their wrongs, ensuring their second chance, their redemption. They. Must. Suffer . . . for a very long time."

"And seven years isn't enough?"

"Not even close."

"Why are they suffering?"

"A curse set in motion a long time ago."

"I have a mind to shorten the time of suffering, Asher." She clenched her jaw.

"What?"

"You mean who." She smiled—crooked, in a hurry.

Asher gazed at Claire. "Cillian?"

"Yes," she admitted.

"Being beautiful isn't a sin, Claire." Hallstatt, Austria—the place of the Devil's Dustbin—also presented a vision of unrepentant beauty so frequently observed in Bavarian villages.

And as far as Asher knew, the devil had never apologized for the existence of his dustpan called Hallstatt, Austria.

Asher believed only beautiful people—such as himself, of course, and the beautiful blonde who sat across from him—should be allowed to live in this place, and in the place modeled after it, The Hive.

Time to clean house . . . but not yet, so Asher changed tactics.

Initiate the Manchurian protocol.

The protocol that would start World War Three, and Claire would be the catalyst. She'd been prepared, brainwashed, to complete a deadly set of actions. War ensured suffering. She smiled. "Claire, I imagine you remember him. That tweedy little orphan boy—who is no longer a tweed or a boy. Cillian Finn." The waitress set their hot breakfast on the table.

"I couldn't forget him." She licked her lips but not because of the food. Claire was still battling anorexia.

"He's a walking work of art—one of Michelangelo's finest sculptures—don't you think?" Bushcroft's skin prickled with desire. He adjusted his tie and cleared his throat, then took the first bite of his breakfast.

"He is."

"When did you first meet him, Claire?"

"In Mongolia. During training. He wasn't much of anything to look at back then." Her right eyelid twitched, and an air of haughtiness cloaked her lie. Asher smiled. Claire Amilee was lying like a politician with a microphone.

Snaring a fish required bait. Cillian was the bait, and Claire was the catfish Asher had brainwashed to act when she heard the trigger words—tweedy little orphan boy.

But what if Asher was wrong about Claire? What if he'd gotten the whole darn situation wrong? No need to show his uncertainty. The magician kept talking, stroking Claire's carnal desires. "Had the Italian Renaissance artist still been alive," Bushcroft said, gesturing narrowly with his hands, "Cillian Joseph Finn would have been his masterpiece, his legacy work."

"Here's what I want to know. How did Daniela Rose snag him?" Claire took another swig of her tea.

"Wasn't sex."

"Is that so?" Claire Amilee cocked her head to the left, and ringlets of her bleached-blonde bob sashayed around the nape of her elegantly thin neck, framing her pretty face.

"Rumor had it, they didn't do it until after the wedding." Asher winked and chewed another bite of his blueberry-drenched pancakes.

"You're kidding me."

"I wouldn't lie to you . . . the question is, would you lie to me?"

She evaded the question. "Maybe Cillian had his own motive for that approach of celibacy before marriage," Claire said, then paused. Her features dipped into a bottomless pool of genuine pity for the orphan.

"Explain."

"Maybe Cillian's motive for withholding sex from his blushing bride was for a different reason than fulfilling some higher Godly calling."

"Whatever do you mean, my darling girl?" Asher held his fork midair.

"Delayed discovery . . ."

"Of?"

"I saw his scars, Asher. They crisscrossed every inch of the back of him." Her voice fell to a whisper. "I saw them—one night when . . ." Her voice was crushed by an unexpected emotion—unquenched love.

"You became too attached, too early," Asher said coolly. *Tsk. Tsk. Tsk.* He wagged his head.

"And you didn't!" Daggered icicles shot from Claire's cold eyes faster than Daniela's bow could fire off a volley of poisoned-tipped arrows.

"You had a mission. You both did."

"It was you, then—you had us separated in Mongolia." She seethed.

"Training for the mission came first."

"He could have been mine instead of Daniela's. How could you!" She slid to the edge of her chair, clenching her fork.

"You could have found him again—before she did. You had the time."

A coolness wiped her face of emotion. She leaned back in her chair. Asher's heartbeat ticked faster. That look, the blank stare, was not passive. It was a declaration of war. She was known to fight like an octopus—arms everywhere until her enemy was subdued. "Cillian never told me exactly how he got the scars. Even after I got him drunk one night during training." The anger in Claire's voice had given way to accusation. She was circling, like a raptor before swooping down to catch its prey.

"Intoxication. That offence could have been punished by a proper flogging, then languishing in the cage."

"If I ever hear that you put Cillian in a cage or flogged him, you'll suffer the same, Asher. Mark my words, so why don't you tell me how he got his scars? And don't hold back any details."

Some people feed off protein, carbohydrates, and fats, but Claire Amilee fed off the fear of others. But so did Asher. He grinned.

Claire Amilee leaned forward, her ample bosom spilling out of her top—on the table, in midair, even launching her teacup toward the center of the table. The hot liquid sloshed over the side of her mug and stained the starched white tablecloth.

Sloppy.

Control those things! The sight of untamed flesh made Bushcroft's stomach roil. *Focus on the beauty of Cillian.* "I did a number on him a couple of times. That's all."

"What exactly did you do?" Her gaze narrowed.

"I marked him." Asher laced his voice with every ounce of narcissistic arrogance he could muster.

"When was this—before Mongolia?"

"It was before—before you. Yes, Claire, the world was spinning on its axis before you arrived."

"Never said it didn't."

It was Asher's turn to lean forward—taunting, threatening in his own way. "I flayed him alive."

"You're proud of what you did to him."

"I am—of him, not of me. I could barely stomach seeing him after I'd meted my rage, but the punishment was necessary—the mission before the man."

"He was a boy."

"He survived to manhood, and not all of the boys did." Asher cleared his throat, exorcising the guilt lodged in the back of his throat that was feeding off his regrets. "He's stronger for it."

"You're twisted."

"I am—but so are you, darling. I wish Cillian were twisted. Boy, we could have some fun."

"What can I say about Cillian?" Claire twirled a strand of hair between her fingers while sipping what was left of her tea.

They sat silent for a while inside the small bakery and coffee shop.

Asher broke the silence. "Nothing—that's what you say."

"I'll speak when I want to."

"No—not now. His remembrance and his presence demand an awe-inspired silence."

"Don't be dramatic. He's not a god."

"Appreciate the art form, Claire, and in his presence abandon all words to the poets."

"Tragic. Romantic. Utterly silly." She was quiet for only a moment. "I have a question."

Talking—it was her addiction. "Speaking so soon?"

"Last question."

"Promise?"

"On my husband's life."

"The Secret Service may have a problem with a death swear being placed on the head of the current president in exchange for a Chatty Kathy's silence."

"My husband shouldn't have been allowed to walk into the White House as a tourist, much less as the president." Claire was audacious in her admissions. "His tribe will get over it."

"Cold as an iceberg." Asher smirked.

"Indulge me with the truth for once, Asher. What did Cillian become—just a billionaire banker camouflaged in a Michelangelo-inspired shell, or did he become something more, something naughtier—like me?"

"You're looking to improve your daydreams?" Asher smirked.

"Maybe. Indulge me."

"He's an assassin, Claire . . . a spy and an Orphan just like you, First Lady Covington. He's my Raven, like you're my Sparrow. Sexpionage. It's nothing new."

"But he kills people too—right?" She waited, hoping to milk more information from this dry cactus.

This cactus's blood didn't run for a full minute. "Sometimes—but only when necessary. He doesn't like to kill, so instead, on most occasions he creates financial situations that make people want to die."

"How?"

"He's an economic hit man, and with a few strategic moves, he can shut down a competitor's economy. No food.

No clean water. No fossil fuel to heat or cool. And the citizens beg for death or assassinate their leader—which is usually the goal of the Sons of Venus."

"He's so unapologetically beautiful, yet so deadly."

"What's beautiful usually is." He nodded.

"I guess it's true then."

"What is?" Asher thought to lick his plate clean. Breakfast was delicious.

"Some invisible hand had fashioned Cillian Joseph Finn into a beautiful man, but it wasn't Michelangelo. The Renaissance artist had never breathed life into anything, making flesh and bone a living soul. According to his Bible-quoting wife, only one possessed that track record—the life giver, Yahweh."

"Not you, too. We're in a café in Hallstatt, Austria, not a Billy Graham crusade." He rolled his eyes. "Take it." Bushcroft pushed a small, leather satchel in Claire's direction.

"What is it?"

"What you wanted and something I need."

"Oh?" She opened the satchel and furrowed her brow as she examined a bloodred stone and a small scroll.

"Your grandfather visited my father in a shop in China when I was a kid."

"China? I don't see my grandfather travelling outside of the good ol' USA."

"Just listen for once. When your grandfather visited my father in China, he spoke of the Bat Creek Stone."

"So?" Claire shrugged.

"I need it, and I need you to go and get it for me. And this seed is payment to you for what I want."

"What is this?" She toyed with the bloodred stone, flipping it through her fingers.

"Let's just say that if one wanted to grow another tree that Eve may want to eat from, that's the seed—"

"Of the Tree of Knowledge of Good and Evil." She finished his sentence.

"Sunday School did enlighten you."

"And gave me a permanent guilt trip." She examined the stone. "What shall we call it?"

"It already has a name. It's called the Philosopher's Stone."

"Then no need to change the name." She blew a kiss toward Asher, and he didn't hide his disgust. "I owe you a favor then, in the form of the Bat Creek Stone. But why do you want it?"

"Somehow this relic, if handled correctly by the Orphan Dreamer, will give America and the rest of the world a second chance, and as I've already explained, I can't have that."

"And the map, what of it?"

"It leads to an ancient mountain in Mongolia; it is where the Eternal Light resides." Asher leaned back in his chair. "I need you to make Sheldon nuke that mountain after you lure the Orphan Dreamer there."

"Find the Dreamer and make her toast, along with the Bat Creek Stone and this Eternal Light." Claire's grin made Asher want to backhand her, but he restrained himself. "What does this Eternal Light do?" she asked.

"I don't know what it does. But the professor wants it around, and I know the Orphan Dreamer believes it somehow is connected to the Bat Creek Stone and giving America its second chance. Professor Jakob told me after a bit of . . . encouragement." Asher removed a long cigar from inside his jacket and rolled it between his right forefinger and thumb. "He's missing a finger."

"Isn't he your family?"

"He didn't need all of them. The man picked his nose. Now he has one less finger to do so with."

"You're insane. Does this Eternal Light have a name?"

"The menorah—the lost, straight-branched original Judean light. It's a necessary artifact to furnish the last Jewish Temple."

"What about the Ark of the Covenant? Wasn't that lost, too?"

"I don't know where it is." Asher shrugged. Claire studied Asher's face and his body language for a full minute.

"Asher, you're still hung up on Berlin."

"As I should be." He motioned with his hand out the window. "There—that pristine lake, Lake Hallstatt. That's where the Nazis hid their treasure—treasure stolen from my people. The locals call it the Devil's Dustbin." Hallstatt Lake was infamously nicknamed that because retreating Nazis had dumped their treasure into its deep, cold waters. "They engineered the death of my people and so many others."

"As you and I are doing and will continue to do."

"Don't be a preacher," he snapped.

"Don't be a hypocrite, Asher." She paused and glared at her breakfast companion. "However, I will see what I can do to find out about the Bat Creek Stone. As for the mountain, nuking it will be easier."

"I know." Asher wiped his palms across his pant legs. "Why are you so willingly doing this for me?" He played dumb, seeing if his Manchurian candidate had been properly triggered. "I mean besides Natalia, no one's ever wanted to do anything for me—they do it because they have to, or else."

"It's fun." Claire shrugged. She stood, shouldering the satchel that contained the desiccated, glass-shrouded seed of the Tree of the Knowledge of Good and Evil, the last of its kind, and the map that would lead to the Eternal Light. "Put out the light—end the world. But before we snuff out

Earth's light, I wouldn't mind discovering Cillian's whereabouts and showing him a good time . . . have you a clue, Asher?"

"Is this your requested favor of me?"

"It is."

Asher scribbled an address on a napkin and gifted it to his Claire Amilee. She licked her lips again, then grinned. After she left, Nomed arrived, taking a seat at the table across from Asher Bushcroft.

Every guest needed a house.

27—The Orphan

The Present, the End . . .
3:47 p.m., Saturday, February 3, 2024
Lake Baikal, Russia

IT WAS ONLY TWO MONTHS until the Great American Solar Eclipse. Camouflage painted Wraith's face in shades of anemic gray and brown, breaking up the pale hue of his skin, and allowing him to blend into Siberia's winter forest.

According to America's spy network, his prey would emerge 1,500 feet due west two hours from now.

He had 1,231 confirmed kills but murdering humans had never felt right, only necessary.

Siberia's frozen tree branches reached toward the ghost with frosty fingers and an open mouth, eager to devour.

He slid the bulk of his body out of the hole, facing the bluster of a snow-packed desert. Cillian had never fared well on damp and frigid nights as a boy. He glanced at his watch—midnight. An acrid taste burned the back of his throat as cold, moist air clung to his face.

Two others approached the target with him, moving through the tundra. Hidden within a gale of swirling snow, they stalked, scanning three directions and covering the 275-degree swath of cleared land beyond their hiding place.

A snowstorm had been promised, and not just any snowfall—a fierce, transient blizzard.

Happy hunting.

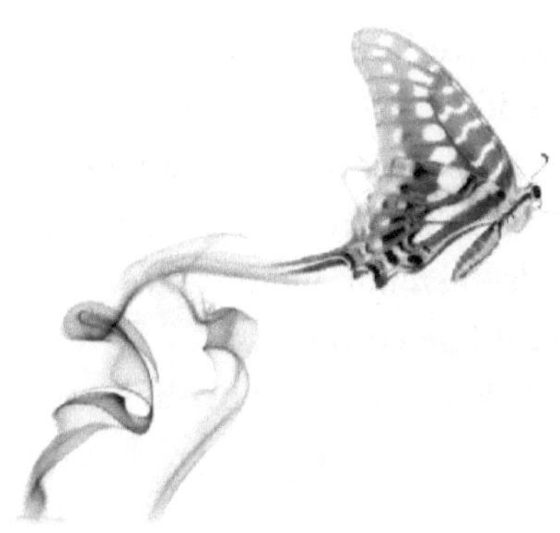

28—Claire

The Present, the End . . .
3:47 p.m., Saturday, February 3, 2024
Lake Baikal, Russia

THE PRESIDENT OF THE UNITED States of America loved to icefish—that was why he married Claire Amilee.

Besides, Lake Baikal would be a beautiful place to die. Claire pondered her plan—how to start World War Three while prolonging the pain of the seven-year Tribulation Period—as she studied the breathtaking view of sea life and encased air bubbles trapped beneath the lake's icy fist.

Lake Baikal would prove to be her husband's final stop on the train called life. Claire smirked. The frozen lake would also be her final stop before she abandoned Earth for the Hive. She required a hiding place, and outer space would do just fine.

After she arrived at the Hive, she would set Earth on fire—Armageddon, the end of "In the beginning . . ."

With Earth eliminated, the universe—her world, the place where Nephilim resided—could stretch out and re-acquire their *lebensraum,* living space.

Cillian would be coming to the Hive soon.

The dissatisfied wife licked her lips, savoring all the possibilities of Cillian—untested waters, but deep and plunging, no doubt.

With a physique like his—six-foot-four, two hundred pounds of chiseled muscles . . . she sighed, needing to again feel his illicit touch instead of imagining it. She hadn't felt it since they both were teenagers trapped inside Bushcroft's Mongolian training camp—the place where beautiful, or-phaned girls became Sparrows and handsome, orphaned boys became Ravens.

Claire Amilee had run away from home after her mother had been murdered. After she finished her training, becom-ing a true Sparrow, she went to college. Years later, she met her future husband, Sheldon Covington.

These days, her husband had become rather soft around the middle, padding his sloppy efforts at making love. Then, after the accident, the attempts ceased.

Wading deep inside Cillian Finn's ocean would be her agenda item number one after she arrived at the Hive. Who cared if the object of her affection joined in willingly? She thumped the syringe, mixing the medication thoroughly.

After he awakened, he would comply for the sake of his family. With red lacquered fingertips, she groped the spine of the cold metal object tucked inside her parka's right pocket—the match to her fire.

Since childhood, Claire had relished destroying things—friendships, reputations, and most of all Daniela Rose

Cavanaugh's happiness. Not every leaf possessed the spine to turn over, forming a new one. As an adult, she hadn't changed. Her destructive habits had only expanded, targeting the destruction of marriages, countries, and even planets.

Claire stood at the edge of the frozen lake, watching Sheldon.

Careless.

Unthoughtful.

He was a man who'd grown accustomed to other people caring for his safety. Her upper lip curled in disgust. Goosebumps invaded her winter-pale skin as she remembered when he'd last touched her. President Sheldon Covington hadn't been a detailed man or a patient man.

She imagined that Cillian—a trained Raven—was patient and detail-oriented.

In Mongolia, he had practiced with her, always tender, patient, unsure if he was giving her pleasure . . . watchful, just the way she liked it. In the end, he'd become a pro in the art of lovemaking, but she'd never told him, always giving him nothing higher than a C+ to keep him humble—and practicing.

Bushcroft hadn't figured out her ploy, or else he would have had her horsewhipped for her deception. She rubbed the back of her legs as though the leather was even now striking her trembling flesh.

29—The Orphan

The Present, the End . . .
4:29 p.m., Saturday, February 3, 2024
Lake Baikal, Russia

THE WIND AND SNOW WOULD be the Orphans' cover when they advanced on the snow-buried tunnel to retrieve Cillian's something—revenge. And NATO's someone—a wayward politician who needed a good spanking.

Ten acres due north, Russian and Iranian soldiers guarded the tunnel that contained his revenge on Claire Amilee, who also happened to be the naughty politician. Land mines, possessed of firepower that Cillian knew would slice his body into shreds, dotted the pathway to the concrete fortress.

His *something* and NATO's *someone* must be found if he hoped to live and see his *someone,* Daniela Rose Cavanaugh, once again.

Would she take him back? Or would she believe every-thing Claire most likely had told her? Like the old serpent, Claire spoke nothing but lies. Surely, Daniela knew this. Claire had bullied his *nighean donn* since they were both children.

His right arm trembled, a four-inch sniper shell rocking back and forth in his partially clenched fist.

"I'll take the first watch. You look deader than Siberia."

"Aye, then," he replied to Sakura.

Leaving his sniper rifle in position and the barrel aimed at the underground entrance, he pushed back into their man-made snow cave.

He closed his eyes and lifted his chin, hoping to catch a whisper of a warm breeze that carried her scent from over 3,000 miles away. Dead leaves rustled as they clung to equally dead branches, but the air around him remained cold, stingy, and lifeless.

No lavender scent wafting through the air.

No Daniela.

His military fatigues were glued to his winter undergar-ments. He flexed his chiseled arm muscles—a gift from the Orphans' training—warming his blood as his teammates kept watch.

The team?

Spook—Cillian's Belgian Malinois.

Sakura—a ninja female.

Ben.

And Cillian. A man of few words, he usually let his eyes do the talking. Some had accused him of adding to the mystery of his persona with his quietness. He hadn't a clue as to what those people meant. Why talk when there was nothing to say? His son was dead, and Daniela was dying or dead, so why was he here fighting?

Adelaide Rose. His daughter. That was why.

A cold sweat sent a shiver from Cillian's head to his toes faster than electric bolts danced across the sky. The wind began to move. The blizzard was coming.

Had his daughter listened to her mother and taken the Bat Creek Stone back to its rightful place? The trembling ceased as he wrapped his fingers around the sniper's shell. A silver coin had once been his crutch, but he'd given it to another, and she wasn't there.

He squeezed the bullet again, trying to suppress the barrage of thoughts that usually came in quiet moments of waiting, like this one.

A sniper had many quiet moments while waiting to kill. Time passed.

"Fifteen minutes are up." Sakura tapped him on the shoulder.

"I'm up."

"What's on your mind?" Sakura asked.

"Murder." A smirk slightly curved the corner of Cillian's mouth. "What's on yours?"

"Getting warm." She rubbed her arms with her gloved hands. "He should be coming out of his hole soon. Let's do it."

His lip curled upward in another uncontrollable body response—a snarl. "Yer eager to kill, Sakura."

"That's a fact. What about yourself?"

"What do you mean?"

"Do you only kill on behalf of your dog?"

"I'd kill for Paul, Spook, or Dan . . ." He looked down.

"Who's this mysterious Dan?"

"No one to you, but everything to me."

"So, you're gay?"

"Not likely."

"Good." She licked her lips as though preparing to devour the main course. "So you wouldn't kill for me?" Sakura reached out and squeezed his bicep.

"Killing excites you, doesn't it?" He shook his head. Pulling away, he massaged the bullet while his moistened eyes belied his rock-hard exterior.

She cocked her head and stared at him; a behavior Cillian found unnerving. "It's not the killing. Death is anticlimactic. Hunting is what makes me feel alive."

Again, he looked in her direction. Almond-shaped eyes held as much mystery as her surprising last-minute arrival inside the Orphans' chopper in Alabama. Cillian hated surprises; his childhood and adolescence had been filled with them, and most had been devastating.

Silence filled the empty space. Cillian looked at his watch—05:32. "You're on my team, Sakura."

"But you hate me because of Mongolia—don't you?"

"That was a lifetime ago."

"A second chance, Wraith." She smiled.

"Aye, then." He nodded then peered through the scope of his sniper rifle.

"My friends call me Saki," she informed him, continuing her unnerving gaze.

"Where are your friends?"

"Not in this hole, obviously." Saki flipped her long, black ponytail over her shoulder. "Making love to it?"

"It?"

She pointed. "The bullet."

"Sakura, focus on the mission," Cillian said.

"What's your angle in making this kill?" she said, ignoring him. She pulled a curved knife from a pocket in her pant leg.

"Freedom. Hope. A second chance for some people I love."

"I doubt you'll find any of that at the end of your rifle barrel." She laughed.

Was she mocking him or trying to lighten the mood? *Assume the best.* Cillian turned away, shoved the bullet inside his pocket, and looked up at the only hint of sky through a hole in their leafy roof. Somewhere high above, hidden within celestial darkness crisscrossed by veins of light, Jake's drone flew.

Jake, the team's eye in the sky, sat in a plush hotel room in Alaska, weaving a drone through clouds and snowfall.

He thought of the virtuous missionary girl he had lost once in Mongolia and now had likely lost to death—his someone. He then looked at Sakura. Virtue, a lost treasure. *But if I had a mirror, I wouldn't see virtue in my eyes, either. Brothels do that to a boy.*

A sour taste filled his mouth; he swallowed.

Cillian shifted his hips. Wet and cold air tunneled into his lungs with each breath—humidity. Was this how it felt to be suffocated? But his thoughts suffocated him more.

"Did your parents dump you or die?" Sakura asked.

"Dump." Without his sights trained on his next victim, that one word propelled his thoughts into a barren land of childhood memories.

The special ops team's name fit him well. He was an orphan, but not without family.

He peeked at the sky.

Paul, Cillian's orphanage brother, was also thousands of feet above him now, sitting in the cockpit of an F-22 Raptor after taking off from the USS *Ronald Reagan* nuclear aircraft carrier. Paul's packages would send fire and brimstone if needed. The lake would melt, and every soldier who remained would sink to the bottom of the deepest lake in Europe.

Cillian pulled his other family member, Spook, close. The dog's black-and-brown coat bristled with every noise and wind change. He stroked the Malinois's back, calming him. *You're okay, boy.*

But Cillian wasn't okay.

Cillian turned to the Orphans. "Target on the move." The ghost lined the man's forehead with the crosshairs of his sight, knowing Ben was measuring the wind and Sakura had squared the target's torso within her weapon's sights.

"Steady . . ."

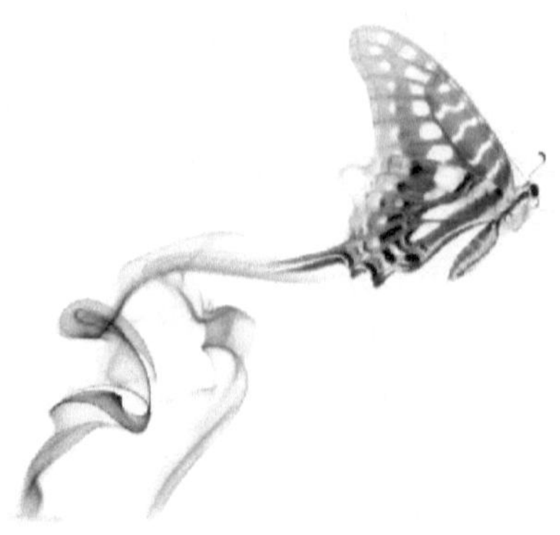

30—Claire

PRESIDENT COVINGTON'S ADVISORS HAD CALLED him a pit bull in a China shop—if those kinds of shops existed any longer.

It was true that Sheldon hadn't won the presidency because he was terribly intelligent, detail-oriented, thoughtful, or even patriotic. Americans had longed for an outsider, a swamp cleaner.

Sheldon's approach to the White House had mimicked the playbook of his and his wife's bedroom. Stale crackers chewed by a rabid dog would've been fresher than their romance. In the sleep aid aisle—that was where their love-making sessions belonged in the grocery store of life.

"Cillian," she whispered his name. Claire grinned from

ear to ear, something she never did. *Don't jinx it, Claire.* A coy grin laced her lips together—a secret secured and puckered, ready for a French kiss.

"Sheldon," she called out in a sensual tone, her voice carrying like a shrill whistle on the sea. No differently than killer whales, she enjoyed playing with her prey before consumption. "There's nothing like fresh air."

"What do you want, Amilee?"

Sheldon sat on a squat chair. Would her body still turn him on? She gripped the hard metal spine of the gun hidden inside her pocket while she approached her washed-up husband from behind. She pressed her pelvis into the nape of his neck.

He leaned forward, creating space between them, and shivered.

Volcanic anger flared inside her chest as arctic winds fingered a path through his tinsel-capped head.

He tugged on his fishing line. "No bite. This is a place of lifelessness. It's a time capsule, stuck in the past and cursed with a leader who was a pain in my butt all four years of my presidency." Claire inhaled and forgot, or didn't care, to exhale. "Truth is, Siberia never did smell like Idaho." Sheldon glanced over his shoulder, not bothering to make eye contact. "But how could it, with Russia's leaders stinking up the east for years?"

Claire's world spun and began to fade around the edges.

Time had run out.

Time to act.

She allowed a loud exhale to escape through her nose.

"It's going to storm, Claire," Sheldon said in an eerily calm voice. As though his words were those of God Himself, snow began to rain down from an ominous sky—silent, stealthy, unpredictable, maybe deadly. "The hibernating bear of Russia is awake now," he whispered. She barely made out his words above the snow.

Time to die. She narrowed her gaze.

Her accomplice, the storm, had arrived. Cold silence closed in all around. She curled her right forefinger around the trigger. A shadow appeared on the horizon. *That's odd.* "Who is that?" It appeared to be a man.

"The man I've been waiting for. But why are *you* really here, Claire?" Sheldon turned and faced his wife, now pointing the gun at his forehead. The snow-laden winds blew in, blustering and tossing a bucketful of snowflakes into her face, temporarily blinding her. She closed her eyes against the onslaught.

Separate the feet exactly nine inches apart. Engage the core—Pilates talk for the abdominal muscles. He'd listened to his wife teaching his daughter the exercise technique. Focus on the target. Aim. Fire. Do. Not. Hesitate.

Aim. Fire. Then breathe, Claire.

Opening its ice-veiled eyes, Siberia would watch as America's former First Lady assassinated her husband at point-blank range.

★ ★ ★

WRAITH SQUARED OFF HIS VICTIM'S head between the sniper scope's crosshairs, then pulled the trigger—a necessary kill to halt the madness before Europe sucked the world into another bloody world war.

★ ★ ★

EYES STILL CLOSED, CLAIRE PULLED the trigger, the details of their marriage flashing before her—the extravagant southern wedding with more gawking strangers than friends followed by a steaming hot honeymoon in St.

Tropez. Then two cycles of failed in-vitro fertilization before Sheldon's ski accident.

Her mind landed solidly upon the task at hand—the bullet slicing through a shower of snowflakes, melting each as the projectile shrieked a litany of curses at the bottled-up failure that was their marriage.

Thump.

Impact.

Cracking, splitting, disfiguring, then immediate death.

Blood, bone, and brains splattered, staining Lake Baikal with the fragments of a life that once was—the life of an American president who loved the idea of an American Dream, her late husband, Sheldon.

A banshee whose breath was formed by ice and snow screeched and screamed in protest of this cold-blooded murder, releasing a deafening thunder of wind. The white-out blizzard joined it in remonstrance.

Stand still. Stand still, Claire repeated in her mind. Being still until the wind died down would prevent her from getting lost in a sea of ice and snow.

Minutes seemed to lapse into hours.

The wind calmed.

All was quiet.

"Finally," she whispered. "Always was all talk and no action." He hadn't fought back or given her what she'd deserved—a hard slap across the backside.

Her father, the ill-regarded senator, had done so on many occasions, before taking so much more. The tension interwoven through the muscles of her shoulders and arms evaporated.

The trajectory of Earth's future had changed, going her way. Forever.

Smiling, the newly widowed assassin holstered her gun,

then circled around the body of her already partially buried fallen prey, determined to study her work. Her smile faded as quickly as it had arrived.

Crimson velvet petals protruded from the upper pocket of the white ski jacket. How had she missed the rose? She plucked the intrusive red flower and examined it, suddenly realizing today was their wedding anniversary.

Oh great, I murdered my husband on our anniversary.

She frowned, relying upon her Botox to squelch the fine lines and crow's feet before her facial muscles attempted to create them. "A rose is so very fitting," she whispered. "I hate roses as much as I detest dogs."

Batting her eyes, Claire raised the rose to her nose and inhaled the sweetness of a long-suffering variety of love—Sheldon's love for her. *Love is patient. Love is kind. Love does not puff itself up.* She ruminated on the fading Sunday School lesson of her childhood.

It hadn't been her fault. Sheldon's skiing accident had changed everything between them. Slowly, Claire rested her hand across her belly. Before his accident, she'd gotten pregnant twice, miscarrying both babies.

Her empty womb and then empty bed had ignited a loathsome grief and silent rage. Love. A propellant toward happiness for some, and a torture chamber for others.

Don't be ugly.

Show some decency, Claire.

She dropped to her hands and knees, spooking powdery snow off Earth's face and revealing the ice beneath. Claire raked the snow to one side, creating an infant-sized grave where she buried the rose, the evidence of Sheldon's long-suffering love, next to his broken body.

"It's bedtime." She turned her back on the grave, then threw his favorite wool blanket, bought from a Hopi woman in Sedona, over the snowy corpse before rolling him up. She looked around.

Where was that shape? Was someone coming?

Her back aching, Claire dragged the concealed corpse onto the sled attached to her snowmobile, then tied him down, crisscrossing the ropes and securing knots. She donned her goggles, mounted her snowmobile, then revved the engine. Relying upon the howl of mournful winds to hide her as she disappeared into the blizzard, she weaved her way toward the bunker, using a compass as her guide.

The Raven would find the lure later this week.

Spook—the Raven's Belgian Malinois—would likely sniff out his president's corpse in record time.

And when he surfaced with the body of her dead husband, two questions would demand answers: Who killed the American president? And why was a dead American president's corpse found in a shallow grave next to the wartime bunker of Russia's president?

Asher's billion-dollar Sky Media would break the story first, fanning the flames on social media, cable news, and other hawkish digital information channels.

A dead former American president found in Siberia after Russia's president invaded a neighboring country: two ingredients that would surely serve up World War Three.

While Earth's low IQ squirrels—humans—devoured the "news," Claire would board Asher's spaceship and fly away to the Hive. Inside any respectable hive, the worker bees must preserve the queen so that she may be ready for Phase Two—procreation. The act was heaven on Earth for Claire.

The skids of her snowmobile threaded fresh snow behind her as she glided across the frozen lake, shooting a tail of white ash as she hummed the old gospel hymn, "I'll Fly Away."

A crack, followed by a thunderous clap.

Claire's snowmobile shuddered.

She knew what was happening. *Don't look back!*

Another clap, followed by more shaking. *Would the ice hold?* Claire tightened her grip on the handlebars. Accelerating into the blizzard, she refused to dab at the rivulet of sweat trickling down her face.

Dread settled into Claire's shoulders as the ice shifted and screamed. She wanted to dump the body, but the Raven must be allowed to find the corpse, setting off a precise chain reaction of her design.

Claire killed the engine, then dismounted—stiff, slow, cautious as to not further disturb the ice. She trudged to the back of her snowmobile, then bent down and peeled back the Hopi blanket.

Blond! That can't be. The dead man's hair was blond, not tinsel gray. She quickly replayed the events of the last hour in her mind.

The blizzard. Snow tossed into her face, temporarily blinding her. The snow partially covering the body, and her distraction while rolling him up. Who was this man wrapped in Sheldon's Hopi blanket? She flipped the murder victim onto his back to look at his face. She gasped. "No! Sheldon, what have you done!"

This was bad, extremely bad. Claire Amilee Underwood Covington had murdered the president of Russia.

Sheldon was alive. But where was he? She looked around the immediate surroundings as if he might be there. She began to turn her snowmobile back to where she'd come from but realized that was a stupid idea.

The frozen lake released a thundering crack, and an icy gash formed in front of her. She mounted the snowmobile, accelerated, then swerved, backtracking for a short distance. She turned again, applied the gas, gained speed, then launched over the Faultline.

As she drove, snow continued to fall around her, softer now, cloaking Asher's Sparrow. She'd been somewhat of a robot, responding to her trigger—the event drilled into a Sparrow's brain by their teacher during the brainwashing period.

And when the trigger conditions were activated, that forced the Sparrow to complete her mission.

Russia's army invading Ukraine was the trigger. But the wrong man was dead—or was it the right one? The shadow of the man walking toward her and Sheldon must have been the Russian president.

But why was he here, visiting her husband as he innocently ice fished in Russia?

Who had sent the president of Russia to this ice fishing location, knowing that Claire and her husband would be there? The CIA? Russian intelligence? Had Asher doubled-crossed her?

"Sheldon, you are a viper." Something animalistic and sensual rose from her gut, consuming her. "Where are you?"

The soft blowing thundered in the distance. *That's not the wind!* The whine of engines penetrated the mewling of blizzard winds. They were coming for her. But who were *they*?

The CIA?

The storm was dying, and so would she if she didn't think fast. Claire gunned the engine, hoping the fuel would last until she had time to stop and refill the tank from the two plastic cannisters attached to her getaway vehicle.

"Help me," she prayed.

But why would God listen to the prayers of a devil's wife? So she bargained with God instead.

Russia's president massacred the innocent people of Ukraine.

An eye for an eye . . . he deserved to die. Besides Ukraine's president is Jewish. Shouldn't I get a free pass? Don't you bless those who bless Abraham . . . and his seed?

31—Legna

A Cosmic Revolution
Immortals—Time without End
03:47 p.m., Sunday, February 4, 2024
Siberia

IN SIBERIA'S SNOWY TUNDRA, CILLIAN sacrificed himself to give Ben, Sakura, and Spook a head start, a second chance. The Russian president's spies had captured Wraith—but not his dog and his team. Success.

Well, a story usually begins as it means to end.

Legna would take care of this one himself. After he secures Daniela's future heartsong, he will arrive in Ellesmere and join Daniela, where she is waiting after that little church fire in small-town America.

Legna isn't God, so he's not omnipresent—present in all places simultaneously.

Cillian is free . . . for now.

With Legna's help, Spook found his master beaten to a pulp, then guided him out of the underground maze of tunnels buried beneath the Siberian winter desert. *He gets into more scrapes than a baker's spatula—but any man determined to protect his family can and does.* Legna laughs on the inside. And as Legna distracted the two sadist guards, Cillian had made his way to the lighthouse—Ireland's Teardrop. His attention is needed there before jet-setting off to the Hive, where the husband and father would prepare a Claire-proof safe place for his daughter and his wife.

His wife—his Daniela—and her present condition . . . well, *faith is the substance of things hoped for, the evidence of things not yet seen.* Cillian would have to sneak his wife and daughter into The Hive. Claire had not invited them.

As for Daniela's illness. Yes, Legna's Master could raise the dead. He raised Yeshua from the grave, didn't He?

The two goons holding Cillian are still inside the dungeon that now holds Legna. Foul water seeps through the stone ceiling of the dungeon, dripping and then gathering into pools of stagnant and mosquito-infested water. A fire in a blackened stone hearth builds in stature and releases a diminutive roar. A steel door featuring a small window is meant to block prisoners' escape.

Legna slouches in Cillian's chair—the hot seat, literally. The sadists have tied his arms to the chair arms, then chained his legs to the legs of the metal chair bolted to the blood-stained concrete floor.

He glances at a clock nailed to the opposite wall as though torture has a time limit. Cillian needs at least a two-hour lead. He could keep these two busy. He inhales slowly, then exhales.

The fireplace roars behind Legna's captor.

The man Legna had mentally nicknamed Beanstalk sits

quietly in the corner smoking. He's the one who had tied Legna's arms to the chair.

"The dog rescued the soldier sitting in your seat seconds before I was to move on to those—my favorite." The greasy-faced man who had chained Legna's legs points at a pair of rusty, blood-caked pliers. "I just had finished using the tie rods, gave him a good beating. By the looks of his back, someone had already cast a bit of fury on him long before I did. Then the dog came, killing that guy." Greasy Face points to a bloated corpse. "Then, you came out of nowhere and spoiled the fun . . . but now, I'm going to spoil you, boy."

"If you must." Legna shrugs.

The accent's thick with . . . Eastern European? Legna studies the soot-stained red brick ceiling. *Russian maybe?* "What kind of dog?"

"A Belgian Malinois." Greasy Face circles Legna. "It was in the nick of time, as the Americans say." He shakes his head. "That beast broke in here, chewed through the plastic arm ties, retrieved the keys to the chains, and took him. Not only did that brute murder our president, but he also has the Bat Creek Stone. We need it, and that pale ghost knows where it is. And I'm guessing you know him since you came to rescue him, so I'm going to help you talk. And then I'm going to cut your tongue out."

Legna stays silent.

"How the heck that dog with its wounded back leg got inside this dungeon—three subterranean floors beneath the Russian winter—it's a mystery more elusive than the Bat Creek Stone."

Legna smiles, then asks another question—nothing more than a distraction. "The Bat Creek Stone?" Legna inquires. "How do you know about that?"

"None of your business," Greasy Face says.

"He's going to die anyways, Vlad," Beanstalk adds. "If you'd like to know, we found out about the Bat Creek Stone and its power to give second chances from Claire Amilee, one of Bushcroft's Sparrows—"

"And America's First Lady." Legna sneers. *Classic Claire Amilee.* "Would you like to share the details?" He laces his voice with a sardonic tone.

"No—don't tell him." Metal slaps against metal as Vlad, the torturer, prepares his tools.

"You're too paranoid, Vlad. Finish heating your gadgets. I have a different interrogation method—good cops, bad cops as, the Americans say. You see, strange man, America must be destroyed for the Mother Russia to take its rightful place," Beanstalk states matter of fact. "And the Bat Creek Stone being returned to Mound Three could give America a second chance. Six-six-six cannot allow that to happen—right?"

"If you say so." Legna nods.

The fire crackles and pops. Smoke rises, filling the room with soot and carbon monoxide, yet refusing to burn Legna's eyes. He forces his eyes not to change colors—not yet. "His name's Spook."

"Whose?"

"Who do you think?" Legna fires back.

"The vampire-pale guy we tortured before you?" Vlad asks then stumbles, barely standing in front of his captive. He reeks of must and stale liquor. *The humans stink—death warmed over!* Legna thinks as he scrunches his nose.

"Please pay attention—"

"Me. Listen to you? Why? You're the blackie strapped to a metal chair—my special chair." Greasy Face spits up flecks of tobacco-stained spit.

Humans, so filthy, Legna thinks then says, "If you had paid attention, you would notice I was answering your former question, telling you the dog's name."

"We didn't ask," Vlad says.

Quickly, Legna closes his eyes, visualizing his other charge, Daniela Rose, she was just fine. Besides, she had a lesson to learn, and if he ran to her side too early, he would only be in the way of her learning that valuable lesson.

So he focuses his efforts on protecting her heartsong—her oily boy's future.

Before the funeral, Daniela had prayed to one day meet her heartsong. And Yahweh had answered that prayer, sending Legna into Daniela's heartsong's future to, let's just say, clean out the cobwebs.

In Legna's world, time isn't divided into the past, the present, and the future.

Time just is.

But the warrior angel required permission to defy time from the One who was timeless—the one Who had no created beginning or ending like His creation. This timeless one's name is I AM, Yahweh.

YHVH usually granted permission—anything for His little darling Rosebud. Legna smiles.

"You happy about something?" Vlad challenges

"No. Just breathing." Legna inhales, knowing that the letters of Adonai Yahweh, YHVH, represent breathing sounds. Also known as aspirated consonants.

When YHVH is pronounced without the intervening vowels of *a* and *e*, speaking God's name, YHVH, sounds like breathing—YH, inhale and VH, exhale.

A baby's first gasp for breath and then his first cry—an inhale and then exhale—speaks God's name.

The deep sigh of that baby's laboring mother calls His

name. A groan—an utterance too heavy for mere words, speaks God's name. Even an atheist, inhaling and exhaling, speaks God's name.

And when a person exhales their last breath, God's name no longer fills their lungs and they die, passing either to a place filled with God's presence—a place of eternal life where breath is no longer required—or a place void of it, a place where breath is suffocated.

Being alive means Legna is constantly speaking God's name, so he just breathes, recharging his power.

Keep the sadistic pair busy. Wraith is still on his way to the Lighthouse to stop the second part of Claire Amilee's plan—a second attempt on her husband's life.

"Who do you *zink* you are?" Beanstalk, the man in the corner, shoots up like a stalk of invading bamboo. "Where do you *zink* you are?" he demands again.

Another accent . . . German?

This human's is thick and guttural. "Wh" pronounced as a "V," and "th" pronounced "z" or "s."

Dressed in an old-fashioned SS uniform, the man raises a lit cigarette to his small mouth. The Russians and the Germans are working together—interesting. "Someone simply asking questions."

"We ask the questions. You insult us, yet you're the one strapped to a metal chair. Something to think about—ya!"

The way humans talk—the tone, timbre, and the use of letters—irritates Legna. "Where are you from?" Legna asks.

"I told you. We'll be asking the questions, ya! Thank you kindly." Beanstalk wilts back into his chair. Spring must be over. Winter's coming. Legna clenches then releases his fists.

But the questioner never asks Legna his name as was delineated in the POW rules: name, rank, etcetera.

Too bad. Maybe he could have lived in the end. "If this

chair's yours, sir, please be my guest and take it back." Legna hadn't quite finished playing with the pair.

Didn't matter, because in a few moments, both would pay—one hundred percent interest add the principal, an eye for an eye, a tooth for a tooth, and a scream for a scream—all for hurting Daniela's heartsong, Cillian, Legna's competition, if romance between Daniela and Legna were even possible.

It isn't.

"You're going to be sorry, blackie," the Russian taunts. *Blackie.* Humans and their incessant obsession with melanocytes. If only they knew.

"I am? For what, pray tell?" Legna shrugs. "Because I haven't done anything—yet." He glances over his shoulder, studying the Russian.

Legna closes his eyes. Is his Master awake and watching his number one in a lineup of seven warrior-agents?

Always.

Okay then . . . Legna smiles—bashful, lip upturned, looking sexy as heck.

The agent nods, surrendering to greatness and the thorough hurting of the German and the Russian—payback, she's not a female dog.

It's Legna, and others like him.

"For He will give his angels charge over us to keep us . . ." Legna recites the Psalms whispered by the man who'd sat in this chair before him as he'd endured the pain until his wife's prayers had touched the heart of heaven on his behalf. Legna was that answer to these broken prayers.

He'd led Spook to his owner's side.

"They've both asked for what's coming, Elohim."

"Yes—they have," the Master whispers into Legna's ear and calms the road-tested warrior. Focusing on his breathing, Legna tucks his lips between his teeth, erasing the grin that's so determined to pop up despite these morbid circumstances.

"Who are you talking to? And what's so funny?" The Russian's beady, pale eyes, lost in his Vodka-puffy face, lock on Legna.

"Not anyone you know."

"Are you praying, blackie?" He belches out a belly full of laughter. "Begging to something unseen to rescue you?"

"Of course I am."

"God doesn't live here, blackie."

"Oh, but He does." Legna breathes in deep, then pours a cup of patronization into his voice. "He's omnipresent, Einstein—which means He's everywhere all the time."

"You think you're so smart." The Russian's laser-blue eyes cut into Legna's face. He prepares his tools in the same way he seems to prepare his appearance, sloppy. Metal clanks against metal—a sledgehammer, knives, a long iron poker, and those bloody pliers.

"Getting down to business, now." Beanstalk eases from his chair.

"Name?" Greasy Face asks.

"Legna. Yours?"

"Vladimir. Surname, Legna?" The beefy, red-faced man named Vlad glances back, his beady eyes peering over the short slant of his thick slab of a shoulder. "We'd like to get to know you a bit more. Wouldn't we, Fritz?"

The man occupying the dry corner of the cave nods. Vlad laughs, as every fool does before he dies, his beer belly heaving as he mocks his lone captive.

"X." Legna shrugs.

"Are you a relative of the famed Malcolm X, comrade?" Vlad taunts Legna.

"Not likely." The man sitting in the corner crosses his right leg over his left. "He's dead, you know." He tilts his head back, inhales and exhales. A stream of smoke adds to the ripe odors freely roaming inside the dungeon.

Humans, still smoking.

Vlad turns his pokers over the fire as though he's roasting a pig. Legna bites his lower lip, containing his mirth. "Malcolm X is too young to be my brother."

"Are you mocking us, again?" Fritz tilts his head to the left as though his head position could possibly lighten the density of his brain. "Vlad, he laughs at us—no?"

Vlad spins around on his boot heels, his grimy shirt crumpling in the creases of his hypertrophied muscles. He stomps over to a rickety table and palms a clouded glass, tossing back his fifth shot of vodka, the Russian's Pervitin.

After removing one white-hot poker, he tosses his chosen instrument of torture to the floor at Legna's feet.

"Sterilizing your instruments with fire and your brain cells with alcohol—clever. I imagine the instruments will still perform their duty, but your brain cells, not so much. Will you remember anything I tell you?"

From his dark corner, the Nazi-wannabe speaks. "Legna, these are the charges I have against you: you have not respected the Geneva Convention. It demands that you give us your last name, too."

"From the appearance of Vlad's tools, I can only imagine that neither of you plan to honor the Third Geneva Convention, comrades."

"Rank?" Fritz stamps his right foot into the concrete.

"Of the third order."

"What? I've never heard of that rank in the American army. Third order of what branch?" Spit flies out of Fritz's cancer-laden mouth.

"Special ops, I guess." Legna shrugs.

"You guess? You do not know?" Fritz wipes the back of his mouth on his shirt sleeve. "You will answer me truthfully. Tell me your serial number." Finally, Fritz suffocates the tip of his cigarette on the leg of his wooden chair. He stands and paces the room, his jackboots beating out Legna's death march.

"One." Legna lowers his gaze, fully aware that his eyes have turned—brightening from a rich midnight black to a shimmering violet accented with flecks of cobalt.

"Afraid of me now . . . ? Ah, as it should be." Fritz rotates his shoulders back and lifts them high. Leaving the poker on the floor, Vlad approaches Legna with a heated sledgehammer. The metal gleams orange, showing off its imperfections.

"And the purpose of the heat, Vlad?" Legna patronizes his captors, having already decided his next move.

"To stop the bleeding." Vlad grins. "Prolong the session. And if the metal's soft enough, it'll become one with your flesh and bone, and when I pull back, I'll rip your whole leg off." He pauses. "Are you ready, Legna?"

"I don't bleed, dear comrade." Legna clears his throat and clenches his fist.

"You will. Everyone does." Fritz towers over his captive, his breath stinking of tobacco and human.

"I'm not everyone." Legna levels his gaze, locking eyes with his imprisoner.

"Yes, you are, and in time, you will scream like a little boy crying for his mommy, just like every other captured soldier does once we've started our business here."

"I don't have a mother."

"Oh, poor boy. An orphan, too? Like the other one?"

Legna clenches his teeth, now annoyed with the endless

chatter. He had other matters to attend to, like Daniela and her second chance.

Vlad slams the sledgehammer into the floor, splintering blocks of concrete and disrupting the mosaic of human-made stains. That would usually get a man talking, but Legna is not a man.

"Still works, comrade."

So predictable. Legna rolls his eyes. Vlad slaps Legna across the face. The archangel grins. Finally . . . an action that authorizes Legna to react. A well-trained soldier follows Elohim's rules—don't make contact until the human does first.

"That pale one wasn't a very nice man." Vlad pauses. "A brown bear would have been kinder. He murdered the president of Russia. We found him in a snow cave."

"So your visit with my friend—it was personal?"

"It was, and then the dog came for him. Don't worry. After I finish with you, and you tell me what I need to know—starting with where the Bat Creek Stone is—then I'll find him again … and his dog. Dog meat is saltier than pig."

"You're wasting time breaking my bones and snatching my fingernails from the root, Vlad." He was delaying the real mission Vlad and Fritz had planned: to go to North Carolina, infiltrate the Cavanaugh-Finn's chalet's perimeter while the man of the house was occupied, and then take the Bat Creek Stone.

They don't know how to break through the security and get inside without setting off all the booby traps.

Cillian had told them nothing.

Legna sitting here is simply a delay tactic. He could have tied them up . . . but that wouldn't have been as fun.

"They tell me the special ops recruits last longer." A wicked grin slides across Vlad's bearded face. He grips his hammer, raises it above his shoulder, and lumbers toward his captive. His eyes carefully study Legna's lithe body, most likely contemplating something like crushing one of Legna's knees first. "I'm hoping they're correct."

Vlad lifts the hammer in both hands above his head, his face flooding with blood and sadistic anger.

"Don't know who *they* are." Legna slowly raises his gaze, leveling his cobalt-violet eyes at Vlad's. "But *they* are liars."

The torturer stumbles backward, confusion registering across his ugly face. Fritz slides forward . . . a bit too much, falling off the edge of his chair.

"I would use my classic introduction of 'do not be afraid,' like Gabriel, my comrade in arms, told the virgin Mary when he visited her on Earth. But to suggest to you two men that you shouldn't fear me would be . . . a lie, too."

"Who are you, blackie?" Fritz spits more than he talks.

Legna continues, "Elohim loathes lying as much as he hates pride." Legna looks at the trembling Nazi-wannabe, foam bubbling around the edge of his mouth. "Cyanide pill. Saves me the trouble."

Legna focuses his gaze on Vlad. "Before Fritz ate his lunch, he forgot to ask me my date of birth, telling me that Fritz is an actor—not a soldier. When a wannabe takes their cues from Hollywood . . . well, they always leave out that every POW must state their date of birth."

Fritz's body seizes, snaking up and down as he releases a bladder full of urine and a colon full of poop.

"What a sight." Legna wags his head. "It'll take him five minutes and twenty-six seconds to suffocate, then die. The movies never get a cyanide death right, either." He does nothing to hide the disdain in his expression. "Vlad, are you an actor, too?"

"I'm a low-level soldier just following the Kremlin's orders, comrade."

"That's what people like you always say when facing a court of moral men—but I'm not a man, in case you haven't guessed." Legna snaps the restraints around his arms and legs.

Fritz screeches as his sallow skin darkens to cyanotic blue. He reaches for his pistol—the coward's sidekick—pulls the trigger, firing off several rounds without the wit to aim at anything in particular.

Legna doesn't flinch or bother to move out of the way.

The bullets would never reach him or penetrate his body. His electromagnetic field protects him. One day, if Daniela fails to satisfy the Bat Creek Stone curse, and the Earth stops spinning, the humans will lose their electromagnetic field currently protecting them from the sun's solar flare. *Get back to Daniela and help her!* "So rude, Fritz. I never had a mother, but you did. And didn't your mother ever tell you, 'don't be rude, and do not forget to show hospitality to strangers, for by so doing, some people have shown hospitality to angels'?"

"Huh?" Vlad's sodden brain refuses to compute simple math.

"If you'd asked for my date of birth, I would have told you that I was with Elohim before the Earth was ever formed."

"You're older than the vampires."

"They don't exist, Vlad—that's pure Hollywood."

"You're a dead man." Vlad reaches for his sledgehammer and swings, missing Legna's knee by inches.

"But you see, I'm not a man. With a friendlier interrogation approach, you would have discovered that my name is Legna, and my species—is angel. But my given name is Raphael. And my surname is the Archangel."

"Serial number?"

"One of seven . . . archangels, that is."

"Rank?" Vlad's whole body is trembling as he brings the hammer down with all his might.

"Chief Archangel." Legna stands, the earth quaking beneath his feet, shaking the bolted chair loose from its metal fasteners.

He sheds his human figure—deep, almost black skin, a boyish face, and a close-cropped afro—and transforms into something otherworldly. His legs shine an onyx black, each shielded with bronze plates. Legna stops the hammer in midair and lifts his captor with it, his feet dangling. After a moment, he drops the man.

Vlad jumps down, scoots backward, then stumbles to his feet before he grabs a thick cloth from his minibar, runs to his fire, and grabs the second iron poker.

Legna spares the silly man any more embarrassment. He reaches out and palms the white-hot poker with his bare hands. "I'll take that."

He tosses the poker to the ground before grabbing Vlad by his shirt collar and pushing him into the chair. "Do you or anyone else know where the man you had before me is?"

"Gone—escaped," Vlad manages to spit out.

"Where to?"

"A lighthouse. We were torturing him, trying to find out if he had the Bat Creek Stone. He didn't talk, and he escaped after the dog came for him."

"Were you going after his wife?"

"Someone was, but not us." He glances at Beanstalk—indeed winter had come, and Beanstalk had died. "Not me!" Vlad vomits up everything he knows, including his dinner of pork, cabbage, and liquor. "Please." He raises his hands. "If you let me live, I-I-I will help you find the men going after his wife, the one they call the Orphan Dreamer."

The slobbering drunk knows who Daniela is—the Orphan Dreamer! Legna's blood runs cold. He narrows his eyes, partly hiding his violet-luminescent eyes.

"That won't be necessary. You will remain in your palatial home, keeping the fire stoked until I get back." Legna walks around the chair. Vlad nods, almost snapping his neck. "If you're lying to me, I'll show you what an archangel can do with his bare hands."

Vlad again vigorously nods.

So agreeable now! Legna eyes the man. "As for your career choice, Vlad. Do me a favor and take some night courses, or something, but stop torturing humans. Tighten up your resume, shave your face, stop drinking, then find another career before you join frothy mouth over there. Capisce?" Legna smiles as he quietly removes the thick door from its hinges and places it to the side.

"Okay. Whatever you say. Bu-bu-but I don't have money for college."

Legna reaches down in his pant pocket and removes a wad of hundred-dollar bills. "That'll get you started. Should exchange nicely." He flashes a smile at Vlad.

It's true. Elohim always gave his human children protection by His celestial creation—His angel army, so that Elohim's kids had the time to make change for the good of all while Elohim's warriors neutralized Satan's human agents and his Nephilim. Time—the balm of justice, allowing good to overcome evil.

"You helped me, so I'll give you one more piece of advice, Vlad. If you can't hack college, become a pig man. You're good at roasting things." The chief archangel ducks beneath the seven-foot opening and disappears into the bowels of the dungeon's tunnels.

He swaggers down the dim, dank hallways, bare bulbs struggling to make their presence known, just like the movies. Soldiers scatter left and right to get out of his way.

"Cillian," he whispers, knowing who Cillian will run into at the Lighthouse—Cillian's devil, a man who had more things in common with him than he knew. "I'm coming, Cillian. Stay strong. Rosebud has prayed for you. She's prayed for many. Polly. Claire. And Emmaline."

What's in a name—a mission, and a legacy?

Legna, a-n-g-e-l.

32—The Orphan

08:01 p.m., Sunday, March 2, 2024
Atlantic Ocean

BENEATH A NIGHT SKY FULLY stocked with stars, deep and dark and cold, the Atlantic Ocean had buried the sun inside its back pocket—the temporary graveyard for nighttime celestial bodies during daylight hours.

Cillian Finn—code name Wraith—abandoned his one-man submarine. He tethered his escape route to the base of the lighthouse before climbing up Ireland's Teardrop to meet the devil incarnate's husband—Sheldon Covington, the President of the United States of America.

Spook tracked ahead, scouting for booby traps and danger.

Ireland's Teardrop—a lighthouse and the final view of the Emerald Isle by 19th-century Irish immigrants escaping the Irish famine. Constructed of granite, the lighthouse was fastened onto rock in the middle of the Atlantic Ocean.

Black waves crashed, lashing granite and rock while reaching up to yank Wraith into its dark depths.

The steel threads interwoven into his muscular frame rippled beneath his wet suit. He moved quietly, each step precise as he stepped out of the ocean as though he were the twin brother of the famed Nephilim—Poseidon, a sea god.

The Irish and the Scottish: these were Cillian's people.

Forbidden to eat their own potatoes.

Irish. English.

Mongolians. Africans.

Asians. Middle Eastern.

Europeans. Indigenous populations.

People.

Inhumanity. The shock and awe of what a human could do to another human—regular folks, not the infamous tyrants of the world.

Darkness was dark until the Light overcame it.

Out of the ocean and up the granite steps of the remote lighthouse in less than a minute, Wraith paused at the top of an island that had been rightfully named *Carraig Aonair* in Wraith's ancestral language.

Carraig Aonair, the lonely rock.

The name was the embodiment of Cillian Finn.

Most days he was an island in the middle of a raging sea, defying the winds whipped up by politicians and other corrupt men who had engineered and manipulated financial, military, and political disasters.

He was a liar—a con man, conning the conners. They believed him to be an economic hitman, exacting their financial carnage of any corporate or national competitor.

In reality, he wasn't their man.

He was more of a janitor and a trashman of sorts. Wraith cleaned up their messes, tipping the world away from chaos and back toward order. And tonight, just before midnight, he was cleaning up the mess of another woman: Claire Amilee Underwood.

Claire was a Sparrow, just as Cillian was a Raven. It's true: a raven was a beautiful bird, but his face flushed with the shame of his youth.

He clenched his jaw, knowing his cleanup effort would protect the last remaining members of his family from Claire's diabolical plan of culling the herd through eugenics.

His service to her would ensure a spot for Daniela and Adelaide in The Hive, protecting his family from the horrors of the Tribulation spoken of in the last book of the Holy Book.

And the capstone of the Tribulation would be Armageddon.

Daniela was convinced that they, as Followers of the Way, would be taken—snatched up, raptured—before the Tribulation, but he couldn't be too careful.

Every man worth his salt prepared a safe future for his family. He had left without telling his wife or his last child where he was going. The assassin's work—his necessary profession and the payment for his freedom and the freedom of his little brother, Paul Ambrose Cole Hansen.

As fate would have it, atop Ireland's Teardrop, the Irish-Scotsman was going to do something cruel and inhumane to another human. His garrote was in his pocket, but he had decided to use his bare hands.

As a member of the ruthless secret ops group called the

Orphans—Sparrows and Ravens—he was used to using his hands.

Long ago, Wraith had made a vow: "Rosebud, I'll be givin' my life for yers, then, so if ye agree to marry me, ye'll ha' two hearts—mine and yers. *Trí na chéile a thógtar na cáisléain.*"

In our togetherness, castles are built.

33—The Orphan

08:01 p.m., Sunday, March 2, 2024
Celtic Sea

"WHY ARE YOU HERE?" WRAITH'S upper lip twisted into a feral snarl.

"You first, pretty boy." Asher Valerian Bushcroft cleared his throat. "Where's Natalia—my sister?" He toyed with the hilt of his knife.

"Gone," Cillian whispered.

"Where to?" Asher rubbed his thumb across the hilt of the knife as though he were spit polishing the matte black handle.

"Dinna know . . . I asked around at the Hive, and that was the agreement—I ask around, and you give my family a ticket into the Hive."

"Everyone needs a family." Bushcroft's fleeting glance from his knife to Wraith's face felt off. He'd never been a man to show a drop of shyness or trepidation.

"Even the cobra and the saltwater croc?" Wraith guffawed.

"Especially the cold-blooded animals like us."

"I'm not like you—never was, never will be."

"As I said . . . everyone needs a family—to know where he's from and . . . who he belongs to." Bushcroft's beautiful gray eyes changed tactics and rested upon the Orphan's equally handsome face.

"Don't look at me." Wraith's eyebrows furrowed into a V.

Asher's face softened. He smiled … and there was something else. Pride, an emotion Wraith had never witnessed from Asher while he looked upon the orphan. "You would have loved her, Cillian."

"Why?"

The slaver owner, media man, chairman of the Sons of Venus refused to answer the question except with an escaping tear that slipped down his handsome face. Bushcroft let the tear linger on his cheek. He wasn't ashamed to cry for his sister. "This . . ." Asher waved the knife around, forming a circle the roundness and size of a grapefruit. "Why I'm here is for our people—for the world. Hitler was an amateur in comparison to six-six-six."

"Our people?" Cillian shook his head. "We. Are. Not. From the same stock of people, Asher."

"At the mention of names such as Hitler or even six-six-six—the enemy your wife has been preparing to fight her entire life—you only focus on two words: our people."

"What's in a name—my name, Cillian Joseph Finn? Like Joseph, I was once a slave—your slave—but no longer . . ."

"Now, you're a prince of Egypt like the ancient Hebrew character in the Hebrew Scriptures? You—an orphan meeting with and advising the President of the United States of

America. The cream does rise, but where did the cream come from?"

Confusion raised Cillian's right eyebrow, destroying his poker face.

"Yes—I've read the Holy Book, too. Thought I might handle Daniela Rose more effectively if I did."

"If you and your Sons of Venus touch my Daniela—"

"You've misunderstood the purpose of the Sons of Venus." Asher raised his hand to brace himself against the rising headwinds.

"I've seen what the Sons of Venus have done to people and places, Asher."

"No—you've seen what Ravens like yourself and Sparrows like Claire have done. You've done the work—not me."

"By your command!" Cillian stepped forward, seemingly setting off an earthquake beneath his tired but determined feet.

"You're a man now with an independent will, and you've chosen how to use your free will, no different than me. Yes, I abused you. I battered you. I and others violated you, stealing your innocence . . ." His voice trailed off as though he might apologize. Instead, he asked, "Are you six-six-six, Cillian? Are you the promised anti-messiah who will bring tyranny and misery to the world?"

"Who is this six-six-six?" Cillian replied.

"Your Daniela Rose has never told you about the antichrist? That's hard for me to believe. Besides, don't you read the Bible now?" Asher flipped the blade into its sheath, setting the business of killing aside . . . for now.

"My relationship with God is none of yer business."

"Fine. Well, Sheldon Covington is upstairs." Bushcroft gestured to the spiral staircase. "Shall we go up?"

Cillian nodded. "You first."

Asher plodded up the steps ahead of Cillian. "Remember this: Time tells all secrets, and she tells no lies. America didn't let us in—but China did. That's why Claire did what she did."

"Us?"

"The Aniyvwiya—the ancient Israelites . . . the Jewish people?"

"I'm not Jewish. I'm a follower of Yeshua."

"By faith, but not by DNA. You wouldn't survive one second in Nazi Germany with your ethnic ancestry—my family almost didn't. We had to get out."

"As I said, we are not from the same stock, Asher."

"Every man is a liar, first to himself." Asher paused his ascent up the stairs and steadied a glance over his shoulder, like a sniper steadying his rifle.

"No—I'm not a deceiver, like you. I know who I am, and ye'll not be definin' me any longer. And as for Natalia, yer precious sister, she's not in the Hive." Wraith smirked. "But you'll never find her. She doesn't want to be found by you. You murdered her—your own sister, Asher."

"You'll tell me where she is!" Asher turned and lunged at Cillian, but the Orphan quickly pinned him to a stone wall.

"Tell me this: what do you know about Claire Amilee?"

"She's a Sparrow trained by me . . . by you."

"I dinna know her verra well."

"But you do know her . . . Mongolia—remember? She trained alongside of you. Of course you remember her, her hair . . . she was shorn like a lamb the first time you met her."

The light bulb flicked on. Guilty as charged. Cillian averted Wraith's menacing glare and released his grip on the man.

Wraith had known his wife's nemesis in a way he never wanted his Daniela Rose to find out about.

A satisfied grin spread across Asher's face. "You see? I'm not the only liar standing in the entrance of this lighthouse." Asher swung a hand dramatically, gesturing to the stone walls. "The Orphans call you Wraith . . . are you a ghost, Cillian?" Asher taunted.

"Part of me." Glaring at the backside of the ghost of his past, Wraith tightened his jaw. The pale skin overlying his chiseled jawline quivered—ripples of a lone wave crossing the Irish sea. He fought to not kill the man. "The part I want to forget."

Pray for your enemies, Daniela had read from the Holy Book. That was overkill when his enemy was Death and Misery incarnate.

"Which part?" Sneering, the small man looked Cillian up, then down. "All of you is beautiful." He turned, and beneath the ghoulish-yellow glow of the rotating lamp of the lighthouse, Asher licked his lips.

"The part you and yer kind touched without my permission."

"That's most of you, Cillian." Bushcroft shrugged. "Did you keep it—the brand?" Now standing three steps above Cillian and towering over the orphan, Bushcroft gestured below Cillian's waistline with a wave of smoke emanating from the tip of the cigar.

"Why do you care?" Wraith clenched his fists into hammers as a wave of nausea threatened to topple him down the lighthouse stairs.

"Maybe I'm sorry for it? That's all." Bushcroft cleared his throat.

"Is that a question? Because I couldna be knowin' the answer, then. Are ye sayin' sorry?"

Bushcroft curtly nodded. Concessions weren't his thing.

"Why d'ye do it, then, Bushcroft?" The Celtic Sea raged

beyond the stone walls of the lighthouse. Damp cold seeped beneath Cillian's dry clothes.

"It wasn't me."

Bushcroft's Texas drawl had never fit the posh, little man, Wraith thought.

"It was the others."

"Ye never take responsibility for anything. Yer not worth the air yer breathing."

"Look if you must know who . . . look to your wife's childhood bully, Claire Amilee. And if you must know why she did it—the decision was somewhat out of her hands. As I said, America didn't let us in, but China did." Bushcroft turned away from the ghost of his past, concealing his emotions, then kept climbing to the one person saving his life in this moment—the president.

Stopping to stand in front of an oddly placed mirror in the middle of the 360-degree staircase, Bushcroft fake-straightened the fuchsia-pink silk tie hidden beneath his ash gray cashmere sweater.

Not a good choice of threads for floating out to sea.

How could the man stand to look at himself? Even the blind rats must be scattering. Cillian's lip upturned into a righteous sneer, disgusted at the small-minded man dimly reflected in the floor-length mirror yet somehow still commanding this space.

Then, he noticed it—the pursed lips, that gasps, the audible wheezes. Bushcroft was using the fashion stop to rest—an excuse to catch his breath. *Smoker's lungs. Make him talk. Make him wheeze. Make him beg for breath.* "Who's *us?*" Cillian pressed his left thumb into the non-sharpened edge of the Smith and Wesson tanto blade and closed the gap between them.

He'd waited long enough.

Earth had enough demons running amuck . . . minus one. "I'll be the ruthless one," he had whispered to his Daniela before making love to her the last time, "pushing back the darkness so ye can be kind. Earth will be balanced, rotating on its axis because of your compassion, Daniela, *a rún mo chroí*—secret of my heart. Trust me, *mo nighean donn.*"

"You're wanting to listen to truth, now?"

"Who's *us?*"

"Us . . . are my ancestors—and yours, too." Bushcroft raised his chin.

Cillian stepped back as Bushcroft admired the reflection of the man now standing behind him. "I was always afraid of falling down the stairs and breaking my neck, then dying a slow death."

"I'll not let ye fall."

Bushcroft smiled. "Reassuring. But before you do that to me." He glanced at the reflection of Wraith's knife. "Listen to me."

"Talk fast. In five more minutes, I'll be late to meet the president." Wraith clutched the hilt of the knife even tighter until the blood left his hand, blanching his skin a hue of anemic gray.

"I-I-I wasn't always this way, you know."

"I wouldna know."

"I was a little boy once, too."

"And?"

"I had to become hard in order to survive." Bushcroft's features rose and fell to match the inflection of his words.

"Yer lyin' to both of us. Ye made a choice, and choices ha' consequences."

"No—I didn't make a choice that night—the night that shaped me into who I am . . . Cillian, the Nazi's trains wouldn't run on the Russian's tracks, and this fact saved us."

The slight tilt of Wraith's head would be missed by most, but not by Bushcroft.

"It's okay to be curious. Like me, you're an intellectual more than you're a brute. That's why I chose you—followed you, captured you, then trained you. As for the German trains not running on Russian tracks—this saved my people—our people."

"For the last time Bushcroft, I'm not *yer* people."

"You're an orphan . . . how would you know who your people are, Cillian?" Bushcroft pronounced Cillian's name Ki-lee-an instead of Sih-lee-an.

The way Bushcroft pronounced his name . . . had Cillian been born to become a killer? "I'm not like you," Cillian whispered, unsure of himself now.

"You murder people, and so do I, but the Aniyvwiya—*the real people, our people*—didn't deserve what they got. They lived in Mongolia by way of Judea before their arrival to Loudon, Tennessee. That's where you're going next, right? Tennessee?"

Cillian swallowed.

"Listen to me." Bushcroft began to tell a story about his family trapped inside the Nazi's death grip . . .

34—Asher

Tuesday
December 24, 1940
Berlin, Germany

YOUR TRAINS WON'T RUN ON our tracks—seven words and a life raft that would save Asher Valerian Bushcroft and his family in the shipwreck that was 1940s Berlin, Germany. But saving the life of a future miscreant carried its own consequences. Redemption—that Christmas message of second chances. It resonated throughout the ages, breathing hope and joy into the darkness of Nazi Germany while shrouding a Jewish family trapped in Berlin—Asher's family. And as long as Asher Bushcroft took breath, he too possessed an opportunity for redemption.

Draped around the evergreen branches of the Bushcroft family's balsam fir, dainty, white Christmas lights glittered brighter than the Milky Way—evidence of the family's attempts at assimilation into Germany's gentile culture.

But assimilation never could completely protect an outsider from the violent whims of a mob hyped-up on Pervitin—the methamphetamine pill was freely prescribed to German soldiers and private citizens during the rise of Nazism.

Earthy scents of pine mixed with cinnamon sticks permeated the family's two-bedroom, second-floor flat. Eleven-year-old Asher curled his upper lip to his nostrils, creating a flap of flesh that filtered out the noxious odors of cinnamon and pine. Asher detested Christmas and its smells, especially this year.

A pool of emotion formed on the lower rims of his eyelids as he stood at the door of the small bedroom and watched his father. Ryland Bushcroft paced from one end of the ten-by-ten boxy, dimly lit bedroom Asher shared with his older sister. Faded paisley bedspreads were tucked in neatly at the edges of the metal-framed twin bed.

Ryland ripped his children's clothes from one dresser, depositing brand-new shirts, sweaters, and drab wool pants into two open suitcases. Asher's father's black, knee-high boots thudded across ash wood floorboards, mimicking the bass lick of an eerie musical death march. Sweat poured down the handsome man's temples. He unbuttoned the jacket of his ink-black SS uniform, revealing a soaked undershirt.

He never stopped packing.

"Papa," Asher dared to ask, startling his singularly focused father. "Where are we going?"

"If we're lucky . . . away."

"Should I tell Natalia we're leaving?"

"She'll find out, Vale." When Asher's father was beyond anxious, he called his only son a shortened version of his middle name, Valerian. The boy hated the nickname as much as he hated Christmas.

Grinding his molars, he forcefully separated his teeth and blew onion breath from his nostrils.

"Life doesn't give you everything you want, son," his father said after noting his ire.

"Should I take what I want, then?"

"Not always the best idea either. Look at the Nazis drugged on Pervitin—not how a model citizen of the world should live, right?"

"What's Pervitin, Papa?"

"Methamphetamine."

"Is that something bad?"

"Makes your mind plum crazy and renders your heart colder than an iceberg. Rots your teeth out, too." Ryland peeled back his cheeks, revealing his full mouth of yellowed chompers. Asher laughed. "Why do you think Hitler and his henchman have teeth blacker than my uniform?" his father asked.

"Because they are devils."

"That, too."

"Yes, Papa."

"No matter what, don't you forget that these Nazis are not superior to anyone. They're pigs, willing to do what another human isn't willing to do, and they're drugged foul animals with no good judgment. Don't play with pigs— they have fun, but you get dirty. And except for tonight—in Adonai's righteous name—vow to never eat the flesh of a pig."

"I promise."

"Good boy." Asher's father rubbed his curly coif like a well-behaved dog.

"Are we Nazis, papa?" Asher pointed at his father's costume.

"No—never." Averting his eyes from Asher's gaze, Ryland dabbed his forehead with a white handkerchief.

"Okay, Papa." Asher forced himself to smile, painting a lie onto the poster of an innocent face. "How do I get what I want from the world?"

"What do you want from the world?"

"The permission to pursue life, liberty, and happiness?"

"Ah, then. That's easy—easier wished for than done. You'll go to America and dream the American Dream."

"Does America allow Jewish boys to dream, too?"

"In time . . . and until then, we'll become as one of them and change our last name."

"I'm Asher Bushcroft. Let the Americans get used to it."

"It's our job, Vale, to shield Natalia and protect her, allowing her to see the world as she wishes . . . full of daffodils, music, and butterflies. And sometimes, we men must eat a bit of crow to do so. Did you know our last name isn't Bushcroft?"

"What is it, then?"

"Our original last name is Rothschild."

"Rothschild," the boy repeated. "What does that mean?"

"Red shield."

"That's boring."

"But clever. I'll tell you the story one day. Your ancestor is Mayer Amschel Rothschild." Asher Valerian Rothschild's father rested his slender fingers on his son's thin shoulders. His father's face darkened. "I'll make this up to you, son."

"It's okay, Papa. I'm going to America to dream."

"How about we celebrate your twelfth birthday in America?"

Asher nodded, not thrilled with the idea of traveling through Nazi Germany but loving the idea of escaping the brown-shirt thugs who roamed Berlin's streets day and night, looking for Jews.

The small boy glanced down at his feet. Even amid a Christmas winter, Asher had been blessed with a summertime pair of feet—feet eager to run, eager to escape World War Two Germany. High heels tapped across wood floors, breaking Asher's daydream into pieces and sending a chill down his small shoulders.

His mother stormed into the children's room and pushed past her son. She looked her husband up and down, never taking the time to hide her disapproving sneer. "Why is your uniform unbuttoned, Reuben?"

"We're leaving."

"Reuben, the ball's tonight, and we've been invited." Reuben was his father's real name, but Germans who weren't Jewish called him Ryland. Only Asher's mother called him Reuben, as though she truly wished her husband dead. Maybe she did?

Secretly, Asher hated his mother for her contempt of his father.

She sucked another drag from her cigarette as she tapped her crimson-red painted nails on the doorframe. *When will the cancer stick finally kill her?* A son who wished his mother dead; what species of animal was he?

"Listen to me carefully, Reuben."

"Stop. Calling. Me. Reuben!" he quietly demanded through gritted teeth.

"It's your name. Isn't it? Its Hebrew meaning—in case you forgot—is behold, a son." She paused, disrespect gloating across her pale face. "More like, behold a coward." A simpering smile seemed to never leave her impetuous facial expression. "You're one of them—always have been." She chuckled as she pointed at his uniform.

"You know why I wear this uniform."

"Do I? Does your son?" She pranced to her son's side and rested her cigarette-free hand on Asher's left shoulder. He pulled away, and his mother pummeled his backside with ten hard slaps. "Don't you ever, Vale!" she seethed.

Asher Valerian stared at his mother, unblinking. His mother looked away, her body trembling, and Asher smiled on the inside.

"Would you throw a winter's dance if they executed me?" Ryland glared at his bride, but she refused to respond. "And what about the children—would you dance on their graves, too? Is that your sole purpose in life, to snuff the Bushcroft name from the face of the earth?"

"Rothschild was your name, and it meant something. I, too, bear the burden of your name, Reuben."

"The burden? . . . Figures. The last name 'Bushcroft' should have been a relief to you. It saved you from the Jewish ghetto where the rest of your family barely exists." Ryland continued his frantic pace, yanking open the closet door and grabbing Asher's favorite sweater. "Here, son. Wear this tonight. It's cold outside."

"Thank you, Papa."

"Now get dressed, Asher. Warm trousers, an undershirt, thermal underpants, and that sweater under your coat." Ryland paused and faced his disapproving wife. "If you could be so kind and find a sliver of time to help save the lives of your own children, I would appreciate your assistance, as then I would not be required to run around like a baboon in heat."

"Don't be overly emotional."

"If I could lend you a drop of empathy." Ryland yawned, but his wife didn't—and neither did his son.

"I will not leave Germany, Reuben." Asher's mother crossed her arms. "This is my home. I'm somebody in Germany."

"As long as they do not know who you really are. I've protected you from too much of our reality—the truth. You're deceived, choosing to believe a lie. You *are* something in Germany: as good as dead."

"I know what's going on."

"Do you?"

"I'm smart, too." *The cry of an insecure, ill-informed woman.*

"I see what you read; propaganda."

"I'm informed."

"No, you're not."

"Do not judge me."

"Because your favorite newspapers and magazines have pretty pictures, you believe what they've written." Ryland approached his wife but stopped five feet short. "Stupid. Stupid. Stupid woman. Living in a world of lies." Ryland's voice raised a half-octave. "I should grant you your wish. I should leave the daughter of Aaron Goldman and take the children with me to America. The only reason we were able to secure papers to leave this hell-hole country is because I. Am. A. Rothschild."

Natalia waltzed into the bedroom, sucking on a Christmas candy as she made her way to her little brother's side. "Mother? Father, what's going on?"

They both ignored their daughter. Asher's father glanced at his two children, his expression registering hopelessness. Panic. Fear.

"Mom? Dad?" Natalia repeated. "Where are you going with those suitcases?"

"Tell them, Reuben." Their mother smirked. "He's running. Your father's a coward, scared of his own shadow."

"A child needs their mother, and this simple fact alone is going to save your vain life from a gas chamber, woman."

"Greta says the rumors about the gas chambers are false."

"Greta? Since when has the neighborhood numbskull gossip become the treasure trove of reliable information?"

"Come, come . . . you've got a fine job. Even been promoted—"

"Is that what you call it? A fine job? A promotion? I. Am. Death." Each word extracted a stream of spit from Ryland's mouth and set it flying in all directions.

If they'd been Catholic, maybe the streams of spit could have been substituted for a delayed baptism. Asher giggled.

"No giggling from you, child!" His mother swung her hips as she sauntered closer to her husband. He stepped back, and her lips curled into a snarl.

Ryland braved a response. "The fine job, as you call it . . . it is no more than survival for my family—my children, my legacy."

"You've never wanted me to be happy."

"I've risked my life to keep you safe, which is better than happy, and all of this was done while I committed unspeakable atrocities against our own people!" he hissed.

"Papa, you've hurt people?" Natalia asked, her innocence striking a visceral chord, her voice angelic in every way. Tears formed in Ryland's eyes.

"And we've been rewarded for your hard work, your sacrifice. Why throw this all away? Be sensible. This rhetoric"—she waved her hands wildly— "it will pass away."

"This?" His hands flew about wildly to match his wife's gesture. "This is a lie. Nothing more than a death trap, as all lies eventually come to be."

"Finally, we have a social life that's the envy of German society. Greta and her husband weren't even invited to the ball."

"Great minds discuss ideas. Average minds discuss events. Small minds discuss people. Waltzing with hyenas isn't an honor. All the powerful Jews have been invited. Don't you see? It's a trap." He paused and glared at her. "Get it now?" He dabbed the back of his neck and his face with a tired handkerchief. "Cracked egg. That's what you are."

Offense registering keenly on her face, his wife marched the last several inches toward her husband and closed the distance between them. She slapped him across the face, leaving long, red marks on his cheek. "I've got plenty more where that came from."

Asher shook his head. Natalia cried.

"Try that speech on a real member of the Gestapo. They may take you up on your offer after they've had a bit of fun."

"Don't you ever disrespect me again in front of the children!" Her proud shoulders retreated from her ears.

"Minor point, woman. We must continue living for that to happen." His face paled as his wife jutted her nose into the air. "You're selfish and evil; not one maternal instinct resides in your rotten, narcissistic bones."

Hatred pulsed through the air between the two. Her slaps had become more frequent, but Asher's father never hit back.

If any woman would dare to slap Asher after he became a man, he'd punch her lights out. But tonight, trembling, Asher backed away until the window stopped his retreat from his parents' fight. He turned and faced the window, pushing aside the sheer curtain. He instantly regretted his choice.

Two men dressed like his father were pounding on a closed door across the street.

A man dressed in rumpled nightclothes opened the door. The uniformed men grabbed him. More soldiers dressed in gray uniforms barged into the house, dragging out a little girl and a woman in nightdresses.

Asher yanked the curtains shut, blocking out whatever was going on outside. "Father, would you kidnap Mister Gutenberg's family—our neighbors?"

"No." He embraced his son and shut a set of thick, tapestry-decorated draperies over the sheer curtains. "I'm not like them."

"What are you like, Papa?"

"I'm a good father." His voice broke. "I've done the best I could in this dreadful place."

"But, Papa—"

"Asher, please don't . . . how could I have known what they were capable of . . . how?"

"I know you did your best, and I love you, Papa."

"I love you too, son." Ryland hugged his only son.

Asher glanced down at his father's spit-polished, black leather boots. Seeing his reflection, he shivered. *If you can't beat 'em, join 'em.* Lesson learned. Clever. Asher smirked. He embraced his father, needing to feel safe. "One day, I'll be just like you."

"Do you have any idea what your father does?" His mother sneered, breaking her son's affectionate trance.

Asher knew.

"Shut up, woman!" Ryland bolted up and raised his hand, preparing to strike his wife. She cowered, and he retracted his hand. *He should have hit her.*

"Please, stop arguing," Natalia begged, then carefully and dutifully packed the most useless item—a violin—inside its case.

Asher didn't chastise his sister. Instead, he locked their

suitcases and dragged them to the front door. "I'm ready, Papa. I'm ready to go to America."

"I'm glad we're leaving. I hate feeling so frightened," Natalia chimed in.

"You'll never feel afraid again," Asher promised his sister.

"You're brave." Natalia kissed her brother's cheek, and Asher blushed.

Their mother's eyes narrowed as she ran her fingers down the slender, gold chain hanging from her neck. A pendant dangled from the chain. It had been a gift from her mother before she died five years ago. The pendant was a six-pointed star. Asher's mother called it the Star of David, but his father called it the Seal of Solomon.

"Take that devilish star off, woman." Asher's father controlled the volume of his voice but couldn't hide his protruding neck veins or the blood red tint flushing his face.

"I'm not going to assimilate, Reuben."

"Assimilate—no, you've done much more. You've embraced the devil's mammon." He extended his open hand. "Give it to me."

"You have no right! Mother gave me this necklace." She lifted her chin. "It's a family heirloom. Natalia's wearing hers." No different than a tattletale, his mother pointed toward the dainty, gold chain hanging around her daughter's neck.

Their father ripped the necklace from Natalia's neck, then dropped it into the bathroom's sink drain. Natalia blinked back tears, and her father kissed her forehead. "It's not worth dying for, Natalia. I'll buy you another one in America. I promise."

"Yes, Papa," she whimpered, and Asher stepped forward with balled fists. "Don't make her cry. Please, papa."

"Not all crying is bad. Tears can precede common sense."

His father looked over at his wife. "Asher, go and retrieve the ham sandwiches from the ice box, then stuff them into your coat pocket. Give Natalia a pair of sandwiches, too. Hurry! We leave in less than five minutes."

"But we don't eat swine!"

"Tonight . . ." Ryland clutched his son's coat lapels between desperate hands. "We eat ham. And if a Nazi stops us and tells you to eat the sandwich, you bite into it without hesitation, licking your lips as you eat. Do you understand?"

"Yes, Papa." The children obeyed their father, even packing tattered Bibles into their suitcases.

Ryland turned slowly and faced his ill-fitted bride. "If you choose to continue wearing that pendant, stay in Germany. It'll save the Nazi's hangman from using his rope. He can string you up with it."

"You don't love me. You never have." Reuban's wife gripped her neck.

All was quiet, except for Reuban's heavy breathing. A long minute passed. "You don't know what love is."

Asher's mother twirled on her pink pumps and strode from the room. Who knew what the real story was behind that pendant? Occasionally, both of Asher's parents had been known to embellish facts.

Quietly, the children finished dressing in layers.

Beneath a starless and cloudy night, Reuben Bushcroft led his children and his reluctant wife down a dimly lit alley to the edge of the city. Beyond a wrought iron gate, they waded with stealth and purpose through chest-high grass.

Please don't let there be any snakes.

Asher's feet were already aching after the long trek when they arrived at the meadow. Hidden behind a cluster of ash trees, a black car was waiting for the Bushcrofts.

Shivering beneath a fresh coat of snow, each slid into

the warmth of the waiting car, puddles of melting snow forming beneath their bums and feet.

The woman in the car explained to the children that she was a member of the French Resistance. She said her mission was simple: to ensure that members of the Rothschild banking family escaped Hitler's reach. In time, repayment would be expected in the form of favors.

Ten minutes into their drive, Asher heard propjet engines whining overhead.

Asher closed his eyes and dared not to look beyond the window. "The planes are German," the French woman said, "but don't worry. I've driven these country roads more times than I can count."

As she drove, she shared her life story. How her parents had left the south of France for Berlin when she was only ten.

Distracting the family with stories and quietly sung melodies, the driver travelled the back roads. She drove, never taking her foot off the accelerator until she had delivered the exiled family to a remote train station on the outskirts of Germany that was not yet overrun by the Nazis.

"Each of you, take your tickets." Four tickets for four scared Bushcrofts.

Asher wondered what would happen to the French woman. He swallowed a mouthful of fear, then asked, "Where will you go, Frauline?"

"Back to help others."

"What's your name? I want to remember you. I want to remember your kindness to me."

"Some call me Moses, in honor of Harriet Tubman and her freedom work, but I mostly go by my given name, Lya."

"Lya." Asher tried the name on his tongue. "Thank you for saving my life." He thought of blowing a kiss, but refrained, thinking the gesture too forward and mature for a young boy.

"Welcome." Lya smiled and gave Asher a wink. "I have a partner, and his name is Legna. He's big, powerful, and brave—don't be afraid if you see him on your trip."

"How will we identify him?" Rueben asked.

Lya laughed. "He'll be the only dark-skinned man in all of Germany, Poland, and Russia."

"Really!" Asher's expression most likely looked a bit gob smacked. "A black man in Nazi-overrun Europe? That's brave."

"He looks like an African prince. You won't miss him. He's very brave . . . and handsome." The strawberry-blonde blushed. She paused and waited, as though she had something more to say but didn't know if she should say it.

"Yes, Lya?" Asher bravely asked.

"Find the Ark of the Covenant, then control the world."

"How?" Asher asked as his father tugged at his arm. He yanked his arm away. "How, Lya?"

"Every path that is to be safely explored requires light. Find the Light—the lamp that lit the journey of the ancient peoples, the Aniyvwiya, as they left Mongolia and escaped to North America."

"Never heard of them." Asher tilted his chin.

"Come, Asher," Reuban commanded.

"You have heard of them, Asher," she said and followed quickly in lockstep, surveying the area, looking for Nazis. "Keep going, Asher."

He nodded as he continued to download her knowledge. "The Aniyvwiya called themselves the real people. They lived in North, Central, and South America before the Spaniards, English, Germans, and Scottish arrived. Many in North America settled in Tennessee and North Carolina, and they were entrusted with the Bat Creek Stone—the keystone that one day will be held by a dreamer who is a descendant of the Aniyvwiya. In that time, after the moon hides the sun from Earth, that dreamer will have the choice to reverse the curse of the Bat Creek Stone that will fall upon the European-invaded lands."

"Karma," Asher whispered as the train waiting on the platform blew its final whistle.

"Yes—so find the Bat Creek Stone first . . ." Her voice ticked up a half octave. "Then, you can abort our peoples' tormentor's second chance."

"I promise I will, Lya." He flashed a freckled-face, sheepish grin, then hustled up the train's metal steps, following his family.

She was pretty.

"You there!" A man dressed in a duster jacket pointed his gun at Lya and pulled the trigger. Asher gasped.

Reuban covered Asher's eyes and escorted his family further into the safety of the slowly moving train. "Father, why?"

"Because men and women still draw breath, son."

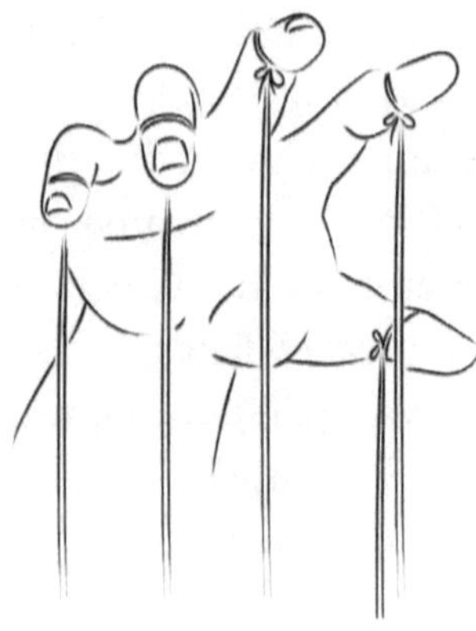

35—Asher

Tuesday
December 24, 1940
Berlin, Germany

WAR WAS—AND STILL IS—A DIRTY business. The Bush-croft family sat on the train, keeping their gazes low as they fled from the Third Reich's claws and its Final Solution. As though humans decided when something they'd never created should die.

Finally, the family of four entered Poland, then fled into Russia.

Second chances.

Redemption.

Salvation.

Trains.

Your trains won't run on our tracks. It was an extraordinary, lifesaving, and war-changing fact that the width of the Russian railway gauge differed from the width of train tracks throughout the rest of Europe. Russia's lines measured five feet wide.

In Germany, Italy, France, and Poland, locomotives ran on tracks that measured four feet and eight-and-a-half inches wide. *Maybe there is a God?*

During the Third Reich's blitzkrieg invasions, their troops would advance into Poland and France, relying upon the supply trains travelling from Germany by each conquered country's railway lines.

They couldn't do that with the Russian railway lines, and this fact saved the Bushcroft family—for now. The Nazis, with their supplies in tow, would have to trudge through Russia on foot to capture Moscow. Luck was decidedly not on the side of the Nazis.

High on Pervitin, the Nazi soldiers marched east in summer uniforms. And if they didn't repent and turn away from their current trajectory, Adonai had a surprise waiting for them.

Existing before time existed, Adonai never threw a Hail Mary. He threw touchdowns with every pass. And this time, His God Factor miracle pass was presented to desperate humans in the form of a hard Russian winter.

Blizzards halted the Nazis dead in their tracks—literally. With a lack of winter uniforms, they froze.

To a demon's senses, hell felt cold, but to a human, it felt hot. The Nazis died while freezing encased in the icy, arctic winter, hell on Earth.

36—Asher

Tuesday, January 23, 1941
Mongolia

THE BUSHCROFTS HAD FINALLY ESCAPED Germany, but Anglo-Saxon nations were not so eager to accept Jewish refugees. In time, however, their Rothschild family connections paid in dividends, paying for and permitting their voyage to China. Many stereotypes would be added to this family's name through the years, but they were just a family.

They journeyed through Mongolia and then to China, until eventually settling in the Hongkew district of Japanese-occupied Shanghai, a ghetto of one square mile. The family was given one million dollars and a tailor shop to oversee in the Hongkew district. But even within the Rothschild family, loans must be repaid—and always with interest.

Clothes weren't the only things fixed inside the glass-front, old-world-reminiscent tailor shop. Asher's father fixed everything from horse races to black-market deals selling stolen artifacts to government and private collectors.

One sweaty Chinese day, a man named Underwood arrived in Ryland Bushcroft's shop. Asher eavesdropped while brushing a recently mended suit. "I need to you to help me get something," the man said to Asher's father.

"What's that?"

"The Bat Creek Stone."

"Why?"

"That stone is my meal ticket—gets me off the in-law's bank roll in the US. It'll let me … let's say, influence future elections. If you know what I mean."

Ryland waved a hand dismissively. "The Bat Creek Stone is a forgery. It's irrelevant, according to most archeologists."

"No, Ryland, you're wrong . . ." Underwood leaned over the wood-stained counter and whispered, "I mean, Reuben. I'm surprised at you—giving the Anglos credit for something so . . . Jewish. That stone . . ." He pointed, then tapped an image of a flat brown stone. Asher stepped onto the small rise of a wooden stool to get a better look. His father glanced in his direction, but he didn't have a shred of discipline for Asher's eavesdropping.

"What does the Bat Creek Stone do for a man like you?"

Don't encourage him, Papa.

"It'll unlock an underground vault where the Copper Scroll treasure is hidden—King Solomon's temple treasure— which includes the all-powerful Ark of the Covenant."

"Tall tales, Mr. Underwood." Ryland ran the length of his tape measure with his smooth fingers as Asher looked on. "I'll design and tailor new suits for you, though—navy and ash gray would look great on you. You're so tall and fit." Ryland was average height, and his son was less than that.

Asher had endured cruel behavior from his classmates, being called a shrimp and the like. Standing with his shoulders back, he had recently eclipsed the fortieth percentile in height for other boys his age—an accomplishment. *I'll become a giant in other ways.*

"Possess the AOC. Control the world—end this forsaken war, too." The customer seemed to have completely forgotten that they were standing a tailor's shop, not a war room.

"America hasn't gone to war."

"You're not American, Ryland . . . so you should do your part and help me end the atrocities across the pond."

"We're in China, not America. We are across the pond," Ryland said. Asher grinned, giving his father a thumbs up.

The man studied the room, his eagle eyes probing every nook and cranny of their exquisite tailor's shop—the exposed wood beams, the fine linens. Underwood leaned over the counter.

"Just find someone to steal that Bat Creek Stone from that Indjian museum for me."

"You mean, 'Indian.'"

"Potatoes. Potatoes. The Bat Creek Stone is a key. I'm telling you." Underwood turned his hand and rapped knuckles on the wood counter.

"Who told you this?" Reuben Bushcroft began taking Underwood's measurements.

"A Chinese girl," he said then puffed out his chest. "She's a descendant of Genghis Khan."

"Nothing special. So many people are. He had five hundred concubines and six wives."

"Busy little plumber, that one." Mister Underwood grinned as Ryland finished the measurements in fifteen minutes. His customer plopped a roll of money on the oak countertop. "For the suit."

"It'll be ready soon." All three of the shop's occupants knew *it* had referred to the soon-to-be stolen relic.

"This is your fare out of this ghetto."

"And you're going to use this key to unlock this secret vault yourself?"

"Naw, the society does the dirty work. I don't open locks. Takes a locksmith." Underwood's usual high society Southern drawl suddenly escaped him, giving way to an improper Southern dialect.

"Sounds about right." He glanced at his son, studying little Asher's innocent face, then took the money. "I'll have the suit ready for you in six months," Ryland said as Underwood pushed his way out the front door.

During their voyage from China to New York, the Bushcroft family stood on the boat deck, watching the Statue of Liberty fill their view.

Asher stared at the beacon of hope until his eyes burned. Blinking just once—afraid to miss a moment of his arrival in the land of the free and the brave—the little boy wiped a trail of tears from his freckled face.

And in honor of the occasion, Natalia removed a violin from its case for the first time since leaving Germany. "For safekeeping, and to seal our love for each other for an eternity."

"What!" Asher's mother stood and started marching over to her daughter. "You're too young." But the rustle of the crowd and the swells lifting the bow of the boat forced her to sit again. "You'd do best to not pin yourself down with any man, especially at your age." She glanced at her husband—or her prison warden, depending on the day—a man who'd been willing to sell his soul to secure a safe place for his family and who now stood listening, mesmerized by his daughter's talent.

"Tell me true, why did the boy give you the violin?" their mother finally asked.

"Our schoolteacher placed his family's name on a list, so Ezekiel gave me his most prized instrument." She kept playing while dutifully explaining to their mother. "And the next day, the men dressed in gray jackets and black boots came for him, kidnapping him from school. They forced him into a truck, where the rest of his family was, and took him away."

Gadgets seemed to turn inside the Bushcroft matriarch's head, finally turning on that rusty bulb. *All wonders to imagine!* Ruth Bushcroft didn't verbalize her newfound understanding, choosing to keep her mouth shut.

Silence.

There is a God!

After the four Bushcrofts stepped onto America's shores, silence became the family's motto and constant companion. The quiet would be their balm after the horrors they'd seen and lived.

That was until a gloomy Thursday morning—December 11, 1941, fourteen days before Christmas—when the madman, Adolf Hitler, threw a temper tantrum and declared war on the United States of America.

Reuben Bushcroft stopped reading his newspaper and slid his specs down his nose. "Play a tune, Natalia." Asher's sister played the sweetest melody on her Stradivarius, "Romance in A Major, Op. 94 No. 2."

After she played the languid tune, Reuben spoke once more, "Favors are meant to be repaid—with interest. We—I—must avenge their deaths, honoring our friends, fighting for the cause of freedom."

"Yes, Papa." Asher and Natalia said in unison.

"And the Rothschild monies?" Ruth Bushcroft did little to hide her smug expression. "Are we to pay that back with interest, as well?"

He ignored his wife.

The next day, Reuben Bushcroft Rothschild joined the United States Army. The thirty-two-year-old man returned to Germany and exacted his vengeance on behalf of the Gutenbergs, on behalf of Natalia's young love. To redeem his own sins against his people.

With his father gone to war, Asher took a different path, embracing his lust for power and brokering deals at his middle school.

After the war, Reuben Bushcroft arrived back in America. He and his underworld contacts stole the Bat Creek Stone for Mister Underwood, placed a replica in its place, and hid the original with a trusted confidant.

One day, while lusting after a pretty girl with sun-bleached hair after losing his sister, Asher Valerian Bushcroft Rothschild opened the door of his heart to his HouseGuest, Nomed. Natalia Bushcroft would pay the consequences of his untamed lust.

And each day after, Natalia had paid for his mistake. Asher remembered what Lya had said on their ride to the train station, as well as Underwood's statement: possess the Ark of the Covenant, then control the world.

But could a boy who couldn't control his lust for a girl control the world?

In time.

★ ★ ★

"'I WILL BLESS THOSE WHO bless you, and I will curse those who curse you'. Payback isn't a female cow, it's a man,

Cillian. Shall we go up . . . to meet the president—together?" Bushcroft's tone returned to cold and calculated now that he had finished sharing his tragic childhood story.

Wraith gestured with his hand for Bushcroft to go first.

Bushcroft chuckled as he climbed the 360-degree spiral staircase that led to the top of the lighthouse. The President of the United States was waiting in a small but posh room. Bushcroft strolled in, cut off the end of his cigar, and relit it with a gold lighter.

The click of the lighter opening and closing sent chills up and down Wraith's scarred back. Bushcroft sucked in a long drag, breathed out a stream of smoke. The toxic cyanide-laden smoke slammed Cillian in the face.

The Orphan coughed.

"The Nazis shouldn't have murdered my people—your people. Nor should the English settlers arriving to North America's shores or the Spanish explorers arriving in South and Central America have murdered the Aniyvwiya. I did join the Sons of Venus, then rose through the ranks, made a deal with the devil to have a second chance with Natalia. Every man needs a family. Natalia's gone, and so are my parents."

"I'm not available, but you're right about one thing, pay-back is a man, a bear. It's me." Cillian gripped his knife, reached back—

"Stop!" The president's voice boomed from across the small room. "Fighting like squirrels over the last nut while the last nut—my wife—is plotting to killing us all."

"You know?" Asher's brow crinkled.

"Of course, I know. I sleep with the woman—don't I?"

Asher glanced at Cillian and shrugged. Cillian's face blushed red, and he slowly nodded. "I guess you do."

"Shut up and sit down, then!" Sheldon's brogans

thudded as he paced the perimeter of the circular room at the top of the lighthouse. "Cillian and I were both in Russia, drawing out what came natural to Claire. She shot the Russian president. He's dead. Now, prepare for World War Three."

"Another World War, Mister President?" Cillian's voice registered sadness.

"Well, son, be glad Claire pulled the trigger, or you would have had to do the deed, killing the Russian president, and his goons would have been on your heels."

"Claire has always been a better Sparrow than I am a Raven."

The president laughed. "Fifty years have passed since America's Fat Man and her Little Boy evaporated two Japanese cities, Hiroshima and Nagasaki, repayment in full for Japan's kamikaze pilots wrecking Pearl Harbor. Wraith, you followed in the tradition of your wife's father by serving in the United States Armed Forces via the clandestine force of The Orphans."

"Yes, sir." Cillian stood at attention.

"Well, we are going to be brave soldiers once again and fight." The president turned and faced Asher. "Asher, you birthed the idea of finding orphans then training them in the art of war, assassination, spy work, etc. to service the Sons of Venus. It's time for both of you to get over your past and fight for the future of America and thus the world! Grow up. Get over it." The president sat down on a worn leather couch and gestured to Cillian and Asher to sit next to each other on a plush, royal blue, velvet couch.

"Guess the first shrink session is beginning," Asher stated wryly.

"No time. You're going to work together and pool your resources. I need you to get that Bat Creek mystery solved."

"What if I already have a partner in the mission of obtaining the Bat Creek Stone?" Asher asked.

"Claire?" The president laughed. "She's double crossing you, my boy. When Daniela dies, somebody needs to be able to step into her shoes. Cillian, do you have the film?"

37—The Orphan

The Present, the End . . .
08:01 p.m., Sunday, March 2, 2024
Celtic Sea

WRAITH HAD DONE SOMETHING CRUEL and inhumane to another human. He had surrendered a cult leader to a rabid animal: Claire Amilee Underwood Covington. The cult leader, Kim Si-Yoon, deserved the punishment. And now, three men would watch the First Lady's work to see what she was capable of before they used her for their last mission.

"It's done, Cil?" The president reached for the object Wraith had removed from his cargo pant pocket.

"Yes, Mister President. Ye may not want to watch it." Wraith gave the president the small reel of film.

"I'll watch it." President Covington loaded the intel. "I've lived with the woman, tolerated her rejection and lies—the cruelest of mental disorders. Claire's ruthless. It would be nice to see what she can be useful for."

"Ye'll never want to kiss her again." Cillian shifted in his seat, sweat flushing his skin.

"I didn't want to kiss her before—no telling where her mouth has been." The president loaded the tape into the player then pressed play. Cillian looked away.

"Why does Claire like to do that?" Asher Bushcroft grimaced as he glanced away from the small television screen too.

"The cult leader forced the five-year-old kid's family to feed him feces and then beat him to death." The president defended his wife.

"Sick." Asher refused to look at the television.

"Before Russia, I spied on Claire, knowing what she'd do. I planted a secret camera and recorded the act on Sheldon's request. She ate the cult leader . . . literally. Of course, after Ki-Soon had a taste of her own medicine." Cillian stroked his Belgian Malinois's head. "There's nowhere to take a shite on this rock, and I dinna want to leave the mess in here. I need a garbage can. Why did you choose Claire to deal with the cult leader, Mister President?"

"Claire," the president whispered his wife's name. "I'd heard the rumors about her . . . tendencies, but I needed to see it for myself. As you know, she wanted me dead, too. How would you feel if Daniela wanted you dead?"

"Dead," Wraith simply stated.

"Bone of her bone, flesh of her flesh." The president paused. "Weird analogy considering what Claire did, but two love birds you and Daniela are. Murdering the Russian president . . . it's going to be a mess." The president got up and began pacing the room again.

"It wasn't personal, Sheldon," Bushcroft interjected.

"Claire had been programmed to murder the Russian president since she went through the Manchurian Program in the Orphan's training."

"But a relief for Ukraine." Cillian grabbed a bottle of water from the posh room's minifridge and drank it.

"Did your sexpionage training program train her to dispose of cult leaders?" Claire's husband asked Bushcroft.

"No—she was a natural." Bushcroft puffed a few times on his cigar, then polluted the air with his cyanide-laced smoke. "Cillian, where were you a few days ago? You weren't at the Hive; I checked the log."

"I had to come back. Take care of some business." Cillian glanced at his boss, the president.

"I never knew Claire to be that good of a shot," Sheldon said, punctuating his words by coughing up a lung full of phlegm.

"You're sick, sir. Why not take the chemo?"

"I'm going to die anyway, but I need to remain as strong as I can in order to control Claire and lead her to water."

"You mean a plate full of the body parts of six-six-six?" Bushcroft probed.

"I needed to make sure she would do it." The president's face was darkening to a sickly green hue. "Can't be brought back to life if the antichrist's body is inside my wife's stomach. Asher, you trained my wife to be the Sparrow that would pull the trigger if Russia's president invaded Ukraine . . . well, he did." If a glare from the president's jaundiced eyes could drip acid, both Asher and Cillian would have melted into gobs of goo.

"But I didn't train her to eat people. So give me some credit." Bushcroft tilted his head and narrowed his eyes as he puffed on his cigar then blew a stream of smoke in Cillian's direction. He winked. "I wouldn't want to be downrange of your rifle, Cillian—my boy, but I'd definitely not want to be down range of Claire's fork." Asher laughs—mouth wide open, shoulders heaving up and down like plunger plunging a stopped-up toilet.

Cillian's pale eyes returned fire with lethal daggers. "I'm not yer boy, Asher."

If you'd like to, continue reading this 300,000-word story, please go to https://www.amazon.com/Orphan-Falls-Running-Wild-Dreamer-ebook/dp/B0CGQ7K5KD/ to purchase Orphan Falls: Part Two.

If you liked the story, consider leaving a detailed and excellent review for future readers.

Thank you!

Bonus Material:

Misunderstood INFJ personality types like Daniela treasured their loyal friends.

It's true.

The world had snubbed, imprisoned, and even murdered those with INFJ personality types: Princess Diana, Martin Luther King, Jr., Eleanor Roosevelt, Nelson Mandela, Mohandas Gandhi, Florence Nightingale, Mother Theresa, and even J. K. Rowling. The quietness of an INFJ was a poison to restless souls.

So here's my letter to Earth's non-INFJs.

To all my non-INFJs,

INFJ personality types are less than 1% of the world's population, but you still may have noticed us. We're quiet, only speaking once we are convinced we have something to say that makes sense and may help someone. So let us be quiet. And don't judge us. We've given a lot to the world; some have even given their lives.

Hi, my name is Daniela Rose Cavanaugh, and I am an INFJ, a personality type known for our deep relationships with a few close friends. But these trusted friends are our rocket fuel and our safe place, so don't mess with them. Friends, please do not break our trust, but, if you do break our trust, expect the INFJ door slam. And no key has ever been cut for that door lock. The locksmith of personalities never invented one.

We have strong intuition and can see the potential in other people. We possess a strong sense of justice and are determined to make the world a better place. Because we are full of passion, if we believe in a cause, we will completely dedicate ourselves to that cause until it is solved.

We don't only dream. We wake up then get out of bed so we can turn our idealistic visions into positive actions. We are not, nor do we think that we are, angels or superior beings.

Adolf Hitler was an INJF personality type, too.

All the Best,

Daniela Rose Cavanaugh
The Orphan Dreamer, an INFJ personality type

Author Biography

J. Nell Brown, the daughter of a chaplain and a teacher, is a Florida native.

Her relationship with Yeshua (Jesus) is fused with experiences in life, travel, extensive Bible study, and people's stories, and she combines all of this to create characters, plots, and settings for her novels and short stories. An involuntary insomniac, Brown practices medicine and writes in her free time.

She is a self-proclaimed nerd and loves all things scientific. Her love of science is demonstrated by her research at Los Alamos National Laboratory, the site for the development of the atomic bomb. She graduated with honors from the University of Florida (U of F) College of Agriculture and received her medical doctorate from the same. After completing an anesthesia residency at The University of Chicago Hospitals, she began practicing in Florida.

Her heart overflows with compassion for people who are hurting, particularly children. A portion of the proceeds from this book will go to the A21 Campaign, a rescue charity for human-trafficked children, and Bethany Christian Academy in Gainesville, Florida, a school that J. Nell Brown attended as a child that promoted love, values, and a solid educational curriculum for children whose parents would not otherwise be able to afford an alternative school education.

Her first nonfiction book, *Shhh, My Father Is Speaking, and I Am Listening*, is about her prayer journey. The Bible is her favorite literary masterpiece. You may follow J. Nell Brown on her author website, JNellBrown.com.

www.ingramcontent.com/pod-product-compliance
Lightning Source LLC
Chambersburg PA
CBHW031306210726

48287CB00005B/1444